Gull Island

Gull Island

Grace Thompson

ROBERT HALE · LONDON

© Grace Thompson 2010
First published in Great Britain 2010

ISBN 978-0-7090-9076-2

Robert Hale Limited
Clerkenwell House
Clerkenwell Green
London EC1R 0HT

www.halebooks.com

2 4 6 8 10 9 7 5 3 1

Typeset in 10/13pt Sabon
Printed in Great Britain by the MPG Books Group,
Bodmin and King's Lynn

Chapter One

BARBARA JONES DREAMED about Bernard Stock and when she woke that September morning in 1917, she was reluctant to let the dream go. Rising out of the narrow bed she shared with her sister Freda, she pretended for a luxurious moment that it was Bernard lying beside her, sharing the single pillow, hogging the best part of the coarse blanket and patched sheet. She searched her memory for the remembered scent of him and imagined it filling the air, mingling with her own.

Pretending it was Bernard's breakfast she would be cooking when she went downstairs helped to throw aside the morning's sleepiness, made her less sluggish as she reached for her long serge skirt and the blouse that needed a wash but would have to do one more day. As she dressed in the gloom of the curtained room, the dream changed to imaginings and continued.

'Do you, Barbara Jones, take this man, Bernard Cedric Stock—' Pity about the Cedric, mind, but it didn't really matter as long as she became Mrs Bernard Stock '—to be your lawful wedded husband?' Oh, I do, I do, I do!

'Barbara! How many more times do I have to call you?' Her mother's voice came up the staircase and startled her from the dream of her longed-for wedding day. Mrs Jones's voice was harsh as she tried to show her anger yet keep her voice low enough to avoid disturbing Barbara's sister Freda.

'All right, Mam, I'm coming,' Barbara hissed back irritably, angry at having to leave her daydream.

'It's late for work we'll all be. And there's me wasting time trying to get you moving! Come down. Now, this minute, I want a word with you, my girl!'

'All right, Mam. I'm coming as fast as I can!'

Barbara came down slowly and braced herself before entering the kitchen, where her mother was poking the fire to encourage the kettle to boil faster. She was sure to have a telling-off for coming in late last night, and Mam could smell drink at twenty paces.

Barbara was seventeen and already blooming into womanhood. Her small-featured, lightly tanned face usually gave the impression of a lively spirit looking for fun and amusement but today was different. She looked weary, the pale blue eyes had lost their usual sparkle and were red-rimmed. Her hair had a natural sheen that made it far from ordinary and this morning it was in its usual plait but feathered with untidy ends, revealing the fact it had not been freshly combed but had been left overnight and hurriedly smoothed to give a pretence of morning grooming.

She forced a smile to deceive the world as she reached the doorway, paused to brush her hands nervously down her ankle-length skirt and straightened the collar of the white blouse. Pushing open the door, she took a deep breath and smiled across at her mother, who was cutting bread to toast against the now brightly burning fire, her face as red as the coals.

'Morning, Mam. There's warm it is and hardly seven o'clock. You going to the munitions factory morning shift or afternoon?' Nervously she didn't wait for or expect a reply but went on, 'Pity for the people in London havin' bombs dropped on them from aeroplanes. Them Germans are clever, mind, even if some of them are wicked and cruel. Fancy taking bombs up in an aeroplane and dropping them on innocent women and children. Terrible it must be.' She frowned a little, remembering that Bernard was in London at the very moment, looking for work. She prayed silently for his safety.

She wasn't at all hungry but she picked up a piece of toast and, spreading it with jam, went on chattering as she took a very small bite. With luck she'd keep Mam from talking until she got through the door. 'Someone just back from there at the party last night was telling us how frightening it was, with the air raids. Policemen and soldiers in vans, cars and even peddling push-bikes shouting for people to take cover.

'Carrying placards too, telling people who couldn't hear what they were saying that there's an air raid on. *Duw*, I'd be screaming in panic for sure, seeing them notices, wouldn't you? Glad I am not to live up there. Pity 'elp them, isn't it?' She hoped that her bright smile and breathless chatter would prevent her mother from giving the usual lecture.

'Pity 'elp you too, my girl. Wicked you are! Didn't your father always say so? Didn't he always say you'd end up bad?'

'Bad? What d'you mean now, for goodness' sake? Forgot to lift the ashes last night? Went to bed without shaking the cloth and setting the table for breakfast? Oh, there's wicked. Don't know how I'll face the vicar if he should call!'

'You can be flippant, Barbara Jones, but being sharp with your tongue won't get you out of this mess!' Her mother's face was so tightly disapproving, the flesh trembled.

'What mess? I only went to Maggie Field's party and stayed a bit late.'

'If that was all you'd done.'

'Mam, for goodness' sake tell me what I've done that's upset you so I can say sorry and get to work. Sacked I'll be if you keep me late.'

'Sacked you'll be soon anyway.'

Barbara looked at the rather burnt toast her mother had removed from the long toasting fork. Always a sign that Mam was mad, that was, her burning the toast. She put it on the bread board with the piece she had half-heartedly begun to eat. She wasn't hungry – after all those ports and lemons the previous evening it wasn't surprising that her stomach was a bit sensitive.

It had been a good party, mind. Well worth the bit of discomfort. Maggie Field had rolled back the coco matting and they'd danced on the bar floor until the dust rose in clouds and they had to stop, breathless, for it to settle. Sixteen of them in a room hardly big enough for six. Dickie Field had played the piano – not well, mind, but loud enough for them to enjoy it anyway. It had been good; such a pity Bernard was in London and had missed it. But it was over and now she had to pay for it by listening to Mam's lecture. She glanced at her mother, who was standing, arms akimbo, a tea towel across her arm, just glaring at her, her greeny eyes more than usually fierce.

'All right, Mam, so I had a bit of a drink. So what? Plenty of girls my age do. After all, this is 1917! The war has blown away all old-fashioned prejudices. Women will be voting soon and then you'll see how the world will change. No more believing men are superior. We'll show them that women can do anything they can.' She reached for her navy jacket that was hanging over the back of the rocking chair and pushed away the tea her mother had poured for her. 'I'll be a bit late tonight – I'm going to the music hall with friends from the shop.'

'No, you won't.'

'What d'you mean?' Barbara stared at her mother, sensing for the first time that this was different from the usual telling-off. 'Mam?' she queried.

'So women can do the same as men, can they? Well, let's see you walk away from an unwanted child the way a man can, shall we? Barbara, you are going to have a baby and don't pretend to me any more because I'm not stupid! I've known this ages and waiting I've been, waiting for you to tell me.'

'What? Don't talk daft!' Half in and half out of her jacket, Barbara sank into a chair with shock. 'How could I be? I'm not married.' Barbara's face was drained of colour and she clutched the table for support. 'Talking nonsense you are.'

'So you haven't been up early to run down the garden to be sick in the lavatory? So you haven't been put off at the thought of an early morning cup of tea?'

'Port and lemon, that's why I've been sick.' Her stomach churned as her mother slowly shook her head.

'Havin' a baby you are.'

'But how can I be? I'm not married, so how can it happen?'

'Doin' wicked things with boys, that's how! Now you'd better get to work and be careful not to let anyone else guess. Do as I say and you'll perhaps be able to keep your job. Tonight, when Freda's in bed and before your father comes home from the pub, we'll discuss what you must do. Go now, you stupid, ungrateful girl, before I swipe you!'

Barbara stared in utter disbelief at her mother, then, with a choking cry, she hurried from the house. How could she have a baby inside her? How did it get there and how will it come out? All she could remember about childbirth was her mother's shouts and screams of pain, and the soothing mutterings of Mrs Block who came to help bring them into the world – and the smallness of the coffins of those who didn't survive. Will it be like that for me? she wondered. Sickness overcame her again, but this time it was brought on by fear.

When she reached the door of the department store where she worked behind the scenes in the stockroom, she hesitated. She couldn't go in. She was sweating with the new bout of sickness that had left her shaking and weak. She was caught in a trap she didn't understand and felt young, utterly alone and very frightened.

She must look awful. If she went in now there would be questions and everyone would get out of her what Mam had just said. But she had to talk to someone; she had to. There must be someone who would tell her how a baby got into her belly. She felt her body. How could something as big as a baby get in there without her knowing? Where was it? Was it scrunched up like an old discarded paper bag? Mam wouldn't be any use. She'd never be able to explain things calmly and sensibly. Mam always coloured up and snapped angry and brief remarks about how stupid she was if she dared to ask an embarrassing question. She and Freda sometimes did it for fun, like when they asked questions about the buttons on men's trousers and what were brassieres and was it all right to say 'bum', if you were talking about tramps in America.

Turning away from the three-storey shop premises, leaning on the warm brick wall for support until her legs regained their strength, she went through the narrow, shabby streets to where Mrs Carey lived. Mrs Carey had nine children – surely she'd be able to tell her how it had happened?

At seventeen, Barbara was as unaware of the facts of life as most of her friends. She knew girls without husbands did have babies and she also knew their children were called bastards and carried the shame of their mother all their lives without even a proper birth certificate. She knew of two girls who were sent away to a special place where they had their babies and came home without them to try and pretend nothing had happened.

But everyone had known. Neighbourhoods didn't change; generation followed generation living in the same houses with the same neighbours. Everyone knew the histories of everyone else and memories were long. Even old Miss Lizzie Green, who was seventy-five if she was a day, was still referred to as the woman who tried to steal Mrs Glyndwr Thomas's husband and had a baby girl and shamed her family.

Mrs Carey's large family lived squashed into two rooms. One room was the kitchen, where all the clothes washing, cooking, meal preparation, family bathing and the thousand other tasks of living were performed. It was also the place where Molly Carey and Henry Carey slept with the youngest of their children. The other room was where the rest of the family slept on mattresses on the floor. This room was divided by a heavy brown curtain between the boys and girls and there was a clout for anyone caught peeping!

From these small rooms, Henry Carey ran a newspaper delivery service and Molly Carey managed to do washing and ironing for other people to earn a few extra shillings. She also looked after other people's children when asked, and was never certain how many should be there at any given time.

When Barbara arrived, Richard Carey, who was almost five years old, was minding his one-year-old sister, Blodwen, bouncing homemade toys on his head and making her smile. Richard had a baked potato in one hand from which he took occasional bites, his face and hand covered with black from the burnt skin.

'Mam's next door if you want her. Will you mind the baby first, while I go to the *ty bach*?' That was the 'little house', the local name for the lavatory at the bottom of the garden. Mrs Carey had heard the visitor arrive and she came in with a surprised look on her tired face.

'No work today then? Never been sacked, have you? Don't worry, plenty of work with this ol' war on, that's one good thing to be said for it. Women can get a job without much trouble. Better paid than laundry and scrubbing floors too.'

'I took the day off but don't tell our mam. I – I wondered if I could talk about something. I have a little problem, see.'

'I think I can guess what that'll be about, *fach*. Only one little problem comes to a girl your age. Been doing something naughty with boys, have you?' She moved swiftly and pushed open the door of the kitchen. 'Clear off, Richard. Nosy-parkering'll do you no good at all! At school you should be, mind. Behave or I'll send you this afternoon.' She tutted extravagantly and smiled at Barbara. 'I kept him home to mind his sister. Best we go out in the yard, the only place where there's a bit of privacy.'

The September day had begun with a misty chill that had cleared to become a bright and mild day. The Careys' garden, a share of a long narrow plot behind six houses, was still untidy with neglected weeds from which struggled the last of the year's crops. The stumps of Brussels sprouts stood in irregular rows like knobbly-kneed dancers, there were a few sad-looking cabbages and leeks, and under the oak trees that all but filled the lower half of the garden newly fallen leaves were spread like an intricately patterned carpet. A corner held a pile of carelessly thrown weeds and kitchen waste intended to be compost, if Henry Carey ever got around to dealing with it.

It was warm and peaceful, the sounds of the street barely penetrating to where they sat beneath the oak tree. After explaining her difficulties, Barbara listened wide-eyed and alarmed while Mrs Carey told her the facts of life, at least, as much as she knew. The gaps in her knowledge they filled between them with guesses and imagination.

An hour later, a dazed, confused and frightened Barbara Jones walked out of the Careys' house and began to walk away from the streets, the familiar and very small area that encompassed her world. She allowed her feet to take her unthinkingly to the beach two miles away, instinctively heading towards the place where she and Bernard often spent their Sunday afternoons.

It was a rock-strewn area of the coast they called *their* beach, where they walked hand in hand and lay in small private places in the rocks. Today it was deserted. Besides the wooden shack which opened on occasions to sell sweets and pop, there were only a few damp and neglected cottages and further inland, one large and imposing house which stretched its Tudor-style walls haughtily up from green lawns and looked across the sea to where an island showed itself, glistening in the late-afternoon sun.

The tide was low, the sea a benign murmur. A causeway led temptingly across to the small outcrop of rocks and greenery and low shrubs, where rabbits lived unthreatened and cropped the rich grass. But Barbara knew from previous experience how quickly the sea crept around both sides of the island and covered the causeway with a dangerous tide where deep pools and uneven rocks made hurrying feet stumble and hidden currents tugged at the legs of the unwary.

She sat there unmoving for hours, unaware of the need for food or even a drink to refresh her. The fact that she carried a child had been a devastating surprise. Even Mrs Carey's explanations had only just begun to penetrate her shocked mind. The revelation was alternately filling her with fear and elation. Now she and Bernard would be married. The fact that she was only seventeen wouldn't be an obstacle – Mam and Dad had been married at her age, and they'd be glad to have one less person in the cramped rooms.

She began to feel chilly and came out of her reverie to see that the tide was almost fully in. A sea mist had fallen, hiding the late summer sun so the island was little more than an outline in the opaque air. Apart from the almost unnoticed sound of the waves, everywhere was silent and she fancifully imagined that she was alone in the whole world. She would stay here in the beautiful, hazy, peaceful place, and Bernard would come and find her and they would walk off into the mist and start a new life without having to untangle the confusion that surrounded her.

But there was no confusion, she reassured herself. All she had to do was wait until Bernard came back from London, explain the situation as Mrs Carey had explained it to her, then leave it to him. They would be married and everything would fit perfectly into place.

She tightened the jacket round her shoulders, appreciating its warmth. The mist had brought a chill to the air. The island was almost lost to sight now and seemed to be floating on the quietly swelling sea. Bernard called the mist that veiled the scene a sea fret. The beach and the island was, he'd told her, a place of sea frets and mysteries. She smiled. Sometimes Bernard talked as if he were reading poetry. Like when he called her eyes sleeping pools of dreamy wonderment. She wasn't sure what he meant but it sounded romantic.

A sound invaded her thoughts and she felt a mild irritation at the intrusion. She recognized the slap of oars on the small waves and the creaking and clunking of wood within rowlocks. Looking out to sea she saw, gradually emerging through the mist, almost as if it were gliding on air, a small rowing boat.

She began to rise, not wanting to talk to anyone. But the man in the boat had seen her and he called, paused in his rhythmic rowing and waved. She stood, half prepared to walk away but suddenly changing her mind and wanting to talk to someone, and in the eerie light she waved back.

'How could you see your way in this? Daft I call it to go out in a little boat in such weather.' Unaccountably she was angry for the risks he had taken.

'I've only been around to the next bay to visit a friend,' the young man replied as he dragged the boat up onto the shingle. 'Here, catch this and tie her to that post, will you?' As she fumbled with the rope he stepped lightly across the rocks and took it from her. 'Here, like this.' Taking the rope, he showed her the way to tie it with a bowline.

She couldn't guess the stranger's age. Perhaps he was younger than herself, perhaps older. She thought he would look the same ten years from now. He was quite small, hardly taller than she was, five feet three at a guess. He was lean, thin even, and his fair hair, bleached almost white by the summer sun, was long and straight, almost touching his shoulders and adding to the illusion of extreme slimness. His eyes, she noticed with fascination, were the colour of the sea and the skin around them was wrinkled as though he spent his days with them half closed against the glare of the sun on the sea.

He wore a shabby jumper from which threads of wool hung in fringes over his hands and across his neck. His trousers barely reached mid-calf and if there had been hems they had been lost for many months, so, matching the jumper, a fringe escaped the carelessly rolled-up ends like a family of spiders having a free ride.

The clothes, she thought with a frown, were misleading. The boy, or young man, was no pauper. His voice was without a strong local accent and he sounded what Barbara's friends would call 'swanky'. There was an air of confidence about him too that suggested he could afford to dress well if he chose. She forgot her recent alarms, her daydreams and her irritation at being interrupted and was filled with curiosity.

'Live near here, do you?' she asked as she followed him up from the now-chilly beach towards the old cottages. 'I bet you live in that posh house beyond the beach with timber beams and dozens of chimneys.'

'That place has been empty for years, although a relation of mine once owned it.' He smiled and gestured towards the cottages. 'These smaller places belong to my father and I stay here sometimes.' He looked at her, his eyes still remarkably matching the colour of the sea moving gently behind him. 'I have the makings of tea if you fancy a cup. You look as though you could do with warming up. No milk, I'm afraid.'

She hesitated, wanting to go but half afraid. 'Oh, I don't think I could drink tea without milk, thanks all the same.'

'Putting in extra sugar helps.' His smile lit up his face, giving it an almost roguish look. 'You don't have to be afraid. I don't bite or pounce on lovely young women.'

She smiled back, intrigued by his almost piratical appearance and casual, easy manner. He was different from anyone else she had ever met. This adventure would be something to tell Bernard about when he came home – something to add to that other news.

The cottage to which he led her was surprisingly neat inside. Built of yellowish stone with a pattern of red sandstone around the windows and doorways, there was a strong smell of dampness as she entered the storm porch but once inside the living room, a chintz-covered chair and a bowl of wild flowers gave the place a brightness and warmth. She stood for a moment, her head hardly moving but her large pale-blue eyes widening and absorbing the unexpectedly pleasant sight.

The young man put a match to the fire and, leaving her to explore, busied himself with a paraffin stove and a tin kettle. While she looked in amazement at the long line of books on a stone shelf, which smelled of damp and showed signs of mildew, he made tea and put the tray on the floor in front of the spluttering fire.

'My name is Luke. Who are you?'

'Barbara. Barbara Jones but I think I'll be changing it very soon.' Did she imagine the slight frown that crossed his face? Was there a hint of disappointment at the news of her marrying? She silently laughed off the vanity and in her embarrassment at the way her thoughts had travelled, she blurted out, 'Mam told me this morning I'm going to have a baby, see, and when Bernard knows he'll marry me for sure. Then I'll be Barbara Stock.'

'What will you do, Barbara, if he – well, if you decide not to marry this Bernard?'

'I don't know,' she gasped. The thought of Bernard letting her down simply hadn't occurred to her. She stared at him. Suddenly all the fears and uncertainties flooded in and she was chilled as if by immersion in icy water. Her eyes widened and her teeth chattered. She crouched nearer to the warmth of the fire, not wanting to look at the serious-faced stranger. Why had she told him? He was staring at her when she eventually looked at him again, the frown on his face deepening.

'Don't let them make you give her away. She's yours and you must keep her, watch her grow and she'll fill every day with joy.'

'She? You think it will be a girl? Funny, I hadn't got round to wondering whether it will be a girl or a boy.'

'It will be a girl and you must call her Rosita.'

'There's a fancy name for a Jones!'

'Jones? Then you don't think this Bernard will marry you?' he asked softly.

'Of course he will! I wasn't thinking—'

'But if he doesn't, you won't let them take the baby away and kill it, or give it to someone else to raise, will you? Please tell me you won't.'

'Bernard and I will be married. She, or he, will be ours.'

'But if he doesn't?' he insisted urgently.

'If you insist on my saying it, all right, if I don't marry Bernard, then I'll keep the baby.' He looked so serious she was laughing, confident in the outcome. 'All right then? Satisfied?'

'Good. Now if you've finished your tea I'll walk a part of the way with you. I have to go back myself soon but an hour won't matter. There are plenty of trains to Cardiff. Are you ready? Your mother will be worrying, especially if you've only just learned about Rosita.'

'Rosita?' She laughed.

'Rosita.' He hugged her and added, 'My mother was called Rosita. I'd like to think that somewhere in the world there'll be a little girl who carries her name.'

They walked back along the silent, mist-enshrouded lanes, the hedges on either side of them like walls separating them from the rest of the world. A cotton-wool world in which they were alone. Barbara was warmed by Luke's company and by his matter-of-fact approach to her situation so that the shock of the morning was becoming an accepted fact and something with which she could deal without difficulty. Apart from the baby and the love and happiness she would surely bring to her, Luke had talked mostly about the sea and the fish he caught and the journeys he would one day make, when the war was over and he was free.

'Free? Good heavens, Luke, look at you, how could you be more free?' she laughed.

'Tomorrow I go back to that other life.'

'You aren't in the army, are you? You don't look old enough.'

'I'll be twenty at Christmas. Christmas Day, in fact. No, the army wouldn't have me – my chest is the problem apparently.'

'Mam has worked in the munitions factory but only for a while. Dad works in a soap factory and grows vegetables. That's the extent of the Joneses' contribution to the war effort, I'm afraid.'

'Nothing so honourable for me. I have a second-hand bookshop. Hardly a blow against the enemy. I did try several times to enlist but they refused me. A friend of mine is in France. His name is Roy Thomas. He and I have been close friends since we were little more than babies. His family is where I think of as home, especially since my mother died. Their home is as noisy and relaxed as mine is silent and disapproving.' They walked on for a while and Barbara waited, sensing his need to tell her more.

'Roy writes cheerful letters but I think the men are going through hell. I wish I were there too. I know it isn't the thing but I miss Roy very much.'

'What d'you mean it isn't the thing? If he's your friend, why shouldn't you miss him?'

'Oh, it's just that our families are so different and ...' He allowed the sentence to hang in the air unfinished and Barbara guessed it was something he didn't feel able to tell her.

'Do you really wish you were out there, in France? I confess I'm glad not to have to face it. Loving friend or not, I'm thankful I'm not expected to go.'

'You're a woman, designed for more gentle things.'

He smiled and Barbara smiled back; the awkward moment had passed. It was the only moment in which there had been any uneasiness between them. She wondered about Roy Thomas, and experienced a slight feeling of envy at the unknown man's ability to spoil the unlikely friendship between herself and this unusual man. But she didn't attempt to bring the conversation back to him.

As they reached the end of the lane that took them away from the beach, they heard voices and the laughter of children. Coming towards them through the hazy evening was a group of youngsters. One was pulling a homemade bogie – a wooden soap box with a long plank for steering and to which old pram wheels had been added.

Barbara smiled as she recognized the Carey family. Richard, the five-year-old, was helping to steer the cart and beside him, fast asleep, was his baby sister Blodwen. A solemn child even in sleep, she was propped upright, jammed in with cushions, the colours of which had faded to a greyish brown. Also in the party were Billie, aged ten, and Gareth, aged seven. The oldest Careys, twin girls Ada and Dilys, were far too aloof to share this escapade. Alun, at twelve, was already chasing girls. Mrs Carey kept her favourite, Idris, close to her, rarely letting him join in any of the activities arranged by the rest.

'What are you doing so far from home?' Barbara demanded.

It was Richard who answered. 'There's bound to be some firewood washed up on the beach so we're getting some for Mam.' He gestured behind him and coming into sight was a second bogie cart pulled by another of his brothers, the eight-year-old Jack. Barbara noted that although only five, Richard was the one organizing the little procession.

'Come back with me now this minute!' Barbara said angrily. 'Your mam'll kill the lot of you!'

'Not without wood.' Richard's jaw was pushed out in a stubborn expression.

'But it's late and almost dark.'

'We've walked a long way for to go home with nothing,' his brother Billie added. 'Come on, you lot, we can cut across the fields from here.'

'The tide's up.' Barbara hoped that would decide the matter. 'Best you come another day.'

Totally ignoring her, the small group dragged the carts up the bank and through the hedge and when the sleeping child threatened to fall out, Luke ran to help them. 'Who are they all?' he whispered as he lifted the ungainly bogie down onto the field.

'They all belong to Auntie Molly Carey, the neighbour I've been telling you about. No sense in any of them.'

'Come on, Barbara, we might as well give them a hand since they're going to do it anyway. Follow me,' he said to Richard the leader. 'I know exactly where the best spots are.' He offered a hand to Barbara and helped her up the bank and into the field, then he lifted the still-sleeping baby from her blankets and cushions on the bogie and carried her across the bumpy surface of the field. The mist hindered their view but Luke knew the way and the rest – led by Richard – followed without question. Bemused, smiling, young enough to enjoy the unexpected, Barbara followed.

Luke worked hard, filling the small carts and even lending them a wheelbarrow which they also filled with some of the larger pieces that wouldn't fit into the bogies. He walked with them to the end of their street, singing songs and making the children laugh when they showed signs of fatigue. His appearance was more piratical than ever when they reached the first of the street lamps. His thin face was streaked with dirt and sweat, his eyes gleamed and laughter showed the whiteness of his teeth against the tanned skin.

For part of the way, Barbara carried the straight-faced Blodwen and Luke gave a piggy-back ride to a very sleepy Richard. He encouraged the others with praise, smiling at Barbara, sharing his obvious happiness at being a part of a family group. Barbara was happy too and her imaginings were of a future filled with outings just like this one. Hers and Bernard's with Rosita and her younger brothers and sisters.

'Roy Thomas's family is like this,' Luke said. 'They're always finding new ways of enjoying themselves, content with simple things and always ready to burst into laughter.'

'Your family are more serious?'

'Sober sides, the lot of them! Mother was different, she was the sunshine of the house, but now she's gone there's very little to laugh at. In fact, laughter is considered to be rather "common".'

Luke pushed the wheelbarrow to the Careys' gate in the back lane, tipped the contents out in the small garden then, with a wave and a blown kiss, he left. His final words to Barbara were, 'Look after Rosita. Keep her safe, she's very important.'

Night had intensified the mist into an almost impenetrable blackness lit only by the filtered light from the occasional street lamp when the rest of the bedraggled procession trooped into the Careys' house They were greeted by screams of relief followed by clouts and recriminations. Leaving them to argue their case, Barbara went home to face recriminations of her own.

The small living-cum-everything-else room of the Careys' was filled so they could hardly move with them all in there at the same time. Somehow Mrs Carey made cocoa for them all and handed the eclectic collection of china around to stretching hands. First to be given his cup was her golden boy, Idris. She knew she shouldn't have a favourite but he was so beautiful and so full of charm how could she help it?

Idris was very different from the other Carey children. His hair, instead of being a shade of brown, was almost yellow and thickly curled so his head was that of a cherub on a religious painting. His eyes were as blue as his father's but with such a gentle and innocent expression that Mrs Carey stood for minutes at a time just admiring her creation with utter joy. The children were given two biscuits each and Idris was slyly handed the broken remains of a third. Richard saw this and smiled condescendingly. Idris was welcome to Mam's special favours. He wasn't a spoilt child like Idris, nor would he want to be. He was already his father's partner, almost a man.

Outside the back gate, where one wall of the *ty bach* formed a part of the boundary, Barbara stood and listened to the lively chatter within the house. She knew that when she went home there would be no cheering welcome. She felt a surge of sympathy for Luke, the stranger who had come into her life and become a friend. She shared with him the isolation of a home where laughter was frowned upon as 'common'. With a last look over the wall towards the lamp-lit room beyond the long garden, she moved away. Now she must think of herself and her baby and of course, Bernard, who loved her and would soon be returning to her.

She remembered the evening's events and smiled despite the encroaching anxiety at the confrontation with her father that must be waiting for her. When she married Bernard, she would create an atmosphere of happiness and laughter just as Auntie Molly Carey had done. Perhaps Luke would be a regular visitor and help show her how.

Chapter Two

FOR THE SECOND time that day, Barbara steeled herself to face her mother's wrath. As she opened the front door of the terraced house she paused momentarily to listen to the sounds from within. Loud conversations were in progress and with a tensing of her jaw she recognized the deep voice of her father. He was either late going to the pub or home early. She wondered apprehensively if he had delayed his regular evening visit to wait for her – if so he'd had plenty of time to build up a rage.

'Hello, Mam, sorry I'm late. Been gathering firewood, would you believe. Me and them daft Carey kids. Over by Gull Island. There was plenty on the beach after last week's storm. Young Richard's idea, it was, mind—' Her attempt to allay the row that was quivering in the air was halted as her father stood up and raised his hand to strike her. He was stopped by her mother, whose pointing finger then told her to sit down. In the corner, hoping she wouldn't be noticed and told to leave, was Barbara's sister Freda.

Mr Jones was not a big man but in the small room he seemed, to a frightened Barbara, to be enormous. She had never seen him look this angry. Normally a mild, indifferent man, he was little more than the furnishings of her daily life but now he looked like a stranger and she trembled with fear.

His pale blue eyes were deep set, deeper now as he screwed up his cheeks to display his anger, becoming lost in the folds. The furious face loomed large as he leaned towards her, and she noticed how fat his face had become. His chin was surrounded by a tyre of fat from which pale bristles were obtruding. He shaved twice each week, on a Tuesday when he and Mam went to the pictures and on Friday when he went to the local pub to celebrate the receipt of his wage packet. She compared him, even in this frightening moment, to the beautiful dark leanness of Bernard Stock and felt a longing for her loved one soar inside her.

'What have you been doing, girl,' her father hissed, 'disgracing us all. Disgusted with you I am! I can't face my mates for the shame of it.'

'No one knows yet, Dad,' Barbara whispered, her voice quivering and sounding like that of a stranger. 'I didn't know myself till Mam told me this morning and I haven't seen the doctor yet.'

'You'll see no doctor!' her mother snapped. 'Best for us all if we keep this to ourselves.'

'But Mam, people are sure to see before long and—'

'No one need know if you do as you're told. You'll see Mrs Block in the morning. I've already told the shop you won't be in for a couple of days and we'll see an end to it.'

'What d'you mean? See an end to it?' What Auntie Molly Carey had told her about getting rid of unwanted babies filled her mind with terrifying images. She looked to her father for support but he, seeing the embarrassment of women's talk brewing, hurriedly prepared to leave.

'You aren't going to take the baby away from me,' Barbara said defiantly when the back door had slammed behind him and she heard his footsteps hurrying down the garden path to the *ty bach*. 'I – I talked to Auntie Molly Carey and she warned me this might be your idea. I'm going to have this baby and when he comes home from London my boyfriend will look after me.'

'If that's what you think you're more stupid than I thought. Won't want to know you when you tell him, you mark my words. Soiled goods you are and who in their right mind would want soiled goods? And what made you talk to Mrs Carey of all people? Fine one she is with her nine kids! And if she knows, then so will half the town by now, for sure!'

There was an uneasy silence as they waited for Barbara's father to return from the garden and go out. 'I'll be back at ten and make sure she's in bed,' Mr Jones said, reaching for his cap. 'If I see her again tonight I'll swipe her good and proper for what she's done to us. Listen to what Mam tells you, you stupid, ungrateful girl. Bringing shame on us all you'll be if you don't listen. Think of your sister if you can't think of your poor mam!' He pushed his way past the clutter of chairs, pouting like a spoilt child, and out into the street, slamming the door behind him.

With Freda still unnoticed and listening avidly, Barbara and her mother continued to argue. They were still at it an hour later when Mr Jones came back from The Anchor and, using the chance to escape further bullying, Barbara snatched the end of a loaf and a piece of cheese and ran to her bed. Eating under the covers, she brushed away the crumbs and curled up, trying to steady her whirling thoughts and be able to sleep. Freda would be up soon; she could hear the hum of conversation below and guessed her mam would soon tell her to get to bed. She screwed her eyes tightly shut. She didn't want to fend off any more questions and certainly not from Freda.

She woke early the following morning and the house was silent as she combed her long hair and washed at the back kitchen sink. Mam was working early that day, cleaning at the munitions factory near the docks. Dad would be on his way to the soap factory, which was on the outskirts of the town, poor eyesight responsible for the army refusing to accept him into its murderous jaws.

He had a long walk before his eight o'clock start and usually left the house before seven. She was grateful for a reprieve from the nagging and her lips tightened as she determined not to give in. Bernard's face came into her mind and beside it that of Luke. They would help her. Between them they would enable her to defy Mam and Dad and the rest of the world.

In a scolding voice remarkably like her mother's, she called up the stairs for Freda to shift herself as fast as she liked and get up and ready for school. Without stopping for more than a sip of water and a crust of toast with a scraping of margarine and homemade damson jam, she left the house. The toast, she noticed with half her mind, was burnt again.

Her mood was different from the previous day. An excitement burned in her until her friends at the shop asked what was her secret. Had Bernard come back? Had he asked her to marry him? Barbara continued to smile mysteriously and promised to tell them soon.

By midday she was far from happy. The initial buzz of early-morning optimism had faded, the remaining smile and the air of excitement was a sham. She wondered how much longer she could argue with Mam and keep Mrs Block at bay, and how soon Bernard would be back to share the burden and reassure her all would be well. She stood staring into space, bringing him to mind. The neatness of his suit and the jaunty way he wore his trilby hat – not a flat cap like her father wore. And his eyes! Those dark eyes, behind tortoiseshell-framed glasses, that glowed when he looked at her and told her he would love her for ever. She needed him so badly now, needed reassurance of his love, needed his support.

Her job that day was to unwind lengths of cloth from the heavy bales and measure how many yards were left, marking the amount in her neat handwriting on the labels. She was strong and quite capable of manoeuvring the bales but today she hated the work, afraid that the tiny baby that she imagined to be like one of the stiff-legged celluloid dolls Freda had once had at Christmas time, with feathers for a skirt, would be distressed by the heaving and lifting.

She wanted to leave the work and sit somewhere quiet, like the beach near Gull Island, and dream of how it would be when she and Bernard had a little daughter to love. Rosita. She savoured the name and wondered anew about Luke, the man with the boat, who had named her.

She stayed out that evening, walking the streets, looking into windows and seeing family groups within and imagining being 'Mam' to a family of her own. Wandering without any real purpose, she walked right through the town and came to the Pleasure Beach. There she mingled with the late-summer crowds bent on having fun, sharing vicariously in their happiness. Buying fish and chips to ease her now voracious hunger, she sat on a bench overlooking the sand and ate with enjoyment.

It was quite dark when she slipped into the house and she hurried straight up to bed before her father came in. She ignored her mother's demands to 'Come down this minute, my girl – you and I have arrangements to make' and lay unmoving until the house was quiet. Then she climbed over Freda's sleeping form and went down and made herself some sandwiches of the cold boiled fish her mother had cooked for her earlier in the evening, covering it with salt, pepper and vinegar from the pickled onion jar.

The next day was Sunday and the day on which she helped her mother with the beds. Thank goodness Dad would be out in the garden. She went downstairs to find her mother already sorting the washing into piles ready for the copper that would be lit early the following morning. To the pile near the copper she added the bottom sheet taken from her bed, having put the top sheet to bottom in the regular manner, but her mother told her to stop fussing and listen.

'Mrs Block will be over later and I want you here so she can decide when you can get the little problem sorted. Don't think you can get out of it, mind, and don't you leave this house for even a minute, my girl. You might not have another chance for her to help. In fact, it might already be too late, heaven forbid. She takes a bit of persuading.'

'*She* takes a bit of persuading? What about me? I *won't* be persuaded! You can't make me. I'm going to wait and talk to Bernard. He won't let you get rid of his daughter, whatever you say. I know he'll want me and our baby and if he doesn't then I'll bring her up on my own.'

'She? It isn't a girl, it's nothing at all – only a small shapeless "thing" and you'd best have it taken away so you can forget it ever happened.'

The first storm of tears broke from Barbara then and between sobs she shouted, 'She is a girl and her name is Rosita and she's mine!' Running from the house she headed for the fields near the railway line where she could sit and not be seen, and think about Bernard. When she went home a few hours later her mother was furious.

'Mrs Block has been and gone. Waited for hours she did and her busy enough for two. Where have you been to, wicked girl?'

'Out!' Barbara replied rudely, dodging her mother's hand and sighing with relief at the reprieve.

A few days later she came home from work and the dreaded Mrs Block was sitting beside the fire. Before Barbara could react, Mrs Block shook her head.

'She looks too far gone to me, Mrs Jones, far too much, but I'll have a look at her and we'll see if anything can be done.'

'You'll do nothing!' Barbara said and giving a low scream of fear she escaped and ran towards the home of Bernard Stock. She had to see if there was news of his return, she had to have someone supporting her or Mam would wear her down until she agreed to accept the ministrations of Mrs Block like so many others had done.

She knew there would no longer be a job at the shop; as soon as her condition was clearly seen she would be asked to leave. Unless someone helped she would have to 'get rid' of Rosita, either before or after her birth. Fear made her tremble so her legs seemed unable to support her as, for the first time, she realized that Luke's hint that Bernard might not marry her was a possibility. She increased her pace and was soon at Bernard's back door.

She was surprised to see that all the curtains were drawn. Surely they weren't all ill? The door opened to her knock and a woman she didn't know stood there. She was dressed completely in black, with a veil of that sombre colour hiding her face.

'Could I have a word with Mrs Stock, if you please?' Barbara asked politely, wondering who this strange apparition was.

'If you've come to offer condolences will you please come back later? The funeral is starting in a few minutes.'

'Funeral? But who died? Surely not another of her sons? This war's already taken two of them. There's only Freddie and Bernard – and he's safe in London, thank goodness. Is it Freddie? Oh, how awful.' The beginnings of motherhood gave added horror to the thought of losing a child.

The black-shrouded apparition nodded her veiled head solemnly. 'The poor woman has lost another son. This time her son Bernard. Up in London he was and now he's dead.'

With a gentle cry, Barbara slipped to the ground in a faint.

She opened her eyes to find a group of strangers surrounding her. One of them, a man in a rather ancient, mildew-rimmed dresscoat and black hat, was patting her face and staring at her through small, thick spectacles. Warm, fat hands were chafing icy-cold thin ones. This was a lady who looked at her with eyes filled with sympathy. 'She's coming round,' she said and other hands came to help her to rise.

'I thought someone said Bernard was dead.'

'Dead. Yes, miss.'

'But he wasn't a soldier. How could he be—'

Confused, she allowed herself to be led indoors but almost as soon as she had been seated and given a drink of water, the crowded room emptied, as horse and carriage arrived at the front of the house bearing Bernard's body. The men dispersed and, standing with the women, she watched in disbelief as the cortege disappeared around the corner, carrying her hopes with it.

Food had been set out on the table and on legs that were still shaking, she walked slowly towards it, past the big Welsh dresser that had been denuded of plates and cups and saucers. Helping herself as there was no one to ask, she picked up some squares of bread pudding and some sandwiches, some cheese and, rather guiltily, some pickled onions and filled her pockets. Her muscles regaining strength, she walked from the house and, her mind a blank, headed for the lonely beach near Gull Island, where she and Bernard had walked and laughed and planned and loved, two miles away.

There was no sign of Luke as, almost an hour and a half later, she stepped into the cool living room of his cottage. She found the kettle and made herself some tea, which she couldn't drink, and apart from the onions, which she ate greedily, she gave the food to the wheeling gulls. Appearing almost lifeless, she stared across at the island. The urge to walk across the causeway and jump off the cliffs on the far side occurred to her but only in a melodramatic way, seeing herself as the scorned and ruined heroine in one of Mam's magazines.

The sun was surprisingly warm; it was just past midday and everywhere was silent. The air quivered with the heat. There was no birdsong, no movement apart from the ever-hopeful gulls and the sea steadily undulating on its relentless, unstoppable journey, its faintly heard murmur soothing and soporific. Uncomfortable as the rocky seat was, she slept.

A mist began to cover the surface of the water as the afternoon wore on, making the sun a hazy ball and the island a place of mystery. She stood up stiffly and walked to where Luke had moored his boat. She took a notebook out of her handbag. She wrote a message for him and, stretching into the boat, put it under the seat and anchored it with a stone. She sat a while longer then set off home to more lectures from her mother.

The sea fret now covered Gull Island and the cold was creeping between her clothes and her skin. She moved as fast as she could between the high hedges of the lonely lane, unhappiness clouding her vision more than the blanketing mist. She had been disappointed not to find Luke there when she needed to talk to him so badly. She felt he had let her down. Her message had been brief, a reprimand: 'Where were you? Bernard is dead. Rosita is safe. Why weren't you here?'

She went first to the Careys' and found the room crowded with all eleven members of the family at home, plus the extra children minded while their mothers worked. The noise they made, all clamouring for a meal, was deafening. Pushing two of her sons off the end of the sofa, to sit on sections of tree trunks that served as stools, Mrs Carey made room for her and handed her a cup of tea.

'Get this down you and when I've fed this lot we'll have a chat.'

She busied herself with a huge saucepan containing soup, ladling it out into an assortment of bowls and basins and handle-less jugs, guiding it around the confusion of raised arms and hopeful faces into eager hands. A chunk of bread was given to each child, Idris first, and Barbara thankfully accepted a share.

Mr Carey had just arrived home. He was still wearing the leather apron with a huge front pocket and carried the canvas bag his wife had made for him to carry the newspapers he sold. He made between ten and fifteen shillings a week, selling them in the street and delivering them through letterboxes. Beside him, having helped for part of the round, was Richard, his willing assistant, already able to give correct change for a tanner or a bob – a sixpence or a shilling.

''Lo Barbara,' Richard called with a salute of a dirty hand.

The bogie cart which Mr Carey pulled on his journey was in the passage near the front door, where everyone had to climb over it to get in or out. Two cats had taken it over for the evening. A dog hid under the table but didn't rise to greet Richard, afraid of being sent away from where he might find a few dropped morsels.

Mr Carey was a kindly man. His weary eyes twinkled in the tanned, over-thin face as he greeted Barbara. 'Got a visitor have we, Molly? There's lovely. A young lady in the house might make this lot behave,' he joked, touching the head of each child in turn. 'Now, what have I got in my pocket today?'

Spoons paused momentarily as they all watched their father slowly dip into his leather apron. He brought out a loaf of bread and a dead pigeon. Handing them to his wife he dipped again and this time brought out some small apples. There was one for each of them, sour, unripe, but hungrily accepted. The rest of the contents of his pocket were three eggs, and some potatoes, still encrusted with the earth from where he and Richard had stolen them from someone's garden.

Once the pocket was empty the spoon returned to the attack and the last of the soup was enthusiastically and noisily finished. The stolen, precious food was put aside by Molly Carey for the following day.

Clearing away and washing the dishes was utter chaos as everyone tried to leave the table at once. The dishes were placed under the table individually, with the saucepan, for the dog to lick, then piled near the bowl of soapy water to be washed.

'Clear off out, the lot of you,' Mrs Carey shouted above the din. 'Barbara and I will see to the pots.' The twins, Ada and Dilys, who were approaching their fourteenth birthday, were quick to move and set off to visit friends. They were making plans and made no secret of their intention of leaving as soon as they had finished school.

When the dishes were washed and order restored, and Henry Carey had gone to spend an hour on the garden, Barbara told Mrs Carey about Bernard's death.

'There's sorry I am, *fach*. I knew, see, but as you didn't tell me who was the father and I didn't like to ask, there was no way I could prepare you for the shock.'

'Mam must have known though.'

'Yes, she knew.'

'What happened?' Barbara asked dully.

'From what I've pieced together from his poor mam's version and what the police told my Henry, Bernard was on a train near London and he didn't have a ticket. Tried to hide, he did. When the ticket inspector started to come down the train he planned to go into a lav with a friend who would show his ticket through a partly opened door so they'd think there was only one person in there, but they were too late and the lav was in use. So, the silly boy tried to jump off the train and, well, sufficient to say he was killed.'

'Why didn't someone tell me?'

'Next of kin are informed, love. Girlfriends don't count, not till you're married are you next of kin. His mam couldn't have known how fond Bernard was of you or she'd have sent a message for sure.'

'She knew.' Barbara's voice was bitter.

'What are you going to do?'

'Keep the baby. Perhaps when Mrs Stock knows it's Bernard's daughter she'll help me. I don't think Mam and Dad will.' She tried to hold back the tears but soon gave way to them and was cuddled in Mrs Carey's skinny arms.

Mrs Carey went with her the following evening to talk to Bernard's mother but they were shrilly and angrily told to leave.

'Keep out of my affairs, Molly Carey, and take that trollop with you! My

Bernard wouldn't have done anything like that! Sunday-school teacher he was, remember. Don't try and put that bit of trouble on *me* or I'll have the police on *you*!'

'Pity you feel like that, Mrs Stock,' Molly Carey said quietly. 'With only one of your lovely sons left I'd have thought you'd welcome a grandchild. I know I would in your place.'

Both Barbara and Mrs Carey thought that as time passed, Mrs Jones would forgive her daughter, accept the situation and allow Barbara to have the child at home, but a few days later Mr Jones won almost a pound on the horses. He'd had a run of good luck which gave him the confidence to take a chance and to his amazement, when he picked out a double both horses had romped home first. He gave five shillings to his wife and with the rest he and his friends got drunk.

Unfortunately, in his inebriated state he told the group of people who were helping him celebrate about his daughter's 'bit of trouble'. Encouraged by his friends' supportive outrage, he came home, threatened Barbara with a tightly clenched fist and told her to leave.

Mrs Jones pleaded but Barbara thought her arguments were less than enthusiastic as she repeatedly reminded her daughter that she had no one to blame but herself anyway and could hardly expect others to be sympathetic. Frightened and unable to think what to do, her mother's words racing through her brain, Barbara walked through the streets the following morning until an advertisement caught her attention. It seemed the answer, at least to her immediate problem.

A week later, in response to the advertisement, Barbara handed in her notice at the shop, said a stiff goodbye to her family, and went to work on a small farm twenty-seven miles away from her home town, on which there were cows, sheep, chickens and geese, and cornfields sloping down to the sea.

Luke was sitting in his Cardiff office staring out at the hazy sunshine and wishing he was on his boat fishing off Gull Island. He wore a sports jacket adorned with leather patches on sleeves and elbows, with a blue and green check shirt, and a plain green tie. He felt a fraud. The clothes were worn to conform to the image people expected when they walked into his shop to buy. If he were to dress in the shabby shorts he wore at weekends and in which he felt more comfortable, more himself, he would fail to persuade them that he was offering a quality service as he took their money. Second-hand books was one of the many occupations where formality was important.

He left his chair and walked over to smile politely as a couple came in to look for a book on formal gardens of the eighteenth century. He led them to the relevant section of shelves and shared their delight when they found what they were looking for, but even at such a satisfying moment, he still longed to be free.

He had been born into a wealthy family and his father initially prepared him to work alongside him in the wine business that had been in the family for three generations. But Luke had never settled into the business with a father who held for him ill-concealed dislike. Luke's happiest times had been the hours spent with Roy Thomas and his lively, affectionate family. It was to them that he had scuttled whenever there was an hour to spare.

Then, when Luke had been approaching his eighteenth birthday, Roy paid a rare visit to him. They were in his bedroom, enjoying a playful fight, and his father had come into the room and in a rage told Roy to leave and never come to the house again. There had never been an explanation.

When Luke's mother had died, Roy had defied the order and come to comfort his friend. Luke had been so shocked by the loss of the one person who had made the house a home, he had been unable to cry. Seeing Roy had released the tears and when Luke's father found them, arms around each other, both with tear-stained faces, his rage almost became apoplectic.

Roy was marched from the house and Luke pleaded for him to be allowed to stay.

'He's my friend and I love him,' he said, and, white-faced with disbelief, he heard his father tell him to leave. In a voice trembling with anger and hate, Luke's father told him he was unclean and not fit to dwell with decent people. When Luke continued to plead, his father hit him again and again.

Luke had been so devastated both by the implication of his unnatural love for his friend, and by his father's intransigent disapproval and embarrassment, that he spent weeks doing nothing more than reel from one bar to another. He was arrested three times for being drunk and disorderly and twice spent time in prison on remand, as his father refused to offer bail. Both incidents were for breaking the windows of his father's house.

His mother would have understood, or at least allowed him to talk about it, but she was dead. So it was his grandmother who had helped start him in a career by introducing him to the wonderful world of books and historical maps.

She had rented a small shop and spent several weeks travelling with him to buy books and maps to fill the shelves, mostly books of little value at first, but gradually he began to deal with more interesting and rare volumes, and almost without thinking he began to specialize in books on gardens and the countryside. He also had room on the walls of his shop for the work of local artists, mostly seascapes.

Once he had accepted the need to work and a purpose to rise each morning, he quickly began to succeed. The second-hand book trade was absorbing, his knowledge grew and he was soon respected and well liked. Having none of the aggression of many and without the domineering and condescending attitude men often showed towards women who worked alongside them, the offer of friendship came from all who met him. But apart from Roy Thomas, who was now away fighting in France, he remained a loner.

His business acumen was strong but in his dealings with people he was patient, helpful and without guile. He smiled a lot and made customers believe he had been waiting just for them to come in and cheer his day, but his smile hid his constant loneliness. Unhappiness, guilt, confusion and, most of all, disappointment at his family's attitude still festered under the veil of quiet contentment.

At five minutes to five he closed the ledger on which he had been working, tilted his chair back and stretched luxuriously. He wouldn't go back to his lodgings; he would send a message to his landlady and go to the beach for a few hours of peace and quiet. With Roy in France fighting a bloody, insane battle there was no one to notice if he was late or, he thought with sadness welling up, to care if he didn't get home at all.

As the train took him to the station nearest to Gull Island, he began to wonder about Barbara. Had she succumbed to the pressures of her family and allowed herself to be led to some dark house where some old woman would perform atrocities on her lovely young body and destroy the life within it? What was it about some families that pride, the opinion of others, was of greater importance than love and support?

Barbara was still on his mind when he reached the cottage and changed his clothes. He saw at once that she had been there. The teapot was slightly out of its precise place and the cup and saucer she had used was out of alignment. He was so fussy; like an old woman, he knew that. Roy often teased him about it.

He ate some stale biscuits and drank two cups of tea then went to the boat. He saw the note at once. The baby was safe, thank goodness. Although short, it was such a bossy note he found it impossible not to smile. Terrible to know Bernard was dead, poor Barbara; but at least the baby was safe. He exuded his breath in a long sigh of relief. He hadn't realized just how important it was.

Surprisingly, it being so late in the season, he went out in the darkness and caught a few mackerel, baked them over a fire and ate them.

Just before he left, as the darkness was complete and only faint variations, black against grey, showed him where the rocks were and the shape of his boat, he sat on the cooling beach, caressed by the offshore breeze, and wrote a reply in the light of his torch, guessing she would go there again.

He wished he had asked for her address. She would be glad of a bit of support and he would gladly give it. He thought it unlikely he would ever have a child, but helping to save this one would in part make up for it. In small, neat letters he wrote: 'Come on Sunday, you know where the tea is kept. Please, tell me your address.'

He put it in the same place she had used but as he walked away, the boat tilted and settled more firmly on the gravel. Before he had reached the railway station, the piece of paper had flown over the waves like a ghostly butterfly.

Barbara found work at the farm very hard. She thought of her anxiety at handling the bales of cloth in the shop and smiled bitterly. Here she was expected to roll fifteen-gallon milk churns, throw hay and animal feed about as if it were cotton wool, and carry buckets filled to the brim with water or milk. She felt constantly dirty and unkempt, rarely having either the time or the energy for washing herself. Then there was the farmer.

Graham Prothero was in his mid thirties. He was a burly man, an inch or two under six feet tall, with a rather flat face, a small round nose, a round chin and a full-lipped mouth that seemed sculptured for laughter – but the suggestion of a humorous approach to life was false. He was immensely strong, with hands that seemed to Barbara as big as shovels. But as is often the case with such physique, he was softly spoken and when dealing with a sick animal those hands were surprisingly dexterous.

He was a childless widower and seemed quite willing for her to take his wife's place in his bed. He hinted at an easing of her heavy tasks if she would … accommodate him.

'If you come in with me and keep my bed warm tonight, I think we might arrange for you to have a bit of a lie-in,' he said one day while she was scrubbing the mud from the dark-grey slate floor of the kitchen. 'What say we let you off the early-morning chores, like? And you can start after a breakfast cooked by me. Worth a change of bed for that, isn't it?'

His soft voice was not pleading; there was a matter-of-fact tone that added to the shock of the words and made her wonder if she had somehow misheard. She went on scrubbing the floor, backwards and forwards, the white foamy lather changing pattern with each stroke. He had come to stand over her as she knelt at her task. Best not to reply, she decided, and it occurred to her how less frightening he was than her father, even though he was far stronger and a great deal bigger.

'What d'you say, then? Give it a go, like? And we'll see how we can improve your days for you. Be company for us both, like, as well as a bit of comfort,' he went on, still in the low, soft voice.

'I like the room you've given me, thank you,' she said without looking at him, afraid to give him a smile which he could interpret, together with the words, as a tease. She tried to continue scrubbing without moving her bottom for the same reason!

'What say we give it a try? Your room if you'd prefer. I'm easy.'

She pretended at first not to understand what he meant, hoping her implied innocence would discourage him. At the end of October, when she still refused, he came into her room one evening and slid under the sheet. She stiffened in alarm. He talked to her as he did with his animals, gentling her like he would a frightened horse.

'Come on, Babs. I know you really want this as much as I do. There's daft it is for us to be deprived of something we both want.'

What should she do, or say? She could hardly run away wearing only a nightdress. His arms enfolded her and be began to stroke her. She still didn't move, afraid now, aware of his strength. What if he lost his temper? She could be killed, buried and no one the wiser. Then his hand reached her swollen belly and he gave a growl of rage and threw himself off the bed.

'You brazen hussy! You've got a baby in there and you didn't tell me! All these weeks pretending such innocence! Get out. D'you hear me? Get out. I won't give a home to a—' He seemed lost for the right word and she lay still as his footsteps stomped down the stairs and into the yard. Night hours passed and still she didn't move; she lay petrified until the clock struck five and she heard him moving about downstairs then go out again. She rose, packed her few belongings and left the farm.

With nowhere else to go, she set off to walk the twenty-seven miles back home. The milk cart gave her a lift for part of the way and for a few miles she sat beside a carter delivering some tree trunks to be trimmed before being sent on their way to a coal mine.

She stopped at a couple of farms to ask if there was work and accommodation but she had no luck. It was evening when she reached home but her father opened the door and swiftly closed it again. She turned away, too weary to plead or even weep, and headed for the one place she might at least have a hearing.

Mrs Carey didn't waste time on too many questions but put Barbara to bed with her girls. Barbara was so exhausted that she slept almost immediately, squashed in with three others, including the one-year-old Blodwen, who wet the bed and didn't stir for two hours.

After further explanations during which Mrs Carey fed her and bathed her blistered feet, she described her life as a poorly paid farmworker and housekeeper to Graham Prothero. The next morning she first went again to plead with Mrs Stock to help her but she refused even to open the door. She felt so weary she thought her baby would simply fall from her, the weight of it was pressing so urgently and painfully down, but she put on her coat, a shawl belonging to Mrs Carey, boots belonging to Mr Carey and walked the two miles to the beach near Gull Island. She went into Luke's cottage and collapsed into the armchair. With an inexplicable feeling of peace, she slept.

When she roused herself it was morning and, stiff from a night in the armchair, she was aware that the place was less tidy than usual. A Cardiff newspaper was spread carelessly across the table and a piece had been ringed in spluttering ink. It announced the death of a Cardiff man, Roy Thomas, in the Battle of Verdun during the month of August. He must be Luke's special friend. Where was Luke? She needed to talk to him, help him over this heartbreaking news. She put the paper on one side and made herself some tea. No milk. She smiled sadly at the memory: 'but it's all right if you add extra sugar.'

Luke came that evening. She glanced at the paper and asked softly, 'Your friend?' When he nodded and turned away she went on, 'Oh, I'm so sorry, Luke. I know what it's like. The disbelief, the pretence that it's a mistake and he'll come walking back, laughing and teasing you for being worried. And that awful moment when you know you can't pretend any more.'

They went out together on the boat and caught fish which they cooked on a fire in the rocks. The evening was cold and they huddled together with Mrs Carey's shawl around them and were glad of the warmth of the fire and of each other. They both talked about their sadness and although Barbara didn't fully understand the loss Luke had suffered, considering it far less than her own, she offered sympathy and the promise of friendship for ever.

He was quiet, thoughtful and kind, far more gentle than the men she had been used to, apart from Bernard, and talking to him was without a moment's unease.

'It's as though we've always been friends,' she told him. 'There's no exploring each other's mood and trying to avoid a word that might offend. As I think of something I can say it without fear of spoiling the moment.'

'I feel the same. What good fortune it was that we came here that day, the day when you first knew about Rosita. It's her we'll have to thank as soon as she's old enough.'

The sound of trundling wheels made them leave the fire and look along the lane. Coming into view through the near darkness was Mrs Carey's son, Richard. He was pulling the bogie on which, propped up against sacks of firewood, sat his small, sober-faced sister, Blodwen.

'Mam asked me to find you and give you this,' he said casually, as if he had walked no more than a few paces to deliver the note which he handed to her.

'Richard. How did you find me?' she asked, taking the scrap of paper.

'Mam and me, we guessed you'd be here. Talks about this place a lot, she does,' he added to Luke. He straightened the little girl on her improvised pram and made her more comfortable. Her expression didn't change, yet Luke thought he saw a glimmer of a smile as her eyes moved to watch them.

'Well,' Richard said, 'I'd best be off then. Mam'll shout if I don't get this one home and to bed soon. Needs a candle she does if she's awake after dark, see, and you know how much they cost. Eight pence halfpenny for a box of three dozen. Damn me proper, you can buy a great big jar of jam for that or a packet of oats to last us the week.'

'He's like an old man,' Luke whispered with a chuckle as Richard turned the bogie and began to walk away. 'And that little Blodwen is a comedienne in the making if I'm any judge.' He raised his voice and called, 'Here, wouldn't you and your sister like a drink before you set off back home? I have some biscuits too.'

Without a word or a change of pace, Richard turned the cart in the narrow lane and came back. Ten minutes later he set off again, with Blodwen wrapped in an extra blanket supplied by Luke.

Barbara didn't open the note immediately. She had only glanced briefly at the writing in the hope it was from her mother. It didn't look like Mam's small neat printing but hope refused to die. Perhaps Dad had written it. That must be it. She couldn't remember ever seeing Dad's writing. It had to be from them. Who else would be writing to her? Surely they had forgiven her by now? They couldn't see her without a place to call home. Not with a baby due in a matter of weeks.

She gripped the paper tightly. Convinced it was an invitation to go back home, she was startled to read that Bernard's mother, Mrs Stock, wished to see her.

Shaking with disappointment, she handed the note to Luke. 'I thought, after all these weeks, that Mam and Dad might have wanted to see me, but they don't even want to know if I'm all right.' She spoke half in sadness, half in anger. 'It's Bernard's mother who wants to see me. I called yesterday and she wouldn't open the door. D'you think she's had a change of heart?

Could she be willing to help me after all?' Barbara frowned. 'Perhaps she thought about Auntie Molly Carey's reminder of how her family is almost gone and will accept Rosita as belonging to her?'

'Go carefully, Barbara,' Luke warned. 'Don't let your disappointment warp your judgement. Don't let Mrs Stock talk you into something you don't want. It would be easy for her to play on your love for Bernard.' He touched her arm to soften the words and added, 'Bernard is still your love, I know that, but he's dead. You and your daughter are what counts now. Please remember that and keep it in your mind as you listen to what she has to say. Your future is little Rosita. Promise me?'

'I promise.'

When Barbara knocked on the door of Mrs Stock's house this time, the door opened and she was pulled swiftly inside by the small, tense woman dressed completely in black.

'Afraid you'll be shamed by being seen talking to me?' resentment made Barbara blurt out. 'Afraid your character will be ruined by my being seen at your door?'

'Now just hold your tongue, you! You're in no position to get lippy with me,' Mrs Stock said with a glare of pure dislike.

'What d'you want?' Barbara asked cheekily. Something in the woman's cold expression had made her lose hope of any assistance. Whatever the woman wanted, it wouldn't be an offer of support. And she wasn't in the mood to grovel. She wouldn't grovel to her parents so Mrs Stock had no chance if that was what she had expected.

'I thought you might like this photograph of my Bernard.' She handed a glossy studio picture to Barbara, who took it but hardly glanced at it. She was watching the woman's face. 'There's something else,' she said flatly. 'I'm willing to adopt this baby of yours. Whether it's Bernard's or not, well, I have my doubts, but me and Mr Stock, we'll give it a home. There, what d'you think of that? Very generous in the circumstances, you must agree.'

In words not normally used by a respectable young woman, Barbara told her no thanks!

Chapter Three

Leaving Mrs Stock, Barbara didn't know which was the stronger
need, to laugh or to scream and shout her rage. It was laughter that
won. Giggling almost hysterical laughter that threatened to tear at
her throat as she tried to hold it back, she covered her face from the curious
looks of those she passed as she hurried through the street towards Mrs
Carey's. First being thrown out by Graham Prothero and now this! What
was wrong with her that no one was willing to support her?

Thank heavens for Auntie Molly Carey and her amiable husband. They
had so little yet they were giving her all they could spare. She was seventeen and there was no one in the world who really loved her. Melancholy
thoughts but they still produced only giggles.

'Well? What did Mrs Stock want then? Nothing useful I'll bet a farthing,'
Mrs Carey asked as Barbara walked in.

Sobering her tense, irrational laughter, Barbara told her what Mrs Stock
had suggested. To her surprise, Mrs Carey looked solemn and not amused.

'Offering to take the baby? Well, I suppose I can sympathize. She had
a letter today, poor dab, from the war office.' Then, as Barbara frowned,
a wild thought entering her head that Bernard wasn't dead but was
coming home, she added, 'Her Freddie is missing in action and we know
what that usually means, don't we? Her last surviving son. Now there's
no one but herself and that soft husband of hers. There's a wicked world
we live in, Barbara. They had a houseful of boys, four of them, and now
they're on their own. So I can understand her wanting Bernard's baby,
can't you?'

'She implied it wasn't Bernard's anyway, didn't she? Said he wouldn't do
… you know, him being a Sunday school teacher an' all.' She saw a hastily
hidden smile crease Mrs Carey's face and went on, 'But I didn't do … that
… with anyone else.' That was funny too and her laughter returned.

'Of course you didn't and she knows it. She can't help trying to keep him
as an innocent child in her memory.'

When a fresh outburst of giggles had ended in tears, Barbara didn't know what to say. She would have been kinder to the woman if she had known about Freddie.

'Seven killed on this street since last Christmas,' Mrs Carey went on. 'Never thought I'd be glad of my Henry's bad chest. And the children being young means they're safe at least from the bayonets and guns of the enemy.' She smiled at Barbara. 'Best you make the most of the baby's early years – they get more and more of a worry the older they get. In their first years it's bad enough, mind. Whooping cough, scarlet fever, diphtheria, consumption, measles and all the rest. Still, best not to be gloomy, and sitting moaning won't get the baby a new coat! Come on, get cracking on those potatoes and we'll get a meal ready. You'll stay,' she said rhetorically, 'and spend the night and for as long as you like, if you can bear the thought of sharing a bed with the others.'

Barbara hugged her and whispered her thanks tearfully. What a day. Tears and laughter and all in the wrong places too. She picked up the bucket of potatoes and washed them ready for peeling. As she began putting them into the large stew pan to cook on the fire, she wondered sadly why her own mother wasn't as kind and sympathetic as Mrs Carey.

'Why won't Mam help me?' she asked. 'If you don't feel the shame of having me under your roof, well … I mean, my own mother.'

'Your dad, he's the one. He's so angry she doesn't stand a chance of talking him round. She'd have weeks and weeks of argument and him giving her less than usual money for food. Done it before he has, when you wanted to stay on at school, remember? He gave her plenty of his lip then, he did, and sulked for weeks, the big Jessie that he is!' She hugged Barbara briefly. 'No, *cariad*, it's not that your mam won't help – she can't help.'

She didn't tell Barbara that Mrs Jones came every week with a few shillings for her to mind until Barbara needed it. There was over two pounds there now, hidden in a tin under some old nails and screws and odds and ends that no one bothered to look at. It was safe there until Barbara was really in need.

Henry Carey came in, with Richard, his usual shadow, behind him. The rest of the family gathered around to see what luxuries he had brought that day. Even the surly twins looked hopeful. The bag didn't contain much but, round eyed, the children applauded each revelation.

'First of all, I found these shoes and thought they might fit Barbara, her having bigger feet than my Molly,' he said, turning to Barbara to explain. 'I try and walk along the back lanes just before the ash cart comes to empty the bins. It's amazing what people throw away. I often find something we can use or sometimes even sell. A bit of carpet, a bowl or bucket that's still got a bit of life in it. Even furniture, a table or chair once or twice, just missing a leg or needing a bit of a polish. Most things only need a bit of a polish.'

Barbara thought of the abandoned rubbish in the yard waiting for Mr Carey to find time for a bit of polish or the right bit of wood to mend it, and she shared a smile with Mrs Carey.

He pulled out a handful of hazelnuts, dropped from a broken bag as someone carried them home, and he shared them between the children. 'And then,' he said with a teasing smile, 'and then I saw, sitting on the ground with no one to miss them, these!' Like a conjurer he produced a cabbage, three carrots still covered in incriminating earth and three duck eggs. Amid cheers he pulled up his sleeve and showed a dog bite, admitting cheerfully, 'I also got this, mind. I had to stick my hand through a fence to get the eggs. Richard couldn't reach luckily or the animal would have had his hand off!' He entertained the family with exaggerated stories about his battle with the dog, which grew larger and more ferocious with every telling.

Helping Mrs Carey by minding the children and accepting occasionally offered work in someone's kitchen when a member of staff fell ill, Barbara survived until the beginning of December. From what she had learned from one visit to the doctor and the information given by sundry 'experts' who had been through the birth of a child several times, Barbara guessed that the baby would be born near Christmas. Luke came to her mind suddenly as she remembered that his birthday was Christmas Day, and she wanted to see him again.

She was surprised to realize that she also missed Graham Prothero and life at the farm. She often sat and stared into space with her blue, dreamy eyes and thought about him. Would it have been possible for her to live with him as his wife? He hadn't suggested marrying her, she knew that, but if she hadn't had a belly full of baby, what then? Would he have considered making her Mrs Prothero?

She rolled the name around her tongue; it wasn't such a terrible prospect. She remembered his strong physique with growing interest, and those large hands that could be so gentle. There was something very safe and dependable about Graham. She felt colour warm her cheeks as she compared him to Bernard and stood up abruptly to push away the excitement of where her thoughts were taking her. No, she still loved Bernard and she always would.

Mrs Carey had arranged for the services of Mrs Block, whom her mother had once asked to perform an abortion, to be available at the birth. That thought frightened Barbara more than the anticipation of pain. What if she killed the baby at the moment of birth?

'There's daft you are, young Barbara,' Mrs Carey said. 'I'll be there, won't I? And I'll promise her an extra shilling if the baby is strong and healthy. Now, does that make you feel better, girl?'

Once or twice Barbara took Richard and a couple of the other children and walked with them to the beach near Gull Island. Mrs Carey was glad to have them 'out from under my feet' for a while, all except Idris, of course. Idris was still beautiful with golden hair that fell in natural curls around his chubby neck. His eyes were as blue as a picture Barbara had seen of a lake in a place called Switzerland.

One Saturday afternoon, early in December, leaving Mrs Carey baking a pie which she planned to fill with swede and potato and a few scraps of leftover meat, and Mr Carey treating himself to a visit to the football game, Barbara walked out to Luke's cottage near Gull Island. Leaving the children making sandcastles on a patch of coarse sand, she went into the cottage, hoping for a message from Luke. She wanted to tell him all was well with Rosita, but the place was neat and tidy and there was no sign of him ever having been back. Leaving another note in case he turned up, she spent a while playing with the children, awkwardly finding a place where she could rest with a minimum of discomfort.

She had brought a loaf and a small amount of jam wrapped in paper and a cloth. They ate it with great enjoyment and quenched their thirst at the pump from where Luke gathered his water, but she didn't allow them into the cottage – that would have been an intrusion, unless Luke gave permission.

When it was time to leave, Richard was missing. Immediately Barbara was in a panic. The tide was swirling around the island and almost covering the causeway, wrapping the island in a wild and murderous embrace. She thought of Mrs Carey's words about her family being safe from the fighting in far-off France. Surely she couldn't lose a five-year-old to the sea so close to home?

Screaming his name in her panic, clutching her swollen belly, she sobbed as she ran around the cottage and the ruins of others nearby, but the waves drowned her call and the seagulls laughed at her. The other children, sensing her fear, began to cry, running with her, pulling on her skirts, frightened but not knowing why.

It was less than two minutes before she saw him casually sauntering out of a ruined building some 200 yards further along the beach, but in those terrifying seconds her mind had sped through the loss of him, finding his body, telling his mother he was dead.

Seeing him alive and unharmed, she ran up and hit him furiously about his head and shoulders. She was crying then as she hugged him better and said she was sorry, trying to explain her fear.

'Come and see what I've found,' Richard said, when they had both stopped crying. 'There's this house, see, and I wonder if I could come sometimes and play in it.'

'No you can't. It belongs to someone,' Barbara explained. 'You can't go in a house that doesn't belong to you, as I explained when I wouldn't let you into my friend Luke's cottage.'

'We wouldn't do no harm,' Richard protested. 'Come on, Barbara, just have a look-see. Or I'll tell our mam you clouted me for nothing,' he warned.

'Oh, all right.' She grinned at him. 'Then we really do have to get back.'

The house had been empty for a long time and there was little sign of previous habitation. Walls once whitewashed were mottled with old paint and moulds in a variety of colours, all drab. The corners of the room were dark with stones and branches and oddment of nets and sacking and vegetation that the wind had brought in. The fireplace was nothing more than a hole, empty of any appliance with which to cook. Rusted metal gave a clue that there had once been a hook on which to hang a cooking pot. Or, Barbara mused, there might have once been a small range or more likely a Dutch oven to stand in front of the blaze. Leaving the other children to play with pebbles on the stone-slabs floor, she and Richard went upstairs.

'Careful, Richard, the wood must be rotten. I don't want you falling through onto the slabs below.'

'Promise not to hit me if I hurt myself?' he asked cheekily.

There were two bedrooms and the remains of a third, which had once been supported by a porch. The porch had gone, blown away by some fierce Atlantic storm, and the floor of the third and smallest room hung at a dangerous angle.

They were all dirt-streaked from the dust of the old place by the time they left but Barbara used the edge of her full skirt and by dipping it into a rocky, barnacle-encrusted pool wiped off the worst of it before shepherding them along the lanes towards home.

She was tired, and decided not to walk the four miles there and back again until after the baby was born. Even Mrs Carey, who answered her many questions as well and thoroughly as she was able, had not prepared her for the cumbersomeness of her body, or the aching back and legs, or the terrible weight between her legs when she had been on her feet too long. She wished she could have seen Luke. He was her lucky charm, her merrythought – not that she had seen many of those! The wishbone, or any other part of a juicy chicken, was not for the likes of her, unless one should crawl, suicidally, into Mr Carey's pocket!

As they passed the turning leading to the railway station, it was almost dark, the moon not yet filled with light, and she hardly looked at the steaming monster that was snorting impatiently at the platform. Blodwen, who rarely wanted to move from her place on the bogie, cried to be picked up to see it and, groaning at the extra strain on her back, Barbara did so.

As the engine pulled away, the lighted carriages towed like a column of fireflies, a figure came down the bank from the station, saw them and called. Barbara waited with fingers crossed in hope and to her delight recognized the small, neat figure of Luke. She was surprised by how different he looked, dressed in formal city clothes.

'Barbara! What good luck. I've been hoping you'd come to see me before this. Is everything all right?'

'Me and Rosita are fine and being looked after by Auntie Molly Carey.' She smiled her delight at seeing him. 'These are some of her tribe as you'll remember. We've been for a picnic.'

'You didn't cross to the island, I hope.'

'No fear. Too many to look after.'

'Don't go unless I'm with you, will you?'

'I won't. Never sure of the tide and with these to look after—'

'I don't need looking after,' Richard protested, bristling with outrage.

Barbara and Luke stood smiling at each other, making inconsequential remarks. Richard watched them, frowning and gathering the others around him, waiting for her to move on. Occasionally he would sigh to remind her they were there and the sigh was echoed by little Blodwen.

'Best I go,' Barbara said at last. 'Pity we didn't meet earlier. Got to get them back for supper, see.'

'Come again soon,' Luke said. 'I'm usually here on Sundays.'

'Soon,' she promised.

It was with undisguised regret that she turned away from him. She glanced back several times to wave at the thin, lonely figure until it faded and became a part of the shadows, swallowed up by the night.

'Is he going to be your 'usband, then?' Richard asked.

'No, he's just a friend.'

She wondered why she had never thought of Luke as a prospective husband. It was normal as breathing for girls of her age to consider the possibility with any new acquaintance. Probably because she still grieved for Bernard Stock, but also because the affection Luke showed was of a different kind. He was a loving friend and she doubted if he could ever be anything more. She also realized that for him it was the same. They had struck up an immediate rapport but although love might grow between them it wouldn't be the kind she had felt for Bernard and never would be.

Too tired to work it out, she said aloud, 'Luke is the one person I can say anything to and be sure he understands. Now, sing, all of you, to cheer ourselves and hurry our steps back home.' They all began to sing with her, 'Show me the way to go home, I'm tired and I wanna go to bed.'

A strong wind began to blow through the bare hedgerow, and the moon sailed along in a clear sky. It filled and shed a soft light that picked out the frost glittering on the leafless branches. The air was chill and the wind made the best of it, finding gaps in their clothes and whistling around their bare legs.

The children in their thin clothes began to wail. Cold, hungry; what was she thinking about keeping them out so late? Fine mother she'd make! Changing the slow song to a march to keep them more cheerful, she sang, 'Jolly good luck to the girl who loves a soldier.' She picked up the youngest, set up the fastest pace the rest could manage and headed once more for the Careys' poor home.

Luke continued to smile until the small group had dissolved in the darkness, the sound of their singing no more than a ghostly echo, then his shoulders drooped and he walked slowly to the cottage. Inside, he lit the paraffin lamp, busied himself making tea then sat in the chintz-covered chair to read his sister's letter.

His heart was racing as he unfolded the flimsy page, hoping for a message of support but fearing disappointment. He had written to her address on the outskirts of Cardiff asking if he might visit her at Christmas and see her children. The reply was brief, stating baldly that he would not be welcome at Christmastime or at any other.

Turning the lamp low, wanting to hide his sorrow in darkness, he sat for more than an hour wondering if, and how, he should kill himself. He ought to make a will. There was no doubt in his mind who should benefit from everything he owned. Barbara and Rosita should receive whatever money the business achieved.

Too lethargic to even walk across the room to put a match to the fire, he wrote down his wishes briefly and clearly and signed them with his full name and the date. Then he cried as he realized he couldn't remember her address or her second name. It was Jones, wasn't it? Or Davies? Or Evans or Thomas? The more he pondered the less he was sure. And didn't a will need to be witnessed? What a fool he was. The document was useless because he was useless!

He lit a match and was about to burn the paper but stopped, blew out the match and threw the paper into a drawer of the desk. Burning it was too much of an effort, he would have to get up to put the ashes in the embers in the grate and he really couldn't be bothered.

He sat in his chair and the lamp flickered and went out, leaving only the unpleasant smell of the burnt oil. He ought to get up and relight it but what was the point? Barbara had friends and didn't need him, his father hated him and his sister wanted to pretend he didn't exist.

Discomfort, that sanity restorer, eventually brought him out of his depression and, shivering with cold, his muscles locked in tension, he forced himself to rise. Like an old man, he moved to relight the lamp and put a match to the fire. There was a shuffling among the screwed-up paper under the criss-cross sticks and as the flames began to slowly curl upwards, a mouse jumped out, shook itself and raised its head as if to reprimand him for disturbing its slumber.

The fur on its back was only slightly scorched and it allowed him to pick it up and place it on the table. The creature was dazed but Luke pretended it was tame and was accepting him as a friend. It seemed very important at that moment to be accepted even by this tiny mouse. He sat watching it, while slowly taking a parcel of sandwiches from his pocket then offering the little creature some crumbs. To his delight the mouse sat up and chewed without any sign of fear.

He ate too, with a pretence of company, and when the mouse had once more disappeared, he opened the door and stood looking out across the glistening sea to the island. The light from the moon made a path that tempted him once again to think of walking along it to oblivion, away from his misery. It was cold with a rawness that seemed to threaten the very skin on his face and he dug his hands deep into his pockets. His fingers closed on a long, narrow box. The watch. It was to have been his gift to Roy this Christmas. He lifted it again and was about to hurl it into the sea but then held back as an idea occurred to him. Once the war had ended, he would go and find Roy's grave and bury the watch there with him.

The decision gave him a sense of purpose he had lacked since the news of Roy's death had reached him and the tenseness around his thin face relaxed as plans began to form. The mouse ran across the floor twice more as he sat quietly in his chair. He slept that night with an odd sense of comfort, knowing he had company.

Mrs Carey was upset. Today she had received the payment from her Christmas savings club. All the year she had been giving sixpence and more when she could, to a woman who called each Friday and marked the amount on a card. Leaving Richard in charge of the children, she had gone to the shops and bought a small gift for each of them – dolls, toy cars, a scarf each for the twins – and with only a few shillings left to buy fruit on Christmas Eve, she had counted and found there was sixpence missing. She was extremely careful with money, always knowing to the halfpenny how much she owned. She knew it had been taken by one of the children. But which one?

She waited until Barbara had brought them home and they were sitting around the crowded table before demanding to know who had taken the sixpence.

'I save all the year so we can make Christmas a bit different from the rest of the year and I won't have you taking more than your share,' she said, her small figure bristling with anger and hurt.

Barbara looked around at the shocked faces looking for a sign of guilt, but it was Idris, the golden boy, at whom she looked longest. 'Idris?' she asked quietly. 'You were here all day and the others were out. D'you know anything about a missing sixpence?'

'Barbara!' Mrs Carey said at once. 'As if my Idris would take from his own mother!'

'Sorry, Auntie Molly Carey, I only thought – him being the only one here....'

'He wouldn't take my money, would you, *cariad*? Now ...' She glared around the table again, questioning them all. On Idris's palm, a round pattern deepened as he gripped the small silver coin tightly. Richard and Barbara watched him, and knew.

The discussion went on for a few minutes, then Idris slid down from his seat next to his mother and crawled across to the hearth. He held up his hand, smiling his beautiful smile, and showed the sixpence he was holding. 'Look, Mam, it's here, dropped in the coals.'

Mrs Carey was overjoyed but Barbara stared at Idris, her eyes full of doubt. She puzzled over why she disliked him so much and wondered also if it were possible to see the future character of one so young.

Ten days later, long after midnight had struck and ended Christmas Day, Luke and the mouse dozed in front of a fire of driftwood, having eaten Christmas dinner together, sharing a chicken, some cheese and a loaf of bread. The mouse had found a comfortable place in the cupboard beside the fireplace and Luke felt beholden to his new friend to come as often as he could to warm the house for its comfort.

Two miles away, in a bed already overcrowded, Barbara lay cuddling her small daughter whom she called Rosita. Rosita Jones, born just before midnight on Christmas Day.

'She's so small. And her causing so much fuss. And look at those legs! She's like a doll with half the stuffing missing,' Barbara said, as she examined the perfect child.

Mrs Carey laughed, her eyes tearful with pleasure. 'Give her time, *fach*. In a month those limbs will be filled out and she'll be the most beautiful baby the town's ever seen.'

'If it had been a boy,' Barbara said sleepily, 'I'd have called him Luke.'

Luke heard about the birth of Rosita early in 1918. It was a Tuesday but Richard didn't complain when Barbara asked him to abandon school and go to the cottage at Gull Island with a note for Luke.

The wind came across the sea with a bite and Richard covered up his head by pulling the back of his coat up and over it, his head in the part where his shoulders should be, arms high and sticking out like antennae. His legs were bare apart from socks which fell around his ankles and disappeared into the over-large boots, but it felt a little better when the wind didn't burn his ears and forehead. Crouched at this odd angle, he walked on, giving the appearance of a deformed alien.

Luke's place seemed empty as he approached the lonely cottage on the isolated shore but as he knocked, then climbed up to look through the window, the door opened and a smiling Luke invited him inside.

'I brought a note from Barbara,' Richard explained, digging in his pocket.

'I thought you might. It's the baby, is it? The little girl?'

'Called her Rosita, she has, mind. There's a name to give a tiddly little squawker.'

'She's a squawker, is she, this Rosita? If she makes her presence known so loudly, she's going to stay. It shows that she's strong.'

'Why d'you live here all alone?' Richard asked. 'Haven't you got no family?'

'None.' The muscles on Luke's jaw tightened and he tried to smile. Then he added, 'Well, there's my friend, of course. Not really family, more a sort of adopted friend.' He knelt down and made a squeaking sound with his lips and after a moment the mouse came out and ran over to his outstretched hand.

Richard moved slowly, instinctively careful not to frighten the little creature, and to his delight, the mouse accepted him and took food from him. The giving of food, such a basic gesture of friendship, gave pleasure and Luke's smile became a natural one.

The man and the boy found each other good company, the spurious adulthood of Richard giving Luke a protective feeling for the boy, Richard seeing in Luke a rare adult who talked to him as an equal and not down to him.

'Did you know that I'm six today?' Richard told him. 'Mam said I can have the cream off the milk in my cocoa, but I expect I'll let Blodwen have it, her being in more need of it, like, being so young.'

'Or Barbara maybe?' Luke couldn't help suggesting.

'She wouldn't take it, not her. Barbara won't take more than she has to.'

'And it's really your sixth birthday? Well, we ought to make today something special. What d'you say to a trip in the boat? We might even catch a small coddling.'

Richard hid his excitement well, nodding briefly and throwing an 'All right then' over his shoulder in the most casual way. But Luke saw the glowing eyes and knew the boy was pleased. He found an extra coat and they set off armed with short boat rods and a tin of lug-worms that Luke had gathered earlier in the day.

Richard found the boat an unbelievably thrilling experience. Luke rowed them around the island and they landed for a brief walk on the soft, downy turf and watched as rabbits hopped about with no fear of them. The air had warmed slightly but was still harsh and the thought of anchoring the craft and sitting to wait for fish to swim to their bait quickly lost its appeal, so after Luke had rowed them further across the bay until they were opposite the ruined cottage, they returned to the beach and the warmth of his home with relief.

Defiant of the cold, they didn't stay inside. Luke made a fire on the shore and they sat in the lee of the boat, draped in blankets, while the flames licked around the driftwood and they talked. They each spoke of their dreams and hopes for a future neither could really imagine.

Luke spoke prosaically of continuing to run his book-selling business without any contact with the family he loved. Richard's future was filled with hopes of a different kind of life to the present one. He described vividly a time where there was plenty of space and where no one needed to be cold or hungry. A future in which the Carey family didn't depend on the varied contents of Mr Carey's pockets.

When the fire died down and shadows began to bring a return of the deepening cold, they went inside and ate several rounds of toast, then they walked along the beach to the cottage Richard and Barbara had once explored.

'D'you own this?' Richard asked. 'You must be rich if you own the other one and rich people always own more than they need.'

'It belongs to no one. The man who used to live there moved away when I was a child.'

'There'd be plenty of room for us in that place.' Richard studied it with his old-young face, one small, skinny leg propped on a rock, leaning forwards, elbow on his raised knee, in the attitude of an ancient philosopher.

'What?' Luke laughed aloud. 'One cough and the lot would be down around you!'

'It's strong!' Richard insisted.

Luke looked at the boy, surprised at the vehemence in his voice. 'Do you really think so, Richard?'

'It's only the front bit that's falling off.'

Doubtfully, Luke went to look more closely at the walls and then, seeing the anxious look on the boy's face and realizing that this was a part of his dream, he nodded. 'You're right. Once that porch is re-built it wouldn't make a bad home.' A look of pleasure lit Richard's young face, and the thin shoulders dropped in relief.

'I got a plan, see,' the boy said.

Luke was curious but didn't ask. If and when Richard wanted him to be involved, he'd tell him.

Among his food supplies, Luke had some Gong soup that cost twopence for three packets. Not much of a meal to offer a guest but at least it only took a few minutes to make and it would warm them. He made up two bowls and filled them with bread and they ate with enjoyment.

Richard had a rather ancient apple in his pocket, which he solemnly cut in half. They curled their faces at the sourness but by dipping it into the sugar bowl ate everything except the core, which they gave to the mouse.

'Give little Rosita a hug from me, will you?' Luke said as Richard reluctantly stood to leave.

'Lucky you are that she isn't living with you,' Richard sighed, tutting and shaking his head in his old man gesture. 'Noisy beyond she is. There's always knocking from them in the next room or them up above complaining and asking us to keep her quiet. Fat chance of anyone getting that one to stay quiet.'

When Richard had gone, Luke sat for a long time on the stony beach near the embers of the fire, staring out at the slowly receding tide. He had enjoyed the company of the boy and now, even though the night air chilled him, he couldn't face returning to the loneliness that stretched out before him once he closed the cottage door behind him.

He kicked the fire into a blaze and threw on more wood. Better out here where he could at least believe in the existence of others even if they were miles away, than shutting himself in the cottage and the unbreakable silence behind a closed door. After an hour, during which he went over the conversation between himself and the six-year-old Richard Carey, smiling occasionally at brief memories, he went in, fed the mouse and went to bed.

The following morning he was wakened early by the sound of someone entering. Curious but not alarmed, he sat up and reached for his clothes and in moments he was on his way down the stairs. To his initial delight, he saw his father standing near the fireplace – tall, well dressed but with such a look of hatred in his eyes that the smile of welcome froze on Luke's face and the contents of his stomach curdled.

'Father? Good to see you. Sorry I was still in bed. I'll soon have the fire lit and some tea made.'

'Get out.'

'What?' Luke staggered as if the man had hit him. 'What d'you mean?'

'Get out of this house and do not come back. This cottage belongs to the family and you do not.'

'But I come here at weekends to get away from town and what harm can I do, just living here for a few days a week?'

'It's a family property and you are trespassing. Your sister told me you were living here and I won't allow it, d'you hear?'

'You can't mean it, Father.' Luke was trembling. He hadn't realized just how much he had hoped that once he and his father met and talked, things would have come right between them. But, as usual, in his father's presence, he couldn't muster his thoughts to even begin. 'I'm your son,' he stuttered painfully. 'I love you and you must love me. How can that not be so?'

'Don't say that word! Coming from your mouth it's unclean. I'll wait outside while you gather your things then the door will be locked and you will give me your key.'

In a daze, Luke went upstairs and returned with his clothes and few possessions in a leather bag. His father refused to take the key from his hand but told him to place it on the table in a cigar box presumably brought for the purpose. Didn't he even want to touch something I've handled? Luke wailed inwardly at the insult. Foolishly, in that moment of anguish, he thought of the mouse.

'I have a pet mouse – he depends on me for food,' he said, stuttering madly.

'No more he doesn't.' His father kicked the carcase of the mouse towards the centre of the room, the mouse crushed with his heel as it came trustingly to greet him. Luke stumbled from the house and didn't see his father leave.

He was absent from the bookshop all that week, having broken the lock and slept in the cottage, guessing his father wouldn't bother to check that he had indeed left. He had to see Barbara and Rosita before he returned to Cardiff, give them an address where they could find him. They at least wouldn't abandon him. But he wondered if even Barbara would turn away from him if she knew how much his father hated him for saying he loved his friend Roy. He knew he mustn't ever mention Roy again, but just hold the happy childhood memories of the Thomas family close to his heart.

He had to wait until Sunday. That seemed the most likely day for Barbara and the children to come. To occupy himself while he waited, he began repairing the porch of the house in which Richard had taken such interest. There were a few tools in the cottage and the remains of the porch were scattered but mostly still sound. He went into town to order wood and cement, which was delivered immediately, Luke himself riding with it on the back of the firm's horse and cart.

Stones for renewing the walls were easy to find and by the time Sunday had come, the porch was as good as new. It was surprising how much the place improved with a good brushing and scrubbing. He even whitewashed some of the walls, taking pleasure in the transformation and enjoying the physical hard work, using it to blot out the expression of hatred on his father's face.

The third bedroom still needed a lot of work but he knew a bag of plaster, strips of skirting board and a few pots of paint would work a small miracle. It was tempting to take another week away from the shop and continue with the tasks he had set himself, but he had to get back. The bookshop was his sheet anchor and without that reason to rise each morning, he would soon succumb to misery and despair.

He bought potatoes from a local farmer on that Sunday morning and put them into the edge of the newly lit bonfire. He watched the lanes and listened for the sound of the children coming. He'd hear them soon and they'd be singing. They were always singing. At three o'clock, with the day already darkening, the potatoes were cooked and he had abandoned hope. Cleaning himself up, he changed into his town clothes and went to the station.

Chapter Four

As 1918 MOVED along on leaden feet, the newspapers continued to print photographs of young men who had been killed, wounded or gassed, or were missing in one of the many battlefields. The list seemed endless, with some mothers begging for news of a missing son and others taking what comfort they could from the words of praise for their sons' bravery and coolness in action. A few believed the oft-repeated words.

For all the mothers it was their little boys they lost, children who had been given a uniform and told they were men. To the mothers they would never be anything but their naughty boys, whom they had expected to come in dirty and hungry from some street game or other.

Food had been rationed in February 1918, when everyone thought the government had abandoned the idea completely and would continue to persuade the country to eat less imported foodstuffs without the law making it impossible to do otherwise. It affected some more than others. Mrs Carey, living in two overcrowded rooms and trying to survive on a very low wage, didn't see the point of complaining when the government demanded two meatless days each week – for her family there had often been meatless weeks. Mr Carey refused to eat margarine when they could not afford butter – he insisted it couldn't be edible as it was cheaper than cart grease!

Barbara felt the war was happening somewhere else, between peoples whose arguments didn't concern her. Cardiff was only eight miles away and she had never been there, so how could events across the sea in a land where they spoke a different language affect her? The only way war affected her was by seeing the letters in the now-familiar envelopes delivered almost daily to families around the street until she thought that there couldn't be any more young men left to die in far-off fields.

Eventually, even those small dramas failed to really touch her. She would shake her head, her lovely eyes filling with tears, and she would say the expected words, like, 'There's a shame,' 'Pity for her,' 'Isn't it sad?', but nothing felt real any more. Bernard was dead and there couldn't be anything as hard to bear ever again.

Bernard's mother came several times to the overflowing house in which Barbara continued to live. Barbara was not happy about her coming but was sympathetic to her need. Each time she came, the unhappy woman sat and criticized Barbara, and nursed her granddaughter, her thin shoulders stooped as she *cwtched* the crying child.

'Always crying she is,' she said in reproof. 'Anyone can see she's unhappy. She's ill fed and just look at her clothes, *ach a fi*! This old blanket she's wrapped in isn't fit for a mangy old dog.' Each time she came she offered to adopt Rosita. Her requests became demands as she criticized Barbara more and more strongly for allowing her child to suffer unnecessary deprivation.

'Stubborn you are, my girl, and an uncaring mother. She'd be brought up in comfort and without having to eat stuff like that!' She pointed to the 'bread and scrape', as Mrs Carey called the bread thinly coated with margarine and the seven-pound jar of jam that had been placed on the table. 'Proper food she'd have and a room of her own and decent schooling too. Not like Mrs Carey's ragamuffins wandering the streets following their useless father! The best is what she'd have with us. Selfish mother who'd deprive her child of all that!'

'It's only Richard who won't go to school,' Barbara defended. 'Like a man he is for all his lack of years, delivering papers and doing whatever else he can to help the family.' But her thoughts were not on winning arguments. Mrs Stock's words penetrated and were causing her to feel guilt. Of all the jewels offered, the thought of a room for her own use seemed to Barbara the most luxurious. Without moving her head she allowed her large, gentle eyes to glance around the overcrowded and very shabby room.

Paper peeling from a corner where rain had penetrated through weakened brickwork. A ceiling patterned with cracks, missing plaster and coloured with endless years of smoke. Wasn't Mrs Stock right? Wouldn't Rosita be happier with her grandmother than with her? What can I offer, she asked herself, except a continuation of this dreary life we're leading?

She rolled her pale blue, dreamy eyes back to the solemn face of Mrs Stock and shook her head. She always had a look of calmness and even now, while her thoughts were in turmoil over her decision, she spoke quietly. 'Rosita's mine. She's best with me.' Whatever happened, she knew she had to at least try and keep Rosita with her. She strengthened her resolve, remembering the urgency on Luke's face as he made her promise never to allow anyone to take Rosita from her. She half smiled, remembering his certainty that the baby would be a girl.

'You can smile and look as smug as you like. It's easy now, being sheltered from reality by the kindness of poor Mrs Carey, taking room and energy she can't spare. Selfish, that's what you are, but I'll have her in the end, see if I don't!'

Looking at the thin-faced, unhappy woman who needed the child as a substitute for the family she had so tragically lost, Barbara vowed silently that whatever happened, Rosita would never live with Mrs Stock. That house might have many things others would call luxuries but there would also be misery, bitterness and a lack of laughter. No, Bernard's mother would never take Rosita, not while she had a tongue in her head to shout a protest.

If only things had worked out on Graham Prothero's farm. Plenty of space there, enough and to spare. Fields for Rosita to wander in and woods to explore. Plenty of fresh food too. Heaven that would have been for Rosita to grow up in – such freedom, she couldn't have failed to be happy. But the freedom was too costly a price – her own in exchange for Rosita's. Besides, she reminded herself, she hadn't been given the choice once Graham had discovered about Rosita. Pointless to regret the decision to leave when there hadn't been one to make.

No, there was nothing to think about with regret. And it was hardly luxury she had walked away from. Best not to invent dreams that were pure fantasy. Although, memories of the place weren't all bad. Hard work for sure, but Graham had been fair in his own way.

Leaving Rosita with Mrs Carey whenever possible, Barbara did several jobs to earn her keep. Working odd hours and taking what work was offered, she managed to pay Mrs Carey for her food and buy the necessities for the baby. Most days, working and bringing up Rosita kept her busy from early morning until she fell exhausted, into her shared bed, late at night.

Mrs Carey continued to help without complaint, but sickly, and with another child of her own on the way, Barbara knew it was only a matter of weeks before that good lady asked her to find somewhere else. Mrs Stock had been right about that, she admitted silently. She mustn't depend on Mrs Carey's good nature for much longer.

There were rumblings of discontent from Mrs Carey's landlady too. She issued frequent reminders that the rooms were overcrowded and the bogie cart and piles of newspapers were a nuisance to other tenants, going in and out past these obstacles.

Noise from Rosita's constant wailing didn't help. Whatever they did to try and pacify her, she cried for most of the twenty-four hours of each day. The walls resounded to the banging of irate lodgers trying to sleep, their complaints reinforced by the landlady's requests to be 'more considerate, if you please. That child is noisy beyond!' The prospect of the whole family being thrown out onto the street was a growing fear.

There were nights when even fatigue from the hectic work-filled hours couldn't keep her from lying awake wondering how she would manage once they parted from the Carey family. Here there was security, with baby Rosita sleeping in the wooden crib made by Mr Carey, watched over with something approaching adoration by Richard.

Now eighteen months old, Blodwen needed him less, so Richard took responsibility for Rosita's wellbeing. He accepted care of her like he took care of everything else: very seriously. It was he who fed her with the bottle of Nestlé milk which Barbara made before she left for work in the pre-dawn dark. He who wrapped some sugar in muslin for her to suck to keep her quiet for a few precious minutes while his mam rested.

Idris rarely left his mother's side and Barbara heard him cry softly, as if trying not to, then admitting that Rosita's crying kept him from sleeping and gave him a pain in his head. Several times during the night, Mrs Carey would drag herself from her bed to nurse Rosita so her golden boy could sleep.

Barbara disliked Idris as much as she loved young Richard. Idris stole from her meagre purse although Mrs Carey refused to accept this. He also stuck his fingers into the tin of Nestlé condensed milk and licked them, so there was often none for the baby's bottle.

Giving up trying to make Mrs Carey believe her, Barbara took extra care of her pennies and hid the milk whenever she went out, telling only Richard where to find it.

In the local fish restaurant, Barbara cleaned fish ready for cooking and scrubbed the yard. Chilblains covered her hands and her ankles but were ignored as she went from the fish cleaning to a house where she again used cold water to prepare vegetables and then wash floors. Summer was coming, wasn't it? And with it respite from the painful condition. Things were bound to improve once summer came. Plenty of jobs then, once the summer visitors started to arrive.

At The Anchor public house, where her father was a regular customer, she emptied toilets and washed the floor of the barn that housed them. A dozen jobs, each unpleasant, earned her sufficient money to survive. She refused nothing. As long as there were hours in the day she was determined to fill them earning money to keep herself and her daughter.

Mrs Jones, Barbara's mother, still gave the occasional florin or half a crown to Mrs Carey to help her daughter, although Mr Jones knew nothing about it. Mrs Carey hid the money and managed without it, knowing that one day soon, Barbara would need money to find a place of her own.

The newest Carey child was born in April, a tiny scrap of a girl they called Meriel. For a while, Barbara abandoned several jobs to look after Mrs Carey. Mr Carey seemed more weighed down by the event than his wife and sat for hours at a time on a chair in the back garden staring at the apple tree as if it could somehow supply an answer to their growing problems. Richard tried to persuade Idris to help with the newspapers but Mrs Carey refused to allow it.

'Not Idris, ask one of the others, Richard, *bach*,' she pleaded. 'He keeps me company and he's helpful beyond with the new baby.'

Richard knew that his useless brother did nothing but he sighed stoically and carried on alone.

One day in May, when she was blessedly free of work, Barbara borrowed an old pram and took Rosita for a walk. The day was clear and sweet-scented with the early blossoms that decorated the trees and hedges, adding a beauty that gladdened her heart. She pushed the ancient pram to the local Pleasure Beach. There, amid other more prosperous strollers, with beautiful clothes and shiny new prams in which warmly dressed children looked out on a comfortable world, she made the decision to leave the Careys.

She had to find a regular job which included a place to live. Otherwise it would mean paying someone to mind Rosita and that would take most of what she could earn. It was a frightening prospect, to strike out on her own without Auntie Molly Carey to support her. Almost as frightening as when her mother told her she was going to have a baby, or learning of Bernard's death falling from a London train.

Briefly, she considered going to see her parents but the idea froze and faded almost as soon as it was conceived. She saw in her mind's eye the expression on her father's face and knew he was implacable. She had seen him several times when she went to clean at The Anchor and he ignored her totally. Nothing would make him change his mind and have her back home.

Once Rosita started crawling, Auntie Molly Carey would find it hard to cope, with a new child of her own and Blodwen, that solemn-faced little girl, whom Richard still treated like a doll and was still less than two years old.

Several of the Carey children were now working. The twins had left the crowded rooms with ill-concealed glee and found places as live-in servants in large houses. They earned little more than their keep and refused to spare even a few pennies to help their mother and their family. Alun and Billie found labouring jobs putting in a few hours after school finished, and Jack and Gareth earned a few shillings delivering groceries around the streets for local shops.

Richard seemed to be the strength of the Careys. He had been helping his father with the paper round and other, less legal occupations, since he was three, but the money he helped to earn was little enough.

Barbara shook off the prosaic musings and took a deep breath, absorbing the tantalizing scents of the afternoon with its hint of approaching summer. Children's voices called, mothers scolded, grandmothers soothed. Here was a place where people came to forget their worries, even the war seemed to have failed to reach this pocket of frivolity.

The sun warmed her cheeks and she closed her eyes for a moment and pretended she was on holiday, staying at one of the smart boarding houses with Bernard, who had just that moment gone to buy her an ice cream. She walked as slowly as she could, while making sure the pram moved enough to prevent Rosita from crying. She felt the need to stay with the cheerful crowd for a while, watching with some envy as grandfathers dug into well-filled pockets to pay for rides for excited children.

There were few fathers present and those that were were in uniform. They stood to attract abuse if they were seen in civilian clothes and obviously able-bodied. Many would suspect them of being conscientious objectors and proclaim their disapproval loudly. She sighed. The war couldn't be forgotten for long, not with almost every family grieving for a loved one.

A group of young sailors strolled along the promenade and children ran to jump up and touch their collars for luck. The sailors good-naturedly laughed and even bent down for the smallest to reach. They were laughing as though they hadn't a care in the world as they went towards the amusement park. Yet they too must have known grief.

The figure-eight was by far the tallest and largest of the rides and it looked precarious, not unlike a half-built building awaiting the bricks and cement that would complete it and give it strength. But as always it was in great demand and Barbara watched as the sailors joined the queue and quickly got into conversation with some girls standing near the ticket office. For a moment, she felt a pang of regret for having Rosita. Girls of her age were having such fun; screaming in exaggerated fright to the amusement of those watching and waiting their turn, as the cars climbed to the highest point then swooped down at terrifying speed, their hair flying in the wind, pretty hats held on tightly, clasped in white-knuckled fists.

She could ill afford it, soon having to face the cost of a room for herself and probably pay for someone to look after Rosita, but she went into the refreshment rooms and ordered tea and a scone. Her eyes became dreamy as she imagined sitting there with Bernard, taking tea with all the time in the world.

Before she had finished her tea, Rosita woke and began crying again, a tight-fisted, red-faced, angry complaint. Barbara looked around apologetically, patting the child's back, and when that did nothing to ease the child's distress she left and walked back through the crowd, pushing the pram and carrying Rosita.

She walked back along the promenade, putting the struggling child back in the pram and jiggling the battered old thing in an effort to quieten her screams. She looked down at the sand where a Punch and Judy show had attracted an audience large enough to block the way to those trying to buy at the stalls set up just below the sea wall. A fight seemed likely between the Punch and Judy men and a couple trying to serve customers with ice cream that was rapidly melting. She paused a moment, expecting and half hoping that the runny ice cream would be thrown at the puppeteers.

There were stalls selling everything from kites, singing birds, balloons, flags and buckets and spades and in one instance, bathing costumes. 'Don't be shy, *fach*, try it on behind the stall, no one will look.'

Barbara looked at passers-by, wondering how different their lives were from her own. Most of the elderly men looked smart but rather warm in their best suits and stiff-collared shirts. Prosperous-looking women with haughty expressions strolled in large ornate hats and thick coats and skirts. She smiled and tried to lift her spirits and share the fun, to forget for a moment or two the predicament she was facing. Perhaps life was a matter of pretence for most people? Like those young sailors, acting as though they hadn't a care in the world. But as she turned away from the thinning crowd and began the long trek home, her forced high spirits plummeted. What could she do to earn money and keep Rosita safe?

Walking back through the quiet streets, an occasional cheery group passed her carrying balloons, small toys and even goldfish in round bowls, prizes they had won in the amusement park. The sound of their laughter gave her a pang of loneliness. She stopped to allow one family to pass her rickety old pram and glanced at the advertisements in a tobacconist's window. One notice caught her eyes and she wrote down the name and address of the shop on the back of a piece of paper torn from a hoarding. 'Housekeeper wanted for farm.' it said. Her experience was hardly great, but she had worked for a few weeks for farmer Graham Prothero, and at least knew what to expect. If she exaggerated her knowledge a little, she might be lucky.

She would write a reply and the next day hand it into the shop to post to the advertiser. It was a solution she hadn't thought of but it was a solution, and the idea of country living for them both was strongly appealing. It would be so good for Rosita. Why hadn't she thought of it? It was the perfect answer. A job where she could keep her baby with her. She continued home with a more buoyant step.

The reply to her letter came by post less than a week later and she opened it with fingers trembling with hope. What a relief it would be for Auntie Molly Carey. Then she glanced at the note and gave a groan of disappointment, recognizing the address of the farm. It was Graham Prothero, from whom she had run away. Or who had thrown her out, as if it mattered which!

How fortunate she hadn't mentioned it to the Careys. At least the disappointment was only her own. Angrily remembering her previous experience and not wanting to repeat it, she threw the letter in the fire and tried to forget she had ever written. But when she returned to the Careys' two rooms after work a few days later, she knew she might have to change her mind.

'Got to go we have,' Mrs Carey said, as, sobbing, she opened the door to Barbara and handed her the baby Meriel. 'Given notice to leave the rooms on Saturday week.'

'Why? What's happened?' Barbara almost fell over the bogie in her haste to get inside and comfort the woman. 'What reason can they have to throw you out?'

'Since when did they need a reason?' Bending over the fire, fiercely stirring the soup simmering in the black, soot-encrusted pot, Mrs Carey took a deep breath to control her sobs and added, 'We'll all have to go on the parish. The children will go into a home for waifs and strays. Separated we'll be, after all me and Henry have done to keep us together.'

'Is it Rosita, crying all the time? Is that why they've asked you to go? If it is, then I've got a surprise for you. I've got a place to go. I can leave and that will settle it.' She patted the distressed woman's shoulder and said brightly, 'I was offered a job in that letter that came last week. It was from a farmer offering me a job. What d'you think of that, then? Talk about coincidence. It was meant to be. I'll go and talk to the landlady now, this minute. We'll change her mind for sure when she knows I'm taking my lovely, noisy daughter from the house.'

'It's no use, Barbara. The rooms are let and the new people – paying more than us, mind – are coming on Saturday week at twelve.'

Richard was sitting on the stairs and when Barbara opened the back door to go down to the *ty bach* he pulled at her skirt. 'Barbara, remember that old house on the beach, the one with the porch all broken and falling about? Why can't we all go there? No one owns it. Gone away they have, the family who used to live there. Luke and me, we started to mend it.'

'You've seen Luke?'

'Not this ages. His cottage is always locked up now. There's a padlock on the door so even if he came back he couldn't get in. I saw the other man come and he had it fixed. I think it was Luke's father, even though Luke always said he hasn't got a family.'

Throughout the winter months Barbara had often thought about Luke but lack of time as well as lack of energy prevented her from walking the two miles to the lonely beach in the hope of seeing him. 'Shall we go on Sunday? See if he's there? If the boat is still on the beach he might have left a note.'

Richard shook his solemn head. 'Looked everywhere I have.'

'We'll go anyway.' Barbara had a strong need to talk to Luke about her half-made decision to go back to the farm. Being outside the limited circle of people who made up Barbara's life, his opinion mattered. She knew he was more worldly and his comments would be honest and helpful. Although they knew each other so slightly, she trusted him to have her interests at heart. Perhaps, she thought with a faint glimmer of hope, he might even think of a better solution than returning to the farm. She shuddered at the prospect of sleeping again under the same roof as Graham Prothero. His persistence would hardly have lessened. He knew who the letter had come from.

'We can look at the house, can't we?' Richard said, breaking into her thoughts. 'We can take the bogie and bring back firewood.'

'Yes, we'll take food and have a picnic – even if it's raining.' A necessary proviso to avoid disappointment.

Five of them set off for the picnic a few days later. With the solemn-faced Blodwen in her undisputed place on the bogie, propped up with blankets and an ancient cushion, they walked through the lanes, singing and laughing with excitement.

Luke was there when they reached the narrow beach near Gull Island. The sound of oars made them turn their heads to see the small rowing boat making its way towards them. The oars lay still for a moment and his hand came up in an excited wave. Breathless, Barbara waited for him to touch the rocky shore and climb out to greet them.

There seemed to be so much to say, both herself and Richard talking at the smiling man in unison, each trying to grab his attention and share their news. Eventually he covered his ears with his hands and laughingly told Richard and the others to go and find some driftwood for a fire. 'I've caught a few small fish,' he told them. 'And we'll cook them on the beach.' He turned towards Barbara, his thin face lined and sad, but lighting up as he smilingly took the sleeping child from her.

'If I'd had a boy I'd have called him Luke,' she said shyly.

'No, and another girl next, too. When you marry,' he said, looking at her for the first time.

Barbara laughed. 'Bernard is dead. There won't be any more.'

'You're young. You'll marry.'

'If there are any young men left to marry after this terrible war.'

Luke's lips tightened at the reminder of the young man for whom he still grieved.

While Luke sat and nursed the baby, Barbara helped the others to gather wood for the bonfire, then when Luke reluctantly handed her back, she watched as he showed them how to cook fish in the large pan he kept hidden. After scouring it clean, he collected more water from the pump and placed the fish in to gently poach. He made no attempt to go into the cottage and, curious, Barbara walked to the door to see if what Richard had told her was true.

Luke saw her and while the fish cooked, watched over by Richard, he told her quietly what had happened when his father had called.

'He'd always disliked Roy and did everything he could to discourage my friendship with him and his extrovert family,' he said. 'A mention of his name brought on furious anger. When I told him I loved Roy, he went berserk, hitting me. Making it sound sordid. But I did love him, and his family, who always made me feel good about myself, and happy to be with them.

'When Roy died I had to grieve alone as I was forbidden to go and seek comfort from Roy's family. His last letter came from a place called Ypres. "Wipers", the soldiers nicknamed it. I'll go and find it one day when the war is finally over. My father can't understand how I found something with Roy and his family that I couldn't find at home.' He frowned for a moment. 'It was there that I was allowed to be myself, I suppose.'

Moments passed and he was unaware that he was holding his breath, wanting her to understand, afraid of her reacting as his father had done, with disgust. Then Barbara turned and hugged him. 'There are lots of ways of loving, Luke. Many kinds of love. All are beautiful. Your father hasn't learnt that. Pity for him, isn't it?'

Arm in arm they walked back to the others. For Luke it was as if a band of steel had been removed from around his chest. He could breathe freely for the first time in many months. What did it matter if his father despised him? If only one person could believe that his love for Roy hadn't been sordid, then the world was not empty. Lighthearted, he helped share out the food and the atmosphere became a celebratory party.

The children whooped and shouted and sang and danced, all except

Blodwen who retained her slightly haughty manner throughout. Luke studied her curiously. She rarely spoke yet she seemed to be watching, taking in everything that was said and done. Was she observing the stupidities of the human race? And would it all come out one day in a great gale of laughter?

While the younger children built houses and castles with the smooth pebbles, Luke and Barbara followed Richard to examine the house. The porch, repaired by Luke, had remained standing and was firm and strong. It was no longer as clean as Luke had made it. Inside there was sand and stones and the dry debris of many years, blown back to its place soon after Luke had brushed it out. The walls and roof appeared to be dry and sound and there was nothing to discourage the idea of the Careys using it for a home.

'I'll sleep there myself for a night or two – better than trying to keep warm under the upturned boat! Next weekend we can work together, fix the windows and make it weatherproof. There's all the summer in front of us, remember, and by next winter it will be as snug a home as anyone can wish for.'

Richard's face was fixed in a tight grin that nothing would move. He watched Luke survey the floorboards and, like a miniature adult, discussed with him the most necessary needs. Smilingly, Luke nodded at the six-year-old's recommendations and made notes on an old envelope.

'You're right, I hadn't thought of that,' he said frequently. Or, 'That's an excellent suggestion, Richard.' And he would scribble furiously on his paper with his scratchy pencil, licking its indelible lead to strengthen the letters.

'He really does have a good idea of what's needed, you know,' Luke said to Barbara when they were preparing to leave. 'He's only six, yet he understands some things so well. And understands things so fast. If he'd been able to have a good education, there's nothing he couldn't achieve.'

It wasn't until the bogie was packed, with the driftwood tucked tightly around little Blodwen, and they were setting off home, that Barbara had a chance to talk to Luke about the possibility of returning to farmer Graham Prothero.

'I'll walk you home and you can tell me how you feel about it,' Luke said. He had intended to anyway, as always, reluctant to say goodbye to this happy, fascinating family. Reaching into his boat he pulled out a thick coat and from its pocket produced two woolly hats, one for himself and the other he handed to Richard, who proudly pulled it on.

As they walked through the gathering gloom, a raggle-taggle procession of shabbily dressed children with Barbara and Luke at the head, in clothes equally ill-fitting and worn, she explained her need to leave the shelter and safety of the Careys and find a place for herself and Rosita.

'But why this farmer?' Luke asked. 'He won't have changed. It's no use expecting him to be different. If you go back it will be seen as tacit agreement to share his bed. Just by returning, you'll be agreeing to his demands.'

'I'll make myself clear on what I expect,' Barbara said with the confidence of youth. 'I'll make sure he understands. Besides, he might not take me when I insist on taking Rosita.'

'Look, wait for a week. I'll try and find something. I hadn't realized how you were situated. I thought you'd stay with the Careys. I should have thought and sorted out something before this. I'll find you and Rosita a place to live. A room and a position where you don't have to do menial tasks for a man like Graham Prothero. Things that do this to your hands.' He reached for her hand and touched the roughness. 'There must be some easier way for you to earn your keep.'

'It's nice that you care, Luke. I'm so lucky having you for a friend. But I can't see anyone taking me in, not anyone decent. If my own parents are too disgusted to acknowledge me and Rosita, then how can I expect a stranger to help?'

'I'm a stranger and I want to help! I can't be the only sane person in the world.'

'You aren't a stranger.' She smiled in the darkness, her eyes luminescent, turning up to look into his face. 'It's odd, Luke, but although you're different – I mean, you talk posh and have an important job of work – we are friends, aren't we?'

'I hope we always will be, Barbara.' He leaned over and lightly touched her cheek with his lips. 'Friends for always.'

'For always,' she echoed, but when she tried to return the kiss, her lips touched his woollen hat and they both laughed. It really didn't matter.

Rosita had been grizzling for a while but then she began crying loud enough to make their ears pop and nothing Barbara could do would pacify her. Luke took the protesting child from Barbara's arms and *cwtched* her under his coat. With a drawn-out, shuddering sigh, she ceased her crying and went to sleep. Smiling, Luke said, 'And we'll be friends too, Rosita and I.'

Barbara began the singing that always accompanied their walks and soon the children joined in, their voices brave and confident, rising up into the night sky. Rosita snuggled against Luke's tattered jumper inside his jacket, and slept on.

The dark lanes changed to pavements, buildings loomed out of the dark and the nearness of other people was a threat to their happy companionship. An intrusion. Their footsteps slowed as they reached the neighbourhood where streets, all similar to each other, gave shelter to large numbers of families. It was no longer a place for singing and apart from their dragging footsteps there was no sound to disturb the early evening. Most were inside eating their teatime meal or discussing the latest war news.

Nearer home there were a few young people gathered around the street lamp where the lamp-lighter had recently passed, touching each mantle with his long pole before cycling on to the next. The murmur of voices was low, fitting their mood, and tiredness dragged at their feet.

Then the air was disturbed in a way that made them stop and cling to each other in fright. They heard screams, sudden and bloodcurdling. Then the shouting of angry voices reached them and the crashing of objects being thrown about. Some atavistic instinct told Barbara it was the Careys before they dared to take one step further and reach the corner of the road.

They ran down to the house and in the pale yellow light from the oil-lamp within, they saw a pile of boxes and odd shapes, which, on closer inspection, turned out to be all the Careys' possessions.

In a now-silent tableau, Mrs Carey, with the new baby Meriel held protectively close, was being comforted by her husband. With the children gathered around his legs, Henry stared at the small collection that was all his family's possessions, in perfect stillness, as though transfixed by a spell.

'The landlady decided not to wait till Saturday,' he told them in a dazed whisper. 'Them new people, they're coming tomorrow.'

Chapter Five

AFTER THE INITIAL explanations and recriminations had been said, amid the cacophony of cries and screams from the frightened children, their first priority was to try and carry their most valued belongings to somewhere the children at least could get some sleep.

'There's a barn on the Cardiff Road,' Henry Carey said, with an attempt at lightness. 'Warm it'll be and there's a good roof if it turns to rain before morning.' They discussed this in low voices, each wondering if they had the strength to carry their pitifully few possessions even that short way.

'It's right on the road, mind,' Mrs Carey said in a whisper. She had no strength to speak normally; all the breath had been forced out of her by the cruel loss of their two rooms. 'Dangerous for the children it'll be, with not an hour going by without half a dozen carts passing, and motor cars and lorries too.'

'It'll be all right, Molly. Get it real comfortable in a few days, once we find a place to have a fire. We'll manage just fine.'

'What about the house I found, Dad?' Richard said, and from the impatient tone of his reedy voice, Luke and Barbara guessed it was not the first time he had suggested it, even though, stunned by events, they had not been aware of him speaking.

'Tomorrow, boy, we'll think about it tomorrow,' Henry said quietly. 'Don't worry us now with your daydreams.'

'Excuse me, sir,' Luke said politely, 'but I think your son is right. Why spend energy getting settled into an unsuitable place which you'll probably have to leave in a few hours' time once the farmer finds you there?'

'But it's miles away. These children can't travel out there at this time of night. It's over by Gull Island!'

'We can,' Richard argued. 'It isn't that far. Be there in no time we will.'

'I'm terrible tired, Mam,' Idris wailed, and Richard glared at him and hissed, 'Be quiet or I'll swipe you proper!'

'Leave him, Richard, he's trying to be brave,' Mrs Carey said, hugging her golden boy.

'Two miles it is,' Barbara said. 'They're all tired but they'll think of it as an adventure, a game, if we put it to them like that.'

'Forget it's night-time,' Luke encouraged. 'Just think of it as hours we can use. Come on, I bet you know where there's a cart we can borrow. With a handcart we'll do it in two journeys.' He turned to Richard. 'Where can we borrow a handcart?'

Leaving the others still standing like the shell-shocked injured waiting for someone to tell them what they must do, Luke took Richard's arm and led him away. They disappeared around the corner of the back lane and within minutes a rumbling of wheels heralded their return with the required item. Still bemused, Mrs Carey sat on the cart hugging Meriel and with her arms around some of the younger children, nursing the mantelpiece clock with several of the hastily packed boxes tucked around her feet. Then she shook her head.

'No, this won't do. Feeling sorry for myself won't help get us settled and that's what I have to do.' Getting down ungainfully from the cart, she added another box of assorted china in the place she had previously taken. The unlikely group moved slowly off, two cats on the sack of bedding, the dog running around barking in excitement. Barbara, Rosita and Mr Carey stayed with the other children.

'I should have told Molly before,' Mr Carey muttered. 'She should have been warned. If only I'd told her.'

'You did tell her. She knew days ago.' Barbara continued to settle Rosita to sleep on the pavement, wrapped in several blankets, then sitting beside her. Blaming himself and talking nonsense, she tutted impatiently. Tired and frightened and worried he must be, but he should be thinking about how to *deal* with what had happened, not trying to think how he could have prevented it. As he repeated his words she felt mildly irritated. For the first time she recognized that Henry was a weak man.

'Knew ages ago I did,' he went on, half to himself.

'Uncle Henry Carey, you *did* tell your wife, there just wasn't time for her to find somewhere else. She told me almost a week ago. She's been asking ever since but there are no rooms to be had, not with all these children. No one is willing to take on these children. It's a large family, you've got remember, even though the twins have gone to live somewhere else and two of the boys have left home.'

She was cold and it would be ages before the cart came back to take them to somewhere they could sleep. She kept touching Rosita to make sure she was warm, and she added another blanket from the pile in the road thrown from the Careys' rooms.

'I knew at Christmas,' he surprised her by saying.

'Christmas?'

'I couldn't tell her, see. I was hoping the landlady would change her mind.'

'You knew you were going to be thrown out and you did nothing?'

'It was when she knew about another baby coming, see. You won't say, will you? I thought the landlady would be too sympathetic to really chuck us out. Molly always pays the rent reg'lar. I was sure she'd change her mind.'

'You knew at Christmas and did nothing?'

'Sorry I am.'

Barbara thought she would explode. She wanted to hit him for his stupidity in allowing his wife and children to reach the present situation, then she let out her fury in a long breath. What was the point? As she had told him, there was no sense in worrying about what had happened today, best to get on thinking about tomorrow.

'The house on the beach will serve for a while. You'll get something before next winter,' she said softly. 'It's near enough for you to keep selling newspapers.'

'It's two miles! I'll have to get a bike!'

Temper flared at his selfish remark but she was saved from replying as the handcart, with Luke pushing a sleeping Richard on board, came back, the dog still in attendance. The rest of the goods were loaded on. It looked precarious but Luke and Richard stacked it as safely as they could.

The night was dry and clear with stars making a pin cushion of the sky. There was no one to see them as they trundled along the silent lanes, except for a fox crossing their path and pausing to look at them curiously, and an owl gliding softly overhead.

They all had a strange, heart-thumping feeling of invading someone else's space as they entered and took possession. Mrs Carey shared blankets and the youngest children were given priority. Each one was wrapped into a cocoon of warmth, then they were rolled together like a row of sausages, giggling until sleep claimed them. By the time they were all settled to sleep in the cold and rather eerie house on the beach, dawn was showing pink and yellow fingers and a calm sea was touched with the glory of it.

The children slept on, but Mr and Mrs Carey and Barbara rose early. Luke was sitting outside, waiting for them to wake. A fire burned close by and a kettle simmered at the edge of it. In an attempt to cheer them, Luke gave them Richard's list of suggestions to improve the house.

'He's had some very good ideas. Give him a problem and he solves it so fast, quicker than me quite often! It's hard to remember that he's only six. He talks and thinks like an adult.'

'Miniature adult is what he is.' Henry smiled proudly. 'Never one to play with other children, our Richard. Spends all his time with me or listening to grown-up talk.'

'Then you'll look at his ideas?'

Mr Carey shook his head. 'I can't think straight, boy, and that's a fact. Best we *cwtch* down here and see what happens. It's all beyond me.'

Henry seemed to Barbara to have shrunk. The responsibility for the disaster was his and no one else's yet he hadn't the glimmer of an idea how to deal with it.

'Richard thought that if the floor was repaired above the porch there would be three usable rooms upstairs and, at the back of the house, a lean-to might make a useful storeroom for wood that can be gathered from the beach,' Luke went on, determined to encourage the man out of his lethargy. 'It wouldn't cost very much, just a few planks of wood and a pound or two of nails.'

'With two miles to walk to work before I start my paper round I'll need shoes with some urgency.' He seemed not to have heard Luke's words as he stared at the battered shoes he was wearing. One had worn right through and was lined with cardboard.

'I have an idea.' Luke ran to his boat and returned with a pair of good-quality leather shoes, old but polished so his own face was reflected in the toecap. 'You look as though you take the same size as I do. Take them, get them tapped and they'll last a few weeks at least. You can get some second-hand boots when you get straight.'

Mercifully, some of the window glass was still intact, although caked with mould and dirt, and Luke had mended others. The back door was missing, probably taken to replace one in another house, Luke thought. But with a screen made from a blanket nailed to the architrave, the house was already looking habitable. 'Shut out the weather and it's a home,' Luke encouraged. There was even a high shelf above the empty hearth on which Mrs Carey placed her clock. Its ticking gave a feeling of comfort to them all and even Rosita slept on.

The sun was well above the horizon, shining and giving warmth to the newly occupied house when Luke left them. He went first to the boat and changed from the scruffy clothes he seemed to prefer and put on his suit, tie, hat and scarf, carried an umbrella and a briefcase and walked to the station with his feet covered only by socks. If anyone noticed his lack of footwear he didn't seem aware of it.

After depositing his briefcase at the bookshop, shoeless and unshaven, he bought himself some shoes and stopped again at a barber's shop for a shave. An hour later he returned to his office and asked his newly acquired and rather surprised assistant for a cup of tea to be sent in with the day's post. Metamorphosis complete, he began to look at his diary and plan his appointments for the day.

He kept losing the thread of what he was dealing with and allowing his mind to drift back to the family on the beach. Poor as they were, he envied them. Needing so much, yet self-sufficient in the things that counted in life, they were easily content. A full belly and the company of each other was all they required to be uncomplainingly happy. To be a part of a family like the Careys seemed to him to be the very essence of contentment.

It was not the same for Barbara; she wanted more. There was a restlessness about her, that strange way she had of glancing around without moving her head as if she were looking at things secretly, unwilling to share her vision of the better things that only she could see. She wouldn't be as easily pleased as the Careys. She coveted another, more comfortable life.

He wondered whether he could help financially but thought not. For one thing, he had very little himself. The business of secondhand books was precarious. More so now he had taken on an assistant, a young woman called Jeanie, who had to be paid every week, however badly he did. There was the constant need for him to travel and buy stock and he used every penny he earned to replenish those shelves, keeping only the very minimum he required for basic expenses. The other consideration was that he wondered whether giving money would help or hinder.

Sometimes giving money unconditionally only made things worse. A little extra gave a false security and that, added to the relief of having cash to spare, frequently led to further debts. And miraculously, debt was something Mrs Carey had somehow managed to avoid so far. A few pounds might give Mr Carey some ease and reduction of his worries but it might also persuade him he needn't try so hard. The Careys' lives were a precarious balancing act and the wrong kind of help might tip them into an abyss. Helping them to help themselves, that was the only way.

There was also condescension in giving money, a feeling which he wouldn't relish, and it rarely helped for more than a few euphoric moments.

Pushing aside the work, he stepped over to the window. His office was on the north side and so shaded from most of the sun. The bright sunshine across the street made his own room seem even darker and he sighed. How he hated being indoors.

Shadows gave his thin face an almost skeletal appearance; his eyes were clear, bright and far-seeing but now they looked deep-set and hooded. He was usually tanned by the weekends spent on the beach but after winter it had faded to a pale and rather sickly pallor. His long fingers pulled at his collar, longing to discard it, but convention insisted on a man in his position wearing one. Today it irked him more than usual, thinking of the Carey children, ragged and carefree, exploring their new home.

He looked out on the busy scene below him. Women walking past with their shopping baskets filled with whatever food they had managed to buy that day, stopping occasionally to look in a shop window, always hoping for a bargain or something in short supply to eke out their rations. A newspaper seller on a corner, speaking in gibberish only understood by other newspaper sellers, hoping someone would be curious and read what the headlines announced. A group of gypsies wandered past offering artificial flowers and hand-carved clothes pegs to passers-by, most of whom shunned them fearfully.

A farm cart went along the street with dirty hay on the back and several net-covered boxes containing young chickens. He looked at the man guiding the horse through the busy mid-morning throng and thought of Graham Prothero. Barbara must do better than that. He took up pen and began writing the names of people who might be willing to help. There were regrettably few.

Living on the beach was more difficult for Barbara. There were the two miles to walk into town and she had to take Rosita. Mrs Carey was engrossed with her newest child and had less time now for the crotchety Rosita. Twice she saw her father as she struggled to her first cleaning job, pushing the crying child in the broken old pram. He turned away, whistling, increasing his pace until he was out of sight.

Once they came face to face, him in his going-out suit and white shiny collar and neat tie, her in ill-fitting clothes badly in need of a wash and strangers to an iron. She paused, wondering if he dared to look at her. The pavement was crowded with early shoppers and they were so close she could see the bristles on the point of his chin where the razor had missed. Rather than pass her he changed direction, head down, and hurried away.

'You pig!' she shouted in tearful rage. The small satisfaction of seeing his face and neck redden with embarrassment helped a little.

Mrs Carey had reacted badly to the trauma of losing her home. With it went the washing and ironing she did for neighbours. It was impossible for her to carry washing to the house on the beach, even if she had the facilities there to deal with the work. And there were no extra children to mind as she was too far away from those she had previously helped. The loss of the few shillings she had earned was devastating. There were so many basic things she needed.

She was still weak from the birth of Meriel and felt she was losing the battle to cope. There was nothing else for it, she decided, one cold, wet morning – she would have to use the money Barbara's mother had given her over the months since Barbara had been thrown out of her home. It had been given, after all, to help as she saw fit.

Amid the jumble of clothes and saucepans and general clutter, she unearthed a tin box. It had a picture of King George V and Queen Mary on the front and it had once contained tea. She opened it, surprised at how light it seemed, and found nothing more than the paper in which she had wrapped the precious coins. Someone had taken them.

When Richard and Mr Carey came home that evening, they were bubbling with excitement.

'Wait till tomorrow, Mam,' Richard said, but he refused to be drawn on the reason for the secret smiles he and his father shared.

'Tell me,' Barbara pleaded. 'I won't say a word. Got a better job, has he, your father?'

'No, but we've decided this will be our proper home. We're not moving on. We're staying here and making it comfortable, just like a real home.'

The following day, Barbara was told at two of the places where she worked that she was no longer required. The baby, who still cried all day and half the night, was the reason she was given. One of them was The Anchor, where her father drank with his friends, and she wondered bitterly if he had persuaded the landlady to ask her to leave.

She wandered around the shops and the large private houses where there were still likely to be servants or paid help. Door after door opened and quickly closed. There was nothing for her unless she left the baby with someone.

Learning of the situation, Mrs Stock offered a solution. 'Leave the baby with me. I'll look after her while you work. You might get a more respectable job of work then, instead of clearing up filth after heaven knows who!'

The cold voice seemed more a threat than an answer to Barbara's problems and she shook her head and turned away. Bernard's mother was not the company she wanted for her beautiful, if noisy, daughter.

'Leave her with me tomorrow and you'll have a better chance of finding somewhere,' Mrs Carey offered, when Barbara went back to the beach house and told her what had happened.

'I can't, Auntie Molly Carey, you aren't well.'

'Better I am, and with nowhere to go, no washing and ironing to do, no neighbours wanting me to mind their children, I'm well placed for an extra one.' She spoke with enthusiasm, guilt at losing Barbara's money making her desperate to help.

The sky was losing its brightness, everything around them fading into a quivering, floating blur so distances were confusing. Gull Island was nothing more than an indistinct outline that might or might not be real. Trees had lost their freshly sprouted greenness and became as grey as the rocks around the house. Rain began to fall, darkening the evening ever further when Mr Carey and a jubilant Richard returned home.

They arrived on a horse-drawn cart borrowed, they told her, from the fruit and vegetable man. On the cart were lengths of wood to repair the room above the porch, together with bags of cement and some sand and a bag of assorted nails and screws, plus a few necessary tools.

On top of the sacks Mrs Carey gasped to see a table, a rocking chair, a square of red and yellow matting and, last of all, an iron fireplace with a hob on either side on which to stand saucepans. Walking along in their wake was an elderly horse carrying an even more elderly man who wore a bucket hat and several layers of coats.

While the children stroked and admired the horses, the old man, helped by Richard with Mr Carey watching with interest, fixed the fireplace. He warned them not to use it for a few days, then, attaching his mount to the back of the cart, he left them having said fewer than a dozen words and an equal number of grunts.

'But where did it come from?' a delighted Mrs Carey asked. Her eyes were shining as she touched and admired her treasures. 'Where did the money come from?'

'Let's say the people who took our home from us helped us get started.' Mr Carey grinned at his son. 'Tell her, boy, tell what you found.'

'It was when we were moving, Mam. They were throwing our stuff out on the road and taking their own stuff in and I found a box with money in it. I knew it couldn't be ours. I thought they owed us that, chucking us out like that, so I took it. Look at all this! We're rich!'

Mrs Carey turned away in shock. The money didn't belong to the new tenants. It was the money she had been given to save for Barbara.

'Aren't you pleased, our Mam?' Richard asked.

'Pleased? Of course I'm pleased.'

'Stealing, mind, isn't it, Mam, and we know that's wicked,' Idris said, his face angelic. 'Richard is wicked. He stole the money and that's wicked, isn't it, Mam?'

'Say wicked just once more and I'll thump you!' Richard growled.

Mrs Carey glanced at Barbara in sorrow. 'But there we are. In this world it's a question of who needs it most, isn't it?'

'That's what our dad said,' Richard agreed stoutly, glaring at his brother.

One day I'll tell her, Mrs Carey vowed. One day I'll explain how I tried to save the money but with the eviction it just wasn't possible. I will tell her, though, so she knows her mam and I did try.

When the new possessions were carried into the house, Idris tried to persuade his father to go with him to see a castle he had built, but Mr Carey sank into the newly acquired rocking chair and ignored Idris as he usually did. He communicated little with his children, except Richard, who was his hard-working partner.

On the following Friday, Barbara found a job, of sorts – a few hours cleaning in a public house, with the promise that one day she might be offered work in the bar. But the landlord firmly refused to allow her to take Rosita. She didn't know what to do. She couldn't ask the kind Mrs Carey to look after her indefinitely, not while she was so unwell.

Determinedly she began knocking on doors to ask if there was anyone who would look after Rosita for a few hours each day. The woman she found was already looking after three others but the house looked clean and tidy so Barbara agreed to bring Rosita to her the following morning.

For a while it worked well, Rosita seemed happy to go in when they reached the woman's door each day and always came out smiling. Then, a couple of weeks later, she went to collect her little girl and the woman smiled and said, 'She's with her gran. Called she did and took her to buy her a little present.'

'What? D'you mean my mother has taken her?' A bubble of painful joy burst in Barbara's heart. At last Mam was willing to accept her granddaughter. She pressed her hands to her chest. She hadn't realized just how much she had wanted this.

'Thanks. I'll go now and fetch her.'

Filled with excitement, she ran to the door of the house she hadn't seen for months and knocked on the door. When her mother answered it there was such excitement that she couldn't get any words out. 'Mam?' she said in a whisper.

The happiness was immediately wiped away as her father's voice boomed, 'Send her away. She doesn't belong here.'

'Rosita, Mam, I've called for Rosita.'

'She isn't here. Why should she be here?'

'Clear off!' her father shouted, hovering out of sight behind the door. 'You and that bastard of yours.' Barbara didn't hear the hurtful words; she was filled with anxiety for Rosita.

'But the woman who looks after her said – Oh my God, please help me. It's Mrs Stock. Mam, Mrs Stock has taken Rosita! Help me, please, she's taken my baby!' Her father's hand came and pulled her mother inside. As the door slammed, Barbara got a brief glimpse of her mother's stricken face as her father shouted at her.

She banged on the door, shouting, screaming, begging for help. Someone had to help her; she needed someone to go with her and make sure Rosita was returned to her. But the door remained firmly closed although she knocked and screamed until she lost all sensation in her knuckles.

Still sobbing wildly, she ran to the house where Mrs Stock lived. Banging on that door produced as little result. The curtains were drawn and the house was locked and appeared to be empty.

She arrived at the Careys' still crying and unable at first to explain what had happened. Miraculously Luke appeared and calmed her and soon had all the facts.

'Don't worry, she's sure to be safe and that's the main thing. Rosita will be safe. We'll soon get her back. No one will take her from you.'

Dressed in his office clothes and with Barbara washed, neatly dressed and calm, they went to the police station and made their complaint. Hours went slowly past as the policeman, seemingly unhurried and lacking a sense of urgency, set about making enquiries. Barbara grew increasingly distraught. Luke sent a message to his assistant Jean that he wouldn't be in the next day and stayed with her, sleeping under his boat and spending the daylight hours with Barbara.

For minutes at a time Barbara screamed her hatred of Mrs Stock, who had cruelly refused to help when she was needed, denied her beautiful granddaughter and was now causing her this agony. She called her all the wicked names she could bring to mind. Luke didn't try to stop her – best she vented her anger on someone and at least Mrs Stock was so far unaware of it.

'I want to hurt her,' Barbara sobbed. 'I want to hurt her and see her screaming like I am, and suffer some of my pain!'

'She lost all her sons, remember,' Mrs Carey said softly.

'That only makes it worse, her knowing how I must feel!'

Barbara and Luke wandered the streets together, unable to rest, and when Luke was talking to the police and trying to find a crumb of comfort to report, she wandered alone. She frequently ran up to look at a baby, imagining she would see the face of her own child. As the day and night dragged by, she would collapse exhausted into a corner of the sea wall, or under a hedge or on the stony beach and doze, only to wake moments later with panic renewed and intensified.

She couldn't go into the house; she felt closer to Rosita if she were outside, as if the baby might be calling her and she would not hear through walls and curtained doorways. Sleep was brief and restless and she would start frequently into wide-awake panic, convinced by some quickly forgotten dream that her baby was dead. Luke was always there to soothe her.

Luke tried to encourage her to talk, to make plans for when Rosita came home, but her mood shifted between uncontrollable sobbing and sitting unmoving as though in a trance, listening for Rosita's cries. Her lovely face was drawn and had lost its glow; her blue eyes seemed larger and full of melancholy.

Richard's contribution was, 'Come back she will, for sure. No one could put up with her yelling for long and that's a fact!'

After two nights had passed without a word, Barbara found herself thinking of all the brown envelopes that had been delivered around the streets of the town. All the grieving they had caused. She began to think of Mrs Stock in a slightly different way and imagined the poor woman nursing her son's child and caring for her with love. All those deaths meant more to her now. Without her baby for three days she was almost out of her mind. How could Mrs Stock have survived after losing her sons for ever? The slight sympathy eased her mind a little.

'At least,' she told Luke, 'I know she wouldn't harm her. She's had enough of death.'

It took three days for the police to find them. The trail began at the railway station, where they had been seen buying tickets, then, after exhaustive enquiries, they learnt from friends that Mrs Stock had an aunt living in Newport.

On the morning of the third day Luke woke and couldn't find Barbara. He searched with increasing concern and after waking Henry and Molly Carey and Richard to help, they found her huddled, shivering and crying outside Luke's cottage, now locked and padlocked. Luke snapped the padlock on the door and took her inside. He lit the fire and made her sip some quickly heated soup and then held her until she slept.

She awoke to see a policeman smiling down at her.

'Your baby has been found safe and sound, miss. And if her yelling's got anything to do with it, she's in excellent health!' The policeman's expression was so full of joy at the happy outcome to the worrying search, she hugged him.

Barbara and Luke travelled with the police to Newport to collect Rosita. The little girl was crying as usual, a sound Barbara would never complain of again.

'How can I ever thank you, Luke?' Barbara sobbed as she held the fidgeting, grizzling child close once they were back home.

'I didn't do anything. It was the police who found her, and quickly too.'

'But you were there. I – I don't know what I'd have done if you'd gone away. I've never needed anyone more than I've needed you these past three terrible days.'

They were sitting on the doorstep of the cottage belonging to Luke's father. Luke took Rosita from her and held her, and she went straight to sleep. She always settled better when he held her. Barbara leaned her head towards him, resting against him in a slumped contentment, her face close to his. Uneasily, Luke moved away and stood, looking out across the water to Gull Island.

'It's all right, Luke,' Barbara said softly. 'I know you don't want love from me, not that kind of love anyway. But I do love you, the way you love Rosita and me. You do understand what I mean, don't you?'

'According to my father, love is an evil emotion, an imp of darkness that should be crushed before it takes its first breath.'

'Have you ever thought, Luke, that your father might be wrong? That the way *he* thinks about love is the one way he can't accept?'

'Mr and Mrs Stock loved their son and tried to love Rosita. That hardly brought happiness, did it?'

'Selfish, over-possessive, that can be another side of the complicated thing called love. What d'you think they'll do now?'

'Move away to hide their shame and grief.'

'I hope so. I won't be safe until they do.'

Barbara knew that the temporary arrangements, with Rosita staying with one person then another, must stop. She and the baby needed a settled life if they weren't to suffer worsening misery. She sat on the windy and grey-shrouded beach one morning and thought about her options. There weren't many and having discarded ones that meant giving up Rosita to be looked after by strangers, there were even fewer.

Luke had returned to town but he was unable to concentrate on work. Barbara and Rosita were constantly on his mind. At seven o'clock on Saturday morning a few days after the rescue of Rosita from Mrs Stock, he made up his mind. He didn't desire her as a man desired a woman, but he cared. Wasn't that a kind of loving? An acceptable substitute? He would marry Barbara and help her bring up Rosita.

The room in which he lived during the week wouldn't do for a family of three, but he'd find somewhere. The first thing was to see Barbara and persuade her of the sense of it. They could use the storerooms behind the shop for a while. Their stock hardly filled the place, even though Jeanie was proving remarkably adept at finding good-quality volumes of their speciality subjects.

He dressed hurriedly and set off for the station. Now he had come to a decision he needed to act on it immediately. He reached the house on the beach at mid-morning and found Mrs Carey sitting on a rock outside the door peeling potatoes. He waved and hurried towards her. A wall of stones had been built around the front of the house and within its boundaries the youngest children played. Meriel was sleeping in a roughly made wooden crib.

'You look very much at home,' he called as he approached her.

'We've been very lucky.' She smiled. 'I've lost my laundry work but the rent we save has meant it's less than a loss than I first thought. The children have a long walk to school but they don't complain. Living on the beach like this gives them a sense of importance in a child's world.' She put down the basket of potatoes and went inside to make him a cup of tea. 'Thank you, Luke. You don't know what this means to us. It's as though we've been transported to another world.'

'Don't thank me! It was your Richard's doing. And I'm glad you like the beach. It has always been my favourite place.'

He sipped the tea for a while, and they chatted about the seagulls and the scavenging crows that had become regular visitors to the lonely dwelling, and the small animals that explored the beach at night in the hope of a morsel of food. Then, unable to contain himself any longer, he asked, 'What time do you expect Barbara? I'd better change into my normal clothes or she'll think you're talking to a stranger.'

'Or that there's more trouble for you to sort out for us,' she said, looking at him with a serious expression. 'What a good friend you are to us all.'

He sensed there was something unsaid and wondered what new trouble they had found. He waited for her to tell him, but she said nothing more although her face was sad and she looked away from him whenever she spoke.

'I'll walk down to meet her. She'll be glad of me taking Rosita from her. She's getting quite a weight, isn't she?'

'Barbara won't be coming, Luke. Gone she has, taken that job with Graham Prothero the farmer.'

Luke turned and stared at her. 'What? Why did she do that? She must have known I'd be back to help her.'

'Afraid she was. Afraid of that Mrs Stock coming and stealing Rosita. Thinking of us, too, mind. I can only just cope although she was wonderful – helped as much as she could with extra money and giving a hand with the work.'

'But I wanted to – I would have helped,' he finished lamely. 'I came here to – oh, it doesn't matter.'

But it did matter. It was another rejection. Barbara refused to accept his help, she would rather face that farmer than take anything from him.

He didn't go to the boat and change into his beach clothes but went straight back to the station. In Cardiff he went first to talk to his assistant, Jeanie. She was a young, newly married woman whose sailor husband was missing, presumed killed. She was hard-working and very capable and he knew what her answer would be when he asked her if she could cope alone.

She readily agreed and he set in motion the legal arrangements to make her an equal partner. Then he went to the recruiting office and, with the aid of a good many lies, enlisted in the army.

He reached France a year after America entered the war and in time for the fierce battle during which the British were beaten back to Amiens. The losses were equal to those at Passchendaele in 1916. He survived physically unharmed but emotionally numbed by the reality of the insane slaughter he had witnessed.

Barbara settled into life at the farm and when she saw how genuinely pleased Graham was to have her back she put aside her doubts and took to the heavy, exhausting work with a light heart. Her muscles were painful with the resumption of the chores, but Graham helped her more than when she had been there before. He seemed tolerant of Rosita, who still made her presence felt by long periods of loud crying and tedious, inexplicable grizzling.

He surprised her with gifts of flowers picked in the fields, and by planting flowers in the small garden at the front of the house for her pleasure. He took her out on walks and showed her things she hadn't seen before, aspects of the countryside that delighted her. Badgers playing outside their sett at night, fox-cubs romping about like puppies, hedgehogs walking with their young families.

It took a while to learn to be still and quiet and have the patience to wait and often accept disappointment, but once she had witnessed something of the secret world existing alongside her own, she found pleasure in every day. When the day's work was finished and they had eaten their supper, he usually sat in his favourite chair and read.

The books on the shelves fascinated her and she picked up several but found them too difficult to understand. So, while he read, she usually sat with a basket of mending or knitting and thought over the day's happenings. The silence was not uneasy, with the humming of the oil lamp and the occasional fall of cinders in the fire; she found life was very pleasant, better than anything she had found in her daydreams.

For Graham, her return was nothing less than a miracle. He knew she was far too young for him and her innocence – even with the baby, which had to prove some worldly experience – made her a person to be cherished and not bustled into a partnership for which she wasn't ready. No, given this second chance, he was determined to exercise patience.

He had been surprised at how badly he had missed her once his anger had abated, for it was anger he had felt. He remembered vividly that strong desire to hit her when he realized she was carrying a child. He knew in that moment of fury that if he gave in to the need to hit her, the beating would have been severe, so great had been his disappointment. He was glad now that he had controlled that urge. When she had answered his advertisement for the second time, he had been overwhelmed with sheer amazement. It must have been meant to be.

He bitterly regretted his harsh and unkind treatment of her, leaving so much of the heavy work to her slender arms, and the way he had tried to force her into his bed. She was young, not more than eighteen, but perhaps if he were kind and thoughtful, she would come to see him not as an older man but someone to whom she could give herself with love.

Barbara was very happy. Respect and affection for Graham grew day by day. He worked her hard but didn't ask her to do more than she could manage and he accepted her unwillingness to move into his bed without causing her any embarrassment. Since her return he had been amazingly kind and had made no further move to be anything but a generous employer.

To her growing delight he took an interest in Rosita, playing with her, making toys and bringing her little treats. Barbara relaxed the last core of apprehension and felt that, hard as life undoubtedly was, it at least offered a respite from the worries of trying to work and find people to look after Rosita. She would stay until Rosita started school. Then things would be easier. Meanwhile, life was full and rather a lot of good fun.

Cautiously at first, afraid of showing the slightest friendliness in case he misunderstood and took it for encouragement, she eased from her early formality in her attitude towards him. Thoughts of leaving faded away. She and Rosita were happy here and she wanted to stay. She could think of no better way of keeping Rosita with her.

The farm kept them busy but Graham took a day off once or twice that first summer, leaving a neighbour to attend to the milking of his four cows, taking Rosita and Barbara for a ride and a picnic on the horse and cart. Once he even took her to the bus stop so she could go back and visit the Careys. 'I know you're always hoping for news of your family,' he said.

Summer gave them longer days and although it also brought more and more work, they had time to talk. He listened with interest and no sign of censure when she told him about her parents and about Bernard and the baby, and the attempted kidnap of the child by Bernard's mother. She told him a lot about Luke.

'Tell me about this Luke,' he said one day. 'I confess I feel a bit jealous when you mention him, yet he wasn't a man you loved, was he?'

The hint of jealousy was disturbing, but when she looked at him he was staring straight into the fire without any sign of tension on his flat face, which was ruddy in the glow from the fire. His book was face down on his knees, his large hands continuing to fill his pipe, and he turned and smiled at her, easily, calmly. 'Tell me about him. He seems a very complex character.'

She relaxed again. She mustn't start imagining things.

'Luke's family didn't want to have anything to do with him. A bit like mine, really.' She frowned; it was difficult to put Luke into a few words. 'His father sounds like a man who is afraid of showing affection and tried to beat it out of his son.'

'Why would he do that?'

'I don't really understand, Graham. But it seems that Luke and his friend Roy were really close; Roy's family was where Luke was happiest. He spent a lot of time with them. His father told him that such a friendship was wrong, wicked even. He said that love was wrong, especially between two boys, but there wasn't any harm in it. He loved the whole family and the happiness that filled their home.'

'Boys often develop a fondness for each other, a close bond that lasts all their lives. Why should that be considered wicked? It sounds to me as though there was something lacking in the father.'

'His father beat Luke rather badly on the day his mother died. He found Luke and Roy with their arms around each other, comfort for one given by the other, both in tears.'

'How old was he?'

'Eighteen.'

'Poor devil.'

'A similar thing had happened when Luke's mother died. It was to Roy and his family he went for comfort and his father threw him out of the house.' She smiled at the big man, who was listening quietly. 'I wish you and Luke could meet, Graham. I think perhaps you, with all your learning, would help him understand and perhaps forgive his father.'

'Forgiveness? I think you're right, clever girl. Forgiveness will have to come before anything else.' He smiled, concentrating on getting his pipe drawing satisfactorily, then lowered his head and returned to his reading.

Graham surprised her one day by saying she looked tired. 'I don't want you overdoing things. I'm going to take on someone to do the heavy work and you can stay indoors and deal with the running of the house. It will give you more time to enjoy Rosita.'

Forgetting her determination not to give him any encouragement to see her as anything other than an employed housekeeper, she hugged him.

'Graham, you're so understanding. I do feel I'm missing the best of her childhood, having her fixed in her pram and dragging her around the farm like I do. It'll be wonderful to have more time to play with her. And I'll be able to deal with the cooking and preserving that I sometimes neglect. Thank you.'

The attention Graham gave her was flattering and well received, but she was very lonely for the Carey's lively family, not having had anyone else to talk to and share a joke with. Visitors to the farm were rare and never came into the house. Perhaps a young man about the place would liven things up a bit.

The boy who arrived a week later to help with the heavy work was not over-bright. Conversations consisted of her repeating his instructions and him misunderstanding. He also seemed a little afraid of Graham, particularly when he was seen talking to Barbara or the baby.

'Pity help him, he's so anxious to please, but I did hope to have someone else to talk to,' she sighed as the young man ran across the field to check on the sheep.

'Are you lonely?' Graham sounded surprised.

'A bit,' she admitted. 'I'm very happy here but I do miss having friends to chat to.' She turned away from him and asked, 'Do you think I could go and see the Careys again?'

He agreed but on the day she planned to go he changed his mind. Thinking about it, she decided it was when she mentioned seeking news of Luke that he had cancelled the arrangement and made her stay. He was short-tempered with her and curt with Rosita. She had obviously upset him.

The sudden change of mood frightened her. Then the slight fear turned to flattery: he was simply afraid of losing her. She wasn't vain, but knew how he had benefited from having her and Rosita sharing his life. His bad mood only lasted a few days but she was hesitant about asking again to visit her friends.

Rosita was a forward child and by the beginning of August, when she was eight months old, she was crawling and pulling herself up on chairs. Barbara was proud of her but exasperated too when she had to watch her every moment of the day. Rosita was unlike her mother, following the dark looks of Bernard, her dead father.

Despite Barbara's efforts Rosita often escaped her care and disappeared, to be found in one of the barns or heading towards the duck pond, where fortunately Graham had erected a strong fence so she couldn't get close. One evening, as Barbara was washing her ready for bed, she found bruising on her back and thighs.

'Graham, look at this. What d'you think happened?'

'You can hardly be surprised at a few injuries, Barbara. The child is always getting into places she shouldn't be.'

'But look. It's lines, as if someone has beaten her with a stick. You don't think that boy has been hurting her, do you?'

'Could have been anything. I don't think it looks like marks from a stick. Imagining things you are. Too anxious altogether.'

'Graham, I'm going to speak to him. And if I don't get a satisfactory explanation I'm going to the police. She's a tiny helpless baby!'

'All right. It was me.' His voice was sharp as he turned his broad back to her. 'It was me. I hit her.'

Barbara felt sickness sweep through her. 'You hit my baby? But why?'

'Come with me and I'll show you.' He led her to the barn. There in a corner was a circular saw and the choppers and sharp knives he used for cutting firewood and for making the swing he was shaping for Rosita. 'This is where I found her this morning when you were collecting the eggs. I had to stop her coming here again. Imagine what could happen if she came with no one to stop her touching all this. She could be killed.' He was watching Barbara's face as he picked up the choppers and touched their sharp edges. Emotions passed through her mind, visible on her lovely face: anger, outrage, then fear and relief.

'I love that little girl just like she's my own. I'd die if anything terrible happened to her. I'd blame myself for ever. You must know that, Barbara. But however she's punished, I'll never smack her again, I promise.'

'You really care for us?'

'You know I do.'

'If you so much as touch her again, I'll leave.'

'I never will, I promise.'

The war ended in November, when Germany surrendered unconditionally, but the world event made little difference to Barbara's life. News was slow to reach the farm, where they rarely had time to listen to the wireless, and when it did, Barbara's only concern was to wonder if Luke had survived it. She wanted to find out and the only chance of doing that was to visit the Careys.

Feeling confident in Graham's growing affection, she asked if she might do so. She watched anxiously for his reaction but he didn't put forward any reason for not allowing the visit or put any obstacles in the way of her leaving for a few days.

Far more effectively, he pleaded for her to forget Luke and the Careys and think of life here, on the farm with him, where Rosita was happy and they were both so badly needed and loved. Without refusing, he had prevented her going.

When, on Christmas Day, Rosita's birthday, he asked her to marry him, she accepted.

Chapter Six

ARRIVING IN FRANCE in the spring of 1918, after alarmingly brief training, Luke had expected to have time to consider his plans for the future. The general opinion seemed to be that the Germans were on the run and all he would be doing was helping to mop up the remnants of a defeated army. It would give him moments of quiet and enable him to think of what he would do on returning home.

Breaking away from everything he knew would be an opportunity to take stock of his life. He needed time to accept the abandonment of his family and the loss of Barbara's friendship and work out what he could expect from the years ahead.

Then he was confronted with the reality of war. Scenes seen in newspapers seemed so unreal in his safe office; articles he had perhaps only half-believed became horrifyingly real.

The small sections of battles seen in small photographs in newspapers and magazines gave no indication of the huge area over which hundreds of men fought and died. They didn't begin to describe the pounding of shells and the explosions of earth and equipment that buried men in seconds, or the screams as dozens of shells came through the air and landed like rain, bringing death and destruction in moments.

He and the few friends he had begun to make were thrown into the frenzied effort to block the enormous counter-attack against the British by thousands of German soldiers brought from other war zones to push them back.

He found himself in the confusion of a battle which changed moment by moment, so he didn't know where the frontline was or from which direction the Germans were coming, or even which direction he should himself be heading. At that terrifying time when he obeyed shouted orders and fired at human beings walking towards him in the grey uniform of the enemy, all he wanted was to survive. The future – if there were to be one – could look after itself.

There were times when fear such as he had never imagined made him deaf to the commands of his officers, blind to anything except his own vulnerability. He was in a pit of lunacy. Dante's Inferno, with mud the killer instead of flames, although there were flames too. These strange forms milling around him, dragging their feet through inches of thick, glutinous mud, covered with the filthy stuff so they no longer looked human, were escapees from a nightmare or an asylum. He was surrounded by maniacs glorying in death, creatures who wanted to kill and be killed.

He was afraid that every breath would be his last and besides the threat of death, there were the twin terrors of maiming wounds. Having left the dubious protection of the trench, he had crawled across land that no longer resembled good earth that had ever grown flowers and food. The stench of it choked him; the all-pervading filth clogged his nose and mouth and throat so he thought he must suffocate.

The noise of the bombardment deafened him and beat into his brain, so trying to think actually hurt, then became impossible. Besides the crump of falling shells, there was the screaming and whistling of their descent and the uproar came at him from every direction, adding to the confusion inside his head. He must be insane; he'd soon be a gibbering idiot. A punishment for saying he loved Roy. He was out of his mind. No one would accept this stupidity unless they were insane.

A crater opened out before him as he struggled forward and rather than make his way around it, he slid down into the depths, towards the glutinous watery mud at the bottom, where two shapes suggesting bodies lay still and half submerged. He slid well below the rim of the crater and holding his position on the slippery side with difficulty, he forced his shaking fingers to reload his rifle. Then he covered first his eyes then his ears with his filthy, stinking hands and tried to think. But there was no excuse for him to remain below the lip of the crater.

He could hardly see, and he knew it was mud, but his eyes stung and he believed he was going blind. He took off his glasses and tried to clean them but every inch of him was covered with slime and he only made them worse. It was like lifting lead, to pull his unwilling body back to where he could see the enemy and fire at them. He desperately wanted to stay hidden. Like many others, he called soundlessly for his mother.

While he fired his Lee-Enfield with manic intensity at the German soldiers who seemed to be approaching on all sides and increasing in number, his mind fretted hysterically with the problem of how he would row his boat with only one arm, or how he would get into it with one leg, or even with none.

Panic ate at him in waves and, in between, guilt made him ashamed of his fear. The others didn't appear to be afraid. They went over the top when ordered to without a sign of anxiety. His father had been right to be ashamed of him; he wasn't a man. Locked in a prison for conscientious objectors, that's where he should be, where his cowardice couldn't create risks for others. He was letting everyone down, crouched in terror on the edge of this filthy shell hole, with only the bodies of two of the enemy for company.

Determinedly he stood up, tears streaming down his face, and looked across the mud to where a column of Germans were coming down a hillside between the stumps of trees that had once been verdant woodland. The men were sliding in the mud and unable, he thought, to aim with any accuracy. Telling himself he was safe, that he could stop them, he aimed at one of the leaders. His arm shook but he saw the man fall.

Moments later, almost an echo of his own actions, he felt a firm thud against his thigh. He had been hit. He wondered if it were a fatal wound and what it would feel like to die. He continued to fire for several minutes then there was another jarring impact and he fell, with a second bullet in his shoulder followed by another sharper, searing pain in his head.

He slowly crumpled and lay at the edge of the crater, the foul stuff inching its way to almost touch his mouth. His mind wandered and he dreamed of being on his boat with the wind touching his hair as the battle passed over and around him, until blissful silence came with the darkness of night.

Exhaustion made him lower his head and at once his nose began to fill with the slime and, coughing, he tried to get up. To his horror his legs were already half submerged. He gave a low scream, remembering seeing horses buried alive in the disgusting stuff. He managed to pull himself out of the glue-like grave and through that crazy night he crawled then stumbled and eventually walked away from the scene of battle.

He had no notion of time, nor of where he was heading, his animal instincts simply taking him away from the danger to where he might rest up and lick his wounds and cleanse himself of the mud and the sewer-stink of death.

He met no one although sometimes he heard distant sounds of activity and once a vehicle passed but, afraid it might be the enemy who would either kill him or commit him to prison, he hid. He slept when he could travel no further, under the remains of a hedge in the slight shallow of a drainage ditch, which was miraculously free of the filthy, clinging mud.

In the early dawn, when the silence was occasionally broken by distant gunfire, he opened his eyes on the smiling, impish face of a woman pressed close to his own.

"'Ello, English boy. Do you think you can walk?' She seemed satisfied by his stuttered response as she looked over his shoulder and called, '*Papa ici, vite.*' Her voice was husky and soothingly low. Behind him footsteps squelched slowly through knee-deep mud and an old man appeared, dressed in the rough clothes of a farmer.

'I need to get back to my line,' Luke said, but when he tried to stand, his head felt twice its normal size and his legs were unable to carry him. Cursing his weakness, he sank once more to the ground.

'Do not worry, *mon petit*,' the woman said. He wondered about the *mon petit* – it was an expression used for small children – but when he roused himself sufficiently to look at her, he realized that to her, he was petite. She weighed about three stone more than his ten and a half and was at least eight inches taller. She smiled widely and in English, said to her father, 'I have found myself an Englishman, Papa. Now what shall we do with him, eh?'

'*Pour commencer nous allons le metre sur pied*,' the man replied with a chuckle. Luke understood that he wanted to get him on his feet and shared her cheerful smile.

Her clothes were brown, her face was brown, her eyes a darker version of that same colour. Her hair was an untidy mixture of brown and grey carelessly combed – if at all. Yet there was something very likeable about her. Even in those first moments of anxiety when he wondered if they would kill him or hand him over to the enemy, he recognized that she was a woman made for laughter and fun.

He stood with the old man's arm supporting him and through blurred eyes looked around the desolate countryside, which was little more than charred and broken tree stumps, ruined buildings and endless acres of churned-up earth. If she could smile amid all this, hers must be a cheerful spirit indeed.

After a cursory examination of his wounds – a deep cut on his thigh, another less serious one, probably from flying shrapnel, across the side of his head, and a channel made by a bullet grazing his shoulder – the old man helped the woman to carry him across the slippery ground. It was exhausting in his weakened state and it seemed like forever before they eventually stopped in the protection of a half-demolished wall.

'Ouf!' the man exclaimed. He muttered something that Luke interpreted as, 'He is heavier than he looks.' Luke shared a smile with the woman.

He washed his glasses and immediately felt better. The woman held out her hand for them and dried them on her skirt, lifting her clothes carelessly and showing a generous expanse of sturdy thigh.

Unbelievably, he was in a small area that was not completely churned up. The farm and most of the animals had survived the fighting that had surrounded them. The farmhouse that faced them was a little way up the slope they were about to climb and was half hidden by a fold in the land. Around it was a patch of green that dazzled after seeing nothing but grey-brown mud.

As they drew closer, Luke saw that the building was damaged; the roof had a large hole in it and the walls gaped where there had once been windows and doors. But from a chimney a thin column of smoke rose and it promised warmth and a place to rest. He was incapable of looking further into the future than to relish those two precious things.

After a wonderful bath, during which the woman walked in and out of the room without any unease, they found him some clean clothes, all of which were several sizes too large. Then they hid him in a barn of sweet-smelling hay, where a solitary horse munched contentedly close to his ear.

A few days later the fighting seemed to have moved further away and they took him into the house. An attic room, giving him a view across the once-green fields, was his home for a few more days while his wounds healed. All were grazing wounds without the complication of bullets embedded. The thigh was the worst but that too submitted to the woman's expert ministrations.

The father moved around the buildings, feeding their few animals but spending a lot of his day just standing looking across the alien landscape, his deep-set eyes full of memories. Martine, his daughter, cooked and cleaned, fed the hens, singing all the time in a surprisingly mellow voice. He was reminded of the Careys, whose singing seemed an echo of hers.

When she had time to spare she would come and sit on the straw-filled mattress and talk to him in a mixture of French and English that had them both laughing within moments of her arrival. With deep regret, he left after a couple of weeks to try and find his way back to his group.

Luke survived the war with a scar on his shoulder and thigh and a patch of white hair where shrapnel had scorched his scalp – the only visible signs of his experience. But the worst scars were hidden, the memories of the hundreds of men he had seen die. The moans of their agony disturbed his sleep. When he returned home, he found it impossible to settle. He was constantly tormented by the faces of men he had killed – none of which he had actually seen. In his tormented mind he saw not wicked and cruel enemy soldiers, only young and innocent young men, like his friend, Roy Thomas.

On Christmas Day 1918 he was twenty-one and, having no family to share the occasion, he went to the cottage on the beach hoping for news of Barbara and Rosita. He broke the fresh padlock on the door and went inside. Nothing had changed, his father hadn't set foot in the place – just prevented him from enjoying it. He sighed and wondered why his father hated him so.

He walked across the beach to find his boat still intact and the Careys living in chaotic squalor in the beach house. He asked after Barbara and Rosita but there had been no news of them since they had moved away. Was it only months he had been gone? The reminder startled him; it seemed like a lifetime.

He noticed that the porch was still standing but the repair to the room above had not been carried out. The wood Richard had bought was still lying abandoned and the room still lacked a floor and a part of its front wall. The money Richard had 'found' and used had been wasted, the lethargic Henry Carey too idle to carry out the simple tasks. Any improvements in their living conditions were those achieved by Mrs Carey and Richard. He shrugged. The Careys survived in the place so why should he persuade them they needed more?

With Richard he went out in the boat and they fished unsuccessfully, content to talk. Luke dreaded the boy asking about the war, but tried to answer truthfully when he did, not glorifying the insane slaughter of a generation of men from many nations.

'Were you scared, Luke?' Richard asked when he was told about the day he was wounded. Here truth slipped swiftly away and Luke shook his head.

'Too busy to be afraid,' he told the boy. 'We had a job to do and we just got on with it.'

Why couldn't he admit to being terrified? Why did he have to lie? The fear had been mind-searing although it had quickly subsided once Martine had found him. But when it fled, it left in its place the guilt. The unforgettable truth was that he had panicked and lost all ability to obey orders, or even to hear or understand them. The shame for his weakness he now covered with lies, even to young Richard.

Perhaps it was the same with others? Guilt making them reply to the inevitable questions with platitudes? He couldn't believe he had been the only one to show such a lack of strength, but he would never talk about it so would never know.

The business of secondhand books continued to grow due almost completely to the work of his partner, Jeanie. The shop was becoming known to collectors and other dealers and postal requests were met with increasing success. Jeanie had done a wonderful job. She had remarried during his absence and her husband came into the shop to help on the days he wasn't working.

Although Luke spent his days in the shop or travelling to buy stock, he was still unsettled. The shop seemed to run without his help and after a few months, he once more arranged for Jeanie to manage without him and set off again for France. He carried with him the watch he had bought in 1917, a Christmas present for Roy, who had been killed at Verdun.

To find Roy's grave had become less important and he doubted if he would bury the watch with his friend as he had once planned. That had been the idea of a silly young man, and after his brief experience of war, that epithet no longer described him. But there wasn't anything else more important for him to do.

It took several weeks to find Roy's grave and when he had done so he still didn't want to go home. No one missed him while he was away. The business continued to succeed. There wasn't even anyone who expected him to write, apart from Jeanie so there was no reason for him to go back. He went instead to find the people who had helped him after he had been wounded.

They hadn't moved from the house where they had sheltered him and were delighted at his return. To his surprise he felt a flood of real affection at seeing Martine again. Large, untidily dressed and laughing, she ran across the yard to meet him. There was no false formality to leave him in any doubt that she was very pleased to see him again. Her lively, happy face was creased into smiles and her low, throaty laughter filled the air.

'You remembered us?' she said. 'Papa. *Par ici vite*! The English boy, he remember us!'

She hugged him and there was a sense of 'coming home', which he had rarely experienced since early childhood. Having no one who cared about him made her pleasure in his company very valuable and she persuaded him to stay, for a few days, then a week, then longer. Her father was the proud recipient of Roy's watch.

Martine was a widow, her husband having been killed during the first months of the war. Although she was in her late thirties, she had no children.

'We owned a café, my 'usband and me,' she told him on one of their many walks. 'It is near the beach at Calais and when my 'usband die, I leave the place and come to look after Papa.' She took his hand and asked pleadingly, 'The café, you will come with me, yes? To see if perhaps there is something left?'

Luke went with her one day, travelling by farm carts, buses and for much of the time walking. All around there were remnants of the battles that had taken place. Metal rusting and distorted so they often had difficulty recognizing its original shape or purpose. The fields were no longer green, but surprisingly the disturbance of the earth had encouraged thousands of dormant poppy seeds to germinate and grow. Many thought it was the blood of the thousands who had died there. The buildings left standing were pitted with shell-fire, some still occupied by families with nowhere else to go.

The beach, once a playground for laughing children, had a sombre mood, echoing with memories of the dead. The devastation was horrifying but after several hours they no longer wept for the tragic losses, they were just numbed by the extent of them. When they reached the part where Martine expected to see the café, there was nothing.

'Where is it?' she asked, throwing her arms wide in theatrical despair. 'Once, my little café stood 'ere.'

'Perhaps you're confused,' Luke said. 'Trees uprooted, the streets reduced to rubble, it must all look very different from when you were last here.' He led the way along the rubble-strewn path along the top of the beach and Martine followed doubtfully.

But Luke was right. A short distance further on they found the building, battered but still standing. The name, Café de Jacques was still readable on the door. They even found the piano in a back room and joyfully, Martine struck a few chords on it.

'Oh, Luke, we will soon have it open for business again. You will stay with me, will you not?'

He answered a fervent 'Yes!' Here he was needed, there was so much to do. At home, no one waited.

Their closeness during the week in which she had hidden him had made them friends. On their reunion the feeling had been revived without a moment of hesitation. Martine had been waiting for him. The visit to see if her café was still there had been delayed until he returned and could go with her; he knew that with certainty now, although she had not actually said so.

Hidden in the attic room of her home as the war began its final stages, they had spent long hours talking and getting to know each other. Now, renewing and building up that companionship, learning about each other, exchanging news of the time between was a delight. They were as natural and honest with each other as if they had been friends for many years, with even their few differences respected and accepted with ease.

Martine was always able to see the positive side of things; laughter seemed to bubble up in her throat. Her husky voice made light of even the most frustrating problems and she sang constantly. To a depressed spirit like Luke, she was a tonic.

Her grey-flecked hair, short and cut like a boy, and the casual clothes she wore that also seemed intended for the opposite sex didn't deter from her feminine attractions. That she was a woman was never in doubt. To Luke she was a perfect companion. Their initial closeness had lasted little more than a week but the briefness of the acquaintance was less important than its intensity.

Luke even tried to make love to her. He saw nothing but loneliness facing him if he returned to his previous life; days spent in the shop and silent hours on the beach to fill the long and empty weekends. To keep Martine it must surely be necessary to share her bed?

His attempt at forming a sexual union had been a failure for them both. Fortunately it didn't seem to matter. Martine found it an excuse for laughter in which he joined with relief.

'*Cela ne fait rien, cherie*, it does not matter! That you are my friend, that is important. Everything else is nothing.' She smiled wickedly and added, 'And now we have the cigarette, yes?'

They hugged a lot and at first Luke found it embarrassing and tried to pull away but Martine insisted and gradually he relaxed into a partnership in which they could both show their natural need of each other's friendship. It was a friendship teetering on the kind of love shared by a man and a woman but never quite succeeding in crossing that haphazard line that changes friends into lovers.

Finding the building less damaged than expected, they both worked to get the café reopened over the next few weeks. Luke began repairs and Martine spent hours at offices gaining the necessary licences and sanctions. Surprisingly, a number of Martine's old customers returned to celebrate with her on the day they reopened. Sadly, it was mostly the elderly or the sick and wounded. All the young men had gone.

By word of mouth news of the opening of Café de Jacques had spread. They planned a really good first night and the local people helped by coming in droves. They both played the piano so took it in turns to lead the singing and serve drinks and food. Few customers remembered how they got home.

If anyone had asked Luke if he were happy he would have been surprised to find the answer was yes. He and Martine ran the café in leisurely contentment, sharing their lives their thoughts and their hopes but not a bed. He played the piano in their little bar each evening and the place attracted a regular clientele that became, for Luke, a substitute family.

Weeks passed into months, months into years, and with the occasional brief visit to check on the shop, time passed in pleasurable contentment, their days filled with hard work but plenty of talk, music and a great deal of laughter.

*

In 1922, the Carey family still lived in the house on the beach but the thrill of the dream come true, a house of their own, so wonderful in that first summer, had changed to despair. The house, seemingly such a safe harbour at the time they had been thrown into the street, was damp and falling apart. Mr and Mrs Carey were both sickly and the children were living half wild. It was only Richard, now ten, who kept them together, and fed.

He rarely went to school and living so far away from the school he had once occasionally attended, the school inspector never quite caught up with him. The rest of the children went to the small village school much closer to their home but Richard had avoided being added to the register. Neither Mr nor Mrs Carey had made any effort to encourage him to go. They both knew how much they needed Richard and seemed unaware of their self-ishness and short-sightedness where their quite remarkable son was concerned. The fact that they were expected to stay at school until fourteen was to his mind ridiculous. He was almost eleven and he had been working in one capacity or another since he was three. Keeping one step ahead of the inspector was a nuisance. Leaving school officially would make things simpler. Roll on September 1926, was his constant sigh.

In the winter of 1926 disaster struck. The solemn-faced little Blodwen and her younger sister Meriel both became ill with what appeared to be a chesty cold. In days they were coughing and wheezing, struggling to breathe and by the time Mr Carey had persuaded a doctor to call at the house so far from his surgery, they were both seriously ill. Although taken to hospital, they both died.

Richard was numb with shock but as self-appointed head of the family he couldn't show it. His amusing little sister, who sat as a silent observer through all their trials and happy moments, was gone. He ached inside and the ache wouldn't go away, whatever he tried, yet he knew he had to be the strong one and carry on with the daily battle to survive. But he envied Idris, the useless one, being cuddled and comforted by Mam, while he went on scraping together the means to feed them all.

For weeks Mrs Carey sat in a chair unable to rouse enough enthusiasm to even cook a meal. Like an automaton, Mr Carey delivered his papers but left more and more of the work to Richard. Richard tried to persuade Idris to help but Mrs Carey's arms would hold her golden boy and, seeing the comfort his mother gained from Idris, he gave up and rose earlier to fit even more tasks into his day.

They were constantly hungry, yet his mother didn't seem capable of dealing with the basic cooking. Again it was Richard, aged ten, who coped. Buying chips several times a week, riding the two miles home as fast as he could on a battered old bike, he delivered the slowly congealing food and made them all eat. Soup and baked beans from tins, plus the chips, kept them going, although his parents seemed thinner every time he looked at them. Gradually, through the summer of 1927, things returned to normal although, for Richard, the loss of his much-loved Blodwen was a constant void that nothing would fill.

He was walking back to the beach pushing his bike one day, carrying packets of chips. As he passed the school, a lady called out to him. Instinctively he wanted to run. She was sure to ask why he wasn't at school and he didn't want that problem, but the bike had a puncture and he didn't want to drop it and run home without it, so he waited while she approached.

'Hello,' she said, smiling at him. 'Are you one of the children who live on the beach near Gull Island?'

'I'm not a child,' he replied defensively. 'I work with my dad, have done these ages!'

'Trouble with the bicycle?' she asked.

'Nothing I can't fix.' He began to move away.

'Your chips must be getting cold – I can give you a lift if you like. Come back and collect the bike later?'

She was right about the chips. 'OK.'

She drove to the beach and avoided asking about his school attendance. She was curious about the boy. 'My name is Miss Bell,' she said. 'I live in the cottage next to the school.'

'I'm Richard,' he told her. 'We all live on the beach, because we like it,' he added defiantly. He didn't want anyone feeling sorry for them.

She didn't ask any questions but was horrified when she got out of the car and walked to his door. The place was nothing more than a hovel. How could they survive? The door stood open and a delicious smell of cooking emerged. 'Mam's cooking pigeon for pie tomorrow,' Richard said proudly. 'Marvellous cook, my mam.'

Some of the younger children peered at her from the doorway and windows, shy at seeing their teacher there. Miss Bell waved to them and said hello to Mrs Carey, who appeared at the door and waved nervously, then she drove away, followed at a distance by the children.

Several times over the following weeks she saw Richard and gradually coaxed him to talk. She emphasized his abilities then hinted that, if he were a better reader and had some help with maths, he might become something really clever – a businessman who could care for all his family and allow them to live without so many discomforts. She concentrated on reminders of how hard life was for his mother.

He began to listen and after a few weeks went into her house, where she lived with her mother, and various lessons were begun. He managed to fit the work, which immediately fascinated him, into his busy days. Miss Bell was impressed by the speed at which he absorbed every new instruction and took great pleasure in his remarkable progress.

The Careys had had no news of Barbara Jones and little Rosita. Richard thought of them often and wished Barbara hadn't moved so far away. Mam would have been glad of her and Rosita these past months, he thought. He liked the idea of visiting the farm and pleaded with his father to take him there.

'Too far, boy,' Mr Carey said with regret. 'Can't spare the time. It'll take a whole day to get there and then see her for only half an hour. Perhaps one day, when we're rich.' Being rich was a joke to Mr Carey, but not to Richard.

'How long have we been living on the beach, Dad? It was when Rosita was born. I was wondering how old she is.'

Mr Carey frowned, his face pale and blue-tinged, in spite of the outdoor life he led. 'Let's see, boy. Born in 1917 so she'd be five and going to school. Fancy that. Five years we've been here.'

'I hope that farmer Prothero bloke is being good to them,' Richard muttered.

'Sure to be. They'll be as happy as anyone's a right to be, with good home-grown food and not having to worry where the next shilling will come from.'

'But we don't know, Dad. Please can we visit? I want to go there and see if she's enjoying being a farmer's wife. It's hard work and she isn't very big, our Barbara. He could be working her too hard.'

Henry Carey had always doubted Barbara's wisdom in returning to that farmer but there was nothing he could do about it, was there? That was always his attitude to problems; he wasn't in the position to disagree with anything people wanted to do. Better to go the way events took you. Besides, fond as he was of her, Barbara wasn't even family.

Legally married they were and her old enough to cope with whatever life handed her. Staying with them in the house on the beach hadn't been much of an alternative to marrying a farmer. Saying she would be happy and well looked after was almost as good as believing it, wasn't it? A bit of pretence helped a fellow to sleep at night. But the niggle of fear for the girl and the baby returned after Richard's spoken concern. He hadn't met Graham Prothero but he'd heard unpleasant rumours about how his sickly and overworked first wife had died.

*

Richard stepped off the train in the centre of the town and headed for the wholesalers. He had money in his pocket to pay for the week's papers. It was the first time his father had trusted him with the money and he felt proud of the responsibility. Unconsciously his hand touched the right front of his coat. In an inside pocket the money jiggled in a satisfying way.

The wholesalers had a counter stretching across the room and behind it, at two cluttered desks, sat two clerks. On one wall there were cubbyholes with numbers on them. He went to the one bearing his father's number and climbed up to feel about on the wooden surface to see if there were any magazines for him to take back. There were only two, special orders, and he rolled them carefully and put them in his pocket.

'Oi! Can you come and see to me? I'm in a bit of a hurry!' he said cheekily to one of the clerks.

'Wait a minute. Can't you see we're busy?' one of the clerks said, pointing to the phone she had just picked up.

'Oi to you then,' he said to the other girl. 'All I want is for you to take my money. Not too much trouble, is it?'

He counted out the money when the girl came forward with the cash box and the ledger, and waited while she filled in a receipt. She took the money and then from outside came a squeal of brakes as a car skidded and then crashed into another, trying to negotiate a corner without giving way. Both girls went to the doorway and Richard's hand slipped into the cash box and came out with a fold of notes.

Boldly he stood with the two girls, a hand on the shoulders of each, stretching to do so, chatting about the stupidity of drivers who insisted on going too fast, making the girls laugh at his adult expressions, and when they had exhausted the subject and there were three customers waiting at the counter near the cash box, he waved at them, gave a final critical comment on the craze for motoring, and sauntered away. When he felt safe enough to stop and count the money, he had £25. A fortune! His savings were growing at an encouraging rate.

He whistled as he stepped off the train and walked down to the beach. Still whistling cheerfully, he gave his father the receipt for the payment.

'I'll deliver the magazines with the evening papers, all right, Dad?' His father put the receipt on the table where it fluttered lightly in the breeze. It was Richard who sighed and grabbed it, and put it on the spike with the rest. 'Got to make sure you don't lose it. Don't want them saying we haven't paid now, do we?'

Mr Carey chuckled. 'You sound like you're the dad, not me.' He whittled uselessly at a piece of wood with which he hoped to fix a broken window frame. 'See anything interesting in town?'

'Only the smartest car you've ever seen. Boy oh boy it was a beauty. Crashed it did, with another coming the opposite way, and them girls ran to the door with as much excitement as if it had been Rudolph Valentino! The driver was dressed like men who fly aeroplanes. Scarves and goggles and leather coat an' all. And a fancy camera slung over his shoulder.' He gave a sigh. 'He must have been carrying pounds' worth of clothes and equipment on his back. Makes you sick how rich some people are and there's us with nothing.'

'No use complaining about that, son. There's some born to be rich and some born to be poor and there's nothing we can do about it.'

That's what you think, Richard thought. Aloud, he said, 'Dad, can I have a shilling to go into Cardiff tonight? Fancy the pictures I do and I think Douglas Fairbanks is on. And there's a film about a motor car ride through North Wales. I'd love to drive a car, I would.'

'Wishful thinking that is for sure. People like us don't even get to ride in motor cars.'

'I have. That Miss Bell has taken me twice into the library and to the office down the docks to talk to the man who does the books. Interesting that was.'

'Well, that's the closest you'll get to owning one.'

I'll have one, one day, see if I don't, Richard promised himself, with a determined smile.

Mr Carey counted out twelve pennies into Richard's hand. 'Deserve that, you do, for all the hours you help me. I just don't know what we'd do if we didn't have you, boy, and that's a fact.' He lowered his voice. 'I thank God you aren't like that useless Idris. Sitting there leaning on Mam, looking up at her with doting eyes. If she so much as moves he falls over.'

'I haven't started yet, Dad. Just watch me. I'll see you and Mam all right one day.'

'For sure you will.' Henry smiled indulgently at his son. What chance did he or any of them have of improving their lot? Paying their way, that's all they were doing. He couldn't afford the shilling he'd just given Richard, but the boy had to have some encouragement to go on helping. If Richard got fed up and left, they would all be done for. Alun and Billie had already found jobs far away.

He called Richard back and said, 'Here's another seven-pence halfpenny. Get a tin of cocoa after your evening round, will you? It warms your mam and helps her to sleep.'

Richard called in to see Miss Bell on his way to deliver his papers. 'Here's the shilling to get that book you said I should read about "counting see" or whatever it's called.'

'Accountancy,' she corrected, and promised to have it by the following day.

It was as the crowds went in at the beginning of the main film that Richard wriggled past the pay desk and slipped through the blanket-like curtains and into the darkness. No point spending ninepence when you didn't have to. The usherettes were frantically reaching out for tickets to fold and tear in half and by standing with a family group, he had easily slipped through unnoticed. Last row but two in the back stalls was the best as he hadn't paid. In the middle of the row. No one would bother him there.

He was whistling when he came out again into the fresh air and someone began to accompany him, singing words to his tune. He turned to see a small, thin man with a long, rather straggly beard, wearing a black beret and steel-framed glasses. He wore wide, cream trousers and a short beige jacket.

'Hello, Richard. It is Richard, isn't it?'

For a moment Richard didn't recognize him then he shouted in disbelief. 'Luke? We thought you must be dead! Where have you been and why haven't you been to see us? It's donkey's years since we saw you and what's with the funny get-up?'

'One question at a time,' Luke laughed. 'Come on, have you got time for a cup of tea and a bun?'

'You bet I have, if you're paying.'

One of the first questions Luke asked was, 'How are Barbara and Rosita?'

'We haven't heard for ages. I've pleaded with Dad to take me there but it's too far. And with the papers to see to early morning and in the evening, there isn't time to get there and back.'

'I have a car,' Luke offered.

'Damn me, you haven't!'

'I'll come for you first thing in the morning and as soon as the papers are delivered, we'll go and find them. I'm going back to France in a couple of days. I only came on a brief visit to check on the shop, so it will have to be tomorrow. Will that be all right?'

'That'll be great! D'you mean I'll really have a ride in a car? I've been in one before, mind,' he added boastfully. 'Miss Bell, the teacher, she's taken me places.'

'You go to school?'

'No fear. But Miss Bell shows me things, like maths and—' He paused, making sure he got it right '—accountancy, and reading as well. She says reading is important if I'm to learn—' Again the pause '—accountancy. I enjoy her showing me but I couldn't go to school – that would be boring and a waste of time.' He looked doubtfully at the strangely dressed man. 'And I can really have a ride in the car?'

'And your father too, if he can spare the time.'

Rosita had started school at the village a mile from the farm. Barbara was concerned as she was not doing very well. Given words to copy from the blackboard on to her little wooden-framed slate, she drew pictures instead. When she did write words they were always different from the ones on the board and she soon earned the nickname 'Miss Stupid'.

Adding and subtracting she managed well enough, particularly mental arithmetic, when the teacher called out the questions, but even so there were days when she achieved nothing, days when all her work was incorrect or hidden under furious scribbling.

The teachers tried to help her but eventually, driven to less and less effort by her rudeness and her lack of co-operation, they put her behaviour down to an inability to learn and gave her pictures to cut out and drawings to colour instead.

'Why are you so difficult?' Barbara asked one day, when Rosita was screaming and insisting she would not go to school. 'You're more like a prickly hedgehog than a little girl! If you'd only listen to what the teachers tell you and do what they ask, school would be fun.'

'How can it ever be fun to be told you're daft? Everyone calls me that stupid Jones girl. They laugh at me. And they make fun of me because I haven't got the same name as my father.'

'I'll come with you this morning and talk to them.'

'No! No. No. I won't go!'

'Rosita, don't be so stupid!' Barbara regretted the word almost before it had left her lips. 'I don't mean stupid, I mean—'

'Him out there, he calls me stupid. The teachers call me stupid and now YOU!'

Graham came to the door wondering what the noise was about and at once Rosita tried to stop crying, her sobs choking as she held her breath. There was that devil in her that refused to cower, though, and in a loud whisper she said, 'It's him who's stupid, not me!'

Graham strode into the room and Barbara stood in front of the now-screaming child.

'No, Graham,' she warned.

Frustrated, Graham stood clenching and unclenching his fists, then stamped out and slammed the door.

Rosita stayed at home that day and Barbara put aside thoughts of the morrow. One day at a time, that was the only way to deal with Rosita.

Luke's car was a small open-topped four-seater and to Richard it was perfection. His father had declined to come so he sat in the passenger seat and allowed his imagination to fly. He would have a car like this and take his mam on trips to see things she had never even heard of. And he would wave as they sped past villagers who would stop and stare in amazement at such a young man owning such a magnificent vehicle.

He asked endless questions about the engine and the speed of which it was capable and twice Luke stopped and lifted the bonnet to explain a particularly complicated reply. As always he was surprised at how easily Richard understood.

The journey took longer than Luke had expected as the way was not signposted, the farm was a small one and it was only when they were quite close to it that people recognized its name and were able to direct them.

It alarmed Luke to see how the expressions of the local people changed to dislike when the name of Graham Prothero was mentioned. He began to have an uneasy feeling that what awaited them would not be pleasant.

Richard smiled and thought only of seeing the look on their faces when he and Luke arrived in this wonderful car. It was green with black mudguards and trim. The leather upholstery was also green and smelled expensive. Richard thought he would have one exactly the same.

It was as the sun reached the summit before its descent down the other side of the sky that he began to think how little time he would have to spend with the two people he looked forward so much to seeing. 'Will we be able to stay a while?' he asked apprehensively.

'A couple of hours at least. Your father promised he would manage the papers this evening so we don't have to hurry back. In fact, we can find somewhere to eat if you like.'

'If I'd like? Will a dog chase a rabbit?'

They drove through the gates of the farm and pulled up near a water pump. The door of the farmhouse opened and a woman stood there, dressed in layers of clothes, as if each one had been added to disguise the tattered state of a previous one, and giving her a bulky appearance. Her once-long hair was badly cut into an attempt at a shingle. It wasn't until she spoke that they recognized Barbara.

'Luke? Richard? But – oh, what a lovely, lovely surprise.'

Luke thought shock was a word better suited to her reaction. She was alarmed. A nervous tic beat like a pulse in her cheek. This visit seemed less and less like a good idea.

'Perhaps we should have written, but we didn't know the address. And I only have a few days before …'

She invited them inside and took off several layers of what Luke now guessed were her working clothes protecting tidy garments underneath She was wearing a simple homemade skirt and blouse, her figure now revealed to be much thinner than when they had last met.

'Come in. Sit down. Oh, it's good to see you. Is that your car, Luke? Come and tell me how you are. Richard, I'd hardly recognize you, so handsome you've grown. This is lovely – I've heard no news of anyone and it's been so long.' A smile of welcome revitalized her tired face and she hugged them both.

The room into which they were shown was neat and clean but bare of any comfort. The chairs and table were wooden and scrubbed so much that the wood stood up in ridges. She went to a cupboard and brought out a loaf and some butter but Luke stopped her, his hand on her thin arm.

'A cup of tea would be nice, but as for food, we are going to eat later. Please, Barbara, just sit and talk to us, that's what we came for, to hear how you are. And Rosita.'

'She has two sisters now – Kate who is three and Hattie now two. They're here somewhere. I'll just call.' She went to the door and called their names and the first to arrive was the five-year-old Rosita, bright-eyed, curious and with an air of tight-lipped defiance that Luke thought odd in one so young. She stood with her chin jutting out as if expecting an argument.

'I didn't smash them eggs and I'm not going to say I did!' Her face lengthened with incipient sobs but her eyes were bright with determination. She went to run back out but Barbara caught hold of her and turned her to face the visitors.

'Rosita, we have visitors, Richard and Luke. Please say hello. Politely, mind.'

'Hello.' She stared at them, wondering if there was the likelihood of a gift. The woman from the chapel sometimes brought them oranges or a slab of homemade toffee.

'We haven't seen you since you were a tiny baby,' Luke said with a smile. 'How old are you now?'

'Five going on six but can I go now or he'll be shouting at me again.'

'Go and tell your father we have visitors, please, Kate,' Barbara said to one of the younger children hovering around the doorway. The two younger girls ran off, leaving Rosita staring wide-eyed at Richard and Luke. She sidled across the room and stood between them. The beard was fascinating. She leaned against Richard and stared at Luke. Her fingers went out to touch the long, fine beard. 'Are you my real father?' she asked.

'Unfortunately not,' Luke replied. He looked across at Barbara to share a smile but she was looking anxiously towards the doorway and seemed not to have heard.

'She didn't go to school today,' she said.

'Remember how she used to cry all the time, Barbara?' Richard said, flicking a thumb towards Rosita.

'He says I'm still a noisy bugger,' Rosita said, glaring at her mother, expecting a rebuke.

'Rosita! That isn't a word we use.'

'He does.' She gestured with her head to the doorway. 'When he talks to me he does.'

Luke bent down and took Rosita onto his lap but as he took her weight she suddenly screamed and held her leg. Instinctively, Richard lifted her dress to see if there was a cut or graze, just as he would have done with his sister, and saw to his horror that the girl's thigh was a mass of yellow and purple bruises.

'It's nothing,' Barbara said hastily, looking again towards the doorway, hearing her husband coming across the yard. 'She's such a clumsy child, always falling. So adventurous, you'd never believe.'

A shadow in the doorway made them look up to see Graham, holding the hands of his daughters.

'Ah,' Barbara said with obvious relief at the interruption. 'Kate and Hattie, Graham, love, come and meet my friends Luke and Richard.'

The three-year-old Kate and the two-year-old Hattie came forward and said 'Hello' politely then ran back to their father. They both had blue eyes like Barbara and Graham. Kate resembled her mother, but Hattie was heavily built like her father, with the same flat face and rounded cheeks and chin, giving a false air of humour. Rosita looked completely different from the others, with dark hair fastened tightly in a plait, and deep brown eyes that looked full of hurt and resentment.

They didn't stay long. It was clear from the attitude of Barbara's large, simmering, quiet husband that they were not welcome.

'Please, write when you have time, Barbara,' Luke pleaded when they were leaving. 'I live in France but when I come home I can pick up letters from the Careys.'

They gave the usual assurances that they would keep in touch, and come again very soon, but on the journey home both Luke and Richard knew it was impossible.

'He hits her!' an outraged Richard said as soon as the car moved out of the farmyard.

Luke agreed but he said, 'Perhaps Barbara is right and she's just clumsy.'

'Clumsy, my foot! I know what a smack with a stick looks like!'

Whatever they thought of the way Graham Prothero looked after his family, there was nothing they could do but leave them to the life Barbara had chosen. They were quiet as they drove home, all the excitement of the anticipated visit ruined.

Barbara cried a little when they left, hiding her unhappiness from Graham and the children. Why did Graham hate Rosita so much? It couldn't be jealousy, not after so long. He was so good to her and the youngest girls; it was only Rosita he seemed unable to tolerate. If only she would behave better, things would improve, she was sure they would.

Chapter Seven

LUKE AND RICHARD got out of the car at the beach in silence, each deep in their own thoughts.

'I'll just say hello to your parents then I have to leave,' Luke said. 'If your mother won't mind me popping in?' He wondered how Mrs Carey would greet him. He had seen how shabby the area around the house was and thought she might be embarrassed by his unannounced arrival, but she seemed indifferent to the state of the place which, when he got closer, was even worse than he had first thought.

The porch he had repaired was still intact but the floor above it had not been replaced. The planks of wood Richard had bought for the purpose were still lying where the delivery man had left them, piled against the sea wall. The nails were a rusting heap.

All around the building rubbish was piled, old furniture mostly, items they had obtained second- third- or fourth-hand and which, when their condition worsened, they hadn't bothered to remove. Good furniture always found a new home and when it had become too shabby for the second owner there was usually a third ready to take it. It was only when the stuff was past repair that it had to stay where it was; there was no one poorer than the Careys who would be glad to take what they had no further use for. In the poorest communities there was the most rubbish, abandoned and with nowhere more lowly to go.

Luke accepted the cup of tea he was offered although it was a jam jar and not a cup from which he drank. Without the others seeing him, he gave some money to Mrs Carey.

'For shoes for Richard and the others,' he whispered, as she was about to refuse. He stayed a while, discussing Barbara and Rosita, wanting to do something but knowing there was nothing to be done. Before he left he went to have a look at the cottage, padlocked and with that dusty air of abandonment that showed how long it had been since anyone had been inside. How stupid that the Careys lived in a hovel and this furnished place was unused.

The boat was still there but that wasn't unused! He looked at Richard, who had followed him on his reminiscent wanderings.

'You can use the boat whenever you want to,' he said with an amused glance, the late sun glinting on his spectacles. 'Just be careful and respect the sea.'

'I should have asked.' Richard had the grace to look guilty for a moment until defiance took over. 'I didn't know where you were and, well, there's fish out there to be caught and hungry mouths here to be filled.'

Luke only smiled wider. 'You know I don't mind,' he said. 'Richard, how old are you?'

'Ten – more like eleven.'

'You should still be in school.'

'What? And leave this lot to starve? I do Dad's paper round most mornings, him being a bit weak till the middle of the day. He often does the evening round, mind. What's the use of schooling to someone like me? I know exactly how much money is owed to us – got the figures up here, I have.' He patted his head, flattening the raggedly cut clump of dark hair.

'You need more than working out what's owed to you if you're going to achieve anything, Richard.'

'Miss Bell thinks I'm clever.'

'So do I, Richard. You are amazing.'

'You ought to meet her. She'll help you if ever you're stuck – she's got plenty of patience if you're a bit slow.'

Three children climbed into the car when Luke finally left, and rode with him to the end of the narrow lane. Then, while the other two ran back shrieking with excitement, Richard stayed for an extra word.

'What can we do, Luke, about Rosita? She shouldn't be there with that man, should she?'

'There's nothing we can do. If it's what her mother wants, then Rosita has to stay. I wish we hadn't gone, don't you?' he asked the serious-faced boy.

'No. I wanted to see her and at least I've done that.'

Luke drove away slowly, waving at the solitary figure who watched until he was out of sight. He was saddened and wished he had not spoken to Richard on the previous afternoon. Some things are better not known.

Before he left for France the following day, he bought two bicycles and arranged for their delivery to Richard and his father. That was something he could do to ease their monotonous, comfortless lives. If only it were that simple to help Barbara and unhappy little Rosita.

*

After Luke and Richard had gone, Barbara thought again about the bruises on Rosita's body. She had pretended long enough. Blood on the girl's underwear from weals on her body, straight lines that could only have been caused by a stick. She had chosen to believe Graham's insistence that she was simply careless.

She had to know, although the thought of what she would have to do once she was certain frightened her. Graham was a good, hard-working man, her inner voice insisted. Although he demanded long hours of work from her, he did much more. He did get angry sometimes and had more than once threatened her with a beating. She had calmed him, promised to do better and he had never actually hit her, but she knew the threat was there. His only real fault was his unreasonable dislike of Rosita. The bruises and cuts were from beatings. She had pretended otherwise for too long.

'They gone then?' Rosita poked her head around the door. 'I liked that man, Luke. He's funny, mind, but nice. Will that beard grow till he can clean his shoes with it?' she asked with a rare smile.

'He's a very kind man. Richard is nice too. I'm glad you weren't your usual cheeky self, love. I was dreading that you'd misbehave like you do when that lady from the chapel comes with a few presents. Now why can't you learn to be that polite with your father? He loves you and would be so pleased if you would only behave a bit better towards him.'

'He hates me because I'm not really his. He says that. When I can't get anything right he says I'm stupid and a truder and shouldn't be here, bothering him.'

'A truder? Oh, you mean an intruder. But how can you be? You're my daughter. Your real father died a long time ago. Your name is Jones, not Prothero like Kate and Hattie, but you were here first. Remember that and you'll behave better, I know you will.'

Graham came in then and Rosita squirmed under the table out of sight.

'They seem pleasant people,' he said, 'but I don't like having visitors. It disrupts the day. Late fetching the cows to be milked, I am, and there's the roots not even started to be pulled.'

'Graham, love, it was only a couple of hours – it can hardly make that much difference.'

He smiled ruefully. 'No, you're right. Truth is, I'm always afraid you'll go away. Seeing someone from your early days might tempt you to leave me.'

'How could I? You and the three girls are my life. I belong here.'

'I – I'd be lost without you, Babs. You know I love you, don't you?'

A low chuckle emanated from under the table and, angrily, Graham pulled out a chair and demanded that Rosita came out. 'Out of there! I thought I told you to gather the eggs? I've been waiting for you to do that since this morning! Now go! If they're hanging about the hens will start eating them and there'll be no stopping them if they start that.'

'I did that hours ago – they're in the pantry!' she said as she scuttled out of the door without turning her back on him, trying to avoid a slap.

'No, you haven't. I don't believe you!' Graham shouted. 'A liar you are as well as useless!'

'She doesn't mean any harm,' Barbara chuckled. 'She has an irrepressible sense of humour.'

An hour later, she saw to her horror that the basket of eggs, which had been gathered that morning, was outside on the ground, tipped up, the eggs broken and, from the footsteps around it, trodden on. She looked anxiously around but there was no sign of Rosita or Graham. Then she heard the sound.

The cane swished through the air and landed on the already bruised body of Rosita. She screamed her fury as she ran to stop Graham's hand.

'Enough! I *won't* have this! You promised me you wouldn't hurt her any more!'

Graham looked surprised. There was no anger on his face, only dismay.

'But she did this deliberately, Barbara. She tipped up the basket of eggs and laughed in my face. She has to be punished. Surely you can see that she has to be punished?'

'You called her a liar and she did gather the eggs this morning as she does every day, even when it's Hattie or Kate's turn!' She reached for Rosita, gathering her into her arms. Rosita was chewing her lip, trying to keep silent the sobbing that wracked her small frame.

Barbara carried her into the house as Graham stood watching, wondering if it was wiser to intervene and apologize for trying to train the girl into obedience or wait until Barbara had calmed down. He knew his wife had never been more furious; he could tell from the way her normally gentle eyes had looked at him. He'd seen reproach and something more. There was determination there and he wondered what she would do.

'Please don't let her leave me,' he prayed aloud.

It was those people who came today, he decided. They had unsettled her, bringing back fanciful memories of the past. She must know chastisement was essential if Rosita was to grow up any use to anyone. She had to have the devil beaten out of her. What good would she be to a man if she was so defiant? She had to be taught to behave. Barbara would see that when she calmed down, for sure.

The next day was market day in the local town and early in the morning, Graham was up, loading the cart with surplus cockerels to be sold. They would be bought to fatten for the Christmas trade and although he would make more during Christmas week, he had decided to sell now and buy a pony for Rosita. Perhaps having something of her own would make her less difficult. He couldn't really afford it, but losing Barbara was something he couldn't face, and her attitude towards him since finding him in the barn punishing Rosita filled him with dread.

'Would you like to come with me to the market this morning?' he asked Rosita when, smudge-eyed and subdued, she came down for breakfast. By the time they had eaten, the cows had been milked and the churn was on the stand ready to be picked up by the local dairyman. Kate and Hattie had already gone to a neighbour, who had promised to look after them until they returned.

'I'll come if you want me to,' Rosita said in a small voice. Barbara said nothing. She hadn't spoken to him since the previous day and during the night she had curled up in a tight unapproachable knot of anger.

Rosita was dressed in her newest clothes, a hat and coat made to match in thick navy cloth, a navy skirt gathered into fullness and reaching well below her knees, and a hand-knitted jumper, of which she was very proud, in a dark plum colour. She wore boots that although not new were in reasonable condition, having been tapped with leather and studded at the toes and heels by Graham a few weeks before.

They set off silently. Barbara tried to sing one of the songs they frequently sang while travelling on the cart, the horse clopping an accompaniment, but the others didn't join in.

'Stay with me, Rosita,' Graham said as he tethered the horse and began unloading the wire-covered boxes from the cart. 'I have a surprise for you and I think you'll like it.' He left the boxes of chickens for Barbara to see to and took the girl's hand.

There were about twenty horses offered for sale. Graham looked at the teeth for an estimate of age, felt the legs and the feet, stood back to look at the overall shape and proportions, watching for the way they reacted to being examined. He didn't want a bad-tempered one. Rosita was all the temper he needed in his life. He stood then, holding her hand, watching while the animals were walked and trotted as the owners showed their animals' best qualities.

'Would you like one of these for your own?' he asked, smiling in anticipation of her delight. 'You and I have to get on, see, and I thought that if you had a pet of your own to care for, and I taught you to ride, well, perhaps we could start off again and be friends. It's what I really want, Rosita, for us to be friends.'

Her brown eyes brightened, the forlorn look washed from her face and she stared at him. Her eyes were so sharp and intelligent, Graham thought. So different from her mother's gentle, dreamy, blue ones. Her face was so unchildlike, and her expression was, yes, calculating. She looked as she always looked when she faced him: disapproving, building herself up for argument and hostility. Even with the offer of such a gift, she couldn't smile at him. He wondered what was going on in that busy mind of hers; what words were locked away behind those tight lips.

'You mean really mine?' she said at last. 'Not Kate's or Hattie's?'

'Just yours. If they want to ride, they can only do so with your permission. There, what do you think?'

The brief look of animation faded. Would this be something else to complain about? Would having this huge creature to look after give him more excuses to beat her? 'Where's Mam?' she asked. 'I want to talk to Mam.' She ran off and left him still looking at the horses and ponies.

'Mam, he wants to buy me a pony.' Rosita said the words dully, without a glimmer of the excitement she felt inside. She was already imagining riding wildly across the fields, thinking of the means to escape when she saw that look in Graham's eyes that always meant a walloping for one thing or another. Perhaps she could ride so far he wouldn't ever find her? The thought allowed a small smile to escape, which was swiftly subdued. 'Mam, will he give me a proper hiding if I forget to brush it?'

Barbara hadn't slept the previous night. She had lain awake making her decisions. For her own safety Rosita must go away. Tears fell every time she thought of parting from Kate and Hattie for a few days, but they would be all right. It was Rosita, Bernard's daughter, who needed her help now.

Leaving Graham to bid for the pony he had chosen, Barbara took her daughter's hand, led her away from the market and climbed aboard a bus just as it was leaving. Silently, Rosita sat beside her mother, seeing in the closed-up face the futility of asking questions. They changed buses in the next town and then caught a train. Where they were going, Rosita had no way of knowing, but she felt excitement growing with every mile they travelled. Wherever it was, it was away from Graham Prothero and the hated farm.

It was Barbara's intention to find the Careys and ask them to look after Rosita until she was old enough to look after herself. She would return to Graham, Kate and Hattie and hope that, one day, when Rosita was past her difficult childhood, they would all be reunited.

They stayed one night in a cottage in Corn Town in the beautiful Vale of Glamorgan and the next day they continued their journey to the beach near Gull Island. Tired, hungry and with blisters on Rosita's feet caused by the ill-fitting boots, they arrived to find the place empty and apparently abandoned.

They went inside and considered staying until the Careys returned. Surely they wouldn't mind? But where were they? There were enough household goods to suggest they hadn't gone for good. Yet there was an air of emptiness that seemed more than the absence of an afternoon.

Recent rain had come through the open door and some magazines left on the floor lay open as if just put down. They were soaked, sticking to the floor, and they tore as Barbara tried to lift them. A curtain had fallen down and mildew showed in its folds. Below the steps was a bicycle, rusted and with both tyres obviously punctured.

She went to look at Luke's cottage. If only he were there. He would know what she should do; he would help, she knew it. But there was no sign of anyone. The place was as dead as the rocks on the beach. There was no evidence of anyone else within miles, the call of the gulls only emphasizing the loneliness.

Angry with the fate that seemed to deny her the slightest assistance, Barbara broke the locks on Luke's cottage with a rock and went inside.

'We'll stay here for a while,' she said. 'Just until the Careys come back.'

'I don't mind if we stay here for ever and ever,' Rosita said, wide-eyed. 'Look at these chairs, Mam. All bouncy and soft and so pretty. Mam, can't we stay for ever? He won't find us here, will he?'

'We aren't running away from your father, Rosita,' Barbara admonished. 'We're just arranging a little holiday for you.'

It wasn't until the next day, when Barbara and Rosita went to town to buy food, that they learned the fate of the Careys. They had all caught diphtheria and that day had been taken to the isolation hospital. Thank goodness they hadn't slept in their house where infection might still be present!

The first thing Barbara must do was collect and deliver the papers, and find someone willing to sell some on Henry's usual corner. Without the few shillings his deliveries made they would be destitute. She went into the house, warning Rosita to stay clear, and found Henry's notebook with his customers listed, together with what they owed.

The bicycle was tempting if only to carry the heavy papers or push Rosita for some of the way; they had walked so many miles on the previous day and her feet were so tender. After trying to manoeuvre the machine's stiffened joints, riding on flat tyres and, much to Rosita's amusement, falling off several times, Barbara decided walking was safer.

The day was spent dealing with the Careys' customers and arranging for the following day's selling at the usual pitch. Barbara succeeded in collecting some of the money owned to the mild-mannered man who was too kindly to insist he was paid – putting others before his own family, she thought, with mild irritation. She hid it in the house for when the family returned.

Days passed and Barbara wrote to Graham, telling him she would be home when she had found a place to leave her daughter. She had no fear of Graham coming to look for them: with no help apart from Kate and Hattie, who were only two and three, he was unable to leave the farm.

Although she was unsure how infections like diphtheria were carried, she knew the symptoms that had appeared regularly in the neighbours during her childhood. As a precaution she kept Rosita away from the house on the beach and every morning she examined the girl for signs of the disease. She asked repeatedly if she had a sore throat, looked in her mouth, felt her glands. Each night, as she put her to sleep in Luke's bed, she sighed with relief that so far Rosita continued to remain healthy.

It was Sunday morning when she went to find her mother and father. Surely now they could forgive her and help their granddaughter? She didn't even reach the house. On a corner she met her father and he stared at her, first in surprise then in anger.

'I hope you aren't planning to visit your mother?'

'Yes. I'm sure she'd like to meet her granddaughter.'

'That's her, is it? Well, you can take it from me there's no welcome for either of you.'

'Who was that, Mam?' Rosita asked as her mother pulled her away. She glanced up and saw tears of disappointment and fury in her mother's eyes so decided not to repeat the question. 'I'm hungry. Can we have something to eat?' she said instead.

Richard and his father were the first to arrive home, pale and even thinner than normal after the fever that had weakened them. They were very pleased to see Barbara and hear what she had been doing.

'Saved the business, you have, my girl, and I don't know how to thank you,' Henry Carey said.

Richard stared at Rosita. 'Run away from the old man, have you?'

'We broke into someone's house and we're living there as if it's ours! Mam just smashed the door down!' Rosita was wide-eyed as she told how her mother had broken the lock.

'She never did!'

'Come and see.' Rosita led him to where Luke's cottage stood and was surprised to see that the padlock had been replaced. Someone had been there while they were delivering the evening papers. Their few belongings had been thrown outside. Unperturbed, Rosita said, 'Mam'll have to smash the lock again, but it won't take her long.'

They walked along the beach and Richard showed her Luke's boat.

'Is he my dad?' she asked. 'The man with the beard and funny glasses?'

'I don't think so. Pity, mind. If he was he wouldn't slap you around like your old man does.'

'Who is my real dad?'

'I don't know but I think he's dead. But I do know who your grandparents are. I heard Barbara and Mam talking about them. Useless they are, the lot of them, so Mam says.'

When he told her their names she asked him to write them down. The piece of paper he found and the blunt pencil didn't make the document seem very important, but Rosita put it carefully in her clothes, tucked away in her only possession, a book.

It was *A Child's Garden of Verses* by Robert Louis Stevenson. She and her sisters loved their mother to read from it. Rosita's favourite was 'The Lamplighter'. Living on a farm, far from any street, the idea of someone coming along each evening to light lamps was a magical thing. She found the page with the aid of the pictures and tucked the piece of paper into the fold.

Freda, Barbara's sister, was surprised to see Barbara and Rosita waiting for her when she came out of work on Saturday evening. It was late as the shop stayed open for longer on Saturdays and at first she didn't recognize them.

'Barbara? Where did you spring from? And is this your little girl? Have you seen Mam?' She was obviously pleased to see them and Barbara was warmed by her smile of pleasure.

'I haven't seen Mam but I met Dad and he told us to stay away. I – I wondered if you could talk to them? I need somewhere to leave Rosita for a while, just until I can get a few things sorted.'

'Come and have a cup of tea and a bun and we'll talk.'

Barbara knew immediately from the closed-up look on her sister's face that it was hopeless but she went anyway. It was good to see Freda again, and to gather news of her family would be some small comfort.

'I'll do what I can, but our dad is very stubborn, as you know,' Freda said when they were about to part. 'If Mam says yes, then I'll come to the beach and find you. If you don't hear anything, well, Barbara, I promise I'll have tried.'

'There isn't anyone else and I have to get back to the farm. I have two other children and a husband who need me. I can't leave them much longer.'

*

Every morning, Barbara left one of the Carey children sitting on a chair near the open door, looking out for Freda. Each day, when she returned with Richard and Mr Carey, there was no news. On Sunday, after the morning papers were dealt with, the day was free. She watched the road almost afraid to turn her head in case she missed that first glimpse of her sister, a promise of help, but the morning passed and no one came. Freda might have tried but she had certainly failed.

Mr Carey sat in the weak October sunshine chewing the end of his pencil and filling in pages of his books. Mrs Carey and Barbara were washing clothes and spreading them on bushes and on the sea wall to dry. Richard and Rosita were out in the boat, hoping for some fish.

Barbara was determinedly not looking along the road, so when the woman appeared it was with a lurch of disbelief that she saw someone approaching. Hope was there for a brief moment then dashed. It wasn't her sister or her mother. It was Bernard's mother, Mrs Stock.

'Mr Stock and I will take the girl,' she said without preamble. 'Your sister told me how she was ill treated. She'll have a good, respectable home with us.'

Barbara's instincts were to refuse but how could she? The Careys were hardly able to care for themselves and were certainly not fit to cope with a lively character like Rosita. And Rosita could not go back to the farm. There were other children waiting for her and wondering why she had abandoned them. She missed Kate and Hattie. Whatever happened, she had to go back to them, just as definitely as Rosita could not. Reluctantly, she walked with a frightened Rosita to the neat, dark little house of Mr and Mrs Stock.

Rosita began to misbehave immediately.

'Is this all there is?' she asked when she had been shown around.

'Better than you're used to,' Mrs Stock replied stiffly.

'Pigsties better than this we've got! And where are the fields?'

'There aren't any fields, child. There's a yard for you to play in.'

'Where?' Rosita demanded, ignoring the shushing of her mother.

'Outside the back door, of course.'

'Call that a yard? The dog couldn't turn round in that little space!'

Barbara left her with strong misgivings. She didn't look back as the bus took her further and further away from her daughter. Before she reached the farm to a jubilant welcome from the girls and an anxious, almost formal greeting from Graham, Rosita had run away.

Three times Mr and Mrs Stock took Rosita back from the Careys, then Barbara came again, collected the wildly furious and frightened child and placed her in a home for waifs and strays.

'Her father died in the war and her mother has gone away,' Barbara told the kindly matron. 'To Scotland I believe. I'm her Auntie Babs,' she explained, adding to the confusion of the unhappy Rosita.

Rosita glared around her, staring at the other girls who had come to watch her arrival. She wasn't going to cry, she wasn't. This was punishment, being locked away in this huge building, but she wouldn't shed a single tear. She wondered what she had done to be punished in this way. It must have been something very wicked for Mam to pretend she was an auntie.

Refusing to hold her mother's hand, Rosita followed the two women as they went from room to room in the enormous building. The matron was dressed in a long, blue and white striped dress, over which she wore a white apron and matching cap. She rustled as she walked and her strong shoes clacked importantly on the bare tiled floors.

Rosita was too distressed to take in much of what they were shown but the rooms seemed frightening. Sounds echoed hollowly. The floors were cold tiles downstairs and mostly bare scrubbed wooden boards above. The place was larger than any she had ever seen, the walls a chilly white and so high she thought they must have been whitewashed barns like on the farm and been piled one on another to make this strange house.

Everything was in rows. Rows of bowls for washing, each with its bar of soap and a towel, rows of lavatories, rows of chairs against long scrubbed tables and rows of beds. She saw several girls who, with their matching dresses and coverall aprons and very short hair, looked as strange as the house. They too seemed to always be standing in rows or walking single file, as if unable to break the pattern.

Then, their tour of inspection was over and she was standing at the doorway and watching her mother leave. She began to scream but the woman dressed in grey who was now in charge of her whispered that if she didn't stop immediately she would be locked in the punishment room. Rosita poked her tongue out at her but remained silent.

Stifling her screams with her hand, Rosita stared after the figure of her mother hurrying down the road and she shook inside. What was happening to her? Why was Mam pretending to be an auntie? She only had one auntie and that was Auntie Molly Carey. She'd better get back to her as soon as possible before this huge house, filled with strange people, swallowed her completely.

Getting up early was no problem for Rosita, who was used to farm life. In fact, she was awake long before the other girls who shared her room and she lay watching the sky through a high window and planning her escape. She wanted to run away immediately – she had wet the bed and didn't know who to tell.

At 7.30 they were roused and like the others, Rosita pulled the covers from her bed, remade it and pulled the covers back for airing. She did it quickly, her small arms stretching across the damp sheet and bundling it so no one knew of her shame. Then she followed the other girls to the room with the row of bowls for washing and was late getting to breakfast and everyone stared. Tomorrow, she decided grimly, I'll use my elbows and make sure I'm first!

She wasn't hungry and the meal of bread and milk didn't appeal, but she ate some anyway and tucked the rest into the pocket on the leg of her knickers. She had to be ready for the opportunity to run, whenever it came.

She didn't go to school on that first day. The grey lady said it was to give her a chance to settle. She sat with the younger children, who were taught by those who had left school. On the second day she walked, in crocodile, with the rest. Biggest at the front, smallest behind, all wearing identical clothes, heavy boots making them look like a centipede.

After a test given by the teacher she was given a desk in the new school. She quickly realized that even here she was unable to keep up with the others. At playtime she ran away and tried to get back to Auntie Molly Carey.

She ran away three times, once being brought back by the local doctor on his horse and trap, once by a friendly policeman and the third time, when she had managed to reach the beach, by Richard.

'Safe there, you'll be,' he assured her. 'Better than with old Prothero for sure. Be patient. Time will pass and when you're grown up you'll be as free as a wild goose.'

'A swan,' she wailed. 'I don't want to be a goose, I want to be a wild swan.'

He was surprised at her vehemence. He couldn't know that crossing her mind was the rhyme from her only book:

Cruel children, crying babies
All grow up as geese and gabies.

She knew she was cruel and had been a crying baby, and she might grow up to be a goose, or worse, a gaby – which she was told was someone simple – but she didn't know what to do about it.

Accepting Richard's advice to be patient and wait until she was old enough to survive alone, Rosita became subdued and surly. She accepted the thick, heavy clothes and the boots she was given with ill grace, hating being made to look exactly like the others. She forced herself to give in to the rules that everyone followed without protest. Giving the impression of silent acceptance, although seething with fear and fury inside, she ignored the attempts at friendship from those sharing the long bedroom and did what was asked of her sullenly and without joy.

At school her record continued to be poor and in the home her belligerent attitude meant she had little chance of making friends. She did have one person to whom she could talk. Surprisingly, the lady in grey, whom she now knew to be Matron's assistant, made allowances for her temper when she could, and tried to help with her written work. In the hours of recreation, when the children were offered a variety of pastimes, she would sit, with chalk and slate, and encourage her to practise writing and reading. Rosita's aim, the clever lady realized, was to read her favourite book for herself and this was the tool she used.

A month after her arrival at the home, the children were invited to a Christmas party given by the local organization in a church hall. They were each given a small gift, handed to them by an elderly man in a Father Christmas outfit. Most of the girls got dolls or books. Rosita pretended not to be interested but hoped for a doll. It might be fun to have a pretend friend. Opening her parcel, which seemed to be the right shape, a smile flickered on her lips. On opening the coloured paper and finding a horse and hay cart, Rosita remembered the farm that was her home and all the anger and frustration burst out of her.

She screamed and kicked those near enough to be a target. Her face was a mask of despair and she pushed away anyone attempting to hold her. She gripped her fists into tight balls and looked for some way of venting her misery. Picking up a vase from a side table, she threw it through the window with a crash that sobered her immediately.

Sobs came then. Why wasn't she with her mother and sisters? Why had Mam said she hadn't got a mother and left her with these strangers? She cried furiously, standing in the middle of a hesitant circle of adults, while the other children kept back against the walls. She threw down the offending toy, gratified to see it broken. Then she poked her tongue out at Father Christmas and ran from the room.

It was the grey lady who found her, led to the corner of the building by her sobs. She picked her up and without a word of censure carried her back to the bus that was waiting to take them back to the home. She undressed her, bathed her and put her to bed. She encouraged her to talk, listening quietly to the release of the girl's bewilderment and pain.

She was allowed to stay in bed the following day and the grey lady came and read to her. One of the girls, called Mary, came too and sat nervously beside her, wanting to talk but afraid of a rebuff. Although they didn't speak, Rosita was comforted by her being there.

On Christmas Day there was a parcel from 'Auntie Babs', but Rosita refused to open it and it stayed in Matron's cupboard for the duration of Rosita's stay.

She ran away once more, early in the spring of 1923, but she was afraid, having forgotten the direction that would take her to Auntie Molly Carey. If she went the wrong way she might find herself back at the farm, with Graham angry with her and raising the cane. The image made her grip her thighs in remembered agony. She sat in the corner of a field for most of the day then went quietly back.

She and Mary became friends, at least as much of a friend as Rosita was capable of at that time. Slowly the months passed with life getting easier. School was still a trial but in the home Rosita became an avid reader, getting much pleasure from reading aloud to Mary and occasionally to others as well.

The anger seemed to have left her, only returning for a brief period after each of Barbara's rare visits. She never referred to Kate and Hattie, frowning and asking who they were when Barbara mentioned them. But she secretly agonized over their abandonment of her. Why did everyone hate her so?

She often took the scrap of paper out of her book and read the names of her grandparents written by Richard Carey. Her grandparents hated her, for sure. Mam and Graham hated her, Graham hit her and Mam let him, then they locked her away. Kate and Hattie never came to see her, or even sent a message when her mother came, so, she reasoned, they must think I'm dead. Or they hated her too and didn't want to see her ever again. She dealt with this by refusing to admit that she had sisters and told everyone she was a solitary orphan, her only relation being Auntie Babs, who hated her.

Chapter Eight

IN APRIL 1928, Barbara began to worry that something was wrong with her eldest daughter. Five years had passed since she had pretended to be her aunt and placed her in the home. The visits she had initially made had ended after a few months. Matron had advised her to wait a while as it always upset Rosita and unsettled her. A renewal of the visits had always been intended but had never happened.

Since then she had written every month and the matron had encouraged Rosita to write a short note in reply. Now weeks had passed and no letter had appeared. There couldn't be anything seriously wrong or Matron would have let her know, but guilt was never far from the surface of her mind and, even with Graham's obvious disapproval, she had to go and see for herself.

On Easter Sunday, she set off with a small bag swinging from her shoulders, leaving eight-year-old, Kate and seven year old Hattie behind. She wore a fashionable long cardigan she had knitted and a long pleated skirt and simple top. On her head was a full-crowned hat with a smallish brim, on which she had sewn wax cherries and a large butterfly made from feathers.

In the bag were a few clothes. Although it wasn't her intention to be away more than a day or two, it was wise to be prepared for the unexpected where Rosita was concerned. She hoped she would just go to the home, discover the reason for the lack of letters, spend a day with her then return to the farm.

She was excited at the break in the monotonous daily routine. She had been increasingly restless over the past months. She was twenty-seven and feeling that life should hold more than the repetitious grind that she and Graham endured.

Graham watched her go, a burly, anxious-looking man wearing thick trousers and a Welsh flannel shirt without its stiff Sunday collar, the sleeves rolled up to the middle of his powerful forearms. He leaned on a shepherd's crook, afraid she would stay away for a long time. Although he stood there until she was out of sight, she didn't turn and give a final wave, which disappointed him.

He stayed for a while longer, half hoping she would come back and give that reassuring wave, aware that he was acting like a child. Then he walked up the hill to check on the sheep. There were still a few waiting to give birth. He stopped for a while where his land dropped sharply down to the river below. Some long-ago land-slide had formed what the locals called the *cwm*.

The wind blew his hair back from his face, revealing the thin line of pale skin around the hairline that the sun failed to reach. He thought of Barbara sitting on the bus that was taking her away from him. He had never felt secure in his marriage; always afraid that her previous life would one day call her back.

He wondered if she would come back this time or was this the day it would end? Would he wait for the buses that came and went and be disappointed? He considered vaguely what he would do. He knew that although she hid it well, she had never been completely happy with him, but they worked well together and apart from the loss of Rosita she had seemed content enough. Perhaps it was him being much older than her that made him always afraid of losing her?

But no. It was more than that. Over the past months she had become more and more distant. Thinking about that daughter of hers for sure. Nothing but trouble that one had caused since the moment of her birth. His frown deepened as he walked on and he hit out angrily at the nettles that barred his way.

He was also afraid that if Barbara did come back the following day, that damned girl would be with her. How could he cope with that madam again? She'd be a bad influence on Kate and Hattie, there was nothing more certain than that. His girls did as he told them and knew what was expected of them. How would they accept the presence of a wayward creature like Rosita? And would he be able to keep his hands off her?

Since Rosita had left them the family seemed, to Graham at least, far happier. But for Barbara, the gap left had never been filled. For a while there had been letters written by the matron in the children's home on Rosita's behalf, assuring her 'Auntie Babs' that all was well and that Rosita had 'settled amicably'. Those words stayed in Barbara's memory and settled unnervingly on her guilty thoughts. 'Settled amicably'? Her wilful daughter? She wondered just how they had persuaded the angry little girl to 'settle amicably' and she feared the worst. Later the notes were written by Rosita herself but they were brief, polite scrawls and, Barbara suspected, written to instructions.

Each letter was a twist in Barbara's heart. She knew she had given up her child for selfish reasons, abandoned her, and worse, pretended she was her daughter's auntie, for the sake of a more peaceful life. Guilt kept her awake at night and she would stave it off, imagining how, one day, she and Kate and Hattie would go to bring Rosita back. But whenever she pictured the scene in her tormented daydreams, Graham would not be there. She would leave the happy vision knowing that while he lived, she and Rosita would never be reunited.

In 1927 the letters had ceased. She continued to write, signing herself 'your loving Auntie Babs', but there were no replies. Rosita hadn't even acknowledged the hand-knitted scarf she had made, or the copy of *Wind in the Willows* she had sent for her tenth birthday.

She blamed Graham. It was his fault Rosita was no longer at the farm. He had beaten the little girl until there had been no alternative to sending her away. He had threatened her safety. It was he who had driven her away. The thought grew until she began to hate the man. He was a cruel monster who had robbed her of her love-child. Gradually she began to avoid his demands. By the time spring came and the sowing was underway, she no longer shared his bed.

At Easter, the weather promised sunshine, and Barbara felt full of optimism as she set off to find Rosita. She would just see that she was all right, and give her the few pounds she had brought for her and the dress she had sewn during the previous winter when the evenings were long and the farm work less demanding.

She wouldn't even suggest she might one day come home. Not yet. When a few more years had passed and Rosita was grown past the difficult age, then she would come and gather her up, take her back and never let her leave again. The dream seemed real now she was on her way, and she glowed with the excitement of the story she invented. She forgot five years had passed and Rosita would now be a leggy ten-year-old, with few memories of the life she had once led on the farm.

The home was a large country house set in a beautiful garden which the children were encouraged to enjoy. Barbara saw several groups of girls sitting with sketch books trying to set down what they saw. The grounds were surrounded by trees and newly unfurled leaves were making a background of a hundred different greens. The lawns were neat and the scent of newly cut grass was delightful. The air was filled with the humming of bees busily searching for pollen, their tiny beating wings filling the garden with the sound of summer.

She went to the little room that was hardly more than a porch to wait for one of the girls to fetch her daughter. The door was wide open, giving a view of the front garden and the driveway. It was very beautiful. Surely Rosita had been happy here?

'What do *you* want? We're just back from Sunday school and I have things to do!'

Rosita's first words shocked Barbara sharply from the euphoric daydream of the affectionate greeting she would receive.

'I – You haven't written. I came to see if you are all right,' Barbara stammered, staring at the tall, thin stranger with dark eyes who glared at her with such intense dislike. She faltered in her words, like a criminal. 'You're – I'm your—'

'You aren't going to say you're my mother, are you?' Rosita gave a supercilious glare. 'A mother? You threw me out, didn't you? Preferred him to me. Then pretended you're my auntie.'

'It was for the best,' Barbara whispered. 'Come out with me. I'll see the matron and ask if we can go out for the afternoon and I'll tell you all about your sisters and the farm. The pony I wrote to you about is still there. Perhaps you could come one day and ride him?' Damn, she shouldn't have said that.

'I don't want any favours! And I don't want *you!*'

Rosita ran off across the lawn, heading for the gate before disappearing in some trees, her skinny legs flying like those of a young colt, her shiny brown hair bouncing with each step.

Barbara sat utterly still, her hands gripping her bag as if life depended on it. She stared out through the door, the spring flowers that filled the borders with the golden richness of hundreds of daffodils now unseen by tear-filled eyes. She was shocked by the reception, which, if she hadn't been so filled with romantic imaginings, she might have expected. To allow five years to pass and then believe that Rosita would run into her arms? What a fool she was.

She dropped her bag and went to stand at the door. A movement at the corner of the wall caught her eye and she stood perfectly still apart from her hand. Slowly the fingers crossed and she uttered a silent prayer. The figure approached her and she turned to smile at Rosita, who glowered back and said, 'You can take me to the beach. I haven't been since you put me in this prison!'

'Which beach would you like to visit?' Barbara asked quietly.

'The one where Auntie Molly Carey lives, of course!'

The matron lent them two bicycles to take them as far as the railway station and this time, both having some experience, they were proficient. The station master agreed to mind them until their return and they stepped onto the train with hope in their hearts. Barbara's hope was to achieve at least an acceptance of her by her daughter. Rosita was tense with excited hope of seeing Richard.

They arrived at the house on the lonely beach in the middle of the afternoon as Mrs Carey was putting a Yorkshire pudding mixture into a frying pan. They still had no oven. Made with Bird's egg substitute it looked appetizing, and the sight of the vegetables simmering on the two hobs and the delicious smell of meat hanging in the Dutch oven in front of the blazing fire made them pleased to accept an invitation to stay and share the meal.

'Funny time to eat for sure,' a smiling Mrs Carey said. 'But by the time the papers are done and my Henry goes to his club for a pint to refresh himself, three o'clock suits us all best. Now, come here, darling girl, so I can give you a hug, Rosita, love. Such a time since we saw you, I'd hardly have recognized you! Tall you are, and quite a young lady.'

Barbara was relieved to see that Mrs Carey looked well and the shelves at the sides of the fireplace were filled with food. Things had obviously improved for the family. Clean dresses and shirts hung behind the door and the windows, now mended, were dressed in cheerful curtains.

But seeing beyond the obvious first impressions, she saw that the house was damp despite the huge fire. The walls were spotted with mildew. Pyramid-shaped patterns of black rising up in the corners showed the extent of the decay, weak places that had been infiltrated by insidious fungus that had been scraped off many times, and which had determinedly recolonized. Floorboards were rotten and Barbara saw that furniture had been wedged to prevent anyone walking on the dangerous areas.

Most serious of all, the walls were cracking, wide gaps that would let in moisture, which in time would increase the damage. Where there was moisture there would be frost. Frost and thawing, expanding and easing, time and again. She knew from the old barn on the farm just how relentlessly that could destroy. The Careys had survived several winters in the damp old place, but would they manage another?

'Where's Richard?' Rosita asked, her voice softer than when she spoke to Barbara. 'I thought he'd be here with the food ready and smelling so good. Better than anything I'm used to,' she added with another glare for her mother.

Mrs Carey looked anxious. 'Richard? Oh, he's around somewhere,' she said airily. 'Now,' she added, quickly changing the subject, 'tell me about yourselves. Barbara? You still at that farm? Where are Kate and Hattie? I've never seen them, you know, although you've told me about them in your letters. Bring them next time, why don't you? And Graham too, mind. Welcome they'd all be.' She glanced at Rosita as she spoke and watched the girl's face tighten with silent anger. 'Well, perhaps not, love. It's our Rosita who's the important one, isn't it?' She hugged the girl and added in a whisper, 'Auntie Carey's best girl you are and always will be.'

Idris, Alun, Billie and Gareth arrived back from their various activities as the dinner was put out on assorted plates and bowls. They looked at Rosita, who glared back at them, tongue fully stretched. Without a word they went onto the beach with their plates and ate their meals huddled in a tight group that left no room for her to join them.

After they had eaten, Mr Carey fell asleep. Mrs Carey gave Rosita an apple then guided Barbara away from the house and sat down against the sea wall. The other children took their plates down to the edge of the sea and washed them. Rosita darted around the end of the wall to listen to what was being said that Mrs Carey didn't want her to hear.

'The truth is, Barbara, we don't know where Richard is. The police have been here three times looking for him and us without a clue as to what's going on.'

'They must have told you what they suspect him of?'

'I think it's burglaries. Henry knows, mind, but he won't say, trying to keep it from me, he is, and him too worried to sleep.'

'Burglaries? Richard wouldn't do anything so stupid!'

'Why not?' There was bitterness in Mrs Carey's voice. 'It's only what Henry's taught him all these years. "Take what you can from those with enough to spare," he used to say. Richard is fifteen now and almost a man. He's only doing what he was taught to do. Remember what Henry used to bring home in his pockets and that bag of his? Starved we'd have been, mind, if he hadn't helped himself to a bit of extra food. Richard doesn't think it's wrong to steal, he only thinks it wrong to get caught!'

'And you think that's why he's staying away? So he doesn't get caught?'

'It's what I think, yes, but where is he? How is he managing? I'm so frightened for him.'

Barbara leaned closer to her friend and whispered, 'Keep talking.' Then, after saying something to encourage a reply, she stood up and peered over the wall, just in time to see Rosita haring along the path towards Luke's cottage.

'Kids, they don't change, do they?' she said sadly. 'She's still as prickly as she ever was.'

Mrs Carey shared Barbara's sigh.

'She needs to be a survivor, mind, like our Richard. Submission is death to all hope. Somehow, I think Rosita and our Richard will never give up hope of something better.'

*

Richard was in Cardiff. It being a Sunday, he was lying low and waiting for the day to pass. Tomorrow the plan he had been nurturing for years was to become a reality. Tomorrow, while Mam delivered the papers for the last time, he and his father would be signing themselves into a secure future.

A tobacconist and newsagents business was available for £85. The rent of the property was cheap and he'd saved enough to pay it for six months. The accommodation, although shabby and neglected, was a palace compared with the house on the beach that he knew was about to collapse. Business was poor too but he knew that, with an effort, it would improve. He wondered ruefully whether his father would rise to the occasion.

The money Richard had managed to accumulate had come from thieving, mostly from market stalls, both stall-holders and their customers. A few shillings or, when he was lucky, pounds here and there, like the time so long ago when he had taken £25 from the wholesalers' box.

The money he most enjoyed acquiring had been from Barbara's father. He had seen him staggering home one winter evening, silly-drunk and alone. While appearing to help him, he had relieved him of two pounds seven shillings and fourpence halfpenny from a back pocket. Nothing before or since had given him greater pleasure.

Lately, he had been more daring and had carried out a series of burglaries, but he knew it was too risky and had to stop. Twice he had almost been caught by the householder and once a policeman had arrived in time to see him and chase him for almost half an hour through the streets and lanes, until he had managed to find a ditch in which to hide. The ditch had been full of water, and the icy chill of it was still fresh in his memory.

He knew it had been his brother Idris, Mam's golden boy, who had told the police where he would be. A few days later, he had accidentally let slip the address of a house he intended to burgle and had watched from a safe corner while the police hid and waited to catch him. Pity it was dear little Blodwen who had died, he thought bitterly. Better for them all if it had been Idris!

He'd been lucky, in spite of his brother's attempts to have him arrested, but luck had a habit of running out. There was enough money now, and as long as his father did his share, things would be comfortable for the Careys at last.

The shop his father would rent was in their own home town. It was in a good position at a junction of the main road amid the shops and the smaller road leading down to the station. Hundreds of people passed on their way to work. He had stood there watching for several days and saw how good the place could become once it was smartened up a bit. The present owner had thirteen cats and the smell was obviously what discouraged customers. Once his mam had cleaned it, the convenience of stopping to buy a morning paper and a packet of cigarettes or some chocolate just before getting on the train would soon appeal.

Beside the awful smell of the place, it looked drab and unattractive. After a month or so business would grow. Mam would soon have it sorted. Dad was a kindly man but without the bite needed to succeed. No, Mam would be the one to get things going, once he'd taught her the business side of things. She might even persuade that useless Idris to help, although that seemed to be too much to hope.

He went to the one café that was open and drank another cup of tea. There was nowhere else to go, nothing to do. He wanted to go home but he didn't dare, not with golden boy Idris on the prowl.

The police couldn't find him now, not with the lease to be signed tomorrow. Once that was done and he had explained the books to Mam, he would go away. Far away, until the hunt for him had died down and his activities had been forgotten.

Barbara stayed overnight in small bed and breakfast accommodation in the town and on the following morning took a taxi to the home to take Rosita out for the day. It was the promise of seeing Richard that persuaded Rosita to spend another day in her mother's company but Barbara didn't mind what the reason was as long as she was given a few hours to reach some kind of rapport with her difficult and resentful daughter.

They met Mrs Carey with Jack and Gareth delivering the last of the papers. The boys, now seventeen and eighteen, looked shifty when Barbara asked about the work they were doing.

'Collecting dole, the pair of them,' Mrs Carey said with a sigh. 'Still, something will turn up for them soon, sure to.'

Both boys looked away and went into the house. Unknown to their parents, they had both signed up to join the army and in a few days' time would be leaving for good.

'Where's Richard?' Rosita asked after hugging the woman affectionately. 'Did you tell him I was coming to see him?'

'He didn't come back, lovely girl.' Mrs Carey glanced at Barbara. 'Stayed out all night he did and Henry and me up watching the tide go out and come back in again without a moment's sleep between us. Gone into Cardiff, my Henry has. Says he's going to look for him, but I think he knows where he is and what he's been doing. Them two are cooking something up for sure. Been into Cardiff time and again, they have, and not a word of what they're doing.'

'We'll come and see you later – we don't want to add to your work by staying. It's a mild day. I think I'll take Rosita to the Pleasure Beach.'

'I don't want to go to the Pleasure Beach, I want to stay with Auntie Molly Carey.'

'But not yet,' Mrs Carey said softly, giving the girl another hug. 'Best you give me the chance to get a meal ready for you all, and give Uncle Henry Carey time to find Richard and bring him home.'

Barbara smiled her thanks at her thoughtful friend.

Barbara and Rosita decided to catch the train into town, then walk across the docks to the beach. Rosita didn't remember passing so close to the huge ships before. She had only seen them on their way, out to sea. They towered above her like manmade cliffs, their painted sides leaning outward, swollen with cargoes and people. There were so many she thought she could have walked across from one side of the docks to the other on their decks. Cork-filled tenders stopped them from scraping their sides against the dockside, gangplanks stretched up to the deck rails where people leaned over and shouted to those below.

She said nothing to her mother and refused to answer when Barbara offered a comment. She just stared at the fascinating world around her. As well as sights, there were the assortment of smells: many kinds of fruit including bananas and oranges, and various types of wood including the sweet-scented cherry wood as lengths of pit-wood were unloaded for the coal mines in the valleys north of Cardiff. She was interested to see coal being exported. It was lifted from the light railway, still in its wagons, which were hoisted up on cranes, then tilted for the coal to be dropped straight into the cavernous holds of the ships.

Men were standing around the dockside in groups, talking, shaking their heads, gesturing to the cargoes waiting to be loaded, cigarettes cupped in curled fists to protect them from the wind that blew in from the sea. Their clothes were torn and Rosita wondered what cargo they had been loading that had ripped the cloth so viciously. She looked at her mother, the question on her lips, but she didn't ask. Instead she tugged at the shredded jacket of a docker and asked him.

'Iron ore did that,' the man told her, and explained briefly what it was and how it was used. He winked at the serious-faced little girl and said, 'Never marry a docker, lovely girl, you'll never keep them looking smart and tidy.' He returned to work, tossing his cigarette into the oily water of the dock.

Cranes swung overhead, lifting huge boxes with ease. Men wrote busily on sheets of paper and shouted orders. Everywhere there was frantic activity, ordered chaos, and Rosita stared in wonderment. Through a pipe in the side of one ship a steady stream of water flowed and Rosita laughed and said, 'Look at that one! It's peeing!' She glared at her mother, daring her to complain at the vulgarity, but Barbara just smiled.

'How can such a thing float?' Barbara said, stopping to look at a Greek vessel. She shivered. 'How can anyone travel on one? I'd be too scared, wouldn't you?'

'No fear! I'd love it.'

Barbara didn't realize that the thought of escape from the institutional life she had been forced to lead was enough to quell any fear Rosita might have had of stepping onto the huge ship.

There was a queue of people waiting for the ferry that was dwarfed by the cargo ships, but seeing the glimmer of excitement in her daughter's eyes, Barbara decided to wait, and they were rowed across by a man who seemed too small to manage the task.

As they walked up the hill from the docks, the scene changed from the business of import and export to holidays and entertainment. The sound of harsh metallic music filled the air, vying with screams and shouts of people having fun, and there was that indefinable scent of sea and warm sand.

They walked through the fairground and Barbara paid for Rosita to try her hand at hoop-la, roll-a-ball and darts, in the hope that she would win a prize to take back to the home, but her daughter was clumsy and awkward, failing to achieve a decent score.

She was puzzled at her lack of skill but decided it was her bad temper causing the failure. Although, she remembered, Rosita had never been very good at school either. Perhaps her lack of ability to learn was the reason for her bad behaviour and not the other way round?

'Never mind, dear,' she comforted, 'we can't all be good at games.'

'Stupid games! These people are all cheats!'

Barbara hurried her away and bought her an ice cream – that was safer.

Walking along the promenade, they went down to the beach, stepping between families who had made themselves comfortable with sand-tables and tablecloths and food spread out around near the mother.

'You didn't bring a picnic!' Rosita complained. 'I've never had a picnic.'

'Yes, you have. Don't you remember how we used to take a basket of food and eat it in the *cwm* below the farm?'

'No, I don't! You must be thinking of the other two!'

'The tearooms are open – we'll have a tray on the sand,' Barbara said gently. They ordered a tray of tea and some sandwiches and cakes, and with teapot, hot-water jug and the necessary china, they walked back to the sands to find a place to eat.

Several children nearby had flags and balloons attached to sandcastle turrets. There were buckets and spades, water-wings and towels lying around the family groups and the scene should have been one of bright colours, yet the formal dress of the trippers made the view a sombre one.

Men wore their best suits and shirts with only a few of them allowed to loosen their neck ties and ease their collars from sweating necks. Most still wore their caps. Women were dressed, like Barbara, in long skirts and heavy cardigans, some laden with winter coats. Neither Barbara nor others removed their cloche hats even when the sun strengthened and they were feeling uncomfortably warm. Many hats were awry after constant easing, giving the wearers a comical appearance that amused Rosita and made her point and laugh much to Barbara's embarrassment.

As they left the beach, Barbara shook her head at a man running around trying to persuade people to take a ride on his small boat but she stopped at the Punch and Judy show, which interested Rosita for a few minutes. There wasn't a moment when she relaxed, smiled or acted like other ten-year-olds, however. Disappointed, Barbara took her back to the station to get a train to the town.

Refusing every suggestion of things to do, Rosita insisted on going back to the Careys' to see if Richard had returned. But as before, Mrs Carey was there with the others but there was no sign of Richard or his father.

'We'll have to go,' Barbara said. 'I promised to take you back long before this.'

'I want to see Richard.' The stubborn look was entrenched on Rosita's small face and her dark, resentful eyes glistened warningly as she added, 'if you don't let me wait, I'll run away again and find him for myself!'

As the evening light was fading, they saw two men walking towards them, but they stopped before they reached the house.

'Policemen they are, and looking for Richard,' Mrs Carey breathed. 'Oh, they'll catch him for sure when he comes back with his father. Oh, why did I insist on Henry going to find him?'

The solitary figure of Mr Carey was seen approaching moments later and he was stopped and questioned by the policemen. He must have satisfied them as, after a moment or two, he continued to walk towards them. A jaunty walk, filled with suppressed excitement. He broke into a run when he saw them all waiting.

'Good news!' he called as soon as he was within shouting distance. 'We own a shop, Mother, and tomorrow we move in and start business!'

'Where's Richard?' Mrs Carey and Rosita asked in chorus.

'Ah, well then, that's difficult to answer. He's gone, see, and with the police wanting to talk to him, I don't think he'll be back for ages.'

Barbara stayed a few more days and Mrs Carey was glad to have her there with so many things happening at once, none of them pleasant. First of all there was the loss of Richard, who was the family's strength. Then they had the noisome shop to clean, and that seemed an impossible task, especially as most of the thirteen cats, whose smells caused such a problem, refused to vacate their home. Then, when they went back to the house on the beach to gather the last of their possessions, it was to learn that Jack and Gareth had left without saying goodbye.

The only intimation of their plans was a note pinned to the tablecloth saying they would 'be in touch soon'. Losing three sons at the same time and each going without the ritual of parting was hard, and Mrs Carey used all her strength in cleaning the shop, wanting to blot out her misery with exhaustion.

On 21 April, Barbara came again and took Rosita into Cardiff to see the King and Queen arrive by train for the opening of the National Museum of Wales. The excitement of the crowds lining the streets and waving flags thrilled Rosita, especially as she remembered that her half-sisters Kate and Hattie wouldn't be seeing it, and she wanted to shout and cheer with the rest. But aware of her mother wanting to see her happy, she did not. Flags filled the air with an undulating blaze of colour, every other face wearing a radiant smile of welcome for the royal visitors.

When the crowds drifted away, they wandered around the shops and Barbara bought some clothes for her daughter. A dress for Sundays and some white ankle-strap shoes with white, pink-trimmed ankle socks. She also bought some Celanese underwear for herself. Impractical and foolish, but it gave her satisfaction to own such delicate things. The woollen skirts, thick aprons, the coarse, practical underwear would still be used on the farm, but knowing she had other ways to dress, other ways to live, would help her cope with the monotony of her existence. The thought of returning to the farm and Graham was less and less enticing. Town was an almost forgotten joy.

At the playhouse, there was a comedy on called *Just Married*. Barbara longed to see it, to be a part of the crowd bent on enjoying themselves, to laugh and relax for a couple of hours, do something far removed from her normal, regimented days. But she had to get Rosita back to the home and there wasn't time. Perhaps another day.

Weary with their wanderings, they caught the train back to town to see Mr and Mrs Carey's newly acquired shop and saw that already Mrs Carey had begun to smarten it up. The smell was still all-pervading but would soon be ousted by the stronger smells of disinfectant and new paint.

The cats roamed around mewing and yowling and Mrs Carey chased them off with a broom, much to Rosita's amusement. Barbara wondered why Rosita could laugh when she was with the Careys but never showed any sign of pleasure when she was with her. Could a child not yet eleven be capable of showing disapproval of her as punishment?

There were several tins of paint on the counter; already newly painted areas were shining in the gas light and the children were occupied cleaning their rooms. Alun and Billie and Idris were arguing about who had the best rooms and who would share with whom. Ada came for the day to help.

Barbara regretfully left them to it and took Rosita back to the home. She watched the girl go inside carrying her gifts and mementoes without a word or a backward glance. She felt defeated by her daughter. Not once had she shown happiness at their being together. She only became animated when she was with the Careys. Out of them it was only Richard who interested her and he was on the run from the police.

Barbara visited again, aware that she was nothing more than the necessary means of getting her daughter out of the home and to visit the Careys. There was never the slightest hint that Rosita took any pleasure in her mother's company. But Bank Holiday Monday would surely persuade Rosita out of her scowling mood. With hope for a successful visit, leaving Kate and Hattie behind again, she took her to the seaside, where holiday-makers were enjoying warm sunshine.

It was mid-afternoon before they reached the sands, after a journey standing crushed with other cheerful passengers on the packed train. Everywhere was filled with happy, laughing people. Barbara became immediately caught up in the spirit of the day, forgetting momentarily the years of working on the farm, and becoming once again the lighthearted young woman she had almost forgotten being. Even the surly expression on Rosita's face couldn't spoil the atmosphere for her.

It was as though everyone was celebrating some great event. The beach was crowded with parties of people who had travelled there by every imaginable means of transport. Besides the sixty extra trains and the buses that unloaded regularly, there were some less usual vehicles disgorging families set on having a good day out. Everything from huge furniture vans and lorries to small cars and bicycles. There were even milk floats drawn by ponies and filled with passengers instead of churns and crates of milk.

Several men had brought mouth organs and banjos and music mingled in a dozen melodies at the same time and people danced wherever there was space to do so. The Charleston was performed high above the crowds on the roof of the promenade, and below, a party of young people danced to their own voices, singing, 'I wish I could shimmy like my sister Kate.'

On the sand, beautifully dressed young women with their elegant partners were unwilling to leave, even after the sun had dropped below the horizon. The mood changed. The women's sleeveless tops that shimmered as the wearers moved were covered in jackets as the air cooled. Beautifully dressed men offered their blazers and white jackets to their partners, draping them around shoulders and using the move to steal a sly kiss. They all looked incongruously smart in such a setting. A number of men gathered driftwood from where earlier tides had left it and lit fires. One brought out a gramophone and the groups gathered near the fires to sing, laugh and then dance some more.

Barbara was grabbed by a man wearing a smooth grey pin-striped suit, from which he removed the jacket, revealing a crisp white shirt and expensive braces. His shirt sleeves were held at the correct length by silver armbands. Laughing, she allowed herself to be led, still clinging to Rosita's hand into the dance.

He tried to pull Rosita into the throng but she wriggled and shouted and he gratefully dropped her back onto the sand, where she sat and glared every time her mother looked at her – which wasn't often.

The man's braces were exactly the same blue as his tie, his hair was flattened back with pomade and his shoes, scuffed already by the sand, were patent leather.

'Surely you must have intended to go somewhere different from the beach?' Barbara asked, giggling like the rest of the crowd.

'Dressed for fun, my dear, wherever I might find it,' he replied, jigging enthusiastically to the music, his fingers tapping out the rhythm on her spine.

Barbara couldn't remember ever feeling so young and excited and she wanted the day to go on for ever. Even Rosita seemed content to sit and watch the unusual scene. But the day did end, as the daylight waned, and she knew she would be very late getting Rosita back to the home.

She told herself that to stay was unfair to everyone, irresponsible, selfish, but eventually gave in to her longing for the evening of fun. She took a delighted Rosita back to the Careys and telephoned the home to say she was keeping her for an extra day. With more apprehension she spoke to a very disgruntled Graham, explaining that both she and Rosita were tired, and that she would be home the following day. She then went back to the beach, filled with a delicious feeling of guilty excitement. She was irresistibly drawn back to the partying people not far from the seawater swimming pool. Another night away from Graham and the girls wouldn't matter, and anyway, she excused, it was far too late to get back tonight, so why waste an opportunity for fun?

Her recent partner seemed to be waiting for her. She walked straight into his smiling welcome as soon as she reached the shelter of the promenade. He took her in his arms as naturally as she had once thought Bernard would have done, and led her down to join the noisy, laughing throng.

It was easy to begin talking to the people and she was soon a part of a gathering around one of the largest bonfires, drinking from assorted bottles of wine that lay about in plenitude, and singing with the rest. Old songs, sentimental songs, popular songs from the music halls and, best of all, slow, romantic ones, with her partner looking into her eyes in the flickering light of the fire and doing strange things to her breathing.

When the fire burned low she settled with the man who had been her partner for the dancing and dozed unselfconsciously, feeling like a seventeen-year-old again.

Laughter disturbed her and she sat up, sleep less important than experiencing this wonderful night. The fire still flickered as fresh wood was occasionally added and shadows could be seen like fringes around the drowsy groups. Music could still be heard and one or two couples were dancing although much more slowly than previously.

'My name is Jim,' her companion said. 'Will you stay for tomorrow? It threatens to be even better than today.' He leaned closer and added against her cheek, 'And tonight the best part of all.'

She hesitated, longing to agree with the implication in those few whispered words. She hated the thought of returning to Graham in that brief moment. She didn't have to tell her new friend about Graham and the girls; she could say nothing. Lying by default, they called it; not as wicked as a downright lie. And it wasn't as if she really planned to do anything wrong, just a bit of innocent flirting. But she couldn't trust herself. So in the end she said a regretful no.

'I'll have to leave first thing in the morning,' she told him. 'I'm expected back by midday. I promised my husband,' she added, forcing herself to say the necessary words.

'My wife expected me back two days ago, my dear, but it's party time and we should have fun,' he replied lightly. He offered her some more of the wine she had been drinking without thought, from the time she had returned. She drank, allowed him to kiss her, then as his hands began to wander, pushed him gently, reluctantly away.

They spent the night with their arms around each other, dozing a little, waking to talk and kiss a little. Jim was so fresh, so sweet and clean; his skin smelled deliciously of soap. She knew she would remember him for ever.

While the rest of the group were still sleeping, huddled against each other in untidy heaps, Barbara slipped away. She wanted so much to stay and enjoy another day of fun but she hadn't the right. Her fun was to be found with Graham or not at all. Groggy with the unaccustomed drink of the evening before, she found her way to the station and caught the first train to the beach and the Careys to collect Rosita and return her to the home.

Rosita complained most of the way back but Barbara seemed lost in a daydream and unaware, so eventually she gave up and sat looking out of the window, ignoring her mother completely.

In a strange way the hours of impromptu holidaying had eased the situation between Barbara and Graham. Knowing there was an escape, that waiting for her was an opportunity for fun any time she wanted it, made it less important. She smiled a greeting when he came out to meet her and that night she returned to his bed.

Winter began early that year. Frosts and even a few flurries of snow came before December began. Graham had increased his flock of sheep and he spent hours up on the hills, checking they were safe. Sometimes Barbara went with him, walking beside him to the hut where he sometimes stayed overnight, when lambing was a full-time activity. On occasions, she left the girls in the care of a neighbour and stayed out with him. Those nights in the silent world of the snow-clad hills, just the two of them wrapped in isolation, were magical, filled with contentment.

Kate and Hattie were growing into quiet, well-behaved children, and she and Graham had reached one of their periodic happy phases. There was no shortage of good food and Graham rarely showed signs of the anger of previous years.

Rosita was safe and cared for. She would grow up and sort out her difficulties without her mother's help. Barbara had slowly accepted that she had been right to send her away, that she was not the one to help her untangle her problems and was able, now, to discuss her behaviour with Graham, who reassured her.

'You always tried to help her, Babs. Done your best you have. She's made it quite clear that your help isn't needed. You have to accept that and then you'll stop worrying.'

'I suppose so,' she agreed sadly. 'Although I still feel a failure where she's concerned.'

'You're needed here,' Graham told her time and again. 'I need you and Kate and Hattie need you. It's here you belong. Rosita will find someone one day and she'll grow into a fine young woman. If she has your blood in her veins she can't do anything else, now can she?'

Barbara fervently hoped he was right.

Chapter Nine

LUKE HEARD OF the death of his father by accident. A visitor to the Café de Jacques brought with him a Cardiff paper, wrapped around a gift for Luke and Martine, a pound of laverbread, the popular Welsh delicacy made from a type of seaweed. The visitor had found the café on his way through Calais while motoring south some years before and since then he had called every time he'd visited France, usually bringing a gift from Wales.

Luke unwrapped the gift, his mouth watering at the prospect of warming the laverbread in a little of the fat from frying bacon. A perfect breakfast. Delicious. He smoothed the paper, intending to read it later, but at once the name of his father caught his eye and he gasped with shock.

'My father. He's dead!' he said to Martine.

'So, you have lost the chance to make up your quarrel. For that I am sad, *cherie.*'

In three days Luke was back in Cardiff. He knew from the newspaper that he was too late to attend the funeral but hoped to visit his sister and perhaps resume normal contact with her. Surely now his father was gone there was no reason to continue with the estrangement between them? He was wrong. His sister refused to see him.

Spending a few days with Jeanie and her husband at the shop, he had an idea and, with Jeanie's willing help, carried it out. Using her to cover his identity, he negotiated to buy the cottage on the beach from his father's estate.

He went by train to see the place although it was not yet his. Before he left the station he looked around him, half afraid his sister would be there, see him, and guess his intentions. Apart from that fear, he felt the usual pleasure at going back and sat for a long time against the sea wall and stared across at Gull Island.

The day was stormy and wild with dead vegetation bowling along like tumbleweed in a cowboy film. The air tingled around him like an angry, tail-swishing cat. The wind gusted spasmodically and threatened to bowl him along with the dead plants. It was exciting and he felt buoyant, hopeful of a good result from his attempts to own the cottage he had always loved.

He returned to France before the transaction was complete but travelled joyfully, knowing that the next time he came home, the cottage, his cottage, would be waiting for him.

Even the knowledge that his sister would have blocked the sale, had she known it was he who had wanted it, couldn't dampen his delight. The cottage was his, to return to whenever he wanted. He planned one day to take Martine there. Perhaps, when they were no longer fit to run Café de Jacques, they would retire there and be happy. He smiled at the thought, yet behind the smile and the image, there was another shadowy picture of himself living at the cottage, but with Barbara and Rosita, not Martine.

Barbara put down the paper she was reading, tucked the small round spectacles in her apron pocket and stared across the room to where her husband was lacing up his boots and tying string around his leg just below the knees. The *yorks*, as the string protection was called, were a necessary addition to his dress. Graham was going out to the barn to tackle the rats. They had been known to run up a man's trouser legs, and, whether the stories were true or apocryphal, Graham wasn't a man to take chances. She smiled at him as he pulled the string *yorks* extra tight, her slow, dreamy eyes showing a rare sparkle. He frowned, wondering idly what the reason was for her amusement, but he didn't ask. Graham wasn't a man to waste words.

He looked contented, she thought; a man living well within his capabilities and looking no further. Apart from periods of half-glimpsed restlessness when she felt a lack of something obscure and unrecognized, she too was far from unhappy. The grain was in, the fields ploughed, and with only root crops left in the ground, life at the farm was slowing down and slipping into the different pace of winter.

While Graham dealt with maintenance of buildings and cleaning up after the busy summer, Barbara was kept busy storing and preserving the fruits and vegetables they had grown for their own use. Apple rings were drying in the cool oven, carrots and beetroot stored in shallow boxes between layers of dry ashes or sand. Jams and pickles adorned the large pantry. Above their heads hung half sides of bacon and hams, salted and then smoked by hanging them over smouldering oak chippings in an outhouse.

Looking around her neat and orderly kitchen, she smiled. It had worked out well for her. Leaving Rosita had been hard but it had been the right thing to do. Kate and Hattie were loved by their father and – here guilt crept into her reminiscences – Rosita had to be better growing up away from him.

She looked across again at Graham as he was about to leave the room. Tall and burly, she hadn't looked at him for a long time. Not properly. She was startled at how old he looked; this year, 1934, he would be fifty. Perhaps he would arrange to celebrate it with a party. Just the four of them, of course. His social life was no more than his market-day meeting and a drink with neighbouring farmers.

She folded her newspaper, with its worrying reports on the rapid rise of Hitler, and the danger to its neighbours from a militant Germany. A head-line caught her eye and she put on her glasses.

'This man Hitler is coming up fast,' she said to Graham. 'It says here that last year he became chancellor and straightaway disbanded trade unions and started arguments about withdrawing Germany from the disarmament conference. Yet he has the support and admiration of the ordinary people, who believe his promises of better things.'

'The man's a marvellous orator, I'll give him that, but that's all he is for sure. Just a bag of ol' wind. He'll soon fade and leave the field open for someone with more sense than to risk involving his country in another war,' Graham replied.

Straightening her glasses, Barbara read on: 'This report says, "He continues to entrance crowds and is the idol of everyone who is truly German. Those who have less right to call themselves Germans are less content. They foresee difficulties ahead." What d'you think he means by that?'

Graham wasn't listening. He was searching the drawer for the scarf that was hanging over the back of a chair in front of the fire to warm for him. Barbara lowered her glasses on her nose and pointed to it with a solitary finger then, refixing her glasses, went back to the article.

Hitler had swiftly assumed the office of head of state, it said, and there was nothing in his way. He would be Germany's autonomous leader, its dictator, with powers wider than anyone could at that time imagine. The words made her shiver, and she thought about Luke.

Barbara didn't normally concern herself with world events but there were constant warnings that Germany was once more posturing for a fight. The lust for power had not been killed by the 1914–18 war, only temporarily subdued. She didn't believe Graham's casual reassurances. Danger there was, without doubt. The reporter had written with urgent insistence. A man like Hitler, who had come up to such a position of impor-tance in the world, would surely not be content to stop and sit on his heels? He was still young and would want more and more.

Seeing her consternation, Graham said, 'If this Hitler bloke wants to involve his people in arguments, best we let him get on with it. We've got more important things to worry about.' It was Graham's usual comment, often repeated in different words each time she tried to persuade him to discuss the news.

As Graham closed the door behind him, Barbara's thoughts returned to Luke. He was living in France and might be involved if Germany and France clashed into conflict again, but she didn't tell Graham of her fears. He never liked her talking about her past. He was unsettled by any reference to people she had once known and from whom she had been taken when she married him. The threat of her leaving him was to him very real, a constant nightmare.

He was unaware that secretly Barbara often thought about Luke; whether he was homesick for the small beach and the cottage and his boat. She knew she was! Even though life was pleasant enough, memories harked back repeatedly to the beach near Gull Island, where she had met Luke and where there had been a special sort of peace.

She searched a cupboard and found some knitting wool. She would make Graham a pair of socks for his birthday in November. Knitting only when he was out of the house would take longer but it would be fun to give him a surprise and the girls would enjoy sharing the secret.

They could make something as well. Kate was quite proficient and could make him a scarf. What about Hattie? She lacked patience and skills. Perhaps she'd better buy him some tobacco for his pipe! She found some red wool and decided that once the socks were finished, she would make scarf and gloves for Rosita and send them for her birthday on Christmas Day.

Barbara had gone to the home to visit Rosita twice during the late summer of 1934 but each time the girl had refused to see her. The matron apologized and begged Barbara to try again, but even though she had tried three times on her second visit, walking the fields between attempts, hoping for a change of heart, Rosita hadn't appeared.

Richard was in a town thirty miles away from his home and working on a building site. He had learned the skills of bricklaying, had mastered plastering to a modest level and was surprisingly good at carpentry but it was at none of these that he earned his living. Thanks to the patience and teaching skills of Miss Bell, he had succeeded in passing exams in accountancy and also business management. He worked for a building firm dealing with various aspects of the business and was also working at other jobs in the evenings to increase his savings. He spent very little, and didn't have a social life, concentrating solely on building a bank account that would one day give him a start in a business of his own.

He sat in a café sifting through the papers sent to him by his solicitor, who was helping him to negotiate the purchase of a small field on which he planned to build one day when he had accumulated enough money to make a start. He often thought of the beach house and the family he had left behind. He knew his mother had made a good job of building the business he had bought for them; he and his father kept in touch by letter and phone calls.

It was Rosita about whom he longed to have news, the little girl, so angry and distressed, beaten by that man Barbara had married then abandoned to live among strangers. He wondered if she was still in the home, or whether she had run away and was somewhere, alone, facing danger, with no one to help her. As soon as he was safe from police enquiries, he would find her and look after her properly.

Rosita was working but still living at the home. After being given the chance to find other, more pleasant work, and being told she was useless, the job she had been given was cleaning and Rosita hated it. Matron had told her kindly but firmly, 'There isn't really anything else you can do, my dear. You do make so many mistakes.'

'I'm not stupid. People just don't explain properly,' Rosita insisted. 'When I was delivering for that grocer I kept missing the signposts – them posts are so high I went straight past. And I couldn't help knocking over that bowl of soup when I worked in the café. The spoon was sticking out and—'

'That's always the case, dear. You are just a bit clumsy and forgetful, that's all. Try not to worry about it. Just do a job you can do and forget trying to better yourself. That only leads to disappointment for a girl like you.'

So the work she was given were only the simplest of tasks and that meant black-leading the grates, scrubbing endless floors and peeling endless vegetables. She flatly refused to consider farm work.

On New Year's Eve, during the final hours of 1934, Barbara was sitting mending some of the clothes Kate and Hattie used for their work around the farm. They were old but still serviceable. It was only silly superstition, she knew that, but her mother had always insisted that any work outstanding had to be finished before the year ended, and that included repairing clothes. The mending basket had to be emptied. It was considered very bad luck to let things lie unfinished after the clock struck midnight.

She glanced at the time. Only a bit of darning on one of Graham's socks after this patch, then she could go to bed.

Graham was walking back to the house. He had left his favourite pipe behind. His clothes were white, the air full of falling snow, blocking out sounds and giving the fields an unfamiliar pattern. He knew the area so well he could have walked it blindfolded and he found the path with ease even though the edges were blurred with several inches of the dazzling white covering.

When he came to the fence above the *cwm*, he looked down and saw a movement, white on white and he knew immediately what it was. That damned ewe again! He had pulled her away from that spot only yesterday. Set on choosing their own birthing place, some of them. This one was determined to have her lamb on the edge of the cliff or commit suicide in the attempt! There was always one awkward one, he mused. Every year there was one who caused him extra worry over their safety. With a sigh, he climbed over the fence and began to walk towards her, his crook in his hand.

Perhaps he would stop and have a warm drink with Barbara when he collected his pipe. She was unlikely to be in bed, he thought, remembering the pile of mending she had undertaken to finish.

His footsteps were already half obliterated as he stood looking down at the ewe.

'Now, old girl, are you going to be sensible and come back with me?'

Barbara banked up the fire. When Graham came back from the hill early in the morning, he would be glad of the warmth. It would only need a lift with the poker and he'd have a nice blaze. She moved the big kettle close to the heat and mixed cocoa and sugar and milk in the bottom of a cup ready for him to make himself a warm drink. As she was about to go upstairs there was a knock at the door. Graham must have forgotten something. But why didn't he just push the door? It was never locked. Perhaps he was taking off his boots and coat before coming in.

She glanced around the room, wondering idly which of his needs it might be. His tobacco? His favourite pipe? Certainly not his sandwiches or his drink. She had seen to them herself as she always did.

When she opened the door it was a neighbouring farmer and he was covered with the snow that was falling fast and silently from the night sky. She was surprised to see the snow. The farm was so isolated that the special muffling effect that was so noticeable in built-up areas – the low purring sound of cars, the whirring of wheels and shouted instructions around vehicles that were stuck – didn't disturb them here.

'Mr Brackley? Come in. What a night! Come in quick and warm your-self by the fire. I didn't know the snow had begun again. What can I do for you?' She turned after closing the door behind him, wondering why he hadn't spoken. 'What is it? If it's Graham you want he won't be in till morning. Up in the fields with his flock he is.

'Graham is … outside,' the man said.

'Outside? Why doesn't he come in?' She stared unseeing into the dark-ness. 'Come back for his pipe, I bet.' She tutted impatiently. 'Tell him to come in before he catches his death. What is it?' she asked, alarmed by silence of the solemn-faced man, who was clutching his hat in gnarled hands.

'I – I found him down at the bottom of the *cwm*, missus. Taking a lickle short cut I was, see. He went over the fence at the top by the looks of things.'

'What are you telling me?'

'Missus, sorry to my heart I am to tell you, your man is dead.' He explained how he had run for help and with the aid of his sons had brought the body home.

'The doctor's on his way, missus. Be here in less than an hour for sure. Now once he's been, how about you and the girls coming back with us for the night? The missus and I will be glad if you'd come. You don't want to be on your own. Not tonight.'

Numbly Barbara shook her head. She was trembling, her arms shaking up and down. Her face had dropped, aged, and she had the look of a stranger to her daughters when they were woken and brought down to be told the news.

'Then my missus will come and stay with you, that'll be best,' Mr Brackley said, his voice stronger now the news had been told. He whistled through the doorway and called his sons to fetch their mam. But Barbara protested.

'No. Thank you, Mr Brackley, but no. I only want the girls,' she said. 'But tell them to come in and have a hot drink before walking back home.' She made them drinks with hands that were still shaking, and sat wrapped in silent, disbelieving shock while they drank it and left.

The rest of that night was simply hours to be got through. Marking time, watching the journey of the clock hands, waiting until people could be told, the arrangements made. There was no thought of the future, just the present, the unbelievable present. In her numbness came bursts of anger. Graham had let them down, leaving them all alone to cope. Why hadn't he been more careful? He had left them all alone and for the sake of a ewe and her lamb.

Kate and Hattie seemed dazed and after being told the news just sat and stared at the walls, then at each other, holding hands and saying nothing. Barbara knew the tears would come and all the questions and recriminations, but she said nothing to encourage them. She had to give herself time to get strong so she could support them fully when the time came.

The deep snow made everything doubly difficult but somehow the news was spread and the arrangements made for the funeral. Neighbours dealt with the animals and offered help in any way it was needed. Numbly, Barbara wrote to tell Rosita that her stepfather had died then, even at such a time she remembered the lie and re-wrote to the matron stating that Rosita's dear Uncle Graham had sadly died.

It was only two days before the news reached Rosita that her 'Uncle Graham' was dead.

'Your aunt wrote to me too and she sounds very distressed,' Matron said kindly. 'She wonders if you might like to go and stay with her for a while? I think she needs some extra family around her.'

'I'll go at once, if she needs me.' Was there sarcasm in the girl's words? Matron couldn't be sure but she was puzzled by the harshness in Rosita's tone.

'Don't worry about your work, my dear. I'll let everyone know you won't be in for a few days.'

Rosita packed her bag and left the place that had been her home since the age of five, and didn't look back. Today she was leaving but wouldn't be going to comfort her mother and those half-sisters of hers who hadn't come to see her once during all the years she'd been away. She was heading for the town and a life of her own.

It was easier than she had imagined to change from Rosita Jones from the home to Miss Caroline Evans, a smart young woman with a future. She went first to a hair-dresser and had her long hair cut into the fashionable shingle. The difference was startling. Her eyes looked huge and her face had a chiselled look that went well with the rather haughty expression she habitually wore. The hairdresser helped with some advice about make-up and Rosita went into a chemist and bought eye shadow, face cream and powder, and some lipsticks. To her utter joy she also bought soap that wasn't carbolic and smelled wonderful.

With the rest of her meagre savings she bought a calf-length skirt, a richly embroidered Hungarian blouse and a long jacket. The outfit was unsuitable for January and she would have to keep the awful coat the home had supplied and the even more awful black lace-up shoes Matron had lent her, supposedly for the funeral. But at least she felt different.

She caught sight of herself in a café mirror and was pleased with what she saw. She looked older, no longer a child needing to be looked after. She bought a packet of cigarettes although she made no attempt to light one. Just having them in her handbag added to her new sophistication. For the first time she was going to be herself, but with a new name. Miss Caroline Evans. How wonderful was that?

Boldly, she applied for a job in a dress shop. Making sure she hid the awful brown coat, she walked confidently in to see the manageress, a Miss Grainger, wearing her new clothes. She carried herself proudly. She was careful about her diction and after a few preliminary questions, which Rosita answered with a mixture of truth, exaggeration and downright lies, she was told she could begin the following day.

Rosita walked around for an hour but the day was chilly. Snow banked up all along the pavement was crisp with the onset of the night's frost. Knowing that a night sleeping outside was impossible to consider, she went back and asked Miss Grainger if she could help her find a room.

The manageress looked surprised to see her back and even more surprised at her request. Looking older than her early forties, she stood behind her desk, tall, elegant, wearing a polite half-frown. Her mid-brown hair was curled into a neat bun, her face was serious but by no means harsh, and there was a gentility about her that Rosita thought she could manipulate.

'I'm from out of town, you see, Miss Grainger. The lady I intended staying with, a dear friend of my mother, has been taken ill. In hospital she is and I've wasted a lot of time visiting her and giving comfort. Now I've left it rather late. Tomorrow there will be no problem. I have plenty of friends who will help, but tonight, I wonder, could you find me a room?'

Miss Grainger was half annoyed and half amused by the girl's impertinence but seeing the smile and the confident assurance on Rosita's pretty face, she said quietly, so the other members of staff couldn't hear, 'A little short of money, are we, Miss Evans?'

'Yes, but only until for now. Tomorrow I'll contact my friends and it will be all right.'

'If it's for one night only, I will allow you to use my spare room. But please, don't tell any of the staff – they will think it very odd.'

They walked back to the house where Miss Grainger had lived with her mother until the old lady had died, and which, she told Rosita, now rattled around her like an over-large cage. She showed Rosita into a cosy bedroom the like of which she had never seen. Rugs on the floors, a thick eiderdown on the single bed and velvet curtains across the window that looked out on a view of the docks.

Miss Grainger watched as Rosita unpacked her few belongings, taking in the carefully mended lisle stockings and the minimal amount of underwear, and offered kindly to lend her a nightdress, dressing gown and towel.

'The rest is following on. I had to wait until I was sure of an address, you see,' Rosita explained in her new, carefully modulated voice, accepting with some trepidation the cigarette Miss Grainger offered. It was foul and she thought her throat was on fire, but she determinedly tried to appear nonchalant and took a second and third puff but soon placed it on an ashtray, and there it stayed.

'If there's anything else you need, please ask,' Miss Grainger offered. She stood for a long time wondering if she had been foolish to invite the unknown girl into her home. It was obvious she had run away from someone, but it wouldn't hurt to give her a few days and see how things went. She could always tell her to leave if she caused any worries.

Rosita was not allowed to approach the customers at first. She had to watch and learn from the other sales girls. She also had to spend time getting to know her stock. When a customer came in for a particular item, she had to have a clear and accurate picture in her mind of all they had to offer.

In the showroom were rails of coats and suits, skirts and dresses. In special glass-fronted showcases on the sales floor there were some beautiful evening gowns displayed with glittering hairbands, evening bags and jewellery. In a corner there were delicate evening shoes, sheer silk stockings, fur stoles and wraps. One gown, Rosita was surprised to see, was in black velvet with a startlingly low front and, from the waist up, no back at all! Some of these special dresses cost fifteen guineas so the cases where they were displayed were kept locked and Miss Grainger had the keys.

In the stockroom below the sales floor, an alteration hand sat at her sewing machine with dozens of cottons and assorted pins and needles, and took in and let out and shortened hems and let them down. There were other rails down there, covered with sheeting, and from these the displays were refilled after sales had been made. It was here, too, that purchases were wrapped.

Rosita had to recognize each material, learn about the latest fashion and be able to discuss the rights and wrongs of dress for every occasion. At first she thought it would be boring but Miss Grainger was encouraging and helpful and her newest assistant soon became fascinated by the variety of both garments and the customers who came to buy. Miss Grainger noted approvingly how quickly she learned and how well she dealt with customers.

The 'stupid' label still hovered around her though. She occasionally brought the wrong garment to the wrong customer and once handed the purchase to the wrong person. The incidents were covered each time by amused laughter but Rosita saw Miss Grainger watching and in her anxiety to please her, made other, less serious errors.

The accommodation problem seemed in abeyance. Miss Grainger had surprised her on the second day after her arrival by saying, 'If you wish, Caroline, you can stay a few more days, just until you find something more suitable.'

'Thank you, that's very kind,' Rosita said in her new voice that went with her new self.

'And,' Miss Grainger added with a chuckle, 'you can stop pretending to smoke!'

A few days drifted on and although Rosita had found a place where she could stay cheaply and which was not far from the shop, she waited until Miss Grainger told her she must leave. At the end of two weeks, she had handed all her small wages to her.

'For my bed and board, Miss Grainger, and thank your for you kindness.'

It was a tricky moment, an opportunity for Miss Grainger to remind her the few days were over, but instead, she handed back two of the seven shillings and said nothing.

Rosita had a way with people that her mother would never have believed. Like Matron and several others if they had been brutally honest, her mother would have described her daughter as an ill-tempered, ungracious character. But in her role of junior sales assistant, she was patient and very polite.

She was only allowed to approach those customers that were considered time wasters, just come to look and finger and dream of owning such beautiful clothes. And at lunchtime, when the staff was reduced, she was occasionally allowed to hone her skills. She encouraged those who came in to try on garments that appealed instead of just looking and sometimes flattered them into buying more than they intended. But Miss Grainger was curious, she knew something was wrong.

'Caroline, dear, why didn't you return the smile when Mrs Prichard-Jones came in just now?' she asked, when that lady had turned away embarrassed at having her smile ignored.

'I'm sorry, Miss Grainger, I didn't see her.'

'Well, just go and speak to her, will you? Just a polite good morning, mind. Don't involve your betters in conversation, that won't do,' she reminded her.

Miss Grainger watched in surprise as Rosita walked to a woman standing near the rail of winter coats before realizing her mistake and walking back again to the counter, where Mrs Prichard-Jones was looking at fur wraps. She frowned and wondered if the girl was perhaps a bit stupid, as the others believed. Such a pity if she were; she was pretty enough and the customers liked her.

She began to watch Rosita more carefully and suddenly the reason for her apparent vagueness came to her. As they walked home together, the rest of the staff now knowing of the friendship between them, she pointed to a hoarding across the road.

'Look, there's a circus advertised. I love a circus. When does it say it's coming?'

Rosita ran across the road and read the notice. 'It's an old one, I'm afraid. It was here months ago.'

'Why did you run all that way? You could have seen it from here.'

'From here?' Rosita laughed. 'No one could read those small letters from here!'

'Caroline, my dear, tomorrow you must see an optician. I think you are fearfully short-sighted.'

Barbara had searched for her daughter without finding even a hint of where she might be. She even went to see Bernard's mother, Mrs Stock, but without opening the door more than an inch, Mrs Stock said she knew nothing about her.

By Easter 1935, Barbara faced the fact that the farm would have to be sold. Without Graham there was no possibility of her and the girls coping with all the work. Besides the heavy work, she didn't have the knowledge. She braced herself to tell her daughters her decision. She dreaded their reaction but instead of tears and distress and begging and pleading for her not to take them away, they were jubilant.

'Does it mean we'll wear shoes all the time and not boots?' Kate asked.

'We'll be able to go to dances and see films and shows!' a delighted Hattie shouted.

Barbara became caught up in their excitement and when a buyer was found, the three of them threw aside the years of drudgery with glee.

They arrived in the town that had been Barbara's home with all their belongings on the back of a cart and rented a terraced house. The size was laughable after the huge old farmhouse. 'But,' Barbara told the girls, 'it's only temporary, just while we get ourselves settled.' The money from the sale of the farm and the animals was put into the bank and Barbara, Kate and Hattie looked for work.

Kate was slim and willowy and rather like Barbara, with the same dreamy eyes and gentle manner. She found work in the local school, looking after nursery-age children, a job she quickly came to love.

Hattie was overweight and followed her father in appearance. Her features, apart from the eyes, were large in the round, flat face. Her hands were wide and clumsy. She had no burning desire for any particular job. Her attitude to life was simple: she anticipated a short working life filled with fun and amorous adventures, before finding a husband and settling down in a home of her own. A factory offered a better wage than a shop or cleaning and she quickly found herself a niche with friends as determined as herself to have a good time.

They saw the Careys and admired their new shop but Molly Carey didn't tell Barbara that she knew where Rosita was, or that she now called herself Caroline Evans.

'We haven't seen hair nor hide of the girl,' she lied, avoiding Barbara's eyes.

Barbara took the girls to the beach where Luke's cottage stood silent and neglected. There was no sign of Luke, although his boat was still in its usual place. While the girls walked on the beach and explored the abandoned house, Barbara sat and stared across at Gull Island. She wondered what had happened to her daughter and felt somehow this was the place where she would one day find her. She wondered too about Luke, far away in France, and young Richard who had disappeared on the day his father had taken on the shop and from whom Mrs Carey had received only a few brief notes.

A sea fret was gathering low over the water, moving out and gradually engulfing the rocky island. She shivered as it cut off the sun. Melancholy overwhelmed her as she felt the chill breeze creep over her skin and she called to Kate and Hattie. It was time to leave. The lonely beach represented the past and there was nothing to be gained by looking back. It was tomorrow where happiness lay, not here with the ghosts of yesterday's woes.

Instead of going straight back to the terraced house where they were settling into a comfortable existence, she went to the newspaper shop again.

'You will tell me if you hear even the slightest hint of where I might find Rosita, won't you?' she asked Mrs Carey.

'I'll always want to do what's best for you and Rosita, you can be sure of that.' The ambiguity of the reply was lost on Barbara.

'Best we tell Rosita that her mam and half-sisters are in town,' Mrs Carey said to Henry later. Henry nodded vaguely, tickled the dog's ear and went on enjoying the comic he was reading.

Rosita was fitted with glasses and, putting them on for the first time, she was startled. Her familiar and fuzzy world was transformed. She walked home wearing them in a state of bewilderment. Everything was so bright and clear. She hadn't realized how beautiful the familiar pigeons were, so many colours and such wonderful patterns on their feathers. Starlings, she saw in amazement, wore fragmented rainbows on their backs. People across the street had faces instead of a pale blur. She spotted people she knew from an amazing distance and they had features whereas before, she now realized, she only recognized them by their clothes or the way they walked.

As euphoria faded, she began to go back over the difficulties of her miserable childhood. She discussed it with Miss Grainger and they realized that poor sight was the reason for much of her so-called stupidity. Copying vaguely-seen shapes from a blackboard was still a painful memory. She'd had no idea until now that there was more, much more to see than the blurred and indistinct images she could make out by screwing up her eyes and looking through the slits.

She remembered going into a shop to buy some sweets her mother had pointed out and coming out of the shop with the wrong ones simply because she hadn't been able to see the label far back in the window. Then there were the buses she had allowed to go past because she couldn't read the destination board in time to raise her hand and stop them.

She had several times waved at people she didn't know, mistaking them for friends, and had been accused of ignoring those she did know and passing them in the street. It hadn't been stupidity, simply her poor sight. She almost screamed in her delight, but her new-found dignity forbade it.

Far from making her unglamorous, the new acquisition became a beauty aid. She fingered the frames with elegant fingers, waving her hands about her face, bringing her large, luminous eyes to everyone's attention. Many of the girls with whom she worked wished they too needed to wear them.

By the time 1939 came, bringing fears of imminent war, Rosita was first sales and earning enough to put money away in a savings bank.

Although she often visited the town where she had been born, she had never met her mother or, to her knowledge, either of her half-sisters; two dull girls obeying their father to please him, and looking at her with a smug smile when she had earned a slap. She doubted whether she would know them if they did meet. It had been so long they would be strangers. She knew they were back, as Auntie Molly Carey had told her. She thought about them occasionally, not without bitterness, and wondered if they would ever meet and, if they did, whether they would acknowledge each other.

To Miss Grainger she told her story. It began when that good lady had discovered her need for glasses. The excitement of seeing clearly and the realization that her problems could have been explained so easily made her pour out the story in a gush of grateful emotion.

She continued to stay with Miss Grainger; the difference in age was no barrier to their liking each other. They read books and discussed them, they saw plays and films and, best of all, it was because of Miss Grainger that she began to enjoy accounts.

It was part of Miss Grainger's job to keep the ledgers up to date and offer them annually for audit. Within two years, Rosita was sharing the work with her and in 1939, when Miss Grainger was taken ill, Rosita did them unaided and was congratulated by the auditors for the immaculate and efficient way she presented them.

'You have an instinctive gift for figures, Miss Evans,' one of them said. 'Have you considered becoming trained for the work? Secretaries with accounting skills can earn a very acceptable salary these days, you know.'

'Thank you for suggesting it.' Rosita smiled confidentially. 'But I plan to run my own business one day. What I have learned will be very useful.'

'Oh? What business would that be? Pretty dresses no doubt.'

'No. A newsagents,' she replied almost without thought. She laughed later as she told Miss Grainger. 'The only people I know who run a business of their own are the Careys so it was the first thing to come into my mind.'

'Selling newspapers and tobacco isn't a bad idea.' Her friend puffed at the Four Aces cigarette held in a large amber holder. 'Smoking is a popular activity and becoming more acceptable. And everyone needs a daily paper. Yes, you could do a lot worse.' She stretched open the new box of twenty and removed the vouchers contained in it. They were saving to send for a pair of Gibsonette-style shoes for Rosita, for which they needed 120 vouchers.

When Hitler's army marched into Poland and war was declared, Luke wasn't very concerned. It all seemed a long way off and could hardly affect the small café that Martine and he continued to run, near the beach in Calais. It wasn't until British soldiers began arriving in France that he began to wonder what he and Martine should do.

'You must leave,' Martine said one morning when, looking very worried, she returned from the market. 'Go now, today. A delay might mean your life.'

'We won't be panicked into anything.' Luke smiled and smoothed the frown from her face tenderly. 'I'll write to my partner Jeanie and arrange for us to go there at the end of the month. But only for a visit.' But he didn't write. He believed that with the German army busy in Poland, France was safe. 'By the time they think about attacking France and Holland, the British will have beaten them back to where they belong. There's plenty of time to think about leaving.'

In 1940 they ran out of time.

'Go tonight, please, Luke,' Martine pleaded.

'We'll both leave in the morning.'

'No, my darling, not we, not us. But you must go.'

'What d'you mean?'

'I must return to Papa. He is a very old man now, and afraid. He needs me more than you do. It is my duty. Please don't try and persuade me different.'

'I need you. You must come with me. We can take your father as well. I know of a small cove where boats are still managing to leave. A few hours' discomfort, that's all. He will come if you explain why we're going. He won't want to live through another occupation.'

'He will not leave, and I can't either. Please, Luke. We'll meet again, I know this, but for now it is *au revoir*.'

Luke still refused to leave without her. He had been so happy in the simple life he shared with Martine. What would he do if she left him? He would never find anyone else to share his life so amicably. 'No,' he said. 'I will not go. We'll live through this together.'

A few weeks later, at three o'clock in the morning, they were woken by furious knocking at the café door. Looking through the bedroom window they saw a group of German soldiers, armed with guns, standing outside. Martine pushed the bed aside, lifted two wide floorboards and gestured for Luke to hide in the place they had prepared in readiness for such an emergency as this. There wasn't much room and it was thick with dangling spider webs and the droppings of mice. For once Luke was glad he was a small man.

The soldiers searched the place and angrily demanded Martine tell them where the Englishman had gone.

'A lover's quarrel,' she sobbed realistically. 'We had a silly quarrel and now he is gone from me! Left me, gone away with hate in his heart and I don't know where. I am desolate.'

Luke stayed under the floorboards all that day. With Martine sitting on the bed above him, watching for the return of the soldiers, they talked.

'Do you not feel 'appy to go 'ome to your little cottage, Luke?' Martine

asked. 'Do memories of your papa still worry you? Death is always difficult to accept, even the death of someone who made you so un'appy.'

'When my mother died, Father told me not to cry,' Luke told her,
pushing a spider's web from across his eyes. 'He said it was unmanly. I
remember Roy coming over and we were hugging each other and sobbing
and my father came and tore us apart as if we'd been caught stealing from
his pocket.'

'*Mon petit*, it must 'ave been 'ard for you then.'

'Roy's family were always touching, hugging. Roy and I used to roll
about on the floor like puppies in mock fights, but if Father saw us I was
punished.'

'I knew this when we first met and I couldn't get close. Kissing and
hugging, they were difficult for you. Your papa, 'e was between us.'

'Even when I was with the Careys, his shadow was there, making me
afraid to show affection the way they all did.'

With his disembodied voice coming from beneath the floor and unable
to look at him, Martine took courage and asked, ''Ave you not thought,
Luke, that per'aps your father was the one with the problem? That he loved
young men, er, what you say, too well? Could he not 'ave been fighting that
all 'is life? If that were so, then wouldn't he be afraid of the same thing
showing in 'is son? You understand what I am meaning, *mon petit*?'

'Good heavens. No!' He took a deep breath, which made him cough,
and it was moments before he could go on. 'My father a homosexual, you
think? That's a crazy idea. He was always—' He went silent, remembering
so many things.

Scenes sped across his inner vision. The time that, being small, he was
chosen to play the part of a woman in the school play. His father coming
to complain and having him taken out of the production. The new clothes
chosen, only to have them thrown away labelled effeminate. So many
things became clear as he thought of Martine's words. It wasn't him, it was
his father. It was his father's burden he had been carrying all these years.
The realization grew like a glorious bubble of joy.

When it was midnight, Martine released him and handed him a small
shoulder bag. 'There is food for three days and little else. You need to travel
light and fast. God speed, my darling. We'll meet again when this is over.'

Luke accepted his fate, not least because he was aware of the danger into
which his being there was putting Martine. He should have gone ages ago.
If he stayed and her lies were found out – he cut off the rest of the scenario.
He couldn't bear to think what might have happened to her if he'd been
discovered.

Travelling at night he made contact with three other Englishmen intent on escape. For two days they hid near the coast, Luke selling his overcoat and shoes in exchange for motor fuel with which they would pay for their passage. They were taken on board a rusting, foul-smelling boat and sent on their way with the fishing fleet.

The boat was old and barely seaworthy. The tackle was red with rust and unmovable, having been left without attention for several years. The wood was so weak Luke found he could dig out chunks with a fingernail. The nets were rotten and fell to pieces when touched. If the Germans stopped them they wouldn't have a chance of bluffing them.

'It's going to be a race between which gets us first, the Germans or the sea,' Luke said grimly. But it was their only chance if they were to escape capture and imprisonment. Luke could face anything but being locked up.

The *Mouette* – The Seagull – was a cranky craft, low at the sides, high in the bow, with a determination to list to port that gave her an odd appearance. Miraculously, after libations of oil, the pump still worked, and pushing and pulling the handle was a continuous task. In mid-Channel they doubted if they were keeping pace with the water seeping in through the weak and uncaulked timbers.

The weather was kind, and fortunately they weren't spotted by aircraft wearing roundels or swastikas, either of which might have fired on them without investigating too carefully who and what they were. Two more days and Luke was standing in his bookshop, smiling at his partner Jeanie, once more without shoes.

Chapter Ten

THE DAY WAS very warm, the sun beating down from a sky that was too blue to see. The crowds strolling through the main shopping street in summer dresses and short-sleeved shirts seemed in no hurry to reach their destination. Time and again, Rosita sighed with impatience as people blocked her way: standing idly around, looking at the temptations offered in shop windows, choosing comic postcards to send back home or just stopping to talk to a friend in the middle of the pavement.

Petrol was free of rationing at last, five years after the end of the war, and already an increased number of holidaymakers were flooding into the town. Most foodstuff was still on ration and the cafés were doing a good trade as people enjoyed a meal without using their precious rations. Queues of customers spilled onto the pavement waiting for tables to be free, adding to the crush.

Rosita looked at her cocktail watch, a present to herself to celebrate her first shop. Her hair appointment was in less than five minutes and she hated to be late, to have to rush in, be fitted with a gown and sit in a chair without taking a moment to compose herself and decide what she wanted the hairdresser to do.

Monday morning wasn't normally a busy time – in fact, most salons were closed, so it was unlikely that the hairdresser was so busy she would have to wait, unless the holidaymakers were queuing there too. The seaside town welcomed and valued its summer visitors and the trippers who came for the day, but there were times when Rosita wished they had chosen a town other than her own!

She saw Auntie Molly Carey approaching and darted into a shop doorway. Later she wanted to see her, but not yet, not until she was ready. The elderly lady walked past and Rosita hurried on, thinking that her much-loved friend was now past the age for retirement. Goodness, how time had flown.

It was June 1950 and she reminded herself with a frisson of concern that she was approaching her thirty-third birthday. It was time she had made her mark and settled into the kind of life she wanted. Thirty-three was an age when most of her acquaintances were head of a growing family. Auntie Molly Carey had had ten children. She shuddered. That prospect was too horrifying for words, and far from the life she wanted for herself. She wanted success and money and a position of importance in the town. Today would see a big step taken towards that goal.

She reached the salon and went gratefully into the coolness and sank into a chair, putting the bag that held her new hat on the small table beside her.

'We are ready for you, Miss Evans, if you please,' the assistant said. 'Cutting, is it? Or just a shampoo and set today?' She pulled out a chair.

'A light trim, please, Megan. And I'll sit at this mirror, in the best light. I need to look my very best today.' Her voice was clipped, authoritative. She had an air of importance that made everyone, including the hairdresser, defer to her wishes.

Megan moved the tray of curlers from the place she had intended to use and moved to the place chosen by Rosita. Bending her client's head forward, she began washing her thick brown hair. Cut well it fell in a short under-roll, it held its shape well and always looked immaculate. Megan wondered about the important meeting that justified the extra appointment that was making Miss Evans a little on edge, but she dare not ask. Miss Caroline Evans did not encourage chatter.

An hour later, with her hair shining and in perfect shape, swinging below a hat of navy blue straw that tilted at an attractive angle to one side of her forehead, Rosita thanked the girl and left. She wore a smart linen suit of pale buttercup yellow that consisted of a button-through dress reaching just below the knee and a straight matching jacket with neat reveres and outside pockets that gave it a tailored look.

Nylon stockings flattered her shapely legs with a blocked heel and a clear, straight seam and her small feet bounced confidently in pale navy sandals that matched the hat. She looked what she was determined to be: a confident and successful businesswoman.

Her appointment was with the bank manager and he showed her to a chair and ordered tea. While he waited for it to arrive he chatted amiably about the weather, the crowds at the Pleasure Beach, which was 'doing better trade than usual with the holiday season hardly begun'. Rosita nodded politely although her mind was not on what he was saying but on the interview to come.

'Well, Miss Jones, about this loan.' She had used her own name for business transactions although no one, apart from Miss Grainger and the Careys, knew her other than Miss Caroline Evans. She noticed his voice had changed. Pleasantries finished, they got down to business.

Unperturbed by the briskness of his manner, Rosita gave him a brief outline of her plans and less than fifteen minutes later she left the quiet office with an agreement to borrow £600, with her shop as collateral and Miss Grainger as guarantor for the rest.

She telephoned her friend and told her the news and they promised themselves an evening of celebration: a theatre followed by supper somewhere grand and very expensive.

With the agreement clutched in her small hand, she caught the bus and, dressed as she was, so unsuitably, she caught a train and went to sit on the beach miles out of town which was so strongly associated with her blighted childhood.

The water was blue, reflecting the clear sky above, and looked tempting, although sea-bathing had never really appealed to her. She took off her sandals and stockings and walked to where the Careys' old house still stood: ruinous, in danger of collapsing at any moment. Sitting on the worn step where the Carey children had often sat to eat their meals, she thought back over the past years.

So much had happened since she had left the home and begun to live her own life. Years in which she had caught occasional glimpses of her mother but had never made herself known. Once, she thought her mother had stared straight through her, but the smart clothes, the glasses and the short hair had fooled her. Her mother and her half-sisters, Kate and Hattie, had left the town now and Rosita had no idea of their whereabouts. She didn't even know if they had survived the bombing during the war. They were part of the unpleasant past. The folded paper on which was written the agreement to borrow £600 was the future.

She had stayed in the dress shop until war had interrupted that comfortable existence and she'd had to choose whether to go into the forces or into a factory making munitions. She chose the factory simply because it offered more money. From the time she had escaped from the home, money had been her god.

Saving, and at the same time managing to give the impression of being used to better things, she ignored girls with whom she had to work, refusing to be accepted as one of them. The time in the factory was time in limbo, a time that had to be lived through before she could make progress.

As soon as war ended and people began to rebuild their lives, she had bought a small newsagents in Station Row and, while still working at the factory, gave a retired Miss Grainger the job of running it. With a young man dealing with the early hours between 5.30 and nine, and giving herself an hour each evening to deal with the books, they had managed very well.

With takings of £38 a week it wouldn't make them millionaires but it was a good beginning.

The sun reflecting off the sea hurt her eyes and she closed them. The warmth made her drowsy and she relaxed. The sea, high on the narrow beach and not far from her feet as she sat on the steps of the derelict house, soothed her like a lullaby. After the sleepless night and the anxiety of whether or not she would convince the bank manager of a woman's suitability to borrow money, she fell into a deep sleep.

She dreamed of Richard Carey, seeing him as the man/child who looked after his family when his kind but ineffectual father could not. He had been so strong and if he had been her brother she would never have been sent away, put in that home away from everyone she knew and cared about. But as she slowly emerged from sleep and dreams, to semi-alertness and fact, she remembered that today she was hoping to cheat him, just a little, and hoped that one day he would forgive her.

Her first thought when she was fully roused after lying for half an hour on the uncomfortable step was whether she had ruined her skirt. Feeling weak and foolish for succumbing to the temptation of a daytime doze like an old man, she looked around hoping no one had witnessed it. Then she rose, put on her stockings and sandals in the ruin of the Careys' old home, and walked briskly to the station.

It was after 5.30 when she went into the Careys' shop. They usually closed at six and Auntie Molly Carey was busy with a last-minute flurry of customers. Rosita stood near the door leading to the living rooms and waited. She looked cool as she always did but her heart was racing with anxiety.

'Go through and put the kettle on while I see to the till, will you, *fach*?'

'I've brought some cakes.' Rosita waved a paper bag. 'How many are home? I hope I've brought enough.'

'Only me and you and your Uncle Henry Carey, *cariad*.' Mrs Carey finished serving the last customer and closed the shop door, leaning on it with a sigh of relief. She looked tired, smaller and more frail every time Rosita called to see her. Rosita told herself she was doing the best for them. The very best.

She put the cakes she had bought onto a plate and looked at the name of the bakery on the torn bag: 'Rees's Fresh Cakes.' But the shop next door was in the process of closing down. Like two others in the same block, it had been sold and awaited its new owner. Rumours wove themselves around the prospective buyers but no one knew for certain who would be coming there when the last cake was sold.

'It's strange how sometimes things go in patterns,' Mrs Carey mused. 'All the shops have remained practically unchanged for years, more than three generations some of them, and now it seems that the whole block is in the process of change.' She felt a stab of panic. Looking at the young woman beside her, she asked anxiously, 'You are sure, love? What if you're making a mistake? What if the area changes so much the business fails? Success or failure is such a precarious thing. If the mix of shops is wrong, the area won't attract regular customers, and none of them will do well. It doesn't bear thinking about.'

Rosita licked her fingers inelegantly, savouring the smudge of cream from the cake, and took a deep breath. She felt a cheat, not being honest with Mrs Carey about what she had learned of the changes, but keeping your mouth closed was essential at times like these. This venture would succeed. She, Rosita Jones, had made sure of that.

'Have you and Uncle Henry Carey discussed it fully?' she asked when she was sitting with both of them later, a second cup of tea in front of them.

'I'm almost seventy,' Henry said, looking at his wife. 'Molly and I both think you're right. It's time we put our feet up and took things easy.' His thin face wore a martyred expression and silently Rosita thought he had rarely done anything else except take it easy! But she smiled, patted his hands sympathetically and agreed.

'You've worked hard all your lives. Now you can enjoy yourselves. I'll buy the shop and you can find a decent place to live.'

'I already have.' Molly smiled. 'Henry and I closed the shop for an hour at dinner time and went to look at it. Down overlooking the sand at Red Rock Bay it is, where we can go for walks, or sit and watch the children playing. Lovely it'll be.'

'Missed the sea, I have,' Henry said with a hint of the offended martyr in his voice again. 'All them years on the beach. Lovely it was, mind, even though it was a bit lonely. I missed it something terrible when we left there, you know. Beautiful it was, living at the edge of the sea. I only came here because it was best for the family.'

Uncle Henry's words left the usual irritation. She loved him dearly but had never been blind to his laziness. It was typical of the man to marvel over what he had gladly left behind years ago instead of appreciating what he had been given, Rosita thought.

'Must have people round us now, though,' Molly Carey added. 'After the years in the shop we'll need company, won't we, Henry?'

'We thought we'd get a dog, now dear old Patch has gone,' Henry added.

'I've seen to all the business side of things,' Rosita said. Then, crossing her fingers in child-like fear, she went on, 'You haven't been in touch with Richard, have you? Oughtn't he to be told what you're going to do?'

'The business is mine,' Henry said with pride. 'The whole bang lot! Richard hasn't been home since I – he got this place for us.'

Molly shook her head sadly. 'Went away before he was sixteen. Get a letter we do, from time to time, and always a card on birthdays and at Christmas. From somewhere up London way they come. But never a sight of him. Not even when he sent the money to buy the property after we'd rented it for years. It was all done through the banks and a solicitor. Not a sight of him, not once.'

Rosita sighed with relief. The last thing she wanted now was Richard Carey turning up and telling her she couldn't buy the place.

They all met at the solicitor's office a few days later and the sale was completed. Rosita went back to the house she and Miss Grainger still shared and told her of her success.

'I agreed that for a month Auntie Molly Carey can stay. They'll continue to run the shop and, during that time, they can get their own house sorted.'

'You still intend to run the shop yourself once they move out?' Miss Grainger queried.

'Why not?'

'It's very long hours and unless you close for an hour or so for lunch, you'll be on your feet from 5 a.m. until 6 p.m.'

'It will be hard, but until I find someone really suitable, that's what I intend doing. I've found someone to help you and I'm looking for someone to do at least part of the days for me.' Her eyes glowed as she turned to look at Miss Grainger. 'I've been so very lucky to have your help all these years.' In a rare moment of emotion, Rosita hugged her friend. 'We're on our way up now, and without you we couldn't have done any of it.'

'Nonsense, dear. If I hadn't happened along, someone else would have turned up. You were destined to do well.'

'Not always. Only after I realized the need for glasses and was shown the fascination of business and accounting – all down to you.'

At the railway station in the centre of the town, a man was alighting from the Cardiff train. He had been travelling for five hours and had left London behind, he hoped for good. The lovely June day was drawing to a close with a chill in the air, making him fasten the buttons of his dark grey overcoat.

Although the coat was no longer new, and a trifle small for his six-foot-three, broad-shouldered figure, he looked moderately smart, with a navy chalk-striped suit and a carelessly fastened blue-grey tie. A trilby covered the dark hair that grew curly and low on his neck. He wore rather gaudy grey leather shoes that would have made Rosita shudder with disapproval. His suitcases were battered and threatening to burst. A pair of braces had been tied round one to prevent his belongings from falling out for all to see. A pity, perhaps, as they would have made an interesting study.

The two cases contained a few items of clothing, bricklayer's tools, several textbooks on building and architecture, a battered enamel mug and, wrapped in greaseproof paper like sandwiches for a picnic, a great deal of money. The largest spirit level was too long to fit in either case and was carried over his shoulder in a canvas bag that had once housed a fishing rod.

Complete with all his worldly possessions, Richard Carey was home.

He didn't go straight to the newsagents, where his parents would have given him a jubilant welcome. With last-minute arrangements and a lot of travelling over the past week, he was exhausted. He went instead to a hotel, where he booked a room. Within thirty minutes of pushing through the hotel room door, he was asleep.

Rosita stood in the Careys' shop with Miss Grainger and began to fear she had made a terrible error of judgement. The place was far more neglected than she had realized. A visitor there ever since the Careys had taken it over, she had become so used to seeing it she had fallen into the trap of seeing nothing.

The shop was clean, the shelves well scrubbed, but more than half were empty. The walls were in dire need of decoration and the stock lacked variety and was far too low generally to satisfy the customers they hoped to encourage. Like everything Henry Carey had tackled, it had been half-heartedly done and what had been achieved was due to his wife's efforts.

The loan was going to be difficult to pay and money desperately needed to build up the business would be hard to find. The books had only told half the story. The stock listed was not there. Henry Carey's book-keeping was as efficient as all the other aspects of his idle life.

'The priority must be stock,' Miss Grainger said. 'If a customer comes in and doesn't find what he wants he won't bother to try us again.'

'You're right,' Rosita said. 'We'll spend a chunk of the bank loan filling the shelves and I'll go back to work.'

'But you can't. Who will run this place?'

'I'll find a girl to work during the hours I'm away. I'll manage the mornings and evenings.'

'Rosita, you really can't do this.'

'Not for ever I can't but for a month or so while we get this place on its feet, I must. I'm not going to give in and accept defeat, not after all our struggles.'

*

Rosita went to see the Careys at their home overlooking the beach later on Sunday after the shop had closed, determined not to allow her worries to show. The takings that first week had been frighteningly small and when she closed her eyes she could see debts and summonses piling up as a footpath to a gloomy future. She had lied to the bank manager and to the Careys so she could buy the shop and she wasn't going to let weakness show now. She held an ace, she reminded herself, and mustn't lose it. She had to survive until changes that were promised came about. Then she would make enough money to start an even better business. Survival until then was going to be a constant worry, balancing on a tightrope above certain failure, but survive she must.

'It's great, Auntie Molly Carey. You've left everything so clean there isn't a thing to do – just open the doors tomorrow morning and there I'll be, a businesswoman with two shops to her name.'

Mrs Carey smiled her pleasure at the praise. 'I worked till ten o'clock for the past week getting everything nice for you, *fach*. Glad you were pleased.'

'I'm thinking of putting in an assistant for a while. I half promised to help out in my old job if they were stuck. You don't know anyone who would do the job for me, do you?'

Mrs Carey thought for a moment and a fleeting idea came and then faded on her lined face. Watching her, Rosita guessed she had thought of someone then changed her mind.

'Who were you thinking of?' she asked. 'Come on, Auntie Molly Carey, I can read you like a balance sheet!'

'Well, I'm not sure. There is someone who is looking for a job but I don't know if she'll be suitable.'

'Tell me where I can find her and I'll decide once I've interviewed her. It was a man I was hoping for,' she lied, 'but a woman would be cheaper and easier to manage. I'd take on a woman for a trial period and see how we got on.'

'I think Kate would accept that. She's a quiet girl but hard-working.'

'How old is she?'

'Let me see.' Mrs Carey stared into space as she worked it out. 'She'd be about your age, I think. Perhaps a bit younger.'

An hour later, Kate arrived at the shop having been brought by Idris, the golden boy, who still managed to survive without working, although he was on the payroll while his parents owned the shop.

Rosita saw her coming through the shop door and felt the years slipping back. She was staring at her mother as a young woman. She turned to Mrs Carey, seeing agitation on her face. Pulling her aside, Mrs Carey said, 'Yes, before you ask, it's your half-sister, Kate.'

Through her shock and anger, Rosita stared at the smiling young woman approaching her. Then, unable to speak, she turned and ran into the room behind the shop. Mrs Carey followed.

'I know I should have told you. I was wrong and stupid. I just couldn't resist the opportunity of bringing you two together. Kate's a lovely girl – you and she would get on if only you'd give it a chance.'

'Does she know who I am?'

'No, I haven't said a word about you. There's no chance of her recognizing you either. You follow your father, Bernard Stock, and there's no sign of your mother in you, not like our Kate, who's the image of Barbara as she used to be.'

Looking through a crack in the door, Rosita stared at her half-sister, her emotions in turmoil. She saw a slim, shy young woman, dressed in a way that disguised her trim figure as if she were trying to hide from the world. Rosita's first thought was, no. This woman wouldn't have the necessary confidence for running a busy shop, but knowing that it was only for a few months, while they got the business on its feet and able to command a good price, she stopped to consider. There would be malicious pleasure in having the girl working for her, to give orders and know all the time that she was the sister who, together with her father and sister Hattie, had ignored her very existence from the age of five. Slowly, she walked back into the shop and held out her hand, watching the woman's face for the slightest sign of recognition. There was none. 'I am Miss Caroline Evans. Do you think you can help me run this business?'

'I'd like to try,' Kate said, smiling. 'My Idris hasn't been well, see, and work has been difficult. If I could earn something regular it will help. Only till he's really fit again, mind.'

That will take for ever, Rosita thought grimly. Thank goodness she'd had the sense to avoid marriage. What a mistake it would have been to become encumbered with an idle husband.

'Have you worked in a shop before?' she asked, trying to calm her shaking limbs. Really, meeting this woman had been worse than when a bomb had dropped on the factory!

'Well yes. I've often helped out when Mother-in-law needed an extra pair of hands.'

'Good she was, too.' Mrs Carey spoke proudly. 'Never needed telling more than once.'

'What did you do before you were married?'

'I worked in a school.'

'Very well. I'll work with you this week, and next week we'll see how you manage on your own. Just for a trial, mind, to see how we get on.' Any sign of malingering and she'd be out, half-sister or not, Rosita decided emphatically.

'Thank you. I'll be here at six for the morning papers.'

'No, I'll do the early shift. I'll expect you at eight.'

Kate hadn't mentioned wages and Rosita thought it wise to remain silent on that matter too. She wouldn't pay a generous wage but would lead the girl on with promises of something better once the trial period was over. If Kate was going to help until Idris felt able to work, she'd be there for a long time!

After Kate had gone to tell Idris the good news, Mrs Carey said, 'I'm sorry. That was a stupid thing to do.'

'Why didn't you tell me my sister was married to Idris?'

'I don't know. I avoided it for a while, afraid of you being upset, then, well, you know how it is, once you start a secret, the breaking of it becomes more and more impossible. I didn't want you to stop coming to see us. We love you like one of our own we do, me and your Uncle Henry Carey.'

'When did they marry?'

'Ten years ago. I introduced them one Christmas when your mam brought the girls to visit. They'd moved to Cardiff for a while see, and I thought that if you two ever met, then would be the time to tell you.'

'They have children?'

'Yes, Helen and Lynne, twins aged nine.'

'You haven't told her who I am?'

'No. Not a hint, I promise. I thought I'd wait and see how you felt about her knowing.'

'I don't want her told. There's no possibility of her recognizing me,' Rosita said bitterly. 'She didn't want to know all the years I was away and I don't want to know now. Right? Abandoned I was, considered a nuisance. And me only five years old. She hasn't seen me since. She didn't visit once, all the time I was in that home.'

'She won't learn who you are from me. You're Miss Caroline Evans. Good at keeping secrets I am,' she said sadly. 'All these years I've known where Richard is. And I haven't been able to tell a soul in case he's still wanted by the police.'

Rosita had been standing, agitated and ready to leave, upset by the recent revelations. Now she sat down again and stared at the woman, dumbfounded.

'You know where Richard is?' she asked, eyes wide with shock. What other surprises would this remarkable day reveal?

'More or less. He's working as a builder. Bricklaying and doing other things as well. Last I heard he'd passed some exam or other. Doing well he is. Got a business of his own, he says. Pity is he can't come and see us.'

'Why doesn't he come?'

'For a long time, he couldn't, afraid of the police catching up with him. Someone told on him, see. Then years passed and he says he doesn't have the time.'

Rosita walked slowly back home, her mind a jumble of confusing thoughts. Richard, her protector when no one else seemed to care, long disappeared from her life but never forgotten for a single day. She frowned as she counted up how long it had been since they had met. More than twenty years. Like her half-sister Kate, he wouldn't recognize her now, although she was certain she would know him the moment they met. If they ever did.

Amid the navy suits, black shoes and white mufflers of the local men in the public house, Richard Carey's clothes stood out. They were more fashionable and well cut. He was recognized as a stranger and curious faces stared towards him and a few braver souls questioned him, warily at first.

'Come far, have you, boy?' a small-featured elderly man asked.

'From a place not far from London,' Richard told him. 'Does it show that I'm not from round here?'

'Well, them clothes wasn't bought round here and that's a fact! Besides, we haven't seen you in here before and a bloke as big as you couldn't be overlooked for long, and that's a fact!'

'Saw you getting off the Cardiff train a couple of days ago,' another voice called. 'Said you was a foreigner then, with shoes that colour, didn't I, Joe?'

'Never seen anyone with grey shoes before. We don't see them around here,' the old man reinforced.

Richard chuckled. A foreigner, and him born not half a mile from where they were sitting!

He bought a round of drinks and left soon after, having amused himself by twisting their questions and his answers so he gave no further details of who he was or why he was there.

'Not one of them spivs from London, are you?' was the parting shot from the elderly Joe. 'My sister saw one of them and he sold her stockings cheap. One had three seams!'

Richard cut off the laughter as he closed the door behind him.

It was lunchtime and Richard had just visited the local Labour Exchange to seek some workmen. Demolition it would be first, then at last his big building project. He had worked for so long to set it up it was hard to believe it was within a few weeks of fruition.

It wasn't proving easy to find the sort of men he needed. Since the war had ended and the country had begun to recover, there had been a surge of new building and qualified men were in short supply. Still, first he had to get the demolition done, and by the time he was ready to employ brick-layers, plasterers and carpenters he would have found them.

He went to the bank to make sure his cheques had been cleared and saw to his satisfaction that he now had a healthy balance. That was beside the money he had not declared and which would soon be put to good use.

Now to visit his parents. He felt a surge of excitement tinged with anxiety as he turned the corner and headed for the small shop he had thought of so often during the years he had been away. It was smaller than he remembered. But he had been fifteen when he'd seen it last and from a child's eye level across the counter it would have seemed enormous. Now, he looked across it and stared at a rather elegant woman who stood beside the till.

'Where's Mam?' he asked.

'I'm sorry?' Kate said with a frown. 'I think you've made a mistake. This shop belongs to Miss Evans.' Attempting a smile she added, 'And I doubt she's old enough to be your mother.'

'Mr and Mrs Carey?' he asked. 'Where are Mr and Mrs Carey?'

'Well, I'm Mrs Carey,' she said suspiciously. 'Who are you?'

'Who are *you* dammit! And where can I find my mother?' Richard was irritated. Was this woman being deliberately perverse?

'I'm Mrs Idris Carey.'

'Oh. I'm sorry I was rude. I'm your brother-in-law, Richard.' He offered his calloused hand, which she took with some trepidation, alarmed by the large and wild-looking stranger. Then he sighed. 'Now will you tell me where I'll find Mam?'

She wrote down the address of the house above Red Rock Bay and suggested he took a taxi. It wasn't easy on the bus and it was difficult to explain how to find it.

'I'll find it. Having a day off, is she? Good of you to help.' Her mention of the shop belonging to Miss Evans hadn't penetrated.

He found a taxi, then changed his mind. If it was some distance away, perhaps he would deal with the final piece of business first. It might be too late otherwise. He hadn't been home for so long, another hour wouldn't matter. Business had to come first.

His purchase of the baker's shop was settled that afternoon and he had already made preliminary moves to buy the grocers on the other side of the Careys' shop. Just that final property to acquire – and that already verbally agreed – and the whole corner would be his.

He didn't go to his parents' house by taxi. He used some of his cash to buy a van. Asking the way and getting confused by the changes the bombing of ten years ago had wreaked on the town, it took longer than expected.

Not used to the van, and somewhat bemused by the casual attitude of other road users compared with drivers in the capital city, he drove slowly. He was cautious of driving too fast, even when the road was clear; he wanted to be sure he had a bargain. He drove carefully, stopping and starting, listening to the engine, checking the various dials and recognizing its idiosyncrasies. He thought it would do until he could afford a better one.

He parked outside the address Kate had given him and surprised his father, sitting on the porch in the early evening sun, dozing over a newspaper, a young puppy curled at his feet.

'Lazy devil. Is this what you call work?'

The shock on his father's face frightened him. For a moment he thought the old man was going to have a heart attack.

'Richard! Richard, my boy!' Henry shook as he rose to greet his son with arms wide, a sob distorting his features. Recovering slightly, he went to the door and called, 'Molly, come quick! It's – it's a dream come true, that's what it is.'

Molly screamed her delight and with both parents sobbing, they went inside. The furniture was familiar, they had changed very little and, as always, his mother's first thought was to put the kettle on and make tea.

'Leave that, Mam, I've got something better, look!' He took a bottle of wine from his overcoat pocket. 'Get some glasses then,' he laughed as they stared at it.

'Wine?' his mother queried. 'It isn't Christmas or anything.'

'Isn't having me home an "or anything" then?'

For four hours they talked, Richard explaining about how he started his business. Finally, he mentioned their new home.

'Why have you moved from behind the shop? You must have done well to be able to buy this.'

'Time we had a bit of comfort,' his father said, avoiding meeting his son's eyes.

'And having that wife of Idris's serving, so you can have a few hours off, that's a good idea. Getting on you are and should have time for yourselves. Still, I'll see to all that now I'm home. Life of leisure and pleasure, that's what you two will have from now on. We'll go out for a meal tomorrow and I can catch up on the rest of the news. Wait till you hear my plans, Dad.'

Henry made noises as if to say something but started coughing instead.

'Tell me, boy, what are your plans now you're back? Home for good, are you?'

'You bet. I've got a surprise for you. I've bought all four properties around our shop and I'm going to knock the whole lot down. This time next year there'll be a spanking new block of flats on the corner where all those shops are. What d'you think of that?'

'You can't!' Molly looked at her husband and instinctively went to stand beside him. 'Richard, love, you can't.'

'Of course I can. Don't worry, Mam, it's all legal and above board. Everything I do now is legitimate. Well, almost,' he added with a grin. 'People are desperate for new homes and planning permission will be easy to obtain now I own all the properties in question.'

'But you don't.' Henry's voice was little more than a whisper. 'Sold it we did. The shop is no longer ours.'

The words so softly spoken seemed to bounce around the room. Richard's eyes opened wide in fright. The shock was so great that lights jazzed at the periphery of his vision. 'You've sold my shop? *My* shop that I worked and stole and saved to buy?'

'Wait till you know who bought it,' Henry said, gripping his wife's hand nervously. He'd known it was wrong. Hadn't he tried to tell her and Rosita it was wrong?

'I don't care who bought it! It wasn't yours to sell!'

'But it was! You told me it was ours!'

'Richard!' his mother wailed as he stormed out.

The door slammed behind him and he stood outside beside his father's empty chair, trembling with disbelief and fear and sheer frustration. What a mess! Would there ever be a way out of the debts this would mean? He turned and glared at the door behind him, kicking it in rage. After all these years of deals, struggles, doing without, working around the clock, sometimes for weeks on end, to have everything ruined like this by his useless father!

What could he do now? He was committed to an enormous loan. The big gamble was lost. At the eleventh hour, Lady Luck was calling in all bets.

Chapter Eleven

RICHARD LEFT THE house he had joyfully entered a few hours before with rage in his heart. How could his parents have been so stupid? The shop had been his, acquired first by stealing and then committing robberies when he was hardly more than a child. Since then he had saved for and bought what he now owned with hard cash. Hours of back-breaking work, living an impoverished life, sometimes in unbelievable squalor and discomfort, always with the minimum of needs. All for the big plan which, because of his father's stupidity and laziness, he was now about to see fall into ruin.

He drove the van back and parked it outside the newsagents, where he could see anyone approaching from either direction as well as the counter inside, and waited. His anger had cooled a little by the time he saw a smartly dressed woman step inside and slip behind the counter. So, it was a woman who owned it. Was that what his mother had been so anxious to tell him? Man or woman, he would go in and tell them that the shop had not been his father's to sell and he wanted it back.

The dissipated anger and the delicacy with which he'd have to deal with a woman, whose help he knew he would desperately need, slowed his steps and made him a fraction less confident. The next few minutes were going to be the most important in his life.

He waited until there were several customers inside before he went towards the counter, to give himself time to look around and decide how he would broach the subject.

The shelves were filled and neatly arranged, the edges decorated with frilled paper. Pens and writing paper filled a corner, a selection of pipes another, with a good display of lighters, fuel and flints close by. A rack of postcards with both comic and local views were on a stand near the window. The cigarettes, cigars and tobacco were on a shelf behind the till, with the small brass scales with which to weigh out half ounces and ounces of the loose tobacco.

The loose tobacco was as he remembered it, he noticed, as he watched a customer being served with an ounce of dark shag. The tall round tin still had a circle of damp flannel on top to keep the contents moist. Behind the neat display of magazines was a glass cabinet advertising Cadbury's. Inside were rows of chocolate bars in their blue wrappers.

Extra lights hung from the ceiling, which also had cards and small gifts on coloured string to entice buyers. The two young women laughed as they served and altogether the atmosphere was of brightness and cheerful friendliness. He was lost. This wasn't the drab little place he remembered. How could he find the money to buy this? His nerves jangled in alarm.

'Can I help you, Richard?'

'Yes, Kate, you can. You can introduce me to the owner, please. I want an urgent word.'

'Caroline Evans,' Kate said with a smile. 'Caroline, this is my brother-in-law, Richard Carey.'

Rosita felt the floor tremble as her body reacted to the shock. She stared at him, unable to speak. He wasn't really looking at her, his dark eyes continuing to look around the shop, wondering at the transformation that he hadn't noticed on his earlier visit. When he remained silent, Rosita attempted to calm herself and she gestured to Kate to leave them.

'I'll make us some tea, shall I,' Kate suggested. 'Nice to have a cuppa before we deal with the till.'

'No, it's all right, you can go. I'll see to things here.' When Rosita finally spoke, her voice sounded to her like that of a stranger. Richard had still not really looked at her. He stood with his hands in his trouser pockets, jacket hanging loose, tie carelessly knotted, gazing about him, obviously waiting for the assistant to leave. Rosita stood, one small hand on the counter, a picture of calmness, and studied him.

He would be about thirty-eight now, and his dark hair was already sprinkled here and there with grey. The well-remembered eyes that were surprisingly blue, although they looked dark enough to be brown, were surrounded by a fine network of lines. But his face looked strong and lean; no sign of him slipping into the obesity of middle age although he was a large man. She thought of skinny Mr Carey and his even thinner wife and wondered how Richard had attained such a size, especially on the poor diet of his childhood.

On the periphery of her vision she saw Kate wave goodbye and she responded, but her actions were dreamlike. After so many long years of imagining him grown to a man, Richard Carey was here, standing in front of her. She was waiting for Richard to look at her, wondering if he would recognize her after so long. She fervently hoped so. It was important.

Richard watched as the shop door closed behind his sister-in-law. He knew he should have said something to her, arranged to go and see Idris, but he couldn't. Not until this shop business was settled. With him it had always been business first.

He prepared a polite smile and turned at last to face the woman whom he would have to persuade to sell his shop back to him, and gasped in disbelief.

'Rosita!'

'Richard.' She wished the counter wasn't between them. If she had been uncluttered by its protection she knew he would have taken her in his arms and hugged her, but he couldn't. Not with the counter blocking her from him. Apart from his parents, he was the only person in the world who might have hugged her and the opportunity was gone. Although her thoughts were still in turmoil, she remained still, her hand resting, unmoving, on the wooden counter.

'When did you get back?' she asked, still in the strange voice. 'Have you seen your mam and dad?'

'They tried to tell me it was you who had bought the shop but I didn't give them a chance.'

'Then you didn't know I was here? You recognized me at once?'

'Of course I did. Mind, I saw you crossing the road and come inside and I confess I didn't know you then. You hardly look the same as that unhappy kid I last saw. But looking at you now, I knew straightaway, even with the addition of glasses and the loss of your long hair.' He smiled, the creases around his eyes deepening. 'You've grown very beautiful, Rosita.'

His gaze strayed to her hand and she knew he was looking for a ring on her third finger. She wished there was as simple a way to find out about him. The state of marriage didn't have a recognizable symbol for a man.

'Surprised that I bought the shop?' She smiled at him, able at last to relax a little. 'It's the second one I own. The other is at the other end of town, in Station Row, run by a dear friend of mine.'

'I'm not surprised that you've made a good life for yourself. When you have a childhood as down as ours, there's only one way to go and that's up. But my shop, well, that's why I came, Rosita. It wasn't Dad's to sell. I want you to sell it back to me.'

She was shocked, hurt, dismayed, but her hand still rested on the counter, the expression on her face still showed apparent calm. She didn't know what she was expecting after he walked in, but it wasn't this.

'You do understand, don't you?' he went on as she didn't reply. 'It's mine and the mistake can easily be rectified.'

Disappointment finally broke the spell he had cast and she tightened her lips and said, 'What? Sell this place? You must be crazy! I'd be ruined!'

'Don't let's talk about it now. Come and have a meal with us. I'm taking Mam and Dad out later – if I don't kill him first,' he added, in an attempt to make her smile.

She shook her head, the slick hair moving then returning to its immaculate place. 'I don't think so, Richard. Today belongs to your parents. I won't intrude.'

He recognized the firmness behind the softly spoken words and shrugged.

'Tomorrow?'

'I might be free in the evening.'

'I'll come here for you at six.'

'Us,' she said and again he felt the edge of her determination. 'My partner will come with us too. If you want to talk business then we must both be included.' She looked at him, wondering if there was a hint of disappointment in his eyes.

'Great,' he said. 'I look forward to meeting him.' He *was* disappointed. Dealing with a man would be more difficult, he thought.

'Her!' she said and saw a brief look of relief on his face.

After he had gone she slammed the bolts home on the shop door and told herself she was being stupid. Why should she even begin to think of Richard coming back into her life after a gap of so many years? Yet it had been her dream. A picture of him as she had imagined he would look was everpresent in her dreams. He was the only person from her childhood she could call a friend.

She pulled herself up angrily. She was nothing better than a daydreaming child, drooling over some hoped-for treat. He was married. Of course he was married. Probably taking his wife to meet his parents for the first time that evening.

She counted the money in the till and put it with the relevant form in the bank's overnight bag. She was glad she had included Miss Grainger in the meeting arranged for the following evening. But, she promised herself, she would dress as attractively as possible. After all, in a life barren of love, Richard was her solitary claim to having once had a boyfriend. She planned her outfit as she walked to the bank and dropped the bag into the night-safe.

Hoping the weather would be kind, she had chosen a summer dress in a floral print that was basically a pale green, with a full skirt, short sleeves and a low, square neck frilled around its edge that daringly revealed the swell of her breasts. She knew that it showed her slender figure at its best. High-heeled white shoes and a small leather bag with long straps to swing on her arm gave just the impression she wanted, casual and easy. A summer straw hat added to the effect she wanted to create. Over her shoulders she threw a white, lacy stole.

Miss Grainger wore a cotton dress too, only hers was navy trimmed with white, with which she wore navy accessories. Her friend looked neat but businesslike, and Rosita smiled at her with affection. 'You're dressed perfectly for the occasion, as always. Tonight, I feel more frivolous.'

To her surprise, Richard wore the same shabby suit that was minus a button and scuffed grey shoes which showed splashes of mud. The shirt was loose, the trousers in need of pressing. He looked as though he were about to unravel and her expression showed her disapproval.

Sensing her reaction, he explained. 'Sorry I haven't changed. I've been in business meetings all day and you don't want to look too prosperous when you're negotiating to buy something.' In fact, he had only the clothes he stood up in and they were second-hand. He had used all his available money to invest in property and equipment.

'Held your meetings in a field, did you?' Rosita stared pointedly at his shoes.

'Building sites are synonymous with mud,' he said with an apologetic smile.

They ate at a restaurant near the old harbour, where boats lay drunkenly in the thick glutinous mud of a receding tide.

It brought Luke to Richard's mind and he wondered if the man had ever forgotten the horrors of the Flanders mud. 'Have you ever heard from Luke?' he asked Rosita.

'Only that he and a friend had a café in Calais. Since the war ended I've heard nothing. I hope he's safe.'

For a while they talked about the beach and the times they had spent with the solitary man, including Miss Grainger in their reminiscences.

As they pushed away their plates and declined offers of coffee, Richard said, 'Rosita, I want to buy back my father's shop.' He tried not to let his anxiety show. Leave something in reserve, he told himself. Pleading would come when all else had failed. 'If I sell Mam and Dad's house I can buy it and give you enough profit to set you up in something similar. What d'you say?'

'No, Richard.'

He shrugged and looked at her, wondering how to deal with her implacability. 'We'll discuss it later.' Again he had felt the edge of determination in the quiet voice and he wondered if he dared explain. Perhaps not. He hardly knew this young woman, so much had happened to them both since the years in which he had been her protector and she his adoring friend. He forced a smile. This was going to be difficult.

He would have to be patient, although finances dictated that patience wouldn't allow more than a week, or two at the most. A month and he would be edging towards bankruptcy and would have to sell all the properties he had struggled so hard to buy.

Coolly, he wondered if romance might be the answer. It wouldn't be difficult to spend some time with her; she was a desirable woman. There was clearly a core of steel within her mind, of course. Perhaps around her heart too, but love had softened many a resistant heart.

They went back to the house, which both women had been loath to sell, even with the prospect of a third shop, and after coffee Rosita left Miss Grainger dealing with the cups and walked with him to the door. She was very aware of him as he leaned over and touched her cheek lightly with his lips.

'Thank you for coming,' he said. 'I like your Miss Grainger very much. You've been lucky having a friend like her.'

'I owe her everything,' she said simply, the words coming from her head while her heart raced and silently pleaded for him to kiss her properly.

He leaned on the wooden gate that had replaced the metal one taken for wartime scrap, and looked back at her. The late-evening light disguised his expression, the trilby hat casting a shadow over his eyes, so she could only imagine the smile as he said, 'Come out with me again, soon?'

'Soon,' she agreed. 'Richard, will you promise me something?'

'Anything.'

'Promise not to tell Kate that I am her half-sister. The name I now use is Caroline Evans, so my real identity hasn't registered with her yet. And of course after so long she doesn't know me by sight. All the years between when I was five and now, neither Kate nor Hattie ever bothered about me. I don't want them to suddenly become my sisters. Not now. Will you promise not to mention who I really am?'

'If you're sure, but I'd have thought that with no family, having someone—'

'Promise me.'

He gave that expressive shrug of his and nodded. 'I promise.'

'Thank you.'

'And will you promise me that you'll think about what we've discussed?'

'Goodnight, Richard.' She turned and went in, closing the door without a final glance.

'He has charm, your Richard Carey,' Miss Grainger said when Rosita went inside. 'D'you think we should sell to him? I think it's more important than he admits.'

'I thought I was so clever.' Rosita sank into a chair and covered her cheeks with her hands. 'When I heard that the other shops in the row were being bought up by a mystery buyer, that ours would be worth a lot more than the true value, I imagined us being able to demand a price much higher than we paid – from an anonymous stranger, a businessman who deserved to have to fight for his profit. I knew that if he bought the others then he was bound to want ours too. I tried to cheat the Careys by buying at a low price before they were approached by this mysterious buyer.'

'Not cheat them, dear. You would never have seen them without. You're a far better businesswoman than Henry Carey and half a dozen others combined. Our second shop is already worth more than we paid, without any deals.'

'But they'd have made more if they'd waited.'

'Perhaps. Perhaps not. I can't see Henry haggling with anyone, can you? No, seeing the money waved in front of his face he'd have sold for less than you paid them, without a doubt.'

'What shall we do?'

'That depends on how you feel about Richard, I suppose. We should wait and, if we decide to sell, see how much we can raise his offer. But he must be stretched financially. There is the possibility that if we wait too long, Richard Carey might lose everything.' She touched Rosita's hand. 'Could you cope with that?' she asked gently.

'No, I don't think I could.'

'Talk to him. Invite him here for a meal and I'll go to the pictures. Whatever you decide will be all right by me. You know I trust your judgement absolutely.'

'Thank you.'

The following day was a Thursday and, pleading a headache, Rosita left the office in the factory where she had worked for almost eleven years and caught the train over to the beach near Gull Island. It had always been her retreat, a place where she could go to think out a problem. Before buying the first shop and when she was working out the best way of approaching the purchase of the Careys' business, it had always been done here, on the lonely stretch of rocky shoreline.

The sun blazed down on the rocks and it was difficult to find somewhere comfortable to sit. There wasn't much shade and in desperation she walked to where Luke's cottage stood, cool and inviting. Without much optimism she tried the door and found it unlocked. Feeling like a thief, she went inside.

Her mother had often talked about this place and the man who lived there called Luke. She remembered him vaguely, a thin, small man with a ridiculously extrovert sense of dress. She smiled, remembering his long beard and the odd spectacles, the casual corduroy trousers and the bare feet in leather sandals. She cast her mind back, seeing him as he jumped into his open-topped car. The leather jacket and the goggles that fitted over his glasses.

She sat in the chintz-covered chair and wondered where he was at that moment and whether he would remember her as readily. Closing her eyes she allowed the heat of the day to fade from her skin in a slow pulsing beat. It was a restful place. Simply furnished, in fact rather sparse, but there were some wild flowers in a vase on a polished table, beside a pile of books, the blooms almost dead, falling across the polished surface in a scattering of yellow dust. Someone came here often.

When she felt cool again, she took out a notebook from her handbag and began to write down roughly what she and Miss Grainger had spent since buying the Careys' shop. To cover what they had invested on improvements and fresh stock, and the cost of the loan from the bank and the legal fees, they would need a couple of hundred pounds on top of what they had paid.

She threw down the pen in exasperation. This is stupid! Selling a business so soon after buying it would be against all business practice. She must refuse. Without the special deal she had hoped to make it was impossible. A business needed to be kept for a few years, nurtured and coaxed along, until the expense of taking over had been met, swallowed and a profit had been made. Unless the buyer was desperate and he needed the property so badly he would pay more than it was worth. She thought that was the case, until she learned that it was Richard Carey who was the desperate person in question. Now everything had changed.

She felt uneasy. Pride at her cleverness, excitement at what she intended to achieve had all changed to guilt in the moment when she had looked up and seen Richard. The move, so smart at the outset, seemed immoral now she knew the buyer. What had been a good business move, to sneak in and buy something she knew someone else wanted urgently, now seemed a terrible cheat. Damn Richard Carey. Why did he choose this moment to come back into her life?

The more she looked at the figures, the more she knew that it was impossible to sell. There were still bills coming in for various repairs they'd had to do. It would be the greatest folly to sell now.

An anonymous builder with a large corporation behind him would have been different. The costs would have been met from a large purse. She had anticipated staying for probably a year, then taking a generous offer and getting out and finding a shop better placed, or even two small kiosks. Now, everything had altered, as if stirred into a mish-mash by a giant spoon. She didn't know what to do next.

The sun was still scorching as she opened the door and went outside. With a stronger feeling of trespass, but knowing Luke would understand, she drew water from the pump and made herself a cup of tea. She remembered her mother telling her about the visits she had made. 'No milk,' Luke had warned her, 'but with sugar it's quite palatable.'

She sipped the brew and washed the cup. It was time to go. There was no point sitting here thinking of what she could or couldn't do; better to go and help Kate with the evening rush. At least that would serve some purpose.

Crossing the narrow road that was little more than a track, she walked slowly along the rough surface of the beach, past the house where the Careys had once lived, jumping from rock to rock, choosing the most difficult route to distract her mind from her worries, until she came to the lane leading up to the station approach. Her shoes were scratched, the leather on the heels torn beyond repair. She was so distressed by the decision she had to make, she hardly noticed.

The station was small and not well used. It had been built to serve the needs of the workmen in the quarry and wood yard, both of which were now closed. The station remained open mainly for the summer visitors although their numbers had fallen, first with the wartime barriers blocking off access to many parts of the beach, then with the growing popularity of holidays abroad for people able to afford the luxury of guaranteed sunshine. Rosita was the only one offering a ticket to the station master who stood as if expecting a rush: uniform neat, shoes as shiny as any soldier's and his ticket machine at the ready.

The train came from Cardiff, puffing and snorting, sending clouds of smoke and sooty specks up into the blue sky, dwarfing the solitary passenger waiting for the monster to stop and allow her to step into the brown and yellow carriage. She found a seat near a window, glad of the escape from the blazing sun and from her thoughts that were getting her nowhere.

She didn't notice a passenger alight and walk off down the approach towards the beach. His small steel-framed spectacles gave him a foreign appearance, although he was Welsh. His beard was long but so thin his narrow face was hardly hidden by its dirty yellow and grey veil. Heads in the carriage turned to watch him pass. The station master nodded and greeted him.

'Evening, sir. Lovely evening.'

'For some, station master, for some,' Luke replied.

Luke had just returned from France, where he had spent a week in a forlorn attempt to find Martine. Since his hasty departure in 1940 he had lost touch with her. He had been back many times and searched the area and the records offices for news of her but she had vanished.

Their café was a ruin, the farm where Martine had lived with her father gone completely under a new housing development. Blocks of flats had grown where there had once been fields, woods and wild flowers. No one knew the whereabouts of Martine, although many remembered the café and the music and the laughter they had shared.

Entering the cottage that afternoon, his senses told him someone had been there recently. The perfume in the air was expensive and he wondered for a moment if his sister had come to investigate the fate of the family's holiday cottage. But no. Why should she come? The place was his now, bought on his behalf by Jeanie, so the family didn't know he was the owner. He reflected with renewed sadness that the deception had been necessary. His sister would have refused to sell if she had known her pariah of a brother was the purchaser. Hatred hadn't ended with his father's life.

He had wondered how to spend his few hours off. The shops in Cardiff hadn't appealed, and he couldn't have stayed in his stuffy flat. Now he was here he thought about fishing, but was too lethargic. It would be deliciously cool on the water but hot work rowing out to a suitable place. He picked up a book and read for a while then walked on the beach, then slept.

As he sat in the chair recently vacated by Rosita, he thought about his life. He was getting old. It was really time to do something about finding Rosita if he was ever to do so. But where could he start? She could be hundreds of miles away. He had made several abortive attempts but the trail had gone cold. He was horrified to realize how many years had passed since he had last tried to find her. His only memory of her was that sad little girl bruised from beatings at Graham's farm.

The evening with Richard did not go well. Rationing was still making meals difficult to plan and Rosita began to wish she had suggested they ate out rather than have to use all her week's meat ration to make a spaghetti bolognaise. She and Miss Grainger forfeited their sweet ration to buy chocolate and scrounged some eggs for which they paid sixpence halfpenny each, and Miss Grainger made them a rich, creamy mousse.

The meal was successful and as they ate they talked, mostly about their childhood. Richard decided to tell her the truth and when they sat with a pot of coffee in front of them, he said, 'If you don't sell me the shop I will be broke within a few weeks.' If he expected immediate capitulation he was disappointed. For a moment they stared at each other, both trying to show their position, Richard pleading, hoping for her sympathy, Rosita cool and determined. Richard decided to explain the situation fully.

'I came out of the army in 1946 with £300,' he told her. 'I bought an old wreck of a cottage with a large garden and knocked it down and built two houses on the plot. With a bricklayer who became my business partner, I borrowed money, delayed paying bills, cut costs how and wherever I could, and finally sold and made a reasonable profit.

'My partner Monty and I survived on as little as was humanly possible for years. We lived in a shed, surviving on fish and chips, apples and beer, and we used every penny we made to buy more land, and we built two larger houses. After that, still living rough, in a caravan by this time, we built a row of five houses, and made enough to get into reasonably sized contracts.

'But instead of acting cautiously and looking for more land, I persuaded Monty to take a big risk. We ploughed all our money into the houses around ... my shop.' He glanced at her as he emphasized the penultimate word. 'I had plans drawn up for a block of flats, the council have given me the go-ahead, and I come home to find my shop, the kingpin of all our hopes, has been sold in my absence by my father.'

'*Your* shop? Come off it, Richard! The deeds and everything else were in your father's name. It was his to sell, so why should I feel guilty?'

'I don't want you to feel guilty, you did nothing wrong. But we were almost family, you and I. Come on, love, you can't really believe you can get away with such a shabby trick, not now you know? Look, I'll see a solicitor tomorrow and get this unfortunate muddle sorted out.' He didn't see her expression change as he went on, 'Just leave it to me – you don't want to worry your pretty little head about this. This is man's work sorting out solicitors and accountants. Relax and leave it all to me.'

It was the worst approach he could have made.

His condescending attitude made Rosita's moments of guilt fade like a sea fret in the sun. Stiffening her back and moving away from him, she said frostily, 'I have no intention of selling *my* shop, Richard. To you, or anyone else.'

'Be sensible. You can't do this to me, Rosita. You can't.'

'Watch me!'

She had been prepared to come to some agreement in which they could both have benefited. The new stock she had bought could have been sold at her other shop and there were properties she could have bought. If it had meant waiting until Richard was able to free the money to pay her, she, with Miss Grainger's approval, would have accepted that. But when he tried to almost bully her with a smile, treating her like some downtrodden, foolish female, she had cancelled all inclination to find a compromise.

'I'm damned if I'll do what you ask,' she said, standing up and picking up their coffee cups, tacitly asking him to leave. 'I am a businesswoman not some poor, quaking little woman afraid to disagree with a tall, handsome male!'

He risked a grin. 'So you think I'm handsome, then?' He stepped towards her, an attempt to put his arms around her apparent in the gesture. She stepped backwards and away from the enticing invitation.

'Nowhere handsome enough!' she snapped. 'And as a business move, a smile and a hug for the little woman doesn't stand a chance of changing my mind! Several have tried that approach before you and got nowhere. Now will you go before I pour the rest of this coffee over your disgusting suit.'

Richard left the house and hurried down the street. From a phone box he spoke to his partner Monty, who was still in London, and explained in brief the problems they faced. 'Can you come down when you've sewn up all the ends there?' Richard pleaded. 'I know you were going to have a holiday, but I don't know how to get around this hurdle.'

Monty agreed and Richard felt easier. Between them they would persuade Rosita to capitulate and let them get on with their plans to build the smart new flats. She would give in, in the end. Unless he and Monty were to be bankrupt, she *had* to agree.

Monty was a widower with two growing sons. He had willingly invested money he raised by selling his house in Richard's business ventures. He had already decided to leave his sons with the aunt who had reared them while he had been in the army, before Richard had made the suggestion of a partnership. The boys were settled in their life and, at seventeen and fourteen, thought of him more of a kindly uncle than a father.

Of the two men, Richard was the one with the real business flare and daring, Monty the equally important small, calm voice. Richard knew that if he failed in this, their largest undertaking, his worst sadness would be for the losses suffered by his loyal friend and partner.

It was not yet ten o'clock, perhaps time to see his brother Idris and get that unpleasant task out of the way. The day had been a bad one from the start, so he might as well end it on the same note!

He had the address of the terraced house on Walpole Street but as he went towards it he decided to sit and cool down before reviving his acquaintance with his brother. The meeting with Rosita had left him tense and not a little angry.

There was just time for a pint and he headed for the public house on the corner. A car passed as he waited to cross the road. It slowed as it reached the junction and he glanced at the driver for the nod that he could proceed. He also saw that there was another person, a woman, slumped down in the passenger seat as if hiding. He was curious and it was only after he had entered the public house that he realized he had just seen his brother, Idris.

It must have been his wife Kate in the car with him. Perhaps she was ill? Abandoning the drink he had bought, he went out and knocked on his brother's door.

'Richard? Come in! I'm so pleased to see you.' Kate stepped back for him to enter. 'What a pity, you've missed Idris. Gone to see your mam and dad, he has. He often goes in the evening, after the children are in bed. Glad of a bit of company, they are.'

It was eleven o'clock when Idris returned and he shook Richard's hand then hugged his wife.

'I'll leave you two to talk – there must be lots to catch up on.' Kate smiled. 'But first I'll make some cocoa, shall I?'

'Hello, brother of mine. I wondered when you'd get round to calling.'

'I saw you earlier,' Richard said in a low voice, staring at his blond-haired, blue-eyed and still very handsome brother. 'Passed me in a car just outside the pub on the corner.'

They looked at each other and their eyes showed there was still animosity between them. 'Did you now? Well, there's a surprise. Pub first, eh? I didn't rate myself and Kate lower in your affections than the need for a pint of beer.'

Idris offered no explanation of the mysterious passenger sitting so low in the car that she was barely visible, so Richard added nothing more. Instead he went straight to the root of his troubles.

'Idris, why didn't you stop Dad from selling my shop?'

'Why should I? They're both old in case you haven't noticed. Time for them to relax instead of minding the shop for someone who hadn't seen them in twenty-three years.'

'Yes, it's twenty-three years since you told the police that I was the one breaking into houses and taking cash, isn't it, Idris? I was just a child, trying to feed us all.'

'I don't believe it!'

Kate returned with a tray and saw the two men glaring at each other like dogs about to close in deadly battle.

'Don't worry, you did me a favour, although I didn't think so at the time. Idris, I need that shop and the new owner is being difficult about selling it to me.'

'She wouldn't be any problem to me!' Idris winked at Kate and went on, 'A bit of a tart like Miss Evans? I'd soon persuade her to be nice to me if she had something I wanted.'

'Idris!' Kate laughed. 'Don't talk about my boss like that.'

Richard tensed his jaw and wanted oh so badly to punch his brother. But he remembered his promise not to reveal to Kate that she worked for her half-sister and he swallowed his outrage. Enmity between Idris and himself would never fade. The air trembled between them even on this, their first meeting for more than twenty years.

Two days later, Richard went to the station to meet the train bringing his friend and partner Monty. He'd hated asking Monty to abandon his plans for a holiday with his sons, but circumstances merited the urgency. The quiet time Monty had hoped for, while the deal Richard had set up was clarified and details settled, was no longer possible. Once Monty had heard of the difficulties, he had agreed to come at once.

His friend's calm face was balm to Richard's troubled mind and as he picked up Monty's suitcases and walked to the van, he felt that already things were improving.

A room had been booked for him at a small boarding house and when he had unpacked, they went to a café, ate, and talked.

'You'd better start at the beginning, Richard. Tell me everything that happened from the moment you walked into the shop we thought was ours.'

Monty was quiet for a while after Richard had finished explaining. Richard waited patiently for his friend to assimilate the information.

'This house your parents have bought, will you be able to sell it easily?'

'I suppose we might, although we're bound to lose money, with legal fees and everything.'

'The first thing we must do is find them a place to rent and put the house on the market.' He frowned then, and said slowly, 'Richard, I suppose they did buy this place? They didn't rent it and put the money in the bank, did they?'

'Of course they bought it. I mean, why would they rent when they had the money to ...' As the words came out of his mouth they lost momentum. Would his father have rented rather than spend an amount of money larger than he had ever seen in his life? The more he thought about it the more likely it became. Throwing the money for their meal on the table, he grabbed Monty's arm and hurried to the van.

'It's the most unlikely hope in the world, but it's the only hope we have! And I won't rest until I've asked.'

Jumping out of the van, they ran down the small streets to the row of houses near Red Rock Bay and banged impatiently on the Careys' door. Richard had a key but he was too excited to search for it. Taking a deep breath, he asked the question that would go a long way towards achieving their goal.

'Seventeen shillings a week we pay rent,' his mother told them, nervously. 'We could have found somewhere cheaper, mind, but we like it here, near the beach and we thought you wouldn't mind.'

'Mind? Mam, I'm as pleased as – Heavens above, you're the best mam a man could ever have!'

He picked her up and danced her around the room, then Monty introduced himself and did the same.

Chapter Twelve

THE FACT THAT the money from the sale of the shop was still available was an enormous comfort to Richard and Monty, but it didn't go any way to meet the real hurdle. Rosita still refused to sell them the property they so urgently needed.

Whenever Richard tried to discuss it with her, he made things worse. Dealing with her was like trying to juggle with red-hot pokers. Appealing to her sense of fair play only added to her determination not to give an inch. Trying the romantic approach only earned him an earful of abuse. If anything, it was the romantic approach that brought out the worst response. To add to his feeling of frustration, the romantic approach was beginning to be less and less a ploy and more and more a reality.

His many creditors were beginning to press. The council were at the point where a decision and a date for the work to commence was an urgent necessity. Sleeping in his parents' spare room, renamed by him as the spare-me-from-this room, on a narrow iron bedstead, with ill-fitting curtains and bare floorboards, was a luxury after some of the places he had called home, but he was beginning to wonder if he would ever achieve anything better.

If only Rosita could be persuaded to give up the shop, things would all slot neatly into place. Everything was poised for him to succeed. If she refused he was going to join the thousands who never quite make it, those with egg on their faces who always end up with nearly-but-not-quite situations in life.

He stood at the top of Red Rock Bay and looked down at the sands. There was no future in looking for a miraculous change of heart. There was nothing more he could do. No words he could find to persuade her. He was beaten. It was pointless to keep going over and over the facts, looking for a chink of hope. He had to face it. He and Monty were finished.

Still staring down at the empty beach, he began to consider the best way to scrape enough money together to give Monty back most of what he had invested. If he could settle his friend's debts and return his investment, his conscience would be at least saved that burden. He got into the van and drove off to look for him.

When he told Monty of his decision, Monty wouldn't hear of it.

'No, Richard. When I became your partner I was prepared to accept the fortunes we might have made. Like a good gambler, I'll accept that we didn't succeed. Now, why not go away somewhere and think about a fresh way to tackle Miss Jones?'

Instead of addressing his many problems, Richard spent more and more time contemplating a life of comfort with Rosita. What if he resold the properties he had bought and went into partnership with her? A newsagent chain was not what he had hoped for in his middle and old age, but it was tempting.

Then he would shake himself out of such a cowardly retreat. No. He would persuade her somehow. She had to give in and let him buy the shop. There was the tricky problem of getting rid of the shops on either side of the newsagent, places they already owned. Selling empty properties in a far from excellent state of repair wouldn't get back what the places had cost when they were still viable businesses.

Back to Rosita. She remained the only one to help them. How could he persuade her? He couldn't go cap in hand and beg. Not to a prickly woman like Rosita. Yet somehow he had to get that last shop and build those flats. Once that had been achieved he would make money at a faster rate than she could imagine. He'd show her what business was all about! But first he had to gain her confidence and persuade her to help.

It was a burglar that changed things in his favour. An unknown person who, like Richard had once done, broke into a house to steal.

The house shared by Miss Grainger and Rosita was on a corner with gardens on three sides. It was empty for long hours of each day, with both women working at the shops and, in Rosita's case, at the factory as well. So it was unfortunate that when the man decided to break in and take what he could find, it was during Miss Grainger's one afternoon off.

She was sitting in an armchair having eaten lunch, her eyes closed, lightly dozing. The tray from which she had eaten was on the corner of the coffee table. She didn't hear the slight click as the latch was eased open, or the padding of plimsolled feet as the man stepped cautiously across the tiled hallway.

There was carpet on the stairs and the man climbed silently and began opening drawers. Bottom one first, so he didn't have to waste time closing them again. He worked quickly and when all the drawers had revealed their contents, he moved to another room. It was when he was on the landing that he disturbed Miss Grainger's sleep. A weak board creaked and she sat up and glanced at the clock, unaware of what had disturbed her.

'Rosita, dear? Is that you?' Groggily she stood up and went into the hall, in time to see the man running down the stairs towards her. He was emitting a low growl of anger at seeing her between himself and the door. Leaping down the stairs at her, he looked enormous.

She ran back into the room and reached for the telephone. The man followed and pushed her roughly aside and snatched the phone, causing her to fall against the table. A chair tipped over, the tray fell with a clatter as the table too overbalanced and fell with her as she tried to support herself. Everywhere there was threat, danger and fear. The noise and confusion surrounded her and entered her mind like a dark cloud.

Everything slowly cleared and it seemed that minutes had passed, then she was staring at the tea leaking into the carpet from the broken teapot. She looked at the man who was staring down at her, panting as though he had been running. Glaring at him, she tried to demand that he leave at once, but she lacked the breath to speak. Her face contorted in a superior expression of outrage, the words forming in her brain, then her eyes showed renewal of fear and her features changed again, from imperiousness to a grimace of pain.

The intruder raised his arm as though to strike her with a back-handed slap but he didn't actually touch her as a severe pain in her chest made her cry out. She was aware of him standing over her, still panting, then of him running out of the house, banging the door back on its hinges. But then everything became dark and vague as if seen through a black muslin curtain, as pain enveloped her again.

Rosita left the factory and went to the Careys' shop to help Kate with the evening rush. Really, she admonished herself, I must stop calling it Careys' shop. It's mine and one day it will have my name above the door. Kate was standing at the door, obviously looking out for her, and as soon as she came in sight, she ran towards her tearfully.

'Kate? What is it? What's happened?' She saw Idris standing just inside the shop and asked with clear sarcasm, 'Your poor husband unwell again? You can go if you like, I'll finish up.'

'It's Miss Grainger, she's the one that's ill! Taken her to hospital they have. Quick! You'd better go quick!'

Not thinking of a taxi in her haste to get to her friend, Rosita ran wide-eyed through the main square, past the park where the thump of tennis racquets could be heard and into the hollow, antiseptic corridors of the hospital. She found a nurse and was told quietly that she was five minutes too late.

'The house had been robbed, my dear. The shock of finding that thief in the house must have brought it on. A heart attack it was. It would have been very quick. She wouldn't have suffered,' the nurse told her kindly, as Rosita changed colour and almost fell. She was guided to a chair. 'Your mam, was it?'

'No,' Rosita said thickly. 'Not my mother. Someone far more important!'

She waited until the medical staff had finished then went to see her friend for the last time. Staring down at the kindly woman who had been such a dear friend and had meant more to her than anyone else in her whole life, she choked back tears and wondered how she would continue without her. The eyes, so intelligent yet always without censure, whatever she said or did, would never smile at her again, the still mouth never share another joke or piece of harmless gossip.

She stumbled from the building and for the first time since she had been accepted as Miss Grainger's temporary lodger, didn't know where to go. She walked around the streets for a while, wondering at the laughter of people she passed. Surely no one should be laughing at a time like this? Then, as the light began to fade on that terrible day, she went to the Careys' house, intending to talk to Richard.

At the doorway, where Henry's chair stood waiting for him to return to its comfort the following morning, she hesitated, then turned and went back to the house. Miss Grainger had family and friends. It was something she could do for her friend – write or telephone to tell them what had happened.

She spoke to the police, who told her there would be an inquest and assured her they were doing everything they could to find the man responsible. She lived through it all as if in a dream.

Three days later the funeral took place, with several of Miss Grainger's cousins and nephews arriving for the ceremony. Friends from the dress shop came too. And some of the Careys, including Kate and Idris, but Rosita was unaware of many of them. Richard had called round several times but she was unable to talk to him, saying abruptly she would see him when the funeral was over.

She had kept herself busy with tasks in the house that had been the only home she had known. Since the death of Miss Grainger, she had scrubbed and polished and cleaned out every cupboard and odd corner so the house was immaculate for that final gathering.

She had no idea where she would live after leaving the house she had entered as a homeless young woman and stayed as a friend. There wasn't a thought in her head beyond preparing the house and arranging the funeral. Everything after that was a blur. She was like a puppet with an unknown force pulling the strings. Visions of a future without her dear friend beside her were cut off the moment they began. It was too painful to bear. Grieving had to come first.

When the men returned from the cemetery, a will was produced and Miss Grainger's final wishes known. The house and its contents were left to a widowed cousin. With the exception of £500 for Rosita to buy a car, the bank account was to be shared between the nieces and nephews.

Rosita held her breath. For a moment she put aside her grief. Now for the business interests. If Miss Grainger's shares in the shops were left to members of her family, she would be back where she had started, but her fears were groundless. The fifty per cent shares in the two shops owned by Miss Grainger were left to Rosita unconditionally, including stock and any money in the business account.

Grief and relief had left Rosita in a daze, not able to go to the factory and unable to help in either shop. A neighbour, Betty Sweeny, who had occasionally helped Miss Grainger in their first shop in Station Row, was asked to run the business and, to Rosita's surprise and relief, made an excellent job of doing so. A week after the funeral, on 30 June, Rosita went to see Richard.

'I'm so sorry,' he began. 'I know how much you loved her.' They were in the living room of the Careys' house and Mr and Mrs Carey had left them alone.

'I don't know what to do. I've had to leave the house, of course. I've moved into a hotel for the moment, thrown my few belongings into the room above the shop. But I have to find somewhere to live soon.' She spoke briskly, hardly looked at him, and she sat as far away from him as the room would allow.

'What about the rooms over the shop? I mean the one in Station Row,' he added quickly. The last thing he wanted was to help her feel more permanent in his own property! 'It's empty, isn't it?'

'Yes, but it's such a mess. It would take ages to clean and decorate and I don't have the time. I don't know how long Betty Sweeny will manage the shop and I still have my factory job.'

'Let me help.'

'I couldn't. I *have* to deal with my life myself. It's the only way I can cope with being on my own. Oh, Richard, she was so much more than a business partner. She was like a dozen friends, one for every occasion, she was my advisor and mother, all rolled into one loving person.' She stood up and he came over and attempted to hold her but she slipped away from his arms and stood staring out of the window.

'Let me help,' he said again. 'At the moment we don't have much I can get on with, not until I've decided on the best way of getting us out of the present mess. So, let's go now and look at the place and then choose some wallpaper and paint.'

They went to look at the rooms and Richard's positive attitude to the gloomy apartment made it seem possible.

The following day, while his workmen made a start on the washing down and painting, she bought a new Ford Anglia for £360 and arranged for driving lessons.

The garage was in the older part of the town amid streets of neat, grey stone houses. In the middle of one street was a school, its paved yard full of noisy screaming children. A public house stood on one corner and a bus stop was close by. What attracted her eyes like a magnet was a shabby shop selling newspapers, tobacco and sweets, not far from the school gates. On its dirty-engrained window was a handwritten notice proclaiming that the 'desirable property' was for sale.

Later that evening, when she went to Station Row, she was surprised at how much Richard and his team had achieved. The skirting boards were all pristine with fresh paint, the walls marked for papering, the ceilings were so white it seemed as though the lights were lit. She smiled, admired the work, thanked him and handed him a folder full of legal papers.

'What's this?' he asked with a frown.

'You can buy the shop back as soon as it can be arranged,' she said. 'I've seen a property going cheap that will do me just as well.'

Richard took the papers and stared at them in utter disbelief. 'I hope you don't think I helped with this place to make you change your mind.'

'If you haven't learned anything else, Richard, you must know you wouldn't have been able to persuade me to do something I didn't want to do.'

'Can I phone Monty and tell him?'

Monty came at once and, after a celebration that became a small party, with food rustled up from the contents of the shop, and a few drinks, the three of them went to look at the property near the school. It was dirty and smelled badly of neglect. The yard outside was overflowing with rubbish including stale food. It was a mess.

Richard felt mean, having forced her to leave the shop she had made so neat and clean, and have to tackle the job of making the school shop habitable. He refused, even to himself, to believe that his persuasions *hadn't* worked. Her decision to sell the Careys' shop back to him was nothing to do with her finding this neglected business; she wouldn't have taken on such a disheartening place unless she had been made to see the importance of his career. Yes, he had talked her into seeing things from his angle. Even a clever woman like Rosita was no match for a man. But he had left her with an ugly task.

The following day, Monty left a present for her. Standing on the counter of the Station Row shop, in front of a smiling Betty Sweeny, was a drawer-shaped wooden container with compartments of various sizes so birthday cards could be well displayed. Previously they had been stacked together in an untidy pile, getting dog-eared and grubby. Rosita wrote to thank him and cheekily asked if he could make another for the school shop!

She gave her notice at the factory and this time she had no intention of going back. Without Miss Grainger, she now had to run the school shop. While negotiations went on, selling the Careys' shop and buying the new one, she transferred stock and bought new ready to fill her new acquisition. The Careys' shop was soon back to its previous empty and dreary look with a lugubrious Uncle Henry Carey in temporary charge.

With Kate sharing the long hours with her at the school shop, and with Richard finishing the decorating between meetings and consultations, Rosita learned to drive. Beside lessons from professionals, it was Idris who spent a few hours each day instructing her.

The first time he tried to put his hand on her knee she smiled and firmly removed it. The second time she pushed it away without hiding her anger. The third time she slapped his face so hard it left a mark that hadn't faded when they got back to the shop. She regretted the slap more than Idris appeared to do when she saw the expression on Kate's gentle face. It was obvious that she had guessed the outcome of the hour's free lesson. Besides the bright red weal on her husband's smiling face, her own was red and dark with anger.

'You can go home with your husband, Kate. I'll finish up here,' she said stiffly. 'Thank you for all your hard work.'

Idris glanced back as he ushered Kate from the shop and winked a brazen eye. 'See you tomorrow when you close for lunch, eh?'

'No, thank you. I'm busy!' What did he think she was – some lonely woman desperate for the attentions of a useless individual like him?

He came into the shop a few days later and gave his wife a smile, then asked Rosita if he could borrow her car to go for an interview for a job. She hesitated. There was something about a new car; it was the most expensive purchase she had made apart from the businesses. The Anglia was beautiful and it was her own and she didn't want anyone else to drive it. She had never belonged to a family where sharing might be acceptable; everything she acquired was solely for her own use. She glanced at Kate's face, saw hope there, and nodded weakly.

'Make sure you drive it with care, and I want it back by one o'clock.

Kate and I have to go to the wholesalers and Monty is coming to sit beside me. I want to see it parked outside and the key in my pocket before one o'clock. Right?'

Idris saluted and grinned. 'Yes, boss.'

'I thought we were going to look at rugs and curtains, Miss Evans?' Kate said.

'We are, but I don't trust your husband with my new and beautiful car.'

'He isn't a bad person, Miss Evans,' Kate defended in her gentle way. 'Silly, perhaps. I mean, he's a bit of a boy, really, never grown up, like. But there, men seldom do, do they?'

'I'm sure he makes you happy just the way he is, and that's what counts.' Rosita turned to pack some birthday cards into the smart new display and thought to herself that if she ever settled for someone like Idris, she hoped someone would have her certified!

At ten past one they gave up waiting for Idris to return with the car, and walked to the new property near the school. Armed with tape measure and a notebook, they made careful measurements and a list of shelves and cupboards they needed, which Richard had promised to have made for them. It was while they were hurrying back to Station Row that Rosita saw the Anglia parked under trees in a narrow lane which led to some old sheds and a few neglected houses. She almost drew Kate's attention to it, then realized that there were two people inside.

'Will you go and open up, please, Kate? I think I'll do a bit of shopping.' She waited until Kate was out of sight then walked purposefully towards her car. She opened the driver's door and demanded that Idris and his passenger got out.

'Miss Evans. What a surprise!' he tried to bluff, smiling at her then at the girl beside him. 'Interview went on a bit longer than expected, so I gave this young lady a lift.'

Rosita glared at the overweight woman, dressed like a tart, who stepped out on the far side of the car, hastily straightening her clothes.

'Hello, Miss Evans. I hope you didn't mind us using your car.' The woman smiled nervously at Idris.

'This is Kate's boss,' Idris said. 'Miss Evans – Hattie.'

He said lots more but, frozen with horror, Rosita heard nothing. Hattie! This overweight, unpleasant-looking woman, with smudged lipstick across her full mouth, was her half-sister! She stared and saw, in the flat face and rounded features, her hated stepfather, Graham Prothero, and she wanted to scream.

She felt anger rising and knew she had to get away from them. What they had been doing was none of her business. She didn't want to think about it, but the dishevelled clothes gave her a picture that wouldn't go away.

Idris was still trying to explain as she pushed him aside and got into the driving seat. The new leather smell was gone. The car felt unclean, no longer hers. She slammed the door and didn't heed Idris's shout: 'Miss Evans! Hang on, woman, you haven't got a licence, remember. Shouldn't be driving on your own.'

She drove to the lonely beach near Gull Island and sat, trembling with hurt and anger, for a long time. It wasn't until she had calmed down that the realization that she was two miles from home and alone in a car she was not licensed to drive dawned on her.

She considered finding a phone and calling Richard but she didn't know where to find him. Sadly she realized there was no one else. Determination tightened her jaw and she reminded herself that she had got this far without depending on anyone. Starting the engine with more trepidation than before, she drove carefully back to Station Row. She stepped out of the driving seat, so tense she thought her teeth would snap. Her forearms and hands ached from the tightness with which she had grasped the wheel; her jaw felt like a vice.

'Sorry I've been so long,' she said to Kate. 'Now shall we have a cup of tea?'

She didn't mention seeing Idris with Kate's sister or explain how she had found the car and brought it back. After all, she told herself, Kate must know what he's like. Why should I add salt to what must be a constantly painful wound?

She tried to remain cool and indifferent to her assistant's problematic marriage but was aware of a growing affection for the quiet young woman. There was something very appealing about Kate's gentle, kindly and hard-working nature, which Rosita couldn't fail to appreciate. She told herself it was foolish to become attached to anyone, that she was better off on her own, safer from being hurt, but the feeling grew.

In November, demolition began on the shops including the Careys' newsagency. Rosita passed her driving test and moved into her new premises near the school. Now the problem of the Careys' shop was out of the way, Rosita and Richard had become more relaxed with each other. They occasionally shared a meal in the evening when they had both finished work for the day.

'We've never really celebrated our good fortune. What about going out somewhere really swish one evening?' Richard suggested when he and Rosita were fixing the last of the shelves in the school shop.

'Where could we go with you wearing that suit?' she teased.

'I'll buy a new one,' he promised. 'Now I have to wear two hats, one for when I'm the mucky and hardworking site foreman and the other for when I'm the slick and smart salesman. I'll need something a bit smart. Shall we go out of town, perhaps to one of the villages where there's a pub with a restaurant? Idris recommended a place called The Old Oak.'

Instinctively Rosita decided she didn't want to go anywhere recommended by Idris. 'Somewhere near the sea,' she said in her emphatic way.

Richard was used to her determined manner and nodded amiably. 'Whatever you want. It's a celebration for us both, not just me.'

'The new shop, you mean?'

'Well, let's say your display of good sense in letting me have my shop back. You recognizing that my plans were the most important.'

'Your ambitions are so much more important than mine, you being a man.' She sounded as if she were agreeing.

'That's it. I mean, I'm employing a dozen or more men, and their families depend on me for survival.'

'And what about my survival?'

'Well, it isn't as if a woman's work is essential, is it? I mean, a woman won't be supporting a family.' He laughed. 'Useful, mind, but it's bound to be less important and more a hobby and ...' Too late, he recognized the steel in her voice and knew he had fallen into a trap.

'I want to be wealthy and independent the same as you and I'll be earning a good income and adding to the lives of people so they don't have to depend on handouts like Idris and—'

He interrupted her, glad of the chance. 'Idris? I know he's a lazy devil, but he's my brother and I've just given him the job of site manager.'

'Then you're a bigger fool than I thought! From a child he's been spoilt and primed for a life without work. Idris is a cheat and will do nothing and take everything.'

'Why are you so hot under the collar about Idris? You can hardly pretend to know him.'

'I know enough. He cheats on Kate for a start!'

'Of course he doesn't!' Richard said hotly, but he knew she was right. He remembered the night he had called at his brother's house after seeing him in a car with a woman. Best to say nothing, deny it. Gossiping would only make things worse – and hurt Kate, who didn't deserve it. 'They're happy, anyone can see that.'

'*He's* happy. Enjoying himself with any woman who's stupid enough to think him attractive, including Kate's sister.'

'I heard Hattie was back. Now come off it, Rosita. Hattie left home wanting to have a bit of independence. She's been staying with Kate and

Idris for a while, so he's probably just being kind. Surely that's understandable?'

'Kind to himself. That's the only kindness Idris understands.'

'We'd better change the subject.'

'Yes, let's go back to you telling me I'm just a silly little woman playing at running a business and I'm really waiting to fall into someone's arms and expect them to keep me in idleness for the rest of my life, shall we?'

Plans to go out and celebrate were abandoned. Rosita went home to her flat and taking a box of chocolates from the shelf, sat and ate them all. A whole month's ration all in one go. Well, so what!

Christmas Day was one of the rare days on which newspapers weren't printed and Rosita planned to treat herself to a really lazy day. She rose at the usual time, though, her body clock refusing to alter for the precious rarity of not having to react promptly to the alarm. She made herself a cup of tea and, taking it back to bed, she contemplated the day off and wondered how best to use it. She might go and visit Auntie Molly Carey in the house near Red Rock Bay.

Christmas was such a milestone in the year. Previous ones remembered for one reason or another, way back into the distant past when most things were a mixed-up blur. It was a time when people gathered together, often a hotchpotch, a most unlikely combination of characters, usually finding to their surprise that they enjoyed the experience. For Rosita it had been nothing more than a brief respite from the repetitive life of the home. There were no family gatherings on which she could reminisce. Her best memories were the years she had spent with Miss Grainger.

From others she gleaned pictures of how Christmas was for most people. Benevolence abounded as everyone shared the celebration with people they hardly thought of during the year, each believing, during that special Christmas camaraderie, that they are the best of friends as they repeated old stories and even older jokes. Rosita gritted her teeth and told herself she didn't want any of it.

She bathed and dressed and looked at the small slice of pork that two weeks' saved meat ration had allowed her. That small piece of meat emphasized the emptiness of her life since Miss Grainger had died. She set it to roast slowly, surrounded by part-boiled potatoes and a couple of stringy-looking parsnips. Cooking was a chore. It was just one of the many reasons she still grieved for her friend, who had always managed to produce appetizing meals from the ration for two, with a minimum of meat and a surfeit of imagination.

Thoughts of Miss Grainger made her melancholy. She was so alone. Kate had invited her to spend Christmas Day with her, Idris and their two girls, Helen and Lynne. Auntie Molly Carey had pleaded with her to join them for Christmas dinner. She pretended she had other plans. She would get through the day without any of them. She wouldn't depend on anyone, ever again.

Why did today matter so much? If she pretended it was a Sunday without the chore of the morning papers it would be easy. Just the luxurious joy of a day without work. But she wished she could go to the shop and rearrange the shelves. After the last hectic hours of Christmas Eve, they were in a mess. But she couldn't. Not today. She had no strong religious beliefs but that was something she couldn't do. To treat it like an ordinary day would have been seen as sacrilegious. Tomorrow, perhaps, another precious day of freedom.

It was a pity she had quarrelled with Richard. She hadn't even thanked him properly for the work he had done in the new shop. He and Monty had made a second card display, and sent one of the carpenters around to fix some squeaky doors and add some extra shelves. She had been most ungracious.

Yes, she decided suddenly. She would go round to the Careys' after dinner and thank Richard, even stay for tea if she were invited. She would also try not to react when his remarks seemed condescending. She would really, really try. Then she thought that Kate and Idris would be there and perhaps Hattie too. Best she stayed away. She would delay her meal until later, and read, and listen to the wireless and – This was ridiculous, she chided herself. Surely a day off isn't something to be used up like a punishment?

A knock on the door at four o'clock startled her. It was Richard, it must be. But it was a neighbour asking if she had a couple of shillings for the gas meter as their chicken wasn't cooked and the gas had run out. Disappointed, she handed over some coins and returned to her living room. She checked on her meal, which was still uncooked, the meat looking smaller than ever, the potatoes greasy and unappetizing. She slammed the oven door and ate a biscuit.

This won't do. What was she thinking of, sitting here like this? Refusing all invitations then hoping someone would come and persuade her to change her mind. She was pathetic! She donned a coat and a headscarf and went down the street, heading for the beach, and bumped into Idris.

'Kate asked me to see if you'll change your mind about coming to Mam and Dad's place.'

'Thank her, will you? She's very kind, but I'm having a lovely time just resting. A day off is a novelty when you work every day, remember.'

'Richard will be there.'

'Wish him a Happy Christmas for me.'

'Shall I come in for a drink?'

'No, I don't think so. I'm just going out as you can see.'

She walked to the car and got in, tempted to offer him a lift back to his parents' to ease her loneliness for a few minutes, but decided it wasn't worth the risk. She could smell drink on him and didn't want the embarrassment of giving him another slap.

She drove around the block and gave him time to leave, then returned to the flat. Richard was sitting on the doorstep, a wrapped bottle of wine in his hand.

'Been somewhere nice?' he asked as she searched for her key.

'I drove around the block to get rid of your brother,' she said in her usual sharp tone.

'Kate sent him. He wasn't trying to – well, you know.'

'I'm glad to hear it!'

He didn't move from the step although he had stood up when she approached. She looked up at him, silently asking him to move so she could open the door. Something in his expression made her heart flip. His eyes had darkened and he was staring at her with undisguised desire.

He followed her in and his presence filled the small room and she was aware of his need of her and of her own failing resistance. The coat he wore was too large, its belt hanging to the floor. She pulled at it to prevent him tripping over and even the cloth of the shabby garment seemed electric, a part of his powerful, sensual aura.

He removed the coat and she saw with half of her mind that he was wearing a new suit. Inconsequentially, as if on a different plane to the here and now, she wondered if he had bought it for their aborted celebration. He was extremely tense and since removing his overcoat he hadn't moved. Perhaps she had been mistaken about his overwhelming need of her and there was something wrong. Panic rose in her. Thank goodness she hadn't run to him. What a fool she would feel if it was trouble and not love.

'Is everything all right?' she asked. He turned to look at her, his eyes so deep set they were almost invisible in the light of one table lamp on a gloomy afternoon.

He pulled her to him and kissed her. She was startled, yet the kiss had been inevitable from the moment she had opened the door and invited him inside. She relaxed in his arms and felt the embrace soften the very bones of her.

'Everything is perfect,' he said before kissing her again.

It was several hours before they opened the wine.

The pork was a cinder and the meal before them was a joke. Richard raised his fork to his lips then threw it down and took her in his arms again.

'Marry me, Rosita. I loved you when you were a girl and I love you now as a woman. I've never loved anyone else. All my life, even at my most lonely times, I was waiting for you to come back into my life. It's a miracle that you did, and were still free. My darling, we'll be so happy.'

Rosita was filled with a joy so intense it blanked out everything except the sight of his face so close to her own. Richard. Her beloved Richard was telling her he loved her. They would marry. She would have someone of her own. Someone to love and to love her. Her heart sang with happiness so his next words took a moment to penetrate.

'There's no hurry, but you might as well advertise the shops straight-away. They'll soon find a buyer. You've done a good job of improving them. Monty and I will soon be on our feet now so there won't be any financial problems.'

'Sell my shops.' It was said calmly and wasn't a question, just a dull reprisal of his words.

'Of course, my lovely Rosita. You won't need them now.'

'What will I do?' she asked in a whisper.

'You'll be at home, my darling, waiting for me.'

'Richard, I can't.' Happiness evaporated and she stepped back from his embrace and stared at him, almost in tears.

'You can invest your money in my business if you like. We'll make you a partner. Monty is bound to agree. There, how d'you feel about that?' He sounded like an uncle giving a child a stick of rock, she thought numbly.

'A sleeping partner, of course.'

'Of course. I don't want you to have a single worry in that beautiful head of yours.'

She was tempted. Oh, how she was tempted by the oldest trick in the world. She loved him and wanted him desperately, but how could she trust even Richard Carey with her happiness and her future? He didn't know her at all, failed to recognize her needs and abilities. Even Richard, whom she had loved all her life, couldn't make her happy for more than a few months. She had to have more than love. Why couldn't he understand?

'No, Richard,' she said in her emphatic voice. 'No, I won't marry you. A businesswoman isn't a fancy dress I wear, a businesswoman is what I am. Accept that, or there can never be a future for us.'

Chapter Thirteen

WHEN RICHARD RETURNED to his parents' house, Hattie could see he was upset. That was good. Cheering up men was something she did well. Smiling, she poured him a drink of the whisky that was the annual purchase in celebration of Christmas and sat beside him. There was an attempt at sympathy in her eyes as she said, 'Quarrelled, have you? There's awful, with it being Christmas an' all.'

'No, we haven't quarrelled. Just a difference of opinion, that's all.'

'What's in a word, eh?' she said in her slow, sing-song voice. 'Cold or cool, stubborn or determined, a quarrel or a difference of opinion.'

'As you say.' He was disinclined to talk, the words he and Rosita had exchanged tearing into his thoughts.

Hattie allowed the silence to grow then said, 'I admire Miss Evans, don't you? Getting on so well and her a woman. She must have had family who helped, mind. She couldn't have done it all on her own.'

'She had no one. She knew what she wanted, made up her mind to get it and went for it with all the strength and determination she could muster.'

'Well I never! Determined, or obstinate, which would you say?' She took his empty glass and stood up. 'Come for a walk, get some fresh air, is it? Do you good it will.'

'Some other time.' He walked away and after saying goodnight to the family who were playing crib and whose faces were red with perspiration and a surfeit of alcohol, he went to bed.

Hattie stood for a while nursing the empty glass then turned to watch Idris. He was wickedly handsome. Pity her dull sister got to him first, but that wasn't the end of anything, not these days. Not if a wife didn't know how to look after a husband proper. Kate had gone home with the children, leaving Idris all alone, poor man. Men like Idris shouldn't be left alone.

She smiled as he groaned and put down his hand of cards. She waved the glass. 'Drink, Idris? Or d'you you fancy a nice walk? Cool you off nice, a walk will.' See what you want and go all out to get it. That was Miss Evans's attitude and she could do worse than follow the same rule.

*

Rosita opened a third shop in a poorer area of the town in early spring 1951. It was little more than a room, with other rooms above and behind it rented out to a family. She asked Betty Sweeny, who had helped out once or twice, if she would consider managing it and Betty agreed at once. The shop took less than either of the others but Rosita had found the challenge was too good to miss and it had come at a time when she needed a challenge to remind Richard who she was. The rent was low and the bank manager and her accountant agreed it worth the risk. Betty nicknamed it 'the kiosk' as it was so small.

After closing the place, Rosita usually hurried home to help Kate enter the figures in the daily books and close the Station Row shop, it being the busiest. It had always stayed open later than the others, mainly to accommodate the men and women on their way home from the six o'clock finish in other businesses in the area.

As Kate was putting on her coat, Rosita said, 'I hear your sister Hattie is still staying with you?'

'Yes. She and Mam aren't getting on very well, and Hattie thought a break and a little independence might be a good idea.'

'Can you cope with looking after another person, Kate? You have plenty to do working and looking after Idris and the girls.'

'Hattie isn't a problem, in fact she's a help. Between you and I she's an awful cook, mind, but she'll get the occasional meal and she always gets the vegetables done and the table set. She's found a job in a factory, piecework on a bench making machine parts. I don't expect she'll stay long.'

'Your husband, he doesn't mind?'

'Idris? Mind? He's got someone else running around after him, waiting on him now.' She laughed. 'He doesn't mind at all. In fact, they seem to get on very well.'

Rosita hid her worries. She wondered if having a word with Idris, warning him off, would do any good, but decided not. When people interfered in the marriage of others, they were usually the one left feeling stupid as the couple closed ranks and put them firmly on the outside.

The business in the kiosk, was slow but it soon began to show an increase with a very enthusiastic Betty Sweeny in charge. Improvement in its appearance would increase the number of customers who came for their morning papers and gradually other sales would grow.

Betty had bought herself a small car to enable her to get to the shop for the early start and was well content with the generous wage Rosita paid her. She was a war widow still in her twenties and, without children, was free to concentrate on her job.

Kate fitted well to the Station Row shop, easily making friends with new customers. She had a long walk home but seemed not to mind. Occasionally Idris would meet her and walk her home, preferring that to fetching the girls from the neighbour who looked after them until their mother arrived.

Rosita continued to enjoy the school shop. Richard had fixed extra shelves and she had added children's books to the stock. The school brought in a lot of customers as mothers called to browse while waiting for their children but the most surprising aspect of that shop was, for Rosita, horse racing.

The public house on the opposite corner to the shop attracted a lot of horse-racing enthusiasts. Before the first race and between subsequent ones, a small, wizened ex-jockey left the pub and went to deliver the bets he had collected to the local turf accountant. The halfway stop for many of his transactions was Rosita's shop. Monty had found the shop was only a few minutes out of his way as he travelled to work and he became a regular customer both for his newspaper and cigarettes, when available, and the race tipster guides.

On the shelf close to the till were small sealed packets containing the day's forecasts of the likely winners. The regulars bought one, opened it and read it then pocketed it with a hopeful gleam in their eyes. The bookie's runner would take their hastily scribbled bets, coins would change hands and the backers would go to the pub to await results. As they got to know Rosita, her shop became a regular meeting place for the Horsey Gang, as she began to call them. They met in her shop and discussed the weights, handicaps of the runners, the successes and failures of the jockeys.

The jargon, at first so confusing, revealed its secrets and she began to understand about each-way bets and odds-on favourites and doubles and trebles. She became used to discussions on whether the going was rough and if certain horses were better or worse on hard-going. When the pub closed at two o'clock, they would stand in her shop, buy more newspapers and read and smoke, discuss the latest results and slide into her back room to listen to the broadcasts of the meetings on her wireless.

Cheers or groans would come from the room and she didn't need to ask about the success or failure of their chosen mounts – she could read it in their faces. Occasionally one of them would have a good win and once, Monty handed her the sweet coupons and the money to buy chocolates, which he gave to her as a share of his good fortune.

It became rather good fun, although she was never tempted to hand over money of her own. That was as stupid as marrying a man who said he loved you but wanted to change you into something he wanted you to be.

*

In April 1951 London was getting ready to celebrate the Festival of Britain, to declare the end of the melancholy of war, open the doors to a brighter peace, and show the rest of the world that prosperity in Britain was on the way. Rosita did some celebrating of her own. She bought a fourth shop.

It was too soon after taking on the kiosk, the accountant warned her of that, but like Richard, she wasn't a person to sit and wait patiently until everything was secure; the risks were a part of the enjoyment. Besides, The Kiosk was only rented – the business was hers but not the building. The rent was easily found from the takings after paying Betty and there was a little to put aside.

As usual, when there was something to celebrate, it was to the Careys she went. Hoping Richard wouldn't be there, hoping he would be, hoping he wouldn't be mentioned, hoping she would have news of him and hoping, so nervously, that he hadn't found someone else.

She was so confused about her feelings for him that when they met she either treated him coolly, like a casual friend, or was so intensely aware of her love for him that she created a quarrel. Her most dreaded thought was that he had found someone and was planning to marry. This was on her mind every time she stepped into the Careys' home.

Uncle Henry Carey was in his usual place by the door, where he would chat to passers-by and read his comics in peace. He gestured with a thumb after greeting her and told her Auntie Molly Carey was inside and half demented. 'She's got something to tell you, *fach*.'

Rosita saw excitement on her friend's face and feared the day had come and she was about to be told about Richard's new love but she was quickly reassured.

'Going up to London we are!' was Mrs Carey's greeting. 'Our Idris and our Richard are treating us. Me, your Uncle Henry, Kate and the children! A trip to London to see the Festival!'

'How marvellous. When?'

'Now soon! Next month, would you believe? Richard is getting the tickets and booking a hotel and everything. Won't it be lovely? Never been to London. They say it's quite big.'

'It is, rather.' Rosita smiled, sharing the elderly woman's excitement. Then the smile faded as Mrs Carey added, 'You'll stay here and mind the house and look after Richard and the dog, won't you, love?'

'Stay and look after—' Rosita laughed. 'Richard doesn't need minding, Auntie Molly Carey! I'll take the dog though. He can stay with me and come to the shop every morning. He'll like that.'

'Richard works long hours and I'd like to think someone is looking after him, see he has a decent meal every night.' She turned a crafty eye on Rosita. 'I can't go if he isn't looked after. Sorry to my heart I'll be to miss it, but I can't leave Richard without—'

'Someone to look after him,' Rosita finished with a chuckle. 'All right, I'll wash his socks, get a meal ready for him somehow and make sure he eats all his cabbage. All right?'

'And there's Idris too.'

There was something in the woman's voice that made Rosita curious. 'Won't Hattie be there to make a meal for him?'

'No, we've … chosen … a week when she'll be away too. Going to a caravan in Weston, she is, with some friends from the factory. So Idris will be on his own, see.'

The words were deliberate. They had *chosen* a week when Hattie would be away. Mrs Carey didn't trust her golden boy any more than Rosita did. She didn't trust Hattie, Rosita's half-sister, either!

'Perhaps Richard and Idris could share for the week?'

'No, *fach*. Never could agree, them two. They'll manage, of course they will, but if you'd keep an eye—?'

'Of course I will.'

They discussed the forthcoming trip for a while, deciding what clothes would be needed for a May holiday, then Mrs Carey looked at Rosita and saw the simmering excitement. There was a gleam in her dark eyes, a fraction more colour in her cheeks. Although she was as neat as always, with her hair smoothly styled and her dress immaculate, there was a relaxed expression on her face and she looked less controlled and formal than usual.

'Was there a special reason for the call, love? Not that you need one, mind. Or did you just come for a chat?'

'I called to tell you that the finance is arranged and I'm soon opening another shop.'

'And there's me gabbling on and never giving you the chance to tell me your news! Congratulations, girl. I'm so proud of you. Pity it is that …' She hesitated, then went on. 'Pity your mam doesn't know any of this. She'd be proud too, for sure.'

'Maybe. But it was when I was five I wanted her to be proud of me. Perhaps if she had been, she would have shared in my success now.'

'I know where she is, mind. I have her address.'

'You haven't told her about me, have you?'

'I kept my promise, love. Although I don't agree with you. She's your mam and whatever she did, she must have thought she was doing the best for you.'

'For herself more like! How could sending me away from her be the best for me? It was Graham Prothero she should have kicked out, not me.' The wound was still raw, Mrs Carey realized with sadness.

'So thrilled with you she was. You were born in our room, you know. Her not willing to—' She quickly changed the subject. No need to remind the poor girl that her grandfather had rejected her too. 'And you were such a beautiful baby. Although you cried non-stop for months on end, she never lost patience, loved you and adored you she did. I can see her now, looking down at you in that gentle way of hers.' She glanced at Rosita to see if her words were having any effect and saw the familiar closed-in expression.

She sighed and changed the subject completely. One day Rosita might listen, but this was not the time. 'Right, then. Tell me about this new shop of yours.'

When the shop had been described and Rosita had explained her plans for it, the conversation returned to the London visit.

'What shall we go and see? Richard gave us a guide book.' She looked around vaguely. 'I dapped it down somewhere.' She found the book and opened it randomly at the list of street markets. 'Love a street market, I do. Has London got any good ones?'

'A few.' Rosita smiled affectionately at the excited woman.

Rosita was leaving when Richard arrived. He was wearing a donkey jacket and the trousers of an old suit tucked into large Wellingtons, which he removed at the door. Cement splashes covered his clothes and spotted his face.

'That's right, I don't want half the building site in my kitchen,' his mother said in mock annoyance. 'Sit down, *bach*. Rosita, make us all a cup of tea, will you? You can tell Richard your news while I go to the shop across the road for some biscuits.'

'What news?' Richard asked as he sat on the sagging old couch. 'Mam mentioned news. I know! You've decided to sell your shops!' He reached out and held her hand. 'I hate quarrelling with you. Come out with me tonight? There's a new restaurant opened on the Cardiff Road.'

'Yes, why not?' She moved her hand from his, smiling nervously, afraid of how he would take it. 'You can help me celebrate my news. I've bought a fourth shop.'

'You've what? Oh, I see. Then my hope of us marrying is just a laugh, is it?'

'I love you, Richard. I want to be your wife but I can't accept conditions as part of the marriage vows.'

'Yet you're asking me to do just that.' He changed his voice to a chant.

'I promise that our marriage will be based on the promise that you'll love, honour and obey, except in the small matter of running a business of your own, which will put me and our relationship second!'

'Why is it such a problem? Your mother worked with your father all her life. They're still together, planning this trip to London – as if it's a second honeymoon, I suspect.'

'Don't you see? It's because Mam had such a hard time of it that I vowed never to let my wife work.'

'So it's pride, then?'

'Yes, pride!'

'Owning three shops and renting a fourth is hardly on the same level as delivering papers and doing other people's washing.'

'Don't demean what Mam did!'

'I'm not. You are.'

Mrs Carey came in, saw the kettle was still cold and empty and tutted dramatically. 'You young people. Never heard of organization? Put the kettle on to boil first, and then talk!'

Rosita put the kettle on to boil on the gas ring. It was always the same. She and Richard were miles apart in their thinking and how could it ever change?

'Going out tonight, Richard, love?' his mother asked. Rosita tensed herself. Was the invitation to the new restaurant still holding?

'No, Mam,' he said sadly. 'Not tonight. Nowhere to go worth dressing up for. I'll stay in and read.'

Rosita was so frustrated and angry she stamped out and walked home, forgetting she had taken the car. Smiling despite her misery, she crept back to the Careys house like a criminal, hoping Richard wouldn't see her getting into it a couple of hours later and driving off. What a stupid thing pride was, and how impossible to ignore.

On Sunday afternoons, Rosita usually spent the treasured free time relaxing. She managed to deal with the weekly accounts on a daily basis with a few extra hours mid-week on her half day. Sunday afternoons were hers to laze and enjoy. Her shops seemed to be a success but she was aware that her social and personal life was at a standstill. Her friends were as few as in the first year she had left the home, apart from the most important one, Miss Grainger, who had left her so tragically. Where was she going? Could Richard be right? Should she give up her ambitions and marry? Settle down to peaceful domesticity and motherhood – if it wasn't already too late?

She tried to imagine it and failed. Then she looked at the tray set for her

solitary lunch and felt a shiver of dismay. That was her future; a lonely existence eating alone, sleeping alone, with no one to care whether she laughed
or cried. She might become rich, but for what? There might be plenty to
share but what was the point with no one to share it with?

From the window of the flat she looked out towards the houses across
the street. The spring day was bright, the sky an amazing blue. It was
Sunday, another week had passed, and she was free. But free from what?
She felt the approach of melancholy.

A picture of the beach near Gull Island sprang into her mind. She hadn't
been there for months. That was the place to look up at the sky, not
through the curtained window of an upstairs flat. She put on a new two-
piece suit in an attractive forest green and a cheerful red polo-necked
jumper with a beret to match and picked up her car keys.

Along the street a van slowed to a stop and Idris, who was driving,
watched as she stepped into the Anglia and drove away. Putting the van
into gear he moved after her. If she was meeting his brother he would
disturb their privacy and if she was alone she might be amenable to a bit
of solace in her loneliness. Either way, the next hour or so could be fun.

Starting a closer friendship with the cool Rosita now would be well
timed with Kate and the girls going to London in a few weeks' time. He
would soon get rid of Hattie if Miss Evans showed any sign of weakening.
Their illicit arrangements could be quickly altered.

Rosita recognized the van as it turned into the narrow lane behind her.
At first she thought it was Richard then reasoned that if it had been he
would have come up and shown himself, not skulked along behind her like
a seedy detective. It had to be Idris. With a sigh for the loss of her planned
walk on the lonely beach, she turned right and right again, and went back
to the flat. Idris she could do without!

Idris didn't get out or even wave. He passed her as she was locking the
door of her car, staring straight ahead. He went to the house where he and
his family lived. Hattie was the only one in.

'Look at this, Idris,' she said, handing him a piece of paper. 'Kate has
written instructions down for things I must do while she's away. I'm
supposed to be going away too, for a week in Weston-super-Mare. Yet I'm
expected to do all this. She's treating me more and more like the maiden
aunt who everyone depends on. I don't want to be the old maid she's trying
to make me.'

'Then don't act like one!' Idris's irritability was apparent.

'What d'you mean?'

'Minding the kids, doing more than half of the cleaning, offering to do
this and see to that. Trying to be indispensable. You're making a deep rut

for yourself and soon you won't even be able to climb out or even look over the edge and see what you've missed. You ought to have more fun while you still can.'

'Fat chance!'

He turned to look at her. Her features had that heavy look often seen in pictures of peasant workers of a century ago. Bovine, he thought unkindly. The sisters weren't alike in looks or temperament. Kate was really rather beautiful, but she was prim about sex and he knew from previous experiences that Hattie was not.

He continued to stare. Earthy. That was the word for Hattie. The description excited him. Earthy, wild, untamed by tedious conventions. Right now, earthy, bovine or whatever, she looked appealing and she was here. Why worry about the prim, cold Miss Evans when he had Hattie living under the same roof and more than willing?

'What are you thinking?' she asked, her head on one side in an attempt at coquetry. 'Feeling lonely with Kate out at the Careys' again? She spends more time at your mam's house than here. And there's all them hours at the shop. Never much time for you, these days. Poor, poor Idris.'

He offered his hand and they walked together up the stairs to her room, where they had been many times before.

Richard knew he had made a mistake in employing his brother Idris to manage the building site office. He was frequently missing and Richard or Monty would find a line of disgruntled men waiting for materials that hadn't even been ordered. Employed to work piecework, the delays were enough for several of his best men to walk off site and find other more reliable firms.

'I'll go back to the office,' Monty offered. He really preferred the tools to dealing with paper and endless forms, but he knew Richard couldn't manage it all. 'It'll be simpler if I do it. Training someone into our ways takes time and you don't have enough of that.'

'Just for a while, then. Thanks.' Richard breathed a sigh of relief. With Monty looking after the office, things would get moving again. And they wouldn't lose any more of their best workmen. Damn Idris and his idle ways.

At first Idris complained to his mother about Richard's unfair treatment of him, but when he realized his brother wasn't going to sack him, only demote him to store man, he relaxed. Life was easy if you only relaxed and didn't press for higher status out of false pride. Pride was for enthusiasts or idiots. Idris was enthusiastic, but never about work.

Monty had found himself a room, where the kindly landlady looked after him well. He was a quiet man who spent a lot of his spare time reading or listening to classical music, a love he had shared with his wife. He also liked to bet on horses, rationing himself to losing no more than five shillings in a week. When he won he would use the money to go to a concert or a variety show in Cardiff.

Besides the shared responsibilities of building the six houses Richard was contracted to do, the men were close friends, each seeing in the other an honesty and dedication to giving good-quality workmanship. They had come through a number of problems together, Monty calming Richard's occasional rages, Richard giving Monty the fullness of a busy and exciting life.

Richard had admitted to the deprivations of his childhood that had forced him to submit to thieving and robbery. He had kept nothing back and knowing his friend understood was a comfort. Richard knew it was best for that part of his life to be forgotten, but things occasionally revived the memories and reminded him of his weaknesses. Or had it been strength, as Monty insisted?

The one thing the men disagreed on was Idris.

'I'm sorry, Richard, I know he's your brother, but I don't like the man and never will. He's crafty and feathering his own nest is all he's thinking of. If he wants something he won't mind who's got the right to it. Take it he will, and smile while he's doing it.'

Richard felt the familiar kick of guilt. How could he criticize? That was how they were brought up, how he had lived as a boy. It was how Richard Carey, House Building and Maintenance, had begun. It wasn't a Sunday school story, his past. And however much he wanted to, he couldn't prevent it from jumping out and reminding him of his own lack of respectability at times.

As though guessing his thoughts, Monty said, 'What he does is very different from what you, as a small boy, did. You were helping your family to survive.'

'See that someone keeps an eye on what he does, will you, Monty? I've dropped his pay to that of a store man but I have to keep him on. He's Mam's favourite and there's Kate and the girls. At least they get a bit of cash from him at the end of each week. I'll just have to hope he finds something less taxing and better paid somewhere else. From what I've heard from that poor wife of his, he rarely stays in a job more than a few weeks. Fancy her having to go out to work.'

'She might enjoy working, mind,' Monty said pointedly. 'A lot of women do.'

*

A sudden storm caused Rosita to slam shut the window in the back room of her school shop, and the glass shattered. Leaving a tray propped up to prevent the rain coming in, she closed the shop at lunchtime and drove to where Richard was working.

'Richard, I've broken a window. D'you think you could send someone to replace it?' She handed him the measurements and added, 'I have to go straight back. I don't like leaving the place with a window missing, in case someone breaks in.'

'Sorry,' he said curtly. 'I don't have time until later. Perhaps one of the men will come after they've finished work.'

'Don't bother!' She snatched the piece of paper back and was about to leave when Monty came out of the temporary site office, a battered old shed that had been set up and taken down more times than a circus tent. 'Can I help, Richard?'

'Monty!' Rosita said with a smile. Beside being Richard's partner, she knew him as a regular early-morning customer.

'Miss Evans. Can I help you?' He laughed. 'It's usually you saying that, not me!'

'There's trouble with a broken window or something,' Richard muttered, glaring at Rosita.

Monty looked at the fighting attitude of the two people and his smile widened. There was tension between them but it wasn't anger. 'I'll deal with your lunchtime appointment with the estate agent. You go and deal with the problem for Miss Evans. All right, Caroline?'

'I'll get the glass. You'd better get back to your precious shop.' He held out a hand for the measurements.

'Don't bother. It's obviously too much trouble. I'll go to the glazier.'

Ignoring the danger of leaving the shop unattended, she drove away and had a huge lunch in a new café in town. When she had cooled down, she returned to the shop to find the window replaced, the mess cleared up and Richard sitting on the step with two early customers.

'I got through the window but I had to wait for you – I couldn't lock the door.' He smiled then and she relaxed and returned it as she served the customers.

'Monty thinks you're a charming person. Efficient, capable and kind. And from what I hear about your Horsey Gang of gamblers, a lot of fun too. I think he was surprised at your display of anger. I told him what a terrible temper you really have, but he doesn't believe me,' he said teasingly.

'A man of excellent taste, your Monty.' She made tea and they sat, between her serving customers, and talked about the forthcoming trip to London arranged for his parents.

'Your mother made me promise to look after you,' she said with a wry grin. 'She thinks you're incapable.'

'So she told me!'

'She's convinced that without a bit of looking after, you'll collapse with hunger and neglect before the week's out.'

'If she knew how I lived in the years I was away she wouldn't believe it. I had to put every penny I could spare into the business. It's been quite a struggle.'

'Nothing worthwhile comes easy. You probably have nightmares about losing it all. You wouldn't want to have it taken from you, would you? Not having come so far.'

'No, I couldn't face seeing all my work slip away. To see it all go would be like losing a part of myself and—' He glared at her smiling face, realizing that she was making a point. He was too edgy to joke, refusing to accept she was teasing him. He stood up and said, 'Oh, and that's how you feel, is it? All the years of struggle to get the shops and I'm asking you to give it all up?'

'What's the difference, Richard? You of all people should know how I feel about parting with something I've built so painfully over all these years.'

He put the empty cup and saucer on the counter and stormed out. She called after him, pleading with him to come back and talk, but his large form moved fast and he was soon out of sight.

After the shop closed she totalled the money and dropped the bag in the night-safe then drove to the beach at Gull Island. Why couldn't she be patient and allow Richard to see in his own time how important it was for her to be a person in her own right? Unless, she thought with that familiar squiggle of fear, he found someone else first.

The island was bathed in the late-evening sun, the day having been sunny and mild. Leaves were slowly showing their tips on the hawthorn along the lanes and blackthorn blossoms were still decorating the hedges like confetti at a wedding. The excitement of spring was in the air as she walked along the rocky shore.

As she passed the uninhabited cottage, she saw a low sports car parked at the side. A man stepped out of it and wished her a 'good evening'. He was dressed in a neat and obviously expensive suit with polished shoes on his feet. Under his arm was a briefcase bulging with papers. Small and slim, wearing horn-rimmed glasses, he smiled before going into the cottage. She felt disappointed. It would have been nice to have someone to talk to for a few minutes. Turning away, she found a sheltered corner that was still warm from the sun and sat down.

It was the cottage once owned by the man called Luke, she vaguely remembered. He had probably sold it and made a life for himself in France. If, she thought with a shudder, he had survived the war.

Ten minutes later, the dapper man reappeared, bearing a tray on which there were two cups of tea.

'Would you mind if I joined you?' he asked politely. 'I quite understand if you want to be alone. This is a place in which to enjoy solitude, isn't it?'

She looked at his face, smooth, as if he had no need to shave. It looked too small for the heavy glasses. Taking the tea, she noted how unworkmanlike his hands were. So different from Richard's calloused ones. He obviously worked with his head and not his hands.

Luke had left behind the rebelliousness of youth, sobered by the events he had witnessed in two wars, and the passing years. His long beard was gone, as was the almost obsessional necessity to abandon at once the trappings of business the moment he arrived at the cottage. He had taken off his jacket and replaced it with a good-quality pullover, but the expensive shoes were the same ones in which he had arrived.

'Have you lived here long?' Rosita asked.

'I've lived around here on and off since I was a child. I was born in that big house behind the trees.' He pointed back to where the mock Tudor house was partially visible through the branches. 'A long time. More than half a century, in fact.'

'I've always loved it here. I come when I have a problem to sort out. There's so much sky, so much space, it makes irritations and frustrations seem less important.'

'And what problems can you have? A pretty young woman like you shouldn't have a moment's unhappiness.'

She smiled at him; there was something comfortably familiar about him. 'I had nothing *but* unhappiness in my childhood. A stepfather who beat me and a mother who abandoned me to a home for waifs and strays when I was five years old.' She looked away and didn't see the smile widen on Luke's face. 'Since I've learned that you make your own luck, things have improved dramatically. Now there's nothing I can't deal with on my own.'

'Except the man in your life,' he ventured.

'How did you know?'

'I didn't. But I'm right, aren't I?'

'Does it show that much?'

'Yes, Rosita.'

She stared at him, wondering at the outstretched arms and the tearful smile. 'You know me? But—'

'I've known you on and off since before you were born, on Christmas Day, my twentieth birthday. My name is Luke.'

'Luke?' She frowned, trying to connect the gentle and elderly face with the faint memory she had of his visit to the farm. A man with funny glasses and a long beard. 'Did you come to the farm once when I was little?'

'Just once. Your stepfather didn't encourage Richard and me to come a second time.'

'But you're different. The Luke I remember was – different,' she finished with a shrug.

'So are you!' He raised an eyebrow and self-consciously asked, 'Can I have a hug? Just one? I've wanted to for so long.' Shyly, a little doubtfully, Rosita allowed herself to be hugged. 'I tried many places for news of you,' Luke went on, 'but I couldn't find a single clue. No one at the farm knew anything about you. I asked Mrs Stock, thinking she might have heard. I even asked your mother's parents but they hadn't changed. The Careys are gone and no one I asked knew where. Perhaps you were hard to find because, like me, you aren't the same person any more. People keep a picture of someone without allowing for time to do its work sometimes, don't they? Where have you been since you left the home?'

She told him some of her story, including the purchase of the shops. 'That's the trouble with Richard,' she said. 'He can't accept that I am a businesswoman and not someone prepared to give it all up and run his home.'

'Richard?'

'Richard Carey.'

'I've lost touch with him, too.' He sighed. 'And Barbara, your mother.'

'I've no wish to see her,' she said sharply. 'Stuck me in a home so she and that Graham Prothero could live comfortably without me.'

'She didn't want to let you go, but she had no choice. I saw what he was doing to you. I felt so helpless and afraid for you and I was glad when I heard you were safe in that place and being cared for.'

'Sorry, Luke, but I can't forgive her.' Her lips were tight, her expression closed in and determined.

'And yet you have to. You can't carry all that anger around with you for ever. Anger and hate are terrible burdens, Rosita, and they get in the way of so much that's good.'

She stood to leave. 'Thank you for the tea. I'm so very pleased to have met you.'

'Rosita, we must all get together and catch up on all that's happened to us. Share each other's adventures. You, Richard, Barbara and me. Soon?'

'Not Barbara. I'm not ready to meet my mother again. I doubt I ever will be.'

'Then you and Richard and me, eh? I'll be in touch now I know where to find you.'

As she drove back from the unexpected encounter, she began to think of Luke as her own discovery. She needn't share him with Richard. Not yet anyway. There was excitement in her dark eyes as she parked the car and locked it. She jangled her keys as she walked towards the Station Row shop, but to her surprise she didn't need them. The shop was still open.

'Kate?' she asked, seeing the young woman standing behind the counter. 'Is something wrong?'

'Well, not really. But there's something I wanted to tell you so I thought I'd wait. Best to keep the shop open while I stood here, so I've taken a few shillings we wouldn't otherwise have had.' She spoke in a monotonous voice as though her mind was elsewhere.

Frowning, Rosita closed and locked the shop door. 'What is it, Kate? You look upset.'

'I had a visit from a lady. She said someone called Mrs Stock was looking for you. Old, she was, at least seventy-five. Rosita Jones she said she wanted, this Mrs Stock. Rosita Jones who'd left the town and gone with her mam to live on a farm with a man called Prothero.' She looked at Rosita and in a trembling voice asked, 'You're Rosita, my half-sister, aren't you?'

Rosita could only nod.

Chapter Fourteen

KATE STARED AT the smart, well-dressed woman in front of her, trying to connect her to the vision of the wild, disliked and unhappy child she could scarcely remember. Seeing the distressed look on her sister's face, she held back all the hundreds of questions that poured into her head.

'You didn't wear glasses then,' she said. 'And your hair, it was a long, thick plait. Your face and hands were always red and rough, as if the wind picked you out for special attention.'

'My face wasn't red when I left the home, it was very pale.' Rosita's voice was harsh. 'I went from one extreme to the other; working out of doors all hours of the day, running around trying to please your father, then going to live in a house where exercise and fresh air were administered in rationed amounts like sweets and stories.'

'The name, Caroline, why did you change it? So no one would know who you were? I didn't know your other name – is it Evans?'

'It's Jones.'

'Mam never said. She talked about you very little once you left. Dad didn't like it; he used to get upset.'

'Illegitimacy isn't something you talk about.' Rosita's voice was still harsh, her eyes glaring.

Kate hesitated, wanting to say something to comfort Rosita but not knowing what. 'The glasses, they're new,' she repeated.

'I'd always needed glasses, although no one bothered to check. It was why I got so many things wrong, but I didn't realize, not until a friend pointed it out. It was so obvious then.' She paused a moment, thinking of Miss Grainger, then went on. 'The hair, well, I intended to be different, so I had to look different. I wanted to be more fashionable. I'd had enough of looking like all the rest, wearing clothes chosen for me by others. My hair was cut in what they called a shingle. Mam got hers styled, didn't she? Pretended she was one of the "flappers" they talked about when she was young.'

'Were you very unhappy there?'

Rosita wanted to cry. She felt vulnerable, weak, like a child caught out in some naughty escapade. Memories flooded back, the days when everyone had visitors except her. Birthdays when there were only two cards, one from the Careys and one – which she threw in the ash bin – from her Auntie Babs. 'What d'you think!' she snapped angrily.

More softly she went on, 'It wasn't your fault, Kate. I know that. I'm sorry but I didn't want you to know who I am. I didn't want you running to tell Mam. You weren't to blame – although I still wonder why you and Hattie never visited me. But Mam *was* to blame. I'll never think differently.' Kate began to speak and she added quickly, 'And I don't want to see her. I hope that's clear, Kate.'

'She works on a farm, not far from where we were brought up, did you know that?'

'No, I didn't. Auntie Molly Carey didn't say and I wouldn't have asked. Why didn't you stay with her? Being brought up on a farm I'd have thought you'd prefer it?'

'I was married to Idris by then and Hattie, well, you know Hattie. She prefers the lively opportunities of town life to the quiet of the countryside.'

'Auntie Molly Carey knows who I am, of course, but you won't tell Hattie, will you? I need time to think about whether I want her to know.'

'What about Idris?'

'No! Keep it to yourself for a while, please, Kate.'

'And I can't tell Mam when I write?'

'No, you can't! Did you know she told the people at the home she was my auntie? "I'm her Auntie Babs," she said. Couldn't even admit she was my mother!'

'I'd better go. It's very late. Will you – will you be all right? I could come back if you want to talk?'

Tears threatened again but Rosita shook her head. 'I'm all right.' She took out a handkerchief and wiped her eyes. 'I'm glad you know, Kate. It will make things easier for me, not having to pick my words for fear of you guessing.'

'That's never been a risk, has it? You rarely talk about the things that really matter to you, do you?'

'Not a word to the others, right?'

Kate put on her coat slowly, reluctant to go. Turning as she touched the latch, she said, 'Oh, I almost forgot. I've made a list of applications for the job of running the new shop. And two people willing to help out here, while I'm in London with the girls and Idris's mam and dad.'

'Thank you.' Rosita took the piece of paper and Kate left.

After Kate had gone, Rosita sat in the semi-dark shop for a long time, still dressed for outdoors, her handbag over her arm. She felt small and mean having been found out and she didn't understand why. Perhaps it was because Kate was such a kind and gentle person and they had built up a rapport that was now probably spoilt. Whatever the explanation, she felt she had let herself down by keeping her identity a secret from Kate all this time.

Luke's words came back to her. He had warned her that continued bitterness would colour the rest of her days with destructive anger. That hatred would spoil every nice thing that happened to her.

Perhaps if she hadn't harboured this hatred her attitude to other things would have been different and Richard would have understood? Had he thought her unkind and cruel? And Miss Grainger? And the Careys?

Suddenly she wanted to see Richard and persuade him to understand. Forgetting everything else, she went to the car and drove to the Careys'. Richard wasn't there.

'He dressed himself up and went out an hour ago. I thought he was meeting you,' Mrs Carey said with some embarrassment. 'Business. It's business, sure to be.'

Rosita didn't want to go back to the flat. She took out the piece of paper with the names of prospective employees on it, and went to the first address on the list. By nine o'clock she had chosen two part-time women to run the Station Row shop in Kate's absence and taken on two more for the new premises. She would continue to manage the one near the school; she needed that pretence of a group of friends that The Horsey Gang supplied.

Outside the shop in Station Row, Richard waited in the van until just after nine for her to come home, then he gave up and went to meet Monty for a drink.

Rosita thought about the woman who had called to find her on behalf of Mrs Stock and, after a few days of consideration, went to see her absentee grandmother. The house was locked up and looked silent with the emptiness a house acquires when the owners are away.

Perhaps they had decided to move and had wanted to say goodbye? Although that was unlikely after the lack of communication over the years. She was about to give up and walk away when a neighbour opened the door and called, 'You looking for Mrs Stock? You're too late, miss. She's dead and gone.'

'Oh!' Rosita didn't feel any sadness, just a mild irritation at having wasted her time. 'I understood she wanted to see me. I must have been mistaken.'

'No, you weren't mistaken. I came to the shop for you, but it's too late now. Although, the solicitor will want to see you, mind. Got something to tell you, he has.'

Two days later, Rosita was informed that her grandmother had left her £1,300.

Money could never repay the debt Mrs Stock owed, she thought, trembling with mixed feelings. The debt the old lady had owed was in time and love, desperately needed over the years. The money was less of a thrill than it should have been, causing instead a renewal of the hurt and neglect. Then she shrugged. It would pay another kind of debt and help the accountant to sleep easier at night. But her feelings softened and she grieved for the loss of someone who should have been an important part of her life. A lonely, stubborn old lady, whose pride had deprived her of a granddaughter to love.

The new shop kept Rosita busy for the next few weeks and she rarely saw Richard. She had said nothing more to Kate on the question of her true identity and Kate had not referred to the subject again. The only change in their relationship was Kate using her new Christian name, Caroline, instead of calling her Miss Evans.

The week before the Careys left for their London holiday, Richard came to see her. Her first thought on seeing him was to wonder where he had been the night his mother had said he had 'dressed up and gone out'. She wouldn't question him. She might not like the answers.

'I had a visitor on the site yesterday,' he said. 'Luke arrived at five o'clock and we went for a meal. I tried to find you but, as usual, you were too busy with your empire-building.'

'Is he well?' she asked, ignoring the last remark. She glared at him, daring him to repeat his accusation that she was too busy for friends.

'He suggested we go to the cottage tomorrow afternoon, it being Sunday. You'll presumably have a few hours off?'

'Not really,' some devil in her made her say. 'I have books to do and – but all right. I can spare you and Luke a couple of hours. I'd like to come.'

'Honoured we'd be.' Richard didn't hide his sarcasm.

'Fine.'

'Oh, and wear something sensible,' he added as he left.

'You mean nothing smart and elegant?'

'That's right.'

Defiantly, she put on a tight-fitting white skirt with an angora jumper in a very pale grey. A blue jacket, severely tailored as she liked them, was thrown casually over her shoulder and a pair of ridiculously high-heeled white shoes completed the outfit. The white drawstring bag with straps hanging over her arm and a blue and white scarf gave a summery impression. She knew she looked good. She smiled as she saw Richard's look of admiration change to disapproval when the van stopped outside the shop. He wasn't going to tell her how to dress!

Luke admired her and said so. Richard's mood darkened.

'I'd planned a sail in my new boat,' Luke told them, 'but from the look of you, it mightn't be a good idea, unless you change into something of mine?'

'No, I'll sit on the beach and wait for you. I'm not very adventurous.' Angry with herself for ruining an afternoon by trying to win some silly game with Richard, she wished she had brought the accounts books with her. At least then the day wouldn't have been a complete waste!

She removed her shoes and stockings in Luke's cottage and, feeling annoyed with herself, stood on the beach and watched as the two men set off down the coast in the small rowing boat to where he moored his newest possession. They were laughing, the sound of their voices coming over the calm water like a reproach.

After a while they crossed the bay before a light wind, waving at her from the deck of the boat which Luke now owned. Again she heard their laughter and her self-directed anger increased and encompassed Richard. If he hadn't been difficult she wouldn't have spoilt her day trying to defy him. Then she reluctantly admitted to herself that he wasn't to blame; it was her own stupidity that had caused her to miss a pleasant hour on the blue sea. Richard had advised her to wear casual clothes – it hadn't been an order! The biter bit, she thought as she sat on the beach in her unsuitable clothes and waited miserably for their return.

They were back after a couple of hours during which she sat and read a book she had selected from Luke's shelves. Luke had brought food and they ate fish and potatoes cooked over a fire in the open, with a crisp salad. Rosita ate little, just listening to the two men talking and laughing, and wondering why she had created a situation in which she couldn't relax and enjoy the occasion with them.

It was dark when she and Richard left and the journey home began in silence.

'Did you enjoy your day?' Richard asked as they approached the first of the houses. 'You seemed very quiet.'

'I have a lot on my mind. Kate knows I'm really her sister. I – I came to tell you and discuss it but you were out.'

'Yes, Mam told me.' That stubbornness from which they both suffered made him hold back on the explanation he knew she wanted. He didn't tell her he had been sitting outside her flat for most of the evening, waiting for her to appear.

'Kate hasn't told Hattie yet and I don't know that I want her told. I don't want to see my mother, ever.'

'It's your choice, but I'd think very carefully if I were you. My father was always a fool but I still love him. Your mother was lacking in confidence, gentle, unsure of herself. She tried damned hard to keep you, under very difficult circumstances, and she failed. So what? Who's perfect? She chose the way to cope with life by abandoning you to a place of safety and going back to Kate, Hattie and Graham. What would you have done, I wonder?'

'I wouldn't have thrown out my child!'

'Not much chance of that happening!' He sounded harsh, his jaw tight with anger. 'Too sorry for yourself. Too afraid of showing a human side. What chance do you have of ever producing a child?'

'Stop the car! I won't ride with you a moment longer!'

He skidded as he clamped on the brakes and brought the car to a squealing stop in a few yards. She got out and turned to him, a clever retort on her tongue, but he slammed the door and drove off without giving her the chance. Fighting back tears of hurt and humiliation, she walked back to the flat on stupid shoes that hurt and the emptiness closed, like a hollow shell, around her.

Hattie was just leaving his mother's place when Richard reached the door and she smiled and said, 'Oh dear, Richard. You look as if you've had a disappointment. There's a shame. Pity for you. That Caroline Evans again, is it? Want to tell me about it, do you?'

The prospect of walking inside and spending the next couple of hours trying to calm himself after the latest argument was an impossibility. He said nothing as Hattie took his arm and pressed against him. The night was already dark and gave a false intimacy between them. They walked towards the silent anonymity of the park, the trees looking enormous with the addition of shadows from the street lamps. Unerringly she led them to where the railings had been broken and without a word spoken they went through.

Hattie was smiling. She remembered Richard's comment about Miss Evans. She made her mind up about what she wanted and went for it, did she? Well, if that attitude was good enough for the frosty Miss Evans, who was she to disagree? Her fingers tightened on Richard's hand as they went through the well-used access.

A week later, the Careys set off for London. To Mrs Carey's entreaty for Rosita to look after Richard, Rosita responded promptly. That evening she went to the Careys' door and put a note through the letterbox. It was a list of seven restaurants where he could get a meal. One for each evening his mother was away. And each one worse than the last.

Kate ushered her group into the hotel where they had booked bed and breakfast. She looked around her doubtfully. It was gloomy but the place looked clean and well run, although the curtains could do with a wash. Turning to help Mrs Carey up the long flight of stairs, she smiled at her.

'Very nice, isn't it, Mam? Richard was so kind to get us a smart place like this.'

'It wasn't easy, mind. Everyone wants to be in London for the festival,' Mrs Carey said, puffing between words. Kate moved ahead of her; it was best not to encourage her to talk while she had stairs to climb. Mr Carey walked behind his wife, even slower than her, Kate thought, listening to his rasping breath.

That first evening they planned to do little more than explore their immediate surroundings. But at five o'clock the receptionist sent a message to tell them their taxi had arrived to take them on a tour of the sights. Richard had arranged it when he had booked the rooms.

At first, Mrs Carey reeled off the names of the places she recognized, her eyes darting from one side to the other, afraid of missing the smallest thing. Marble Arch, Nelson's Column, the Houses of Parliament: she shouted out the famous landmarks, her eyes widening as she took it all in, her voice high-pitched with the thrill of it. Mr Carey nodded modestly as if he had arranged the whole thing for her delight.

All the time, Kate coaxed her when she missed something, and her words were echoed by the girls. The good-natured taxi driver laughed and added to their minimal knowledge with a running commentary.

Mrs Carey was so exhausted that she was in bed and asleep before Kate's two daughters. Kate sat with her father-in-law after the others were settled and they pored over maps and information booklets, planning their itinerary for the following day. At ten o'clock, she held out the festival guide to ask his opinion on something and saw that he too had succumbed to the long day and had fallen asleep. Gently she woke him and guided him to his room.

She went down the wide, carpeted stairs once more, this time to phone Idris and tell him they had arrived safely. He greeted her call with a casualness that hurt her. His mind seemed to be on other things. She thought she heard whispering in the background as they talked and she put the receiver down with a frown on her face. She was obviously mistaken. It must have been the wireless as Idris had said, yet she could have sworn it had been Hattie's voice she had heard.

'Would you like to talk to Richard?' she asked Mrs Carey the following morning. When Mrs Carey accepted with pleasure, she used the excuse to phone the site office. Monty answered.

'His mother would like to speak to Richard,' she explained.

'Sorry, Mrs Carey, but Richard isn't here. I'd try phoning him here at say, eight o'clock? I'll make sure he's here then.'

'My husband, is he there? I'd like a word, please.'

'Well now, Idris hasn't been in since Thursday. When he didn't turn up on Friday we thought he was seeing you off but he hasn't been in since. Nothing to worry about, I'm sure. He must be a bit under the weather, like.'

'Oh, he didn't say when – Thank you, Monty. Sorry to have troubled you.'

Putting aside her worries about Idris's behaviour with an effort, she smiled at Mrs Carey. 'Sorry, Mam. Richard isn't there and neither is Idris. Both out, busy as bees, like always. Monty suggests we try Richard at the site office tonight.'

'Nothing wrong, is there, Kate?' Mrs Carey's sharp eyes had noted the frown in Kate's usually placid face.

'No, nothing wrong, just that Idris hasn't been at work and I wondered why. He didn't say anything about being unwell when we spoke.'

Having given her accommodation and booking to a friend, Hattie sat in bed on that Monday morning, forty-eight hours after she should have left for Weston-super-Mare, with a smile of utter satisfaction on her face. The sound of cheerful whistling came from below. Idris was cooking breakfast, which they intended to eat in bed, Kate's bed. Idris had decided he too would have a holiday and didn't intend to go to work at all that week. He had seen his wife and daughters off on the train and had found little difficulty in persuading Hattie to spend her holiday with him. He was now cooking breakfast which, although they intended to eat it in bed, wouldn't be a prelude to their getting dressed.

The whistle of the kettle was added to the rather tuneless sound made by Idris and when it stopped she heard footsteps coming up the carpeted stairs. She burst out laughing as Idris entered the room with an improvized chef's hat made from a towel and another across his arm. He wore nothing else. He carried a tray on which two plates of bacon, fried bread and some rather crinkly-edged eggs floated in fat.

'Breakfast is served, madam,' he said, balancing the tray. He slid back into the bed he had recently vacated.

'The rations, Idris! Kate will notice if you've used all the rations!'

'Left these rashers for me, she did. They had to take their ration books

for their stay in London but she saved last week's so I could have a nour-
ishing breakfast. What does it matter if I use it all the first day?' He
chuckled. 'Poor Kate. If she only knew.'

Hattie thought Kate would know. Accidentally, or on purpose, she
would let the information slip the moment her sister got back from
London.

Richard was sitting in his bedroom too, but he was alone, with only books
for company. The business was thriving, everything going to plan, growing
at a remarkable rate. He would soon be able to buy himself a house, build
one perhaps. He put down the pen he was using to make notes and sighed.
If things had worked out as they ought, he and Rosita would be designing
one together, choosing furniture and planning a smart kitchen, but it was
useless to think about it. They were always at loggerheads. There was no
possibility of them ever agreeing long enough to plan a picnic, let alone a
life together.

He thought about food and smiled grimly when he remembered the list of
eating places that was Rosita's way of 'helping'. A glance at his food
cupboard with the small allocation of bacon, one egg and a few sausages that
his mother had left made him shudder. He couldn't face stuff like that and
filling up on slice after slice of bread. Rosita was right: he'd better eat out.

Walking up to the main road he abandoned the idea of a solitary meal
and decided to call on Monty. The food at the bed and board, where he
lived, was hardly cheerful. He might welcome an excuse to go out to eat.

They found a place that offered pie, mash and peas and ate with the
solid look of refuelling rather than with enjoyment. Richard told Monty of
the list pushed through his door by Rosita and the man looked at it and
laughed unsympathetically. 'She's a delightful girl, your Rosita. All the
customers think the world of her.'

'She isn't *my* Rosita,' Richard growled.

'Then it's time she was.'

'I thought so once but it's hopeless. Every time we meet we end up
rowing. She's too strong-minded ever to learn to share my life. We want
different things.'

'Then you'll have to rethink what you want and what you expect of her,
won't you?'

'I want marriage, children, a wife waiting for me in a pleasant home with
a meal ready when I get home.'

At this, Monty roared with laughter so loud that other diners turned
their heads to share the joke. 'You've chosen the wrong one there, haven't
you? Rosita is an exceptional woman and damned good businesswoman –

you can't expect her to change overnight into a housewife, content to concentrate on nothing more than your home and comfort! For many women that's what they want and they're more than happy with it. They do it brilliantly, make an art of home-making, but not your Rosita.'

'Stop calling her *my* Rosita!'

'I suppose I'll have to. Unless you do something soon, she'll be some other lucky devil's Rosita, and more fool you for not grabbing her while you have the chance!' Showing what was for him rare irritability, Monty stood and went to wait at the exit.

For a while they walked silently along the pavements, their feet in unison but their minds going separate ways.

'What can I do to persuade her to marry me, Monty?' Richard asked at last. 'Dammit, I love the woman, but I can't get under her protective shell. Whenever we start talking about a future together, she storms off in a temper.'

'Perhaps it's a question of picking the right place. You need somewhere where she can't storm off, don't you?'

Richard began to smile as Monty expounded his ideas.

In London, the Careys were exhausted. For the sake of Kate's girls, they went first to the Battersea pleasure gardens then to the children's zoo – and the boating lake – and the funfair. Feet began to drag but they persevered, determined to give the girls all they wanted from the visit.

The grotto was Mrs Carey's favourite although she wished she were taller so she could see more.

'I love the Temple of Winds,' she said as they sat eating lunch in the splendour of the gold and white pavilion buffet. 'There's clever it is to have each wind bringing the sounds and scents of its origin.'

'The north wind was best,' Kate and the girls agreed. 'That was magic, with the whisper of sleigh bells, howling wolves and the scent of pine forests.'

'And the east wind, that was good too, mind. Wafting scents of oriental spices and temple bells ringing far away.'

'What was your favourite, Dad?' Kate asked Mr Carey, then she shared a smile with her mother-in-law; he was fast asleep.

'Can we see the clock again?' Helen pleaded. Leaving Mrs Carey watching over her husband, Kate pushed her way through the ever-increasing crowds to the Guinness Festival Clock. Movement after movement held them enthralled, with an ostrich popping out of a chimney, a sun, a zookeeper ringing a bell, a mad hatter trying to grab fish, everything so fascinating it was impossible to fully appreciate first time.

When Mr Carey was gently roused, Mrs Carey attempted to make their way to a few exhibits he might enjoy. She was small, and the rest of the happy visitors seemed like giants. The crowds were so intense she doubted if she would be able to see anything without Kate there to make a space for her. All she could see as she and Henry, hand in hand, struggled towards the Far Tottering and Oyster Creek Railway, were the backs of men's shirts and women's dresses.

Giving up the unequal struggle, they collapsed into a fortuitously vacant seat in the Aviary Restaurant and slowly recovered enough for another onslaught into the delights around them. When they eventually found the bandstand where they were to meet the others, they both looked so exhausted that Kate insisted on going back to the hotel.

Hiding the fact from Mrs Carey, Kate had tried several times during the day to phone Idris. There was no reply and in desperation she rang Richard and asked him to go and see if everything was all right.

'Typical! Idris is a damned nuisance to worry you like this,' Richard said without preamble. 'You know what he's like, Kate. He's just taking a holiday from work. It isn't the first time he's let me down and I doubt very much if he's ill. There's been a light on when I've passed at night, and although he hasn't bothered to let me know he won't be in, I haven't any fears for his wellbeing! But,' he added, as she began to argue, 'I'll call on my way home from work this evening, then I'll phone the hotel. All right?'

On his way home, Richard was passing the school shop just as Rosita was locking the door. He stopped, touched the van's horn and waved. 'Fancy coming for a meal later?' he shouted, but a car changed gear as it reached the corner and his voice was lost to her. She waved back with a brief, irritated movement of her arm and walked away from him to where she had left her car.

'Damn you, woman.' Richard slammed the van in gear and drove off, overtaking her as she was starting the engine.

'Bad-tempered devil,' Rosita murmured, wondering at his impatience to be off without a word. He needn't worry, I'm not desperate for a friendly greeting from him, she told herself. But her heart was aching as she watched the van hurl itself at the corner and disappear with another squeal of brakes.

Richard slowed and parked at the kerb. This won't do, he told himself. Driving dangerously wasn't the answer to his frustration. Continuing at a more sensible speed, he drove to his brother's house and parked outside.

There was no response to his knock and, irritability returning, he went around the corner into the lane and tried the back door. It was open and, after calling, he stepped inside. For the first time he began to feel alarmed.

Perhaps he had been wrong and Idris was ill? Moving faster now, he walked through to the kitchen, the living rooms and, there being no one there, up the stairs.

Anxiety increased as he looked in one room then another, his footfall silent on the soft-carpeted floors. There was no point in looking in the third room; the small back room was Hattie's. That was bound to be empty with Hattie in Weston-super-Mare, but perhaps he'd better check?

As he touched the door handle his brother's voice called: 'All right, Richard, I'm coming.'

He must have heard the van, Richard thought, but why is he in that room? He knew from his brother's loud call that Idris thought he was downstairs. Unashamedly he bent his head and listened at the crack in the door. Voices. Whispering voices. He must have a woman in there! Unable to control his anger, he pushed the door and stared at the bed. Entwined together in the sheets were Idris and a red-faced Hattie.

Not waiting for excuses or explanations, he hurried back down the stairs and out of the house. The sight of his brother with his wife's sister was imprinted on his mind like a horrible nightmare. What could he tell Kate?

On the day the Careys went to the South Bank exhibition, the crowds were unbelievable. Great enthusiasm and the determination to pack as much as they could into the day had changed by midday to numb tiredness that made them search for cafés and, when they were fortunate enough to find a chair, sit, ease off their shoes and stare, bewildered by the crush of good-natured humanity around them.

Missing out the series of exhibitions telling the story of the Land of Britain, they struggled through the Dome of Discovery, forced along at the pace of the crowd rather than choosing their own. They managed to see something of its displays depicting the discoveries of man through the ages, and marvelled at man's endeavours and the hardships endured in searching the world for new knowledge and riches. In simple ways, the carefully designed displays explained the way science had added to their learning by research and curiosity.

Mr Carey declared he was fascinated more with the structure of the dome, with its 350-feet span of shining aluminium roof, than the exhibitions.

'I'll wait for you outside,' he said as they approached the exit. 'Over by there, near the river.' Arrangements were hurriedly made as enthusiastic revellers forced them inexorably towards the exit. Henry found a seat near Nelson Pier, watching the comings and goings of excited families, and waited for them to emerge. He felt desperately tired. Afraid of spoiling the holiday for the others, he said nothing, but each morning he dreaded leaving the hotel and setting off on another exhausting day of sightseeing.

Richard rang and told Kate that Idris was off work with a slight cold. He found it impossible to keep the harsh anger out of his voice and Kate thanked him and guessed that Idris was perfectly well, but not inclined to work. Kate silently thanked Rosita for giving her the chance to at least earn enough to keep them afloat. She loved Idris but knew she would never be able to rely on him.

Towards the end of the week, Hattie and Idris discussed Richard. They had said very little after seeing him burst into the room where they had been making love. Idris had laughed it off. 'About time he was educated into the joys of love,' he said. 'I bet he doesn't know what to do when he gets that hard-faced Caroline Evans on her own.'

'And she's too stiff-necked to help,' Hattie added. But although they joked, they were both anxious to know what, if anything, Richard had said to Kate. Their concerns were in opposition although neither would have admitted it. Idris hoped Richard would say nothing. He didn't want his comfortable marriage ruined. Hattie wanted desperately for her sister to know what had happened during her absence. She wanted Kate and Idris to part. Idris was handsome and he was fun. She wanted him, not on rare occasions like this, but openly and completely.

'Richard won't say anything,' Idris said a few days later, believing it was what Hattie wanted to hear. 'He needs me for one thing. I'm a pretty useful member of staff now. There'd be one hell of a mess if I left and he knows that if he gives so much as a hint to Kate or Mam, I'd go, leave him in the lurch, and he wouldn't want that.'

Idris continued to give Hattie, a willing and devoted audience, the impression that he was undervalued and hard-working; an opinion Hattie believed completely.

'If only the business was yours, Idris. There's your brother doing well and making money like fun and not even making you a partner. I bet someone like Miss Evans wouldn't work like you do and get so little back.' She happily ignored the fact that he hadn't left the house all week apart from necessary forays to replenish food and drink. 'Go out and get what you want, that's her motto. Pity we can't all be that determined. But you ought to speak to Richard. A partner you should be. After all, blood is—'

'—thicker than water?' Idris finished for her. His eyes sparkled with humour. 'You think that brother should help brother and sister help sister?'

'Well yes. It's only fair.' She looked at him, her mouth slightly open, waiting for him to say what was obviously waiting to be said. She twitched her lips, preparing to laugh, then closed them promptly as he said, 'What d'you say to the fact that Miss Caroline Evans is *your* sister? Your half-sister to be exact. Rosita Jones is her real name. D'you think she should make you a partner in her business then?'

Hattie's face lost its colour. She put down the glass of wine Idris had poured for her and stared at him, waiting to be told it was a joke.

'True it is. She's the sister that your mother threw out, got rid of into a home, when she was five years old.'

'But she can't be! Caroline Evans? Not Prothero.'

'Daft ha'porth! Graham never adopted her, did he? Illegitimate she is. Her father was Bernard Stock, killed in the First World War, so I understand.'

'Why hasn't she said something?'

'Kate found out a few weeks ago and told me. Made me promise not to say, but, well, you're her sister and I thought you should know.'

Hattie was quiet for a long time, absorbing the startling news. Idris put on a record and tried to persuade her to dance to Victor Sylvester's strict-tempo orchestra, snapping his fingers to the rhythm, but she shook her head. This would take a lot of getting used to. But she took malicious pleasure in the memory of taking Richard into the park that night. At least she had got one over the stuck-up bitch there, hadn't she?

'Funny, isn't it?' she said later, as she prepared vegetables for their meal. 'Your brother with plenty, my sister with plenty and us, well, we're not exactly rolling in money, are we? Doesn't seem fair.'

'If Richard doesn't marry, my girls will probably inherit at least some of his money. What about Rosita? Who'll get what she leaves? Not your mother, for sure.'

'Forget about Rosita,' she said slowly, selecting potatoes to prepare. 'She'll probably leave everything to a cats' home! But if Richard dies before you, then his money will come to you, won't it?'

'Not very likely. There are plenty of us Careys, remember. Eight of us kids left and about twenty-four grandchildren floating about somewhere. Spread about the globe but still in touch with Mam and Dad. Why should he single me out? Richard hates me. He always has. I was Mam's favourite. Anyway, it won't make any difference how many we are. He'll marry Rosita one day, have kids and neither you nor I will see a penny of it.'

'Unless we find a way of keeping them apart?' Hattie peeled potatoes in her slow way, but her mind was speeding and her dull eyes showed pin-points of excitement. Then she dropped her knife and said, 'There's a tin of

Spam in the cupboard. Let's have that with some chips. I don't feel like cooking tonight. Let's go back to bed instead.'

The evening before the Careys were due back from London it rained heavily. Running from the car to the shop on her way home from Station Row, Rosita covered her head with an old raincoat she kept in the car and with her view inhibited, bumped into Richard, who was waiting in the shop porch.

He held her tightly and before she could free herself or protest, he kissed her. The coat fell from her and she lost herself in the unexpected embrace. When he released her she looked at him, breathless and wide-eyed.

'Are you in a tearing hurry or can you spare an hour to come and try one of the restaurants on your list?' He was smiling, remembering her terrible choices of places to eat.

'I don't know.' She was flustered and confused by the effect of his presence and the surprising fervour of his kiss. She needed time to think and compose herself. 'I have to – I have lots to do,' she amended.

'An hour, that's all. One little hour.'

'All right. I'll just take these things in and check the books and—'

'Now, Rosita. Now.' It was raining heavily and he protected her with his coat and guided her to the old van. Covering the shabby passenger seat with his coat, he helped her in.

Her mind was in turmoil yet she found herself trying to think which restaurants were on her list. Was it the pub-cum-café on the way to the Pleasure Beach? Before starting off he kissed her again. Her mind wrestled with confused emotions, her head reeling with this masterful approach. She tried to speak, to at least pretend to be in control, but he silenced her in the most perfect way. Would it be the Pleasure Beach or her final sarcasm, the lorry drivers' pull-up on the road out of town? Surely not. He wouldn't take her there, a muddy parking place, a prefabricated building housing a steamy café where china was so thick it would take a muscular lorry driver to lift it.

'What are you smiling at, darling?' Richard asked as they drove through the gloomy streets.

'Just wondering which of the places I suggested was the one you chose.' She couldn't see through the window but just knew he would take her somewhere smart and expensive.

It was the lorry drivers' café!

'Richard! You can't mean it!' she protested, but he ignored her and, opening the van door, hauled her out with little ceremony.

The rain continued to pelt down and crossing the churned-up parking area meant her stockings were splattered with mud and the shoulders of the thin jacket she wore were soaked through. Her glasses were spotted with rain and the moment they entered the café they steamed up completely. Taking them off to polish them, she glared at Richard but he seemed unperturbed by her anger. In fact, he was trying unsuccessfully to hide a smile.

'Find us a couple of seats and I'll fetch the food,' he said. Leaving her to struggle through the crowd of burly lorry drivers, staining her light-coloured clothes on their rain-streaked waterproofs, he made his way unperturbed to the counter. She sat fuming with anger and was hardly aware of the interested looks and nods and whistles from the other diners.

The food he brought looked worse than she expected and she glared at Richard again, about to protest and say that she couldn't eat it. He seemed completely unaware of her furious glances; he smiled and began to eat. She sat for a while, the knife and fork untouched beside her plate. She wanted to leave, to stalk out with head held high, an expression of utter disgust and fury on her face, but miles from anywhere and in such weather, she couldn't.

Her protests subsided; there was nothing she could do except humour him until he took her home. Her rage was gradually abandoned when she realized she hadn't eaten since breakfast. Trying to keep the look of disgust on her face, she picked up the cutlery and began to eat.

To her surprise it tasted good and without a word passing between them, but with Richard smiling affably to all, they emptied their plates.

'Now,' Richard said firmly as they reached for the thick china mugs filled with strong tea, 'you and I will talk.'

'About what?' she asked ungraciously, determined to revive her disapproval of the venue.

'About us.'

'If it's about me selling the shops—'

'First things first, you irritating and irritable woman. I love you and I want to marry you.'

Around them conversations ceased. They had everyone's attention, although they were too aware of each other to notice.

Rosita felt the stirrings of her need for him that were never far below the surface. 'Richard, we'll never agree. I'd make you unhappy, you know it.'

'I couldn't be more unhappy than I am now, with us apart and fighting every time we meet.'

'You demand too much of me.'

'I want you to live with me as my wife. Everything else will sort itself out if we use that as a starting point.'

'Living together we'd fight more, not less.'

'Not if I accept your need to run your businesses. I will understand, Rosita. I do understand. I've been so full of old-fashioned principles and pride, I couldn't see how stupid I was. Why should I expect you to give up what you do so well and settle for being a housewife and mother?'

'You mean it?'

'I mean it, my darling girl.'

'I want that more than anything, but are you sure you can cope with me as a businesswoman? I won't be able to put you first all the time.'

'Let's start by showing the world we're a couple. Over the next few weeks we should be able to sort out our differences, then we can announce our engagement. What d'you say?'

'Go on, miss, tell the bloke yes!' The harsh voice of a man on the next table made her turn her head and there, in a row, were four smiling faces who had obviously been listening to every word.

Richard knew it was a dangerous moment. He saw the conflicting emotions crossing her face. She could have stood up and shown her displeasure. Knowing how stubborn she could be, he thought it even possible for her to stalk out and walk the seven miles home through the rain. She was quite capable of such an action. But she didn't. She burst out laughing.

'Of all the romantic proposals ...'

The diners cheered. 'Go on, then,' one of them called. 'Tell the poor bloke yes! Put us out of our misery!'

'Yes, Richard, I'll marry you.' She intended to say more but her words were lost in the uproar. The story had been passed from table to table until the fifty or more men were raising cups and mugs in noisy toasts from the extremely polite to the plain ribald, accompanied by sauce bottles thumping on tables. In moments diners left their tables to come and shake their hands and wish them luck. Their health was drunk, with tea replacing champagne, and everyone was clearly delighted with the unexpected celebration.

They walked to the door through a cheering, laughing crowd whose voices could still be heard when they reached the van, and whose waving arms could be seen through the steamy windows of the café.

'I knew you'd say yes, if I chose the place with care.' He laughed. 'Captive in a place like that, you *had* to listen to me. You couldn't do your favourite trick of stalking off.'

'I did want to,' she admitted.

'I know. I could see it in your face.'

He helped her into the van, managing a few kisses as he did so. They drove through the steady downpour for a few miles then he stopped the van. Taking her in his arms, he said, 'You've promised to marry me and in front of dozens of witnesses. Now you can't change your mind.'

'I'll never want to, Richard. Never, never, never.' But they couldn't kiss. Not properly. They were both laughing too much.

Chapter Fifteen

RICHARD REACHED HOME in a state of euphoria. Rosita had agreed to marry him. Some time in the distant future as yet, but she had agreed. Silently he thanked Monty for his sensible advice and patted himself on the back for taking it.

Monty had been right about choosing a place from where she couldn't walk away and he chuckled as he remembered his friend's advice to get the proposal in first: 'Forget conditions, you're asking the girl to marry you, not interviewing her for a job!'

He had stayed late at the flat in Station Row and they had talked about the future, not in the usual way, each trying to score points off the other, but calmly, working out how their businesses would be made to fit their lives, leaving them time for fun.

He was smiling as he collected the dog for his nightly walk and, although it was past midnight, he took him further than usual, enjoying the peace and silence in which to contemplate the future. He went along the well-known streets, made unfamiliar by the late hour. Shadows made the buildings look misshapen; the silence made his footsteps extra loud so he trod with more than usual care. Occasionally he would start as a cat left a pool of darkness to run without sound, and cause the dog to growl threateningly.

Strolling towards Idris's house on the way back to his parents' house he began to imagine telling his parents. They would be pleased to know that he and Rosita were together; he knew that was something they had both hoped for. He glanced up at the lighted bedroom of his brother's house and frowned. Only one room was lit: a bedroom. He wondered if the two of them were there together and thought it more than likely. Idris wasn't the sort to be put off by him knowing.

He would have to do something about his brother. This affair couldn't continue. Mam would find out and this was something she wouldn't be pleased to hear. In fact, he wondered if she'd believe him if he told her about finding Idris in bed with his sister-in-law. Ruefully, he thought Mam would rather believe he'd had a mental aberration than believe Idris – her golden boy – capable of such a thing.

As he turned away from the house, the light upstairs was extinguished and he deliberately closed his mind from the problem of Idris and his sordid affair. Tonight was a night for thinking of himself and Rosita. 'Come on, boy, you've sniffed there long enough.' He tugged on the lead. 'Time to go home.' He urged the dog forward once more and walked on.

It was evening before Rosita could go to the Careys' and hear about their visit to London. She was greeted almost tearfully by Mrs Carey.

'You're all right, Rosita? Oh, I'm so glad to be back. Thought all sorts of terrible things were happening, I did. A week from home is such a long time – it seems we've been away for months! But it was lovely, mind. That London place is full of such beautiful buildings and oh, the shops!' She chattered on, wiping away the tears and hugging Rosita between telling her some of their adventures.

'I've never seen such lights! And that big-huge river. All the boats and buildings were lit with coloured lights and oh, the funfair! You can't imagine how splendid it all was. And that Skylon above it all like a magic wand making it all happen. Best of all was when the whole place was lit up at night. Beautiful beyond it was.'

'It made us realize how long we'd been in the dark all those war years,' Henry added. 'The girls thought it was fairy land. They didn't want to come home, those two. And remember the fireworks, Molly?'

'Every night a fireworks display filling the sky and reflecting in the lake. Oh, Rosita, love, you ought to try and go.'

Rosita tried to tell them several times that London was where she and Richard might go for their honeymoon, but she didn't have a chance for a single word before Mrs Carey was off again on some description of her exciting week. Telling was part of the fun, she knew that. Time for hers and Richard's news later, she thought with a chuckle, when the travellers had calmed down.

Mr Carey made them some tea and brought out some biscuits they had bought in Fortnum and Mason. 'And the tea—' he began.

'Bought off ration, would you believe,' his excited wife interrupted. 'Off a street trader!'

'Street trader!' Mr Carey said scornfully. 'He was one of them spivs!'

'Well, whatever,' Mrs Carey chuckled. 'I only know I haven't had a better time in all my life.' He sat back on the couch and fell asleep.

Richard arrived and Rosita and he greeted each other with a light-hearted kiss.

'Well, would you believe it! They're greeting each other as if they've been apart longer than us!' Molly Carey grinned. 'Stopped quarrelling, have you?'

'I hope so, Mam,' Richard said, looking at Rosita.

The descriptions and memories were repeated with embellishments for Richard to hear but all the time Rosita could see Mrs Carey was waiting for someone and guessed it was Idris, her favourite child. When there was a knock on the door and a shout, she saw the woman's face light up and she wondered what it was about Idris that made people admire him. Why couldn't they see beyond the handsome features and the fair curly hair? Compared with Richard he was nothing.

Idris was followed by Kate, Hattie and the girls, who filled the small room with their excited chatter. Yet, Rosita realized, there were undercurrents of unease. She looked around the family, trying to decide where it came from. The twins, Helen and Lynne, were glowing with excitement, their faces full of nothing but happiness.

Her eyes alighted next on Kate, calm, gentle Kate, and saw a smile that was strained. Kate had a bag of gifts in a colourful carrier bag with the logo of the festival on it and as soon as they settled in chairs, cushions and on the floor, Mrs Carey reached for a similar bag from under the table. Soon the room was like Christmas morning, with discarded tissue paper and assorted wrappings covering the floor. Excited fingers tore and scrabbled and revealed souvenirs of the visit to the capital. Helen and Lynne were included, to their surprise, as their mother gave them each a new shoulder bag. Rosita admired the small model of the Skylon she had been given and Richard frowned at her over the heads of the others and gestured towards his new Festival of Britain tie, with something akin to horror.

'To hold your trousers up,' Hattie whispered. Richard glared at Idris, the brothers exchanging looks of such fury that Rosita took Richard's arm in a protective gesture and pulled him away from the rest.

'You feeling fit again, Idris, love?' Molly Carey asked her favourite son. 'Richard said you've been sick.'

'Yes, Idris,' Richard said loudly. 'Ready for work next week? Or are you too busy with … other things?'

'I'm fine, Mam, and yes.' He spoke to Richard but didn't look at him. 'I'll be there on Monday.'

'Your light was on late last night, considering you're supposed to be ill.'

'Chasing a fly,' Idris replied hastily. 'Gets on your nerves something chronic when one is buzzing round the room.'

'Chasing something,' Kate said quietly.

The air was filled with unsaid things and Rosita looked at Kate in alarm.

What had she found when she had returned home? Something to make her gentle face sad and for her tongue to have an edge of reproach rarely heard. She had the look of a puppy who had been unfairly whipped. To take attention away from the unhappy woman, she turned to Hattie and asked, 'What about your holiday, Hattie? You don't look very tanned after a week at the seaside.'

'And you didn't send a card,' Kate said.

'Stayed in, didn't I? Sick I was and hardly left my room.'

'There's a shame,' Mrs Carey said at once. 'All that money and you no better off for it.' She shook her head and tutted sympathetically. 'You might just as well have stayed home.'

For some reason Rosita didn't understand, the words hung in the air. Richard's head jerked around and he glared at Idris. Rosita frowned as the brothers continued to stare unblinkingly, one challenging, the other with an air of defiance. It was obvious they shared some guilty secret.

Then she looked at the red-faced Hattie, who was looking at the floor with self-conscious scrutiny. Slowly her eyes focused on Idris, who was thumping the cushions of the armchair, beating time to some silent dirge of his own. In that brief moment of time, Rosita knew that the problem, whatever it was, involved Hattie and Idris. But what could it be? She remembered seeing Hattie and Idris in her car and wondered if they had done more than a bit of furtive kissing. But no, Idris wouldn't be that stupid. Perhaps he had 'tried it on' with someone and Richard had discovered it? Or worse, perhaps Kate had somehow learned of it.

Unaccountably, Rosita felt shame. Idris had certainly 'tried it on' with her and she had ignored it. Why hadn't she faced him and told him that if he didn't behave she would tell his mother? For an adored son like Idris, that might have been enough to warn him off. Or at least make him think twice about having an affair while his wife and children were away from home.

'Idris wasn't alone while we were away, Mam,' Kate said softly. 'I found evidence that he'd had … company.' She didn't say female company but it was implied by the seriousness of her expression.

'Never!' Mrs Carey gasped. 'Oh, Kate, love, you must be mistaken. Not my Idris.'

'I had a few pals around, that's all, Mam. You'd think, listening to Kate, I'd done something real wicked. Thieving or burglary.' He smiled at Richard, unable to resist reminding Richard of his early career.

'Oh, just some friends!' His mother looked relieved. 'Well, now, you can't blame him for that, Kate, him being unwell an' all.'

Kate didn't say any more, unwilling to upset her mother-in-law, knowing perhaps that whatever revelations she announced, they would be twisted into something innocent.

The party broke up soon after, and Idris and a pale, silent Kate took their girls home. Hattie followed them at a slight distance, as if unsure if she should. Richard and Rosita stayed a while, wanting to smooth over the disquiet of the previous moments. Perhaps now they could tell his parents their news. In his chair, Henry Carey snored rather noisily and their derisory laughter was also loud, glad of the chance to release some of the tension.

'What was up with Kate and Idris, then?' Mrs Carey asked. 'I know there was something, so don't try and tell me different. Is she angry with him because he didn't keep the house tidy? Or for leaving dishes piled up in the sink? Men are like that. Always have been and always will be. She shouldn't start a row when she's been away for a week. Now isn't the time.'

She didn't seem to expect answers so Rosita and Richard stayed thankfully silent.

Rosita gathered up the last of the wrapping paper and Mrs Carey made tea. Richard sat staring out of the window, wondering what would happen between Kate and his foolish brother. It had spoilt the homecoming. He had imagined the family sharing his delight when he announced that he and Rosita were planning to marry. Now the event had been soured. Damn that brother of his.

Richard glanced at his father, who seemed safely asleep, then quietly told Rosita about finding Idris in bed with another woman. To save her distress, he didn't tell her the woman was Hattie.

'And Kate knows?'

'She's guessed.'

'Poor Kate. I thought she meant a woman, from the way she said he's had "company" in her absence. Auntie Molly Carey will never believe it, you know. He's a fool, that brother of yours. Imagine Kate's humiliation discovering that while she was away, Idris was finding comfort with another woman. Poor Kate. I won't know what to say to her tomorrow. It's such – such an insult.'

Richard thought of how much worse it would have been if Rosita had known who the other woman was. He hoped she would never find out.

When Mrs Carey came in with a tray of tea, she stopped beside Henry, whose snores had ceased, and nudged him.

'Tired out, he is. Slept a lot while we were away. I think all the walking and pushing our way through the crowds was too much. He loved every minute, mind,' she added, not wanting Richard to regret arranging the holiday for them. 'Never seen him so happy.'

'Wouldn't it be better to get him to bed, Mam?' Richard suggested. 'He doesn't look very comfortable, slumped like that.'

'Here's your tea, Henry. Come on, *cariad*, push that stupid dog off and drink this. You'll never sleep tonight, dozing at this time.'

There was no response and she placed the cup and saucer on the table near him. It was ten minutes more before they realized Henry Carey was dead.

The rest of the night was a blur. For a few moments, after realizing he was gone from them, they all sat, unmoving, numb with the suddenness and shock. When Mrs Carey did move it was like an old, old woman, completely different from the bird-like brightness she usually displayed.

Rosita helped Mrs Carey take the dog away and cover the face of her dead husband, while Richard made telephone calls. Idris came back and hugged his mother, bringing forth her tears. He sat beside her, his arms holding her, and Richard was grateful to him for being able to give some comfort to his stunned mother.

It took half an hour of that dreadful, uneasy silent waiting before the doctor came and declared Henry dead. Then, more waiting, interspersed with a visibly shaking Mrs Carey making tea that no one wanted but which they all drank.

Rosita went straight from the Careys' house to the shop to open up and sell newspapers. Her first customer was Monty and she told him what had happened.

'Can I use your phone?' he asked. She heard him telling Richard that he would deal with everything that day and call to see him after work that evening.

'It was such a shock,' she told Monty. 'We were laughing at him, sitting there nursing that dog of his. And all the time he was ...'

'Best way to go but hard for those left behind.' The platitudes always came more easily than original remarks and were somehow more reassuring.

'We were looking forward to telling them all that we're getting married,' Rosita said in a lull between serving customers. 'It would have been a cause for celebration, and now ...'

'Now you can keep it to yourselves for a while and enjoy the privacy of it for a while longer. My congratulations to Richard on his good sense in ... capturing you. He's a lucky man.' He smiled, winked and left. She was sorry to see him go. He was a kind man and she wished he could have stayed a while longer to allow her to talk.

Customers kept her busy for the next hour and a half as workmen and then business people filed in for their morning papers and cigarettes. The businessmen were followed by mothers buying magazines and spending their sweet ration. The small coupons had to be cut out of the ration books and put into a tin to be counted later and exchanged for fresh stock, a job Rosita hated. Restless and unable to think of much besides the death of Uncle Henry Carey, she tackled the irksome task to keep her fingers and at least part of her mind busy. She threaded them onto cotton with the aid of a sewing needle, separating every twenty coupons with a cardboard disk to make counting easier. At 9.30, during a lull, she made herself some coffee.

Richard rang to tell her that the undertakers were there. She sipped the warm drink and allowed her thoughts to return to Monty. He was such a good friend to Richard, someone he could rely on, very much as she had depended on Miss Grainger. She knew he was fond of her too and seemed genuinely pleased that she and Richard were intending to marry.

The funeral took place on a warm June morning and after dealing with the morning papers, Kate and Rosita closed the shops and went to the house near Red Rock Bay to stay with Mrs Carey while the men went to the graveside. A surprisingly large number of people turned up. The house was crowded with people wanting to show affection and sorrow. Yet there were tensions within the family.

Kate pointedly ignored Idris. Rosita noticed that her sister Hattie was absent. So were the rest of the Carey family. None of Mrs Carey's children were there apart from Idris and Richard.

'They've all written to say they're sorry to miss the funeral,' Mrs Carey told Rosita, but she didn't sound convincing. Richard had given the task of contacting them to Idris and she guessed he had probably left it too late for arrangements to be made. If Mrs Carey noticed the absence of Hattie she didn't say anything. There were so many people milling around she might not have noticed. Rosita found herself in charge of handing out cups of tea to the women, while Richard and Idris poured stronger drinks for the men. Hands appeared and were filled with a cup and saucer, hands connected to people she rarely looked at, the crush was so great.

At two o'clock the last of the mourners left and Mrs Carey stared around the empty room in disbelief. From the moment of Henry's death the place had been constantly full of people. Now they were gone. Her eyes rested on the armchair where Henry had spent a lot of his time.

'From now on it'll only be me,' she whispered to Rosita and Richard. 'Once there were twelve of us, can you believe that? Now there's only me. At night when I wake, the bed will be empty and I'll be alone. In the day, whenever I have something to say, there'll be no one to listen. Or care about my opinion. No one to touch me or to give me a hug. Will I ever get used to it?'

She seemed to have forgotten that Richard still lived there, and neither bothered to remind her. After all, she was right, she was alone. She was alone because Henry was no longer there.

There were no words. Rosita hugged the elderly lady, who seemed to have shrunk in the past few days. Richard put an arm around them both and for a long time they stayed together. Mrs Carey went through the people who had come, seeing them as a procession before her eyes. Suddenly she said with bitterness, '*She* didn't come.'

'Who, Mam?'

'Barbara, of course. Rosita's mother. You'd have thought she'd come after all me and Henry did for her.'

Rosita felt an almost painful shock at the mention of her mother.

'How could she have known?' Richard asked.

'Because I wrote to her, that's how!'

There are always feelings of guilt around at a funeral, Rosita thought as she continued to hold Mrs Carey. Words regretted and words unspoken that should have been said. In the atmosphere of grief at the funeral of Uncle Henry Carey, whom she had loved as much as a father, guilt for her deliberate neglect of her mother stabbed like a knife. Richard seemed aware of her thoughts and moved to pull her closer.

Was it just this moment of sentimentality that made her feel shame and remorse? Or was it the reminder that time was passing, that the generations were beginning to change, with one going and another moving up to take its place? One day her mother would die and then it would be too late for a change of heart. For those brief moments she seriously considered making contact with her. After all these years, wasn't it time to forgive? Forgetting was impossible, she knew that, but surely she was a big enough person now to forgive?

It could be speedily and simply done. All she had to do was mention it to Kate and something would be arranged. Perhaps a meeting at Kate's home, with Hattie there to help things along? On neutral ground in a restaurant with a meal to edge away their initial strangeness? It would be so easy, but easier still to leave it and do nothing.

Life settled back into a routine. 'Like one of those snowstorm scenes,' Rosita said to Richard. 'The ones you shake and release thousands of flakes then watch them land once more, slightly different but normal enough to appear the same; safe and familiar.'

'I'm worried about Mam, though,' Richard told her, helping himself to the Oxo-flavoured casserole she had prepared for their evening meal. They were in her Station Row flat and, it being Saturday, Richard knew he could leave his mother because Idris and Kate would be visiting her. The weekly arrangement had quickly become a regular habit so neither Rosita nor Richard ever questioned it or checked on it; they just accepted it as a part of their new togetherness. Saturday evenings and Sunday afternoons were theirs.

'I go as often as I can,' Rosita said. 'And always stay for a cup of tea and a chat. I think she faces each day as if it were a long expanse of empty space to be filled.'

'Rosita, d'you think we could make a date for our engagement? It would be something good for Mam to look forward to. She loves a celebration and you know how she loves an excuse to cook, and fill the house with people.'

'Have an engagement party?'

'Now. Very soon.'

'I don't know. I'll have to think about it.' She didn't look at him, knowing the disappointed 'little boy' look on his face would have made laughter inevitable and she wanted to tease him a little. Love and laughter are good companions. Solemnly she refilled their wine glasses. 'Richard? Persuade me,' she coaxed.

Now it was his turn to tease and for a few heart-stopping seconds she waited. She looked at him in alarm. Had she misread his mood? Was he upset by her response? Then he jumped up and held her so tightly she couldn't move – not that she wanted to.

As Richard had predicted, Auntie Molly Carey was overjoyed at their announcement.

'Pity Uncle Henry Carey won't be here,' she sighed, 'but never mind, this is a glad occasion, not one for sorrow and regrets. *I'm* alive to see it and that's what I must remind myself! Every day is a blessing when you're my age.'

With the newspapers being an everyday occupation, it was impossible to arrange a day off, so they decided to have the engagement party on a Sunday afternoon, 14 July.

'Like cows you and your papers are, Rosita,' Mrs Carey said with a laugh. 'Cows can't go on a five-day week either, now can they?' Her words, with connotations of the farm where Rosita had lived so unhappily, brought her mother to mind. This engagement party was an excellent opportunity to invite her mother and shake off the ghosts of the past, but

Rosita determinedly ignored it. One day, but not yet. She wasn't ready yet and wondered if there would ever be a time when she was.

Whether it was the prospect of marriage and, if she were fortunate, children, or simply the passing of time, Rosita began to warm a little towards her mother. Perhaps, when the wedding was arranged, she would contact her. With Richard to support her it would be easier than when she was alone. The thought grew and was embellished with imagined scenes in which her mother would hug her and everything bitter and unpleasant would miraculously melt away.

By the time the engagement party was only a couple of weeks away, she was teetering on the point of writing to her and arranging to meet, just briefly. If their meeting went well then she could come to the party. It would be a good time to revive the damaged relationship, with everyone in celebratory mood and no time for long conversations of the soul-searching kind.

On Wednesday evening, with only eleven days to go, she was still trying to make up her mind. She had said nothing to Richard, but thought she would broach the subject with Auntie Molly Carey, the recipient of so many of her secrets and problems. Her intention to go there immediately after closing the shop was altered when she found Kate's handbag on the counter. Instead of going to the Careys' house, she would call on Kate and return it.

At Walpole Street, near to Kate and Idris's home, there was obviously a party going on and for that reason there was no room to park near the front door. So, finding herself closer to the lane, she went through the small yard and, finding the back door half open, she stepped inside. The soft sandals she wore made no sound.

The day had been hot. After an absence of more than a week, the sun had returned to shine brassily down out of a blue sky. Stepping out of the brightness, the kitchen was dark and for a moment Rosita's eyes couldn't pierce the gloom. When she did focus, it was to see a couple on the couch against the far wall. They didn't look up, unaware of her arrival. The sounds they were making made clear their complete absorption in each other. Beside them a radio played softly.

Rosita was so shocked that even if she had wanted to speak she was unable to utter a word. Idris lay sprawled along the couch and, on top of him, her position leaving Rosita in no doubt as to their activity, was her half-sister, Hattie.

Afterwards she was to wonder at the speed with which the various thoughts, memories and facts fell into place. So this was what Kate had come home to! The 'company' Idris had entertained was his wife's sister.

Hattie hadn't been to Weston, but had stayed behind when the others had gone to London.

Hattie and Idris! It was obscene! She gasped, paused a moment as though to berate them, then ran unnoticed down the path with a choking sob.

On the way to the car she saw Kate, who had gone back to the shop for her handbag, realized what had happened and returned. Rosita walked with her to the front door and stood talking to her, to allow the couple inside time to separate. Only when Idris sauntered out, casually dressed, and kissed his wife, did she leave.

Hurrying back to the car she decided that Idris and Hattie must get their kicks from the risk of being caught. There was no other explanation. She wondered whose idea it had been to make love where they would have to run to the stairs as soon as they heard Kate's key in the lock. Hattie might be trying to take Idris away from Kate, but Idris might just be vain enough to believe Kate would love him however badly he behaved.

It took several days before she could face going to the Careys' house. The thought of meeting either Idris or Hattie there was too terrible to contemplate. She didn't tell Richard of her discovery, although she suspected he already knew.

She did eventually go to talk to Auntie Molly Carey. It was memories of the death of Uncle Henry Carey that made her decide to arrange a meeting with her mother before it was too late. Her opinion of her half-sister Hattie was a separate issue. What she thought of Hattie was nothing to do with reviving her relationship with her mother. Regretfully, Idris was Kate's to deal with. All she could do was be ready to offer support.

For a long time she thought about the proposed meeting. Auntie Molly Carey was the one to advise her, and after all, she had known them both all their lives. But when she eventually came face to face with Barbara, what would she say? How would they react to each other after so many years and after so much had happened to them both? Days passed and she said and did nothing about it. Then, before she could even talk to Mrs Carey, the matter was taken out of her hands.

Kate was waiting for her when she arrived at Station Row one evening. She wondered if Kate intended to talk about Hattie and Idris, whether this was the discussion she had been dreading.

'Come up to the flat if you've something to talk about, Kate. We'll have a cup of tea, shall we?' She knew she was delaying it, but what could she say to this woman to comfort her when she had been so terribly let down by her husband and sister?

But it wasn't about Idris and Hattie.

'Rosita, Mam is coming to see me at the weekend. Will you come and say hello?'

Rosita just stared at her. Preparing herself for offering words of comfort, she was completely thrown. Kate went on, 'I know you'll need time to think about it after all these years but really, you should see her. Time is passing. Mam's over fifty and already feeling the dread of drifting into old age without you, her first and best-loved daughter.'

'Best-loved!'

'Yes. You were the flesh and blood of her true love, Bernard – that was his name, wasn't it? She loves us all, but you the best. I've always known that.'

The desire to punish her mother was still causing her stomach to tie itself into knots. But Luke's voice seemed to cross the miles and warn her that this might be her very last chance. He had warned her gently one day of leaving it too late and the hatred within her wouldn't have an outlet and would continue to ruin her happiness.

'All right, I'll come.'

She regretted the words as soon as Kate had left but knew she had to go through with it. If they failed to make any bridges she needn't ever see her again. It was that thought she clung to as the day approached.

Richard was pleased when she told him but played it down and was matter-of-fact about the whole thing, knowing that a wrong word could make her change her mind. As the hours passed, she became more and more nervous. The day before she and her mother were to meet, she decided, on impulse, to go and talk to Auntie Molly Carey. She'd say she didn't know what to wear. Yes, that would do for an excuse to talk to her.

Driving down to the house near Red Rock Bay, she expected Mrs Carey to be alone. But the living room was full. She heard voices before she had reached for the knocker. Richard answered the door and after kissing her, said, 'Kate, Idris and the girls are here.'

'Then I won't stay. I only wanted a chat with your mam. It will keep.' They exchanged a few words, a brief kiss and parted.

As she walked back to the car, Rosita was stopped by Hattie stepping out in front of her. 'Can we talk for a minute?' Hattie said and, without waiting for a reply, she got into the car and turned to stare at Rosita. 'I know who you are,' she said. 'Bursting to tell you I've been, for weeks, but I wanted us to be alone.'

'Oh,' was all Rosita could manage. Somehow Hattie discovering her secret made her meeting with her mother less attractive.

'I've got a bit of a problem, see, and I thought, you being a woman of the world, like, you'll advise me.'

'Hattie, I don't know you. To offer advice to someone you don't know is asking for trouble. You and I would tackle a problem in an entirely different way. Now, if you don't mind I'd rather you talk to someone else. I must go, I really am busy and—'

'Always busy, rushing here and there. Must be great having a life of such importance.'

There was no envy in the words. Her face showed genuine admiration. Cautiously, expecting the subject to be the affair with Idris, Rosita said, 'I'm not the one to help you.'

'Yes, you are. Following your rules I was. Going all out for what I wanted, just like you said, so you're a bit responsible, see.'

'What?'

'Well, it's like this, see. I'm going to have a baby and, well, I don't know what to do about it. I thought you, being so worldly and everything, you'd help me make up my mind.'

'Make up your mind about what?' Caution deepened. She wondered if she were physically strong enough to push her overweight half-sister from the car, and decided she wasn't.

'I don't know whether to have the baby or not,' Hattie continued, smiling. She seemed oblivious of Rosita's growing anger.

'I don't want to hear this!'

'You don't have to have the baby, I know that. There's plenty of choice. I've got to think about what's best for me.'

'If you're thinking about an abortion then I don't want to hear! Do you understand? Go to a backstreet *Gwrach* and murder your child if you must, but don't talk to me!' Rosita's voice was warningly low but Hattie was blissfully unaware of the distress she was causing.

'Get rid of it? I had thought of that. Having a baby would spoil my life quite a bit. It wouldn't be much fun having to drag a child around with me everywhere I went, would it? Me not being married an' all.'

'I think you should go! Now, this minute!' Rosita saw an image of her mother talking exactly the same way as Hattie was now and all her unhappiness was rekindled in a way it hadn't been for years.

Hattie chattered on, oblivious of Rosita's growing pain and anger, her silence convincing her she was talking to an interested and admiring audience of one. 'The man, the father, like, he won't marry me. At least, I don't think he will. So the sensible thing would be to lose it and try and forget it ever happened. Get on with the rest of my life. Don't you think that's best for me?'

'That's between you and your conscience,' a trembling Rosita managed to say.

'Of course I could have the baby, then get it adopted. Or fostered might be better!' She looked as though the idea had just occurred. 'Then,' she went on, 'one day, when I'm older I could find her and—'

Rosita leaned across, opened the door and asked her to leave, giving her a fierce but ineffectual push. It was clearly Idris's baby and choking misery as well as compassion for Kate, whom she had grown to like very much, made it impossible to listen to any more.

More importantly, Hattie had confirmed the reason she hadn't wanted to see her mother all these years. Hattie was exactly the same type as Barbara, thinking the same thoughts as when Barbara had discovered she – Rosita – was on the way. Rosita was shaking as she imagined her mother discussing whether or not to allow her to live and if she did, then whether it might be nice to let someone bring her up and return her when all the problems had faded. History was repeating itself.

She used both hands and pushed a protesting Hattie from the car and drove off, tears stinging her eyes, her throat threatening to burst with held-back sobs.

Around the corner she stopped and allowed the tears to fall. How could she ever meet her mother with anything but hatred? Barbara's own daughter was growing up exactly the same as her mother had been: calculating, callous and self-centred. She closed her eyes and saw in her mind a kaleidoscope of memories, mostly of Richard, showing him at various stages of his life, growing from a boy to a man. She opened her handbag and took out the faded and creased photograph of Bernard Stock, her father. At least she didn't carry the blood of the harsh and unkind farmer, Graham Prothero.

Starting the engine again, she felt isolated from everything; unreal, invisible and completely alone. She knew how her mother must have felt about her; she had been unwanted, a nuisance, a burden to be discarded as soon as possible. Hattie's attitude was the same as Barbara's had been. She had no right to be alive. She didn't belong to anyone or anywhere. If only she could drive non-stop until she had left everything behind again, just like when she had run away from the children's home and met Miss Grainger. Perhaps it would work again but this time she would emerge as an independent woman with no memories to hold her down and prevent her from being happy.

She drove out of town to the quiet beach near Gull Island and stepped out onto the rocky shore. The tide was far out and her feet took her onto the seaweed-slimed causeway towards the island without thought. Her mind was still ringing with the words spoken by Hattie and which, in her distress, she imagined spoken thirty-four years before by her own mother.

Slipping and sliding, cutting her legs on sharp rocks and barnacles, she felt nothing, although blood ran down her legs and gathered in her shoes. The sun was long gone, leaving a darkening sky and making way for a storm. Clouds rushed towards her, approaching from the west, carrying moisture from the wide expanse of the Atlantic ocean. But her surroundings were irrelevant; unseen, unfelt and no longer of any importance.

The wind, a forerunner of the approaching storm, lifted her jacket and touched her skin through her undergarments, but she disregarded the chill. Dark swirling water began to fill the space around the island and deepen the pools. Fish and small crustaceans eagerly searched the replenishing tide for food and Rosita walked on without reducing or increasing her speed. The whole journey was a dream.

When she was a few yards from the island shore, the tide deepened and with added strength it sucked and pulled at her legs. It seemed determined to force her out into the wicked race of water coming at speed around the rocky outcrop of land, where she would be immediately out of her depth and in waters so irresistible she would be helpless to choose her own destiny.

She didn't care; nothing mattered any more. Her eyes were staring but seeing nothing. The spray had covered her glasses with an opaqueness that inhibited her sight but she didn't notice. Yet, there was, deep within her, some instinctive seed of survival that forced her to deny the greedy water its prize, and pull herself towards safety. She held on to the jagged rocks and tore her hands as the water tried to dislodge her. Straining every muscle, she battled against the enormous force of the sea and inch by inch pulled herself towards land.

When she eventually dragged herself out onto the beach, she was waist-deep in water and the waves touching the rocks and bouncing in every direction leapt and frolicked and soaked her completely. She was exhausted and crawled to lay on the sand until she felt the tide touching her feet. Then instinct prevailed once more and she crawled higher up the beach and stopped when she reached the reedy grass on the higher ground.

Cold, wet and without food, she was alone and no one knew where to find her. She wasn't worried. It simply didn't matter.

Chapter Sixteen

LUKE SPENT SEVERAL days each week travelling to sales and book fairs and other shops, buying stock or collecting pre-ordered items, but when the weather was good and he was at home, he often went to the cottage straight from the bookshop. He usually rang his housekeeper before mid-afternoon so she would know whether or not to prepare a meal for him. There were no other arrangements necessary.

On the day Rosita talked to Hattie, he had arrived at the beach near Gull Island early and parked his car out of sight at the back of the cottage. He walked for a while then, as he sensed the approach of the storm, he gathered driftwood for the fire and prepared for a cosy evening in with his books. Even in mid summer, a fire was friendly company.

He didn't see the Anglia arrive or see Rosita's staggering walk across the rocky neck of land to the island. While he sprawled in front of a roaring fire, a drink at his elbow and a book in his hand, he had no thought of there being anyone out on the storm-swept protuberance of land only yards from where he idled the hours away.

The storm was a violent one. As he sat and read, Luke was constantly aware of it as things began to roll about outside the cottage and occasionally bang with a suddenness that made him start. Once he went out to rescue a bin that was rolling first one way then another and threatened to go on all night. Outside, the night was black, with rain coming down in solid torrents and blanking out everything beyond his nose. He was soaked in the few moments it took to anchor the bin. He paused though, and looked towards the turbulent water and the island. Both were unseen; only memory told him they were there.

It was almost midnight when he stretched, considered setting off back to Cardiff, then changed his mind and decided to stay the night. The weather was really wild, the wind pausing now and then before lashing at the walls in increased fury. More unseen objects were rolled about before its angry breath. Better to stay where he was, warm and comfortable, rather than risk driving through the lanes and perhaps meet a fallen tree, or worse, be hit by one. Better to rise early for the six-mile drive to the shop.

He liked the sound of a storm when he was inside. The cottage was old but solidly built and he could laugh at the wind, locked away from its power, cheating it of its intention to do harm. He thought of the people who were out in it, seamen most of all, and policemen and emergency services, and he was thankful.

Before he settled into bed he stood by the window and looked out over the sea. The island was invisible in the darkness apart from the fluorescent white of angry waves as they reached the beach. Tomorrow, he thought idly, would be a good day for collecting driftwood.

Rosita struggled to find protection from the waves that were breaking with increasing force over the cliffs of the island. She had to move although the effort was daunting. Every time she rose to her knees, the wind pushed at her and once succeeded in rolling her over with a casualness that was terrifying. The noise was deafening, an orchestra of ululating wails, sudden slamming, weird howls that sounded animal-like and a whispering, threatening drone. The fury of movement and sound convinced her that this was a night she wouldn't survive.

She dragged herself to where a slight overhang of rock gave at least the presence of shelter and cursed herself for her stupidity. Her clothes were soaked and she huddled miserably against the rock face and tried to pretend they were not. 'Richard,' she sobbed. 'Where are you?'

It was impossible to sleep with the wind slamming and threatening to move even the solid rock against which she sheltered. She wondered if Luke were in the cottage and thought not. It was usually weekends when he came. The reminder made her shiver with increased panic as she realized there were hours before morning gave even a slight hope of rescue. I am alone, she thought, engulfed with melancholy. No one even knows where I am. Too weak to walk back across the causeway. How can I hope for rescue?

Idris was not a happy man. For a while it had been fun to have an affair with Hattie but things were turning sour. Kate had guessed and was threatening to leave him. That would never do. He needed Kate and he didn't want to be parted from Lynne and Helen. He would have to tell Hattie goodbye and suggest she find somewhere else to live. It was over and he hoped she would be as willing to end it as she had been to begin it.

He had always courted danger in his love life. The imminent threat of discovery had been the spice he needed to fully enjoy any illicit relationship. The most exciting had been Hattie. Being Kate's sister was enough at the beginning; the enormity of the idea, the danger it encompassed, had kept him awake night after night until he had approached her and found her willing.

Then risking making love to her in the house while everyone thought he was alone, while his family were in London. Creeping about and ducking under windows as they moved about from room to room, exaggerating the dread when someone called and Hattie had to run, giggling, her plump body clad only in a towel, up the stairs.

Best of all was the evening they had made love in the kitchen, while Kate was walking back to the shop to find her handbag. Listening for her return and holding Hattie in his arms until the very last moment, when Kate touched the lock with her key. That had been fantastic!

He was waiting for Hattie now. Kate was out and they were hoping for one of their joyous sessions. He decided they would make love for the last time before he told her it must end, but she came in with an expression on her face that knocked his romantic approach for six.

'Idris, I'm going to have a baby,' she blurted out as she opened the door.

'Bloody hell, Hattie! You could have told me gently, not shot it at me like that!'

'Sorry, but I've been trying to say something for days and, well, it's a hard thing to tell anyone, isn't it?'

'What will you do?'

'What are *we* going to do, surely?' she replied, looking at him with those dark eyes he had once thought attractive and now seemed dull and unpleasant.

'Sorry, love, but I won't leave Kate and the girls. If you tell her about me I'll deny it. You can't prove anything, we've been too careful for that. Today I was going to tell you "goodbye", anyway, and ask you to find somewhere else to live.'

'Idris! You don't mean that!'

'Damned right I do. It was fun, mind. I can't deny that. You were a lot of fun, but that's all it was. If you weren't careful enough to avoid this mess, well, I'm sorry but it isn't my mess – it's yours.' On impulse, suddenly remembering some cash he had in his pocket, intended to pay a large bill for Richard, which he had forgotten to do, he said, 'I can give you some money.'

She stood and stared into space as though in a trance. He took a roll of crisp white fivers from his pocket and held them out to her. They belonged to Richard but he'd get over that little problem somehow.

'You mean you won't leave Kate and marry me? Or even share a part of your life with me?'

'That was never on the cards and you know it, so don't start any fancy nonsense with me.' He was still speaking pleasantly, his tone the same as when they had shared intimate moments.

'What will I do?'

'Go and see your mother, I suppose. First you ought to get a place to live. I want you out of here as soon as possible. There's always some advertisements in the window of Rosita's shop. Why don't you stroll up there now and see if there's anything you fancy? You've got money – that's better than you expected, isn't it?'

'Then it's all over? Everything?'

'You knew it couldn't last, Hattie. We both enjoyed it and now it's time to end it.' He attempted to kiss her but she pushed him away with surprising vehemence and ran from the house.

Her thoughts were in turmoil as she walked the street, battling against the fearsome wind, careless of the torrential downpour. She tried to consider how to deal with the frightening prospect of being an unmarried mother. The storm reflected her mood. There was a raging storm both outside her and within.

The shame was just a part of it, although that was bad enough. Heads would turn as she passed and she would catch sight of shared glances and disapproving nods. She'd be used as an example to make other girls aware of the dangers of loving too well and too soon. How would she cope with it all?

Hattie wasn't one for looking further than the present. Enjoyment was fleeting and to be savoured to the full. If she had considered where the affair with Idris was taking her, she would have believed he would stand by her, tell the world they were in love, not just lovers. After all, she must mean more to him than Kate or he wouldn't have started an affair in the first place, she reasoned – incorrectly.

She needed a man, a man who would marry her, but how could she find one now, in this state? Thoughts of all the chances she had missed while she was sharing Idris with his wife made fear change to anger, and calmly, coldly, she decided on the best course to take. The first step was to talk to Rosita again. A woman of the world, she'd know how to deal with the dilemma. She was unaware that as she was thinking of her, Rosita was in danger of losing her life in the storm that raged around them both.

At the school shop the next morning, there was a queue of angry customers waiting for Rosita to open. Among the first was Monty and after ten minutes had passed and she still hadn't appeared, he knocked on the door of a neighbour who sometimes helped out. She had a spare key and at

Monty's request, went up to find the flat empty. Soon the customers went off with their purchases and Monty, who had noted the absence of her car, was watching the road anxiously.

What could have happened? Rosita would have made arrangements if she had intended to be delayed. Efficiency was important to her; she wasn't the kind to forget something as important as opening the shop on time. When half an hour had passed, he rang Kate. She knew nothing and, running in growing fear, he went to find Richard.

Richard tried his mother, then after several abortive enquiries, he rang the police at Monty's urging. 'It might be a false alarm, Richard, but if it isn't we're wasting precious minutes.' He had been aware of Rosita's absence longer than Richard and his fears had grown at a faster rate.

It wasn't until Monty pointed out that although it was only seven o'clock in the morning, Rosita was already an hour late opening the shop, and she might have been missing all night, that Richard realized how worrying it was. Then, learning that her flat was empty and her car wasn't to be found, he felt the churning of real ice-cold panic.

He went back to the office to liaise with Monty and between them they phoned or visited everyone they could think of who would know where she might have gone. It didn't take very long; the list of her friends was not enormous. She was always too busy working to make a lot of friends.

'What about Luke?' Monty suggested. 'Could she have gone there?'

'Unlikely. He lives in Cardiff. She would have said if she planned to visit him and I'd have gone too – he's my friend as well, remember.'

'But he has a cottage near?'

'Yes, but – Dammit, it's worth a try.' Glad of something to do, some purpose to take away the feeling of impotent frustration and rapidly growing fear, Richard threw himself into the van and drove off.

Rosita had managed to sleep a little but was fully awake long before the queue had formed outside the school shop. She had never been so cold. Huddled against the unyielding rock, she tightened the flimsy jacket around her shoulders, watching for the first rim of light to appear on the horizon. The early darkness, with its promise to imminent change, took her back in memory to the farm.

She remembered getting up on frosty mornings and going into the barns to feed the animals and remembered how glad she had been of their warm bodies and the breath that floated from their mouths and made pictures in the still air. She could have grown to like the farm, if her mother had supported her and stopped Graham from hitting her.

There were rare occasions when Graham had taken her with him onto the hills to check on the sheep. She had liked that and had taken an interest in what he was doing, young though she had been at the time. She remembered wanting to please him, make him like her as much as he liked Kate and Hattie, but some devil inside her refused to let her reveal it. The battle between wanting him to like her and the imp that showed only her worst side went on within her.

The worst side always won. Trying to punish her mother and Graham had only hurt herself; she must have known that, but had been too young to deal with it. Perhaps, she mused, if Auntie Molly Carey had been around, things would have been different. Richard's mam was one of the few people she could always talk to.

She became aware of company. Hundreds of gulls had settled on the sheltered side of the island during the night and now the winds had eased, they were cackling and calling, preparing to leave. They rose in groups of a dozen or so at a time, joining the rest wheeling around her, creating a deafening hullabaloo, before setting off across the still-turbulent waters in search of food.

The grass was shining in the pre-dawn light and rabbits were grazing quietly around her. She squeaked with her mouth to coax them closer but they ignored her and went on feeding.

She had to get up and walk back to the beach as soon as the waters parted. If anyone were to see her, she would have to get to the most likely spot *to* be seen. The saddest thing was, no one would miss her until morning and then it would only be a line of disgruntled customers wanting their 'twenty fags and my paper, love'. What I want is a bath and a cup of tea, she thought miserably. Ben Gunn, she remembered, had wanted cheese when he had been rescued from that mythical Treasure Island.

Her ankle was swollen and rather stiff. If she was going to make her way back to the causeway, she ought to start. She looked at her watch. Four o'clock. Plenty of time; it was still too dark. At five, she began to make her way slowly down from the shelter she had found and crawled to the middle of the grassy plateau above the beach. The tide was out. It seemed impossible that all that swirling water had gone. She had to get across as soon as she could now it was light, and the prospect made her ankle throb in anticipation of movement.

Luke woke early and couldn't return to lazy slumber. It was irritating not to be able to sleep when it was pointless to be awake. He sat up in bed and read, tried again to close his eyes and rest but eventually gave up, washed in the large china bowl and went downstairs. He made tea and went out into the glistening dawn. The air was clean and sweet; the storm had moved on but there were still sudden gusts that rattled loose metal somewhere and made it screech and grate complainingly.

The night had left a litter of fallen branches and assorted rubbish around his doorway. It had also left a newly washed array of brilliant greenery: the leaves of stunted trees near the cottage were dust-free and polished. He stood and admired nature's handiwork for a moment, then pushed the larger pieces of wood away from the door with Wellingtoned feet and went onto the beach.

A gust of wind hit him as he left the lee of the cottage and made him stagger. The noise seemed far less than when he had been inside but the wind was still fierce enough to block all other sounds. A stick flew up and hit him as he went to check on his boat.

He had been right about the driftwood. For a while he worked methodically, putting the largest pieces in a pile ready to be sawn into useable lengths and filled a woven basket with smaller pieces. He looked across at the island, realized his glasses were covered in salt, cleaned them and looked again. The grass beyond the beach was a very bright green in the early-morning light. Perhaps he would walk over and see what the storm had brought. It would mean being late but there wasn't anything Jeanie couldn't deal with; she was a very capable person.

He stood enjoying the still-blustering wind and the sense of being the only person in the world. Then he thought he saw a movement over on the island. Not a fisherman, surely? Not in weather like this. It must be flotsam. It was amazing what turned up on the sea's edge after a strong wind and high tide. But he continued to stare.

There was something waving in the wind. An edge of cloth? A sack, perhaps, caught in the rocks. Then the object moved and he saw something waving rhythmically. There was someone out there! There must have been a shipwreck. He looked around wondering how best to deal with the emergency. The boat? Or walk? The boat would be risky and would mean going a long way following the shore before making for the island to avoid the strong currents. But if the figure was an injured man, how could he get him safely back? Better run to the phone box, but no. This was his person. He was here and it was up to him to perform the rescue.

A motor boat would be the answer. He waved back frantically until he was sure the person had seen him then disappeared into the cottage before hurrying towards the next bay, where the water was always deep and where he moored his boat. He prayed as he ran that the boat hadn't been damaged by the storm and was relieved when he found it apparently unharmed. He had taken a blanket and as a precaution an extra anchor.

The engine started without fuss and he headed for the island, warily avoiding the dangerous currents that pulled so fiercely.

Throwing the anchor overboard, he jumped into the swirling water, waded ashore and walked to the figure lying on the sand.

'Rosita!' He stared in disbelief at the bedraggled and exhausted woman. 'Whatever possessed you to—' He wasted no more time in explanations and recriminations; taking off his sweater he gave it to her, and also the jacket he wore, and wrapping her in the blanket he carried her to the boat.

He was filled with remorse as he turned the boat towards the shore. Why hadn't he sensed she was in trouble? He had always believed he had an extra sense where Rosita and Barbara were concerned. He had lain in his bed, complaining about not being able to sleep, and all the time Rosita had been out there in desperate risk of hypothermia and death. He smiled reassuringly at her.

Dressed in his jumper and with her hair awry, her face devoid of make-up, Rosita was startlingly like her mother. Her colouring was different – she obviously followed Bernard Stock in her brown eyes and darker skin – but seeing her now was like turning back the pages of time and seeing Barbara as she used to be, shabbily dressed and surrounded by the unruly Carey mob.

His heart ached with happiness at the memories. Why hadn't he snatched the opportunity when it offered itself? Euphoria changed to harsh truth and less happy memories flooded back as he stepped out along the road back to the cottage.

Because his father had frightened him with fears of his unacceptable sexuality, that was why. He hadn't had the knowledge, maturity or confidence to realize his father had been wrong. It had taken Martine to make him accept that. He smiled at Rosita again. 'We'll get you to hospital within the hour,' he said softly.

Fixing up a simple crutch to support her injured ankle, he helped her to the car after wrapping her in extra blankets and feeding her hot soup to continue the warming process. She was dressed in a pair of his trousers and several jumpers, a scarf was wrapped around her head and Luke thought she looked utterly beautiful.

'You're so like Barbara,' he said in admiration. To his alarm she reacted strongly.

'NO! I'm NOT like her and never could be!'

'All right,' he soothed, seeing her face tense with the threat of tears. 'Not in spirit, I know that. Barbara was far too unsure of herself to manage what you've achieved, but just now and then, an expression ...' His voice trailed off. Rosita was determinedly not listening.

As they turned right at the T-junction at the end of the lane, Richard was hurtling towards them from the left. They missed each other by less than a minute.

Richard searched and, finding Rosita's car, he wailed in his grief and drove straight to a telephone box to tell the police of his find. He stood and stared across at the island until they came, convinced she was dead. He answered their questions mechanically and then watched as they went over and searched the small island.

Numb, drained of all emotion, he prepared himself for confirmation of his fears. He felt lightheaded and deathly ill. The world was going on around him without him taking part. He saw the men walking methodically over the higher area of the island, pushing vegetation aside with sticks at each step. Now and then, one would pause and bend down. Each time that happened, his heart would leap painfully as his body came momentarily back to life.

All he could do was wait for the words he dreaded. They would find her body, he knew they would. When a motorcyclist arrived with the message that she was safe, and in hospital, he didn't believe him for a moment, so certain was he that she was dead.

'Are you sure?' he asked stupidly.

The following day, Rosita came home with nothing more than a strapped ankle to show for her stupidity. She sat propped up on her couch while Richard fussed and watched her every move.

'I never thought you were such an old hen,' she teased.

'I never thought you had less sense than a day-old chick!' he retorted.

The flat was full of visitors for most of the following three days. Besides Richard and his mother coming every moment they could spare, there was Monty, Kate and of course Luke, who wouldn't leave until he was certain that she was all right.

On one of the rare moments when there were just the two of them, Richard asked why she had been so foolish. Rosita didn't try to explain. She couldn't talk about what Hattie had said and the way she had revealed her casual attitude to the new life within her. It was bound up with Rosita's unfortunate childhood and very painful. How could she explain the disturbed memories and thoughts that had caused her to be so careless about her own life? She did tell him Hattie was expecting a baby.

'I didn't ask who the father was but there's no doubt, is there? It must be Idris, your oh-so-charming brother.'

'There was something going on, but I didn't want to tell you,' he said. He didn't develop the subject. Rosita stared at him, surprised at how shocked he looked.

'Now,' Richard said brightly, 'Mam wants to know what she can make for your tea.'

'Poor Kate,' Rosita whispered sadly.

'Poor you! It's yourself you should be thinking of now, not other people's problems. It's just you and me, Rosita, that's all that matters now. Remember that, won't you?'

Between them were thoughts unshared that isolated them from each other. Luke, to whom she had told everything, insisted she discuss it with Richard but she refused. The time wasn't right. Instead, she created added enthusiasm about their engagement party, now only days away.

With the shops running satisfactorily, Rosita luxuriated in a few days of doing nothing. Three days before their engagement was to be announced, Richard called with the books from the shops. Her ankle was still painful but she put away the stick she had been using, determined to cope.

'On Monday I'll be back at the shop,' she told him.

'Only if you come out for a meal tonight and prove your ankle is strong again, and if you agree you'll need an assistant for a while,' Richard said firmly, and for once she didn't argue.

They went to see Mrs Carey on their way to the restaurant, Rosita laughing at the awkward way she walked.

'There's lovely!' was Mrs Carey's greeting. 'On your feet again. And thank goodness too.' She brought a chair forward. 'How about a nice cup of tea, then?'

'We can't stay, Mam. We're just off to eat. There's a table booked for half an hour's time.'

'Come tomorrow and stay longer?' She turned her head enquiringly, like a little bird, Rosita thought affectionately.

'Tomorrow for sure,' she said.

'Was that the door?' Mrs Carey said a moment later. 'What a night for visitors. Now who can that be?' she chattered on, asking herself questions and guessing answers. She went to the door and came back with Hattie.

'Glad you're here,' Hattie said. 'I saw the van go past the house and guessed you were coming here. Got a bit of news, I have, see. I'm going to have a baby.'

Mrs Carey sat down suddenly and stared at her. 'Getting married then, are you?' Her first thought was relief that she would be getting from under Kate's feet, unaware that she had already left.

'Well, it's up to him, really.'

'Who?' Mrs Carey demanded. 'Tell us the father's name.'

Hattie turned and smiled sorrowfully at Rosita. 'Sorry, Rosita.' Into the silence she added, 'It's Richard, see.'

Rosita stared at the tableau of people, frozen by shock. Then, with a low scream, she left the room. Richard moved then and tried to stop her but she pushed him away from her as if he were unclean. 'Don't touch me!' Somehow she reached the street and getting into Richard's van, ignoring the wrenching pain in her ankle, she drove to Gull Island. 'Please be there, Luke,' she repeated time and again like a mantra.

There was no car parked beside the cottage or behind it. Luke wasn't there. In her distress she blamed him for not being there, blamed Richard for letting her down and blamed her mother for having a daughter like Hattie, a daughter so like her mother she made the same mistakes as Barbara and dealt with them in the same blundering way.

She sat looking out across the water to the little island that was bedecked with jewels that were in reality her own tears. She drove back to Station Row and left the van beside her Anglia. Richard could come and fetch it but she wouldn't let him in.

Hearing his footsteps, knowing instinctively it was him, she went to the top of the stairs and waited while he knocked and knocked on the door. He opened the letterbox and shouted through.

'Rosita! Aren't you even going to listen to what I have to say?'

No, she said silently. Being on my own is the safest way to live.

She ran a bath, soaked for a while then went to her lonely bed. This, she thought to herself, is all my future holds – work and hours spent alone – but at least it won't be peppered with heartache.

A knock at the door the following evening started her heart racing, within her a tiny core of hope. Yet she didn't for one moment consider talking to Richard. She went to the top of the stairs and looked down. A hand came through the flap and waved at her. It was Luke.

'I've brought a gift for your engagement,' he told her when she opened the door. 'When will you have the party? A pity it had to be delayed, but if you will go on survival tests in the middle of a storm—' He saw from her face that something was wrong. 'Rosita? What is it?'

She told him calmly and without a break in her voice and felt proud of her strength. Instead of sympathy, Luke stared at her in disapproval.

'You ran off and didn't even allow him to speak? You saw Hattie and Idris together, didn't you?' His voice was low but disapproval was clear. 'I thought you loved Richard?'

'I did – I do – but there's no future for us now. I can't bear to think of him with that ... that creature.'

'Didn't it occur to you that she might be lying? You know it was Idris she was having an affair with.'

'He was one, yes, but how many more? She named Richard.'

'A single man would be a better bet for her, surely, than a man married with two children and his sister's husband at that.'

'He must have been with her or there would be no point in naming him.'

'You didn't even ask him.'

'I panicked.'

'You're so afraid to trust people, yet when have your friends let you down? Never!'

'Hattie is like my mother, callous and uncaring.'

'We won't argue that point now, although I can never think of Barbara that way.' He put down the parcel he carried and took her in his arms. 'Rosita, you have to start trusting people or your life will be as barren as—' He almost said the fields of Passchendaele, a thought never far from his mind. 'Or your life will be barren of happiness and love.'

'Love makes you vulnerable.'

'Life without it is a sham. See your mother. Start picking up pieces instead of throwing them away.'

'I can't.'

'Then talk to Richard. Ask yourself who would be the most likely to lie. Richard or Hattie?' He handed her the gaily wrapped parcel. 'Open it.'

She did and found a beautiful cut-glass bowl. The light shone on it and it glistened in myriad rainbows.

'Many facets, all fascinating,' he said quietly. 'Like relationships.' He hugged her. 'Be careful not to waste too many more years in resentment, Rosita. Time has a terrifying ability to speed along without us being aware of it. Talk to Richard.' As he left the flat he added, 'Then talk to your mother.'

Richard's reaction to the news was to lock himself away from everyone and lose himself in work. He went out chasing new contracts, advertising for extra workmen and interviewing office staff. Then, when he learned that Idris couldn't account for £300 paid to him by a customer, he sacked him.

His mother thought it was unfairly done, as Idris insisted the money had been taken from his pocket while he fixed a puncture. But Richard refused to listen to him. There was sadistic satisfaction in telling Idris he was useless and a liability.

'Fine one to talk,' Idris complained to Monty when he went to collect his things. 'Him of all people. How d'you think he got started? Stealing! That's how. Wanted by the police he was, and probably still is!'

He watched the expression on Monty's face, hoping for anger and shock, but Monty nodded and said, 'I know all that, Idris. You can't harm him by spreading that old story. He went to the police years ago and they had nothing on him. They were suspicious at the time though because someone—' He looked pointedly at Idris '—someone reported him and set the police thinking he was guilty. I wonder who that was, Idris? Know anything, do you?'

Idris shrugged and smiled amiably, his innocence an almost convincing act. 'I didn't take the money. I put my jacket on the ground and as usual, a crowd gathered – you know what it's like.'

'Perhaps, but I don't think the £300 was the reason Richard asked you to go, do you?'

'No, he's been looking for something to whip me with for months. Never wanted me working for him in the first place.'

'Can you blame him? You're a lazy bugger, Idris. He's been overpaying you and you've done as little as possible to earn it.'

'Yes, I suppose I am lazy. I'm fun as well, mind.' Idris smiled and the wicked amusement in the startlingly blue eyes showed once again how his charm could work wonders.

'Here's the address of a friend of mine,' Monty said. 'A builder who's looking for a man to run the stores. It might suit you, no hard work, a bit boring perhaps, but you'll find ways of dealing with that, won't you?'

'Thanks. I'll get round the boredom. Any good-looking office girls there? With spectacles and long legs?'

'Don't start before you even see the place,' Monty groaned.

Monty told Richard what he'd done and Richard shrugged. 'It's up to you. He's my brother but I don't think I'd recommend him to anyone I wanted to stay friends with.'

'I did it because you were unfair. You've no proof he took the money.' Richard looked at him with a raised eyebrow. 'All right,' Monty admitted. 'I did it for Kate. She needs the wages he brings in.'

'I was glad of an excuse. I wanted him out of here. I can't look at him without wanting to hit him.'

Idris took the paper with the name and address and when he was interviewed he was given the job. Then the following day a letter arrived telling him he would not, after all, be needed.

'It's Richard's doing! He's pushed his nose in and got me sacked before I even started!' he told his mother. 'I'll get him for this!'

'Idris, love, Richard wouldn't do that.'

'Wouldn't he just! And what's he been saying to my Kate? Kicked me out she has.'

'What d'you mean?'

'Put some clothes in a suitcase and changed the locks on the doors, that's what she's done. My case is outside, Mam. I can stay for a few days, until I talk her round, can't I?'

Idris spent days just lolling around being spoilt by his mother and trying to think of the best way to pay his brother back. In his mind he twisted the facts around in a confusion of truth, daydreams and wild imaginings so that the trouble with Kate, the loss of the job and home, the baby carried by Hattie, were all due to Richard's interference. Richard and that snooty bitch Rosita. It had all been fine until she had come back into their lives.

After the shop she managed had closed in the evenings, Kate usually went straight home. One morning in late July, when the weather outside was heavy with the threat of thunder, she closed the door and went to see Rosita.

'Kate! What a nice surprise.' Rosita smiled as she opened the door of the flat. 'Stay for something to eat?'

'No. I'd better get back. I only wanted to tell you I might not be able to get in tomorrow.'

'Is anything the matter?' Rosita's thoughts immediately went to Idris. What trouble was he causing now?

'I feel rather ill. I'm aching in every joint and my head feels fit to burst.'

'A few of my customers are ill with a summer flu, I hope you haven't got that. Look, leave it to me, I'll find someone to come in. Just have a couple of days in bed and rest quietly.'

'Thanks. I'm sorry to let you down. I know how awkward it is when one of us is off.'

'That's my worry, not yours. Come on, I'll drive you home.'

When she had finished the routine jobs she did every evening, Rosita sat and thought about Kate's words. She was vulnerable with just the minimum staff and three shops and a kiosk to run. If someone was ill there were a few people who would step in, but the whole thing was dangerously fragile. And what about herself? How long did she want to go on working twelve hours at the school shop, only to come up to more work?

She took her thoughts to bed and with a notebook on her knees began to work out the finances of a complete change to the running of her businesses. Not the least of her priorities was the thought that if she and Richard ever got back together, she had to make herself free to spend time with him.

Since the announcement by Hattie that Richard was the father of her unborn child, she and Richard had hardly met. When they did come face to face, usually at his mother's home, they spoke like strangers, neither giving or taking an inch. After several embarrassing and upsetting confrontations, Rosita avoided calling on Mrs Carey when it was likely that he'd be there.

Idris was pleasant when they met and treated her to a friendly welcome. He even went back to the school shop to repair plaster around a window after Rosita mentioned it to Mrs Carey – a job he had attempted twice before. For Auntie Molly Carey's sake, she responded to him in the same manner. She didn't want to risk upsetting Mrs Carey, the only one in her life, beside Luke, she felt able to love.

It had been several weeks before she felt able to ask the whereabouts of Hattie.

'Given up her job and gone to stay with your mam,' Mrs Carey told her. 'Best for her to be miles away, after what she did to us.'

'Her and Richard,' Rosita reminded her.

'Well, yes indeed. And there's my poor Idris. He's in the wrong too, mind, but there, she must have led him on, her staying in that house when we were away, not going to Weston like she told us. Wicked girl she is.'

'Hattie stayed with Idris all that week?' Rosita was startled at the casually stated remark.

'Like I said, she's a wicked girl. Cancelled her holiday and stayed there with Idris and him not strong against temptation, being a man an' all.'

'Yet Hattie said Richard was ... responsible. Can she have been lying?'

'I think we'll have salad tonight, too hot for anything more. Or shall we be lazy and go for some fish and chips? Stay and eat with us, *fach*. Richard and Idris will be back soon. Idris went for a job today. In Cardiff it is. I hope he doesn't get it, mind – better off staying in your home town I always think.' Mrs Carey's chatter showed her determination not to discuss Idris and Hattie any further.

Idris and Hattie alone in the house while Kate and the children were in London? For a whole week? It was impossible to believe that Idris was not responsible for Hattie's condition. The scene she had witnessed was hardly mild flirting. And Richard had hinted at knowing something too. Shame for her instant rejection of Richard flooded through her, chasing other thoughts trying to escape. Somehow she had to face Richard, and say she was sorry, and ask him for another chance.

She put off the meeting, wondering whether to write or phone, or simply go and see him at work. Days passed and to avoid making a decision she worked on the new set-up for her business. Kate was still off work and having a temporary manager in the Station Row shop meant extra hours each evening dealing with the accounts and the ordering and the thousand things Kate did so efficiently.

Then Betty Sweeny in The Kiosk rang to say she was ill and unable to work. Trying the usual people who helped on occasions, she failed to find someone to take over. In desperation she rang Richard. She wished she had spoken to him earlier instead of contacting him to ask for help. Why had she delayed?

'What is it, Rosita?' His voice gave no hint of pleasure at her call.

Making her voice as formal as possible, fighting back the longing to see him, she said coolly, 'Several of my staff are ill with this summer flu and I wondered if you can think of anyone who might help.'

'Oh, business, is it? I'll put you on to Monty.' Without further word he passed the phone to his friend.

'Monty, I'm sorry to worry you with this, but I have a problem trying to find someone to open the kiosk tomorrow. You don't know anyone who might help, do you?'

'Let me have a think,' he said.

'There's a part-timer who will help but I desperately need someone for the afternoons.'

'I think I have an idea.' He asked how she was, whether her ankle was now sound and warned her to be careful not to catch the flu, then rang off. She replaced the phone with a feeling of dread. Richard would never forgive her, not now. She couldn't remember a word of what Monty had said.

A young woman phoned an hour later and explained that she was a neighbour of Monty's and she had worked in a newsagents before. They met, liked each other and, with Monty's recommendation too, she thankfully accepted her help. The phone rang again, this time from someone else saying she had the flu and she too would be unable to get to work.

Running between one shop and another to deal with the busy periods and help the inexperienced staff, she somehow survived the next ten days. By that time, she had also made her preparations to ensure that such a situation never happened again.

The money from her grandmother, Mrs Stock, was a safety net and she silently thanked the proud old lady for her generosity. What a pity she hadn't been kind until after her death. A little friendliness earlier would have meant a more contented and fulfilled end to her days. Why didn't I break down the old lady's barrier of pride while I had the chance to give something in return? she grieved. But the money had been a wonderful gift, giving her the chance to put right the weaknesses in her widely expanding business.

When Kate returned to work in August, the middle of the busy holiday period, Rosita asked her if she would accept overall responsibility for the shops. 'Each of the shops will have a manager, and you will oversee the whole chain,' she explained. 'And by the end of the year there might be another. I have my eye on a small kiosk that's worth considering. Will you come with me when I go and look at it?'

They discussed the plan and agreed that two part-time assistants for each shop, plus a couple of casuals, would give them some overlap should illness again disrupt the businesses.

'As soon as everything is running satisfactorily, perhaps I'll take a holiday,' Rosita said. With Richard if I can persuade him, she added silently. But where to start? If they weren't speaking, how could he be persuaded to try again? Why had her first call after weeks of silence been to ask for his help? It would make convincing him that much harder.

Chapter Seventeen

CIGARETTES WENT UP by one penny on a packet of twenty in August and although the price of matches didn't alter, the number of matches in a box was reduced. As usual there were the regular grumbles about depriving the working man of his pleasures, but the complaints faded and the increases were soon forgotten.

Although they moaned at first, none refused to buy, Rosita thought wryly. Men, and an increasing number of women, would always find the money for what they wanted. She was different; spending as little as possible and sinking every penny back into the growing business was such a habit, she wondered with some sadness if she was still capable of enjoying herself like most people.

There was certainly more money circulating now, she noticed. Luxuries were being snapped up more quickly and her stock took advantage of the fact that things like fountain pens and lighters, that had been impossible to find during the war years, were being offered by enthusiastic reps.

How fortunate she had been to start in business just as the gloom and austerity of wartime was beginning to ease – even if she couldn't take advantage of the foreign holidays and better clothes that were coming into the shops. Since clothes rationing had ended in 1949, people were becoming more fashion conscious and, although always smartly dressed, she felt she was being left behind.

Sweets were still rationed, but other shortages were easing. Newsprint scarcity had kept newspapers limited to a few pages through the war and the forties, but now papers and magazines were thicker and new periodicals appeared at intervals. The new comic, the all-colour *TV Comic*, which cost fourpence, quickly became a favourite, with Muffin the Mule, Mr Pastry, and Prudence Kitten.

Television was the new craze and while people were still complaining about lack of money, more and more houses were sprouting the large H aerials on their roof. Perhaps soon she would be able to ease restrictions on herself and treat herself as a reward for her endeavours. A holiday, perhaps? She sighed and went to straighten the magazines on the counter. Perhaps. But not yet.

Christmas seemed to come earlier each year and by the end of September some shops were already starting to show small, almost apologetic displays of cards. Rosita was negotiating to take over her second kiosk. It too was near a school, this time in Beach Street not far from the Careys'. There was a public house close by and a fairly large bus stop. Like the others it was run down but she could see the potential, once she had put her mark of excellence on it. There was something else: now her sisters knew who she was, there was no reason not to put her name on the shops. Over each of the premises would be the name:

Rosita's.
Newsagents, Tobacconists and Confectioners.

She decided to start the Christmas activities as a celebration of opening the new shop. If she were to compete for the extra business that the gift-buying season brought, she couldn't drag too far behind the rest. There was no point in waiting until many of the customers had found what they wanted elsewhere. But it would add to the excitement if she waited until at least the beginning of November, when the new kiosk would open. Besides, it seemed unfair to the children to start the excitement too soon.

The schools returning after the autumn half-term was the signal for the rush to begin and on one hectic Sunday, Rosita and Kate went around the shops and the two kiosks and decorated the windows with tinsel and cotton wool and put the Christmas stock on display.

A letter arrived for Rosita among the post at the Station Row shop and, recognizing her mother's writing, Rosita gave it a cursory glance, saw it was congratulations on opening her new premises, then threw it in the bin. Clearing up later, she took the note out of the rubbish and smoothed it out. She would take it to show Auntie Molly Carey. The letter was an excuse to call and Richard might be there.

Since her refusal to listen when he tried to explain about Hattie and himself, they had hardly exchanged a dozen words. When they met, he immediately muttered some excuse and left. Christmas Day would bring another birthday and the reminder that she was approaching an age when most people accepted the fact that, for them, marriage and motherhood were fading from the scene, distressed her.

She had chosen a career and in doing so had given up all the chances of having fun that most young people enjoyed. Every penny had been scrupulously put back into the business. Now she was well on the way to making a real success of it all, but there was a risk – which she had ignored. Renting the second kiosk, when she hadn't fully recovered from the previous purchase, had not been wise.

She had gone against the advice of her accountant by increasing her business so fast. She was severely stretched financially. But with the economy buoyant she felt the risk was justified. A few more years and she would be safe from the dread of poverty. Poverty in old age was still her greatest fear, despite a Health Service and an old age pension.

Starting to build a business, she had put aside marriage as less important. Richard Carey had been her only dream and he was gone from her life with only a few memory snapshots to comfort her. Time had passed so quickly and she had found herself at the age when the time for finding love had gone, almost without realizing it. The decision had been her own; there was no one in the background whom she could blame. Like her friend, Miss Grainger, she would travel the rest of her life alone on a lonely road. She hoped she would be as content.

It was in this mood of melancholy that she went to see Mrs Carey bearing the letter from her mother. Richard wasn't there. In fact, Mrs Carey was alone and trying to fix some decorations into the ceiling by balancing dangerously on a stool.

'Auntie Molly Carey!' Rosita scolded. 'Come down now this minute and leave this to me. You don't want a broken leg for Christmas, do you?'

'I wanted it to be a surprise when Richard and Idris come in.' Mrs Carey smiled at her. 'But glad I'll be to sit and watch a young woman do it for me.'

'Not so young,' Rosita said lightly, stabbed by her recent thoughts.

They had the inevitable cup of tea before they recommenced the decorating and as they finished their second cup, Rosita handed Mrs Carey the letter.

'She wasn't as terrible as you think, you know,' Mrs Carey said as she refolded the single page. 'Seventeen, that's all she was. Half your age. Imagine, finding yourself alone and with a baby coming, a father who refused to mention her name and a mother too afraid to disagree with him. Her mam tried to help, mind. She sent money around whenever she could, a few shillings now and then. Without Barbara knowing, of course. He wouldn't have let her do even that. I kept it in a tea tin with a picture of George V and Queen Mary on the front. I was meaning to give it to her when she found a place of her own, but ...'

Suddenly making up her mind, she told Rosita how Richard had found it and, believing it belonged to the people who had taken their rooms, spent it on wood and stuff to make the house comfortable. 'Barbara's mam did what she could, see. It was her father who was stubborn. Wouldn't let her mam come and see how she was coping, or even see you when you were born. On her own, Barbara was, and her only seventeen. Uncle Henry Carey and I did what we could, though it was little enough.'

She looked at Rosita, and the quiet concentration on the young woman's face encouraged her to go on. 'D'you know, she didn't even realize she was expecting. And when her mam told her she had no idea how it had happened. There's daft it seems now, but it was true of many young girls at that time – 1917 it was, with the war taking so many young men.'

Mrs Carey had tried to talk about Barbara many times but Rosita had closed her mind to any plea for understanding. Resolutely she had reminded herself that she had been abandoned to the children's home because her mother had chosen that farmer Graham Prothero instead of her. For the first time, she began to think of her mother as a frightened young girl. She waited for Mrs Carey to talk some more.

'Her mam would have helped, mind. As I said, it was her father, see. Shamed he was and couldn't see further than that. Embarrassed at his mates knowing and know they did, of course – there was no keeping secrets around where we lived. Neighbours knew the ins and outs of everything then. Yes, things would have been very different for young Barbara Jones if it hadn't been for her father.'

'Fathers!' Rosita said disparagingly. 'What trouble they cause. Mam's father turning her away when she needed help, me with a stepfather who beat me.' She thought of Luke then and added, 'And there's Luke. His father bullied him because he was afraid Luke was – you know, preferred boys to girls.'

'Luke was happy for a long time with Martine, so he couldn't have been harmed that much, mind,' Mrs Carey defended. 'He knew you had to forgive and accept that we aren't all perfect. Best not to dwell on the failings of your parents but get on with making your own mistakes! We all make them.'

'Luke was told to get out and never contact the family again. His father said that and Luke was only twenty. Told him he was all sorts of awful things. Luke was so miserable to be pushed away as though he were a leper, because of some fantasy in his father's nasty mind. Mam, me, and Luke. What is it about fathers?'

'I suppose my Henry was far from perfect.'

'No, not Uncle Henry Carey. He was a lovely dad.'

'Weak, mind. But there, it was him being weak that made Richard strong and so determined to succeed.'

'And Idris?' Rosita dared to ask. 'Can he use his father as an excuse?'

'Oh, well, it was different with Idris, *fach*. Never had a chance he didn't. He'd have been better placed if his father hadn't been so hard on him.'

Rosita smiled and watched the old lady's wrinkled face frown in defence of her golden-haired favourite. Rules or generalities, Idris was always the exception. She smiled again as she tried to imagine Uncle Henry Carey being hard on anyone.

'You ought to go and see your mam, Rosita,' Mrs Carey said as they began on the decorations.

'One day.' Then, deliberately changing the subject, Rosita pretended to slip and laughed in alarm. Soon they were laughing at idiotic things, the laughter genuine.

With the ceiling hung with glittering showers and the walls bedecked with swoops of brightly coloured garlands and cheerful banners, Mrs Carey started on the Christmas tree.

'I'd better give up,' Rosita said as, still laughing, they looked at the crooked shape of the final banner. 'It looks as though the room was decorated by a drunkard!'

'I quite agree,' said a voice and Richard came into the room. His face was rosy with the cold frosty weather and he wore an overcoat, a trilby, leather gloves and a woollen scarf. A smile, and the outdoor freshness, made him even more attractive than usual. A shiver of longing trailed through Rosita's body, aching desire in its wake. She tried to catch his eye, persuade him to at least share a smile.

But his smile faded and he asked, 'Why didn't you leave it for me to do?'

'You don't like it?' With dismay making the laughter fall like a stone, Rosita thought, here we go again, our first words and a threat of argument.

'It's all right, but you're pretty thoughtless, Rosita. I don't think Mam should be climbing about on chairs at her age.'

Wordless with anger, Rosita hugged and kissed Mrs Carey and reached for her coat. 'I'll see you soon,' she said, opening the door to leave.

'You will come for Christmas dinner, won't you?' Mrs Carey pleaded.

Running out of the door, Rosita didn't reply. She'd rather have a cheese sandwich in her own flat than watch Richard's disapproving face over a table filled with goodies!

The cold air hit her like a thousand knives as she went outside and she tightened her coat and ran to where she had left the car. She heard footsteps behind her and knew it was Richard. She turned to face him, prepared for further disapproval. 'I wouldn't let your mother do anything dangerous!' she snapped. To her consternation he was smiling.

'Rosita, I'm sorry. I don't know why I was so unreasonable. I know how much you love Mam. It's just that the moment we meet I'm on the defensive. Please, can we go somewhere and talk?'

She nodded and, getting into the car, she drove them to where a gaily lit café window offered warmth and a table to share.

'I want to talk about Hattie's baby,' he said when they had a pot of tea and toasted teacakes in front of them.

'No, I ...'

'Please, Rosita, listen to me or we'll never get things straight between us.' He held out his teacake and she took a bite. 'The truth is, the baby could be mine. I'm not perfect and there was an occasion ... I haven't led a blameless life. I'm nearing forty, for God's sake! But I believe that as Hattie had been having an affair with Idris for several months and I – well, I was careful, the chances are that the baby is Idris's and not mine.'

Her eyes widened as she prepared to speak but he offered the cake again to prevent her saying anything and she took a huge bite, and chewed it elegantly as he went on.

'Perhaps it doesn't make any difference. The baby being mine or not, if you know I was involved with her. I can't blame you if you feel that way. The sad thing is, I don't even like her. It was when you and I seemed to be getting nowhere and, well, I was glad of the pretence of someone caring, I suppose. Sex can make you forget, for a while at least.'

He had been looking through the steamy window as he spoke and now he turned to her. She had opened her mouth a little for a further bite but couldn't hide the incipient, hopeful smile. She had thought this conversation through many times in her head and knew that, whatever he said, however he explained, she wanted to forgive him. She loved him, wanted him, no matter what his faults were. If it was pride versus loneliness there was no contest.

'My brother has a lot to answer for. I was glad to see him gone from the business. He treats Kate so badly I can't bear to look at him. Something happened that gave me the reason to tell him to leave.'

Rosita quirked an eyebrow, silently asking him what had happened.

'Three hundred pounds went missing. He said he hadn't taken it, that it must have been stolen when he removed his jacket to deal with a puncture on the van, but I didn't believe him.'

Rosita spoke at last. 'Funny, I'd never have thought Idris was a thief. Unreliable, workshy, a womanizer, but never a thief.'

'You think I was wrong?' He took a deep breath to begin convincing her but she fed him a piece of cake; his turn to be silent.

'You know him better than I do, but weren't you grasping at the opportunity to get rid of him?'

He nodded and chewed then said, 'It was a heaven-sent opportunity, that money going missing. He's worse than useless, he's a liability.'

She reached for another piece of cake but he held her hand. 'Why are we talking about my brother? I want to talk about us getting back together.'

'So do I,' she said. 'Oh, Richard, so do I.'

After that evening, when they talked and talked, and laughed and ended the day sharing their happiness with Mrs Carey, everything seemed set to work out between them. Even the frequent appearances of Idris, who was trying to persuade Kate to talk to him, wasn't enough to spoil those few joyous days.

Kate was cool and indifferent to her wayward husband's entreaties while Mrs Carey hovered anxiously trying to translate what they said to each other and explain away any misunderstandings. Rosita and Richard were oblivious to it all; they were rekindling their precious love for each other.

Christmas 1951 was a magical occasion, although there were a few sad moments as Mrs Carey remembered other Christmases with Henry always beside her. Ada, now forty-eight, surprised them with a flying visit. She was still housekeeper to the family she and Dilys had originally left home to live with so long ago. Messages came from the boys, all with regret at not being able to see her, all claiming a life too full to spare a few days or even hours.

The family gatherings, walks in the cold, crisp winter air and making plans for their future filled the time contentedly for Rosita and Richard. It seemed that at last their troubles were behind them and they could look forward with hope. They were so happy, it seemed the world shared their joy.

On New Year's Eve, when the shops had closed, Rosita waited for Richard and he arrived with a basket packed with chicken pies made by his mother, and two flasks of hot soup. He drove the two miles to Gull Island and there, on the freezing cold beach, the wind beginning to howl, offered her an engagement ring.

'Let's marry as soon as we can,' he said. 'We've wasted too much time already. I want us to have children, so you'll have to make arrangements for your shops to be run without you.'

'I already have. There's nothing to hold us back from a happy life together.'

They found kissing an odd experience in the biting cold, with their lips blue and their noses threatening to snap. The island looked uninviting with an Arctic wind lifting dead vegetation and throwing it about in wild whirl-winds of ferocious power. The wind cut through the layers of clothes they wore and chilled them the moment they left the protection of the van.

Romantic it might be to propose marriage on their special beach, but the impracticalities soon made them lose their enthusiasm for solitude.

After attempting to warm themselves by drinking the hot soup Mrs Carey had supplied, they went to see if Luke was at the cottage and were relieved to see smoke issuing from the chimney.

'We've got news,' Richard said as Luke opened the door and invited them to sit by his huge wood fire.

'And about time too!' Luke hugged Rosita and kissed her cold cheek. 'You two should have married years ago.' He looked at them with slight embarrassment on his face. 'That *was* what you were about to tell me, wasn't it?' Behind the large horn-rimmed glasses his eyes wrinkled with relief when Richard nodded.

After congratulations and when details of their plans had been discussed, Luke smiled and said, 'I have news too. I've finally traced Martine. She's coming here.'

'Wonderful news!'

'I'm so glad,' Rosita added. 'Shall we make it a double wedding?'

'I don't think so,' Luke said, a shadow of sadness on his face. 'Too much time has passed.'

Rosita and Richard left soon after, having thoroughly warmed themselves. As Richard ran off to bring the van closer, Luke said, 'Now would be a good time to go and see Barbara, Rosita. Time to let some sunshine into dark corners.'

'One day, when I'm ready,' she replied.

'Soon,' he insisted. 'If you leave it until it's too late, that will be more guilt and regret, more burdens for you to carry.'

But Rosita was too happy to worry overmuch about a mother who had almost faded from her memory and become a stranger. Now, when she thought of Barbara, she saw a picture of Hattie in her mind, a greedy, self-centred Hattie, grasping everything she wanted without a thought for others, indifferent to the unhappiness she caused.

The only one not to offer congratulations and good wishes as news of the engagement spread was Idris. He tried to ruin things by putting in little jibes when Richard and Rosita talked of their plans, reminding them of their age and the unlikeliness of having a child – a subject that, with Hattie's situation common knowledge, seemed not to embarrass him at all but which seemed to give him added pleasure.

He wished something would happen to prevent the marriage but could think of nothing he could do to cause further trouble. In a fantasy, he began to imagine planning Rosita's death. A trickle of fear spread into a torrent as the idea filled his many idle moments. If only he dare – such a pity she hadn't died on that island. If only she could be persuaded to go there again, and this time with Luke too far away to help....

'It isn't fair, Mam!' Idris was marching up and down in his mother's living room. Weeks had passed since Richard had last helped out with money. 'Ruined my chances of getting another job, he has. He accused me of stealing, he did! If that isn't hypocritical, considering how he got started, tell me what is!'

'Richard didn't say you stole that money,' Mrs Carey said firmly. 'He said you were careless in losing it.'

'He thinks I pocketed it, I know he does, he as good as admitted it too, only he made sure no one heard him say so! But where is it? If I stole it then what am I supposed to have done with it? Damn it all, Mam, I haven't got the money to buy a packet of fags!'

Mrs Carey opened her purse and gave him half a crown.

'If he didn't think me guilty why did he sack me?' He put on his hurt-little-boy expression.

'He was upset with you and that wicked Hattie for – you know – the way you two carried on. Her fault, mind, I know that. But you shouldn't have done what you did. Richard's fond of Kate and was upset at the way you treated her. Perhaps that was the real reason, I don't know.'

'Self-righteous bugger! And him no better than the rest of us.'

Since Kate and Idris had separated, Kate had been in the habit of bringing any letters for her husband to the shop with her and arranging for someone to deliver them to Mrs Carey. In the rush and muddles of spring cleaning, and arranging the stock for the new season, the post became mixed up and a letter from Luke, addressed to Rosita and Richard, found its way into a pile addressed to Idris.

Idris pushed it to one side, intending to give it to Richard when he saw him, but then he became curious. It would be easy to explain that he opened it by mistake. He was interested to learn that it was an invitation for Richard and Rosita to visit Luke at the cottage and meet Martine. Martine was coming to England and intended to visit Wales after a short tour of the London sights. They intended to be away for five days, returning the day before the day of the invitation. Idris made a careful note of the dates.

Idris read and reread the letter. A plan that seemed to have been hovering in his mind, just waiting for the final ingredient, was now complete.

Copying Luke's rather large handwriting was easier than he'd imagined.

The new, forged letter was brief and worded in similar style, asking Rosita only to meet Luke and Martine on the island on Sunday, a week before Luke's original invitation. Luke's cottage would be empty and he would be 200 miles away. It was, he had written, to plan a surprise for Richard and had to be kept a secret.

Something happened a few days after he had handed the letter to Rosita with apologies for having opened it in error, an event which threw the whole country into turmoil and grief. King George VI died in his sleep.

All entertainments closed down. The radio played only serious and sombre music and everywhere windows were dressed in the purple and black of mourning at the passing of a much-loved monarch – a man who could have left the capital for a safe refuge during the terrifying bombing of London but had chosen to stay and share his subjects' danger. Like many others, Rosita felt the loss of a figure who had been steadfast and strong during those awful years.

Rosita immediately changed her window displays for something fitting the occasion and found pictures of the King and his Queen with which to decorate the displays, together with pictures of the young Elizabeth. The newspapers she sold all bore boldly black-rimmed messages of sympathy to the Queen Mother and Queen Elizabeth II.

So great was the shock and sadness that Rosita almost forgot the arrangement to meet Luke and Martine. She had already made her excuses to Richard and in a sudden rush she picked up the scarf she had bought as a gift for the Frenchwoman and drove to the beach where the island stood isolated and still, half-hidden in a chill sea fret.

There was no one at the cottage and the tide had not yet cleared the causeway. Surprised that Luke had made a mistake about the tide, she sat in the car and waited for the water to recede so she could get across. That would be at midday according to the tide table she had consulted.

She was nervous, every inch of her wanting to stay away from the island. She shuddered involuntarily, remembering her previous experience when she had been in danger of dying of hypothermia. Only Luke could have persuaded her to cross the slippery causeway again. Perhaps that had been his idea, she mused. Perhaps he had asked her to go there to live down any residual fear she had of the place. She looked across, hoping for a glimpse of him to reassure her. She had a strong urge to abandon the plan and go home, but she couldn't show Luke she was afraid, could she?

Luke and Martine must already be there, having reached the island by boat. She stood and stared, even waved in case they were watching and waiting for her, hoping for a sight of them, before beginning to cross the wet, dangerous path. It wasn't a cheering prospect to walk over the slippery rock alone. And draped in mist, the island looked far from enticing. She shivered as vivid memories of the last time she had been there returned to frighten her. Perhaps, knowing how Luke loved a bonfire, they were gathering wood and preparing to light a friendly beacon for her. But although she looked across repeatedly, no smoke issued up into the cold, misty air. It seemed that her guess had been wrong and they hadn't gone out to wait for her. So, where could they be?

She turned and walked back to the cottage, half-hoping that they had changed the plan and were waiting for her in the comfortable living room, the thought of one of his huge log fires increasing the dread of crossing to the cold mist-wrapped island. But the cottage was still as silent and empty as before. She looked for a note to tell her the plans had changed but again she was disappointed.

She found the key which Luke allowed her to use and went in to wait. By the look of the tide there was another half-hour or longer before she could begin to cross. There wouldn't be much time out there and back before dark.

Much as she dreaded to walk to the now eerie island, she knew she had to go. She trusted Luke and didn't want to let him down if he was planning something special. She stood and looked out of windows that were encrusted with salt. Although not yet midday, it was gloomy and winter clouds hung low over the sea. Really, this seemed less and less like a plan prepared by the careful and sensible Luke.

Luke had met Martine at Dover and although they ran and hugged each other like loving friends, they both sensed almost at once that things were not the same as when they had shared the running of Café de Jacques. Martine looked the same as he imagined her – older, of course but still with the wide and wicked grin that had always cheered him.

'Luke! You have lost your beard! Have you framed it to hang on the wall to show your grandchildren?' she teased. 'And your spectacles, they are enormous! Like the ears of Mickey Mouse!'

He responded to her teasing with a smile and for a moment hoped their meeting would recover from the initial numbness.

She was dressed more smartly than before and it surprised him a little. She had always shown little regard to her appearance and the neat check suit and matching coat and hat looked odd. For a while they pretended, laughing and exchanging news of their separate lives, but the magic had gone.

They hugged and kissed but time had played one of its cruel tricks and made loving friends into strangers. There was stiff formality where there had always been relaxed camaraderie. There was excessive politeness in their conversations. Martine spoke less English, her lapses into French adding to the separation. They spoke of past friends and each had to think deeply before remembering. Worse, Luke pretended to remember when the name meant nothing and he suspected the person was known to Martine after he had left her. Words dried up and others were left hanging in the air unanswered, unanswerable.

The hotel where Luke had booked a room was not grand. He had chosen a quiet place not too close to the centre of London and having travelled there by train, he showed her to her room and left her to bath and change. They arranged to meet in the dining room.

'I hope it's all right with you, Martine,' he said, 'but I didn't book anything for tonight. I thought our greatest need would be to talk. Tomorrow we'll go out on the town. Shops, dinner and a theatre, whatever you wish.'

'*Parfait, mon petit* Luke.' Although her smile was as warm and loving as always, there was something in her eyes that made him suspect that all was not well.

'There is something wrong?' he asked later, when they sat eating fish à la Bretonne, fish in a delicious sauce containing celery and leeks and carrots.

'I am so very 'appy to see you again, why should there be something wrong?' she asked. 'Are you not pleased I am 'ere?' Her accent was more pronounced; she took time finding the English words.

'Delighted, my dear Martine,' he said. 'I hope to persuade you to stay for ever.'

'For ever, it is a long time, yes? Time changes everything, us included.'

'We've grown older.' He smiled. 'At least, I have. You look the same as when I said goodbye, so long ago.'

She touched his arm affectionately. '*Merci, cherie*,' she whispered.

They spent five days in London admiring the splendid buildings, many still wearing the scars of bombing, they wandered in the parks and along the Serpentine and the majestic Thames. The afternoons were spent at exhibitions, evenings at the theatre, but whatever they did there was an atmosphere of strain. Luke knew without being told that Martine wished she were somewhere else. His enthusiasm was false; Martine's was soon abandoned completely.

'Shall we forget the rest of the week and go straight to Cardiff?' he suggested as they pushed their way through the crowd around Buckingham Palace. 'London can be very tiring and perhaps five days is enough at one time.'

'Luke, *mon cher ami*, I 'ave enjoyed everything you 'ave planned for me.'

'But?'

'I think I should go back to France.'

'Go back? I was hoping you'd stay longer, not go back sooner. In fact, I'd hoped you'd never go back.' But even as he spoke, he knew he was deceiving himself.

'It's best that I go.'

Arguing seemed pointless; she was only saying what he had detected. She no longer felt comfortable with him and it was best they faced it. The love and affection they had once held for each other was no longer there.

Changing her ticket was easy and he saw her off on the train that would take her to Dover with mixed feelings. There was disappointment but more than that, there was a sense of failure. He had failed to make her see him as the same person who had left France ahead of the German advance twelve years before.

Yet there was a sense of relief too. He had been showing a tourist around London, nothing more. Once she had gone, he spent the days searching bookshops and by Saturday he had gathered an alarmingly large collection. He thought he would stay over the weekend and see another play. It was a long time since he had treated himself to a holiday and Martine leaving was no reason to abandon this one.

Late on Saturday afternoon, he changed his mind and, struggling into a taxi with his books packed in boxes, he went to Paddington and caught the train for Cardiff. He would arrive late but he would have a lazy day on Sunday to recover. He remembered his invitation to Richard and Rosita to meet Martine. He would have to cancel, but there was plenty of time. A whole week.

He felt unashamedly lighthearted as he travelled home and stepped inside his house, where the spare room had been decorated for Martine's visit. New covers on the bed with curtains to match had been chosen by his housekeeper. A freshly washed rug beside the electric fire. Flowers in a vase were drooping but he knew they would have been changed in time for Martine's arrival. He took the sour stems from the water and threw them into the bin. A funereal bouquet for a dead friendship.

On Sunday he felt restless. His intention had been to rest but he woke early and dressed before seven o'clock. He was in limbo, having planned to visit a few places with Martine until the following weekend and arrive back in time for her to meet Rosita and Richard on the seventeenth. Now, with a week in which to inform them of the change of plan, he wandered around the house unable to decide how to spend the day.

He was tired, but he couldn't sit still. Eventually, after a light lunch he set off for the cottage. It was a way to use up the afternoon. Tomorrow he would go to the shop and see what had happened during his absence. His mind wandered over the books he had bought. They would need pricing and entering in his catalogue, the titles checked to see if any were on customers' request lists.

He was surprised to see Rosita's Anglia parked near the beach. Getting out of the car, he looked around for a sight of her. The tide had parted, leaving access to Gull Island free but he didn't even consider her walking across on a day like this, with low cloud shortening the day and the island half lost in mist. She wouldn't have gone there, not after her last experience.

He went to the cottage and as soon as he stepped inside he knew she had been there: perfume on the air and a chair slightly out of place. But where was she now? Unable to see her, he walked briskly up to the end of the lane and with increased anxiety, ran to the station and phoned Richard.

'Isn't there something very secret going on this afternoon?' Richard chuckled. 'Rosita only hinted – you know how difficult she finds it to keep some things to herself. I understood she was meeting you and Martine?'

'Not today.'

'But I got the impression she was meeting you on the island.'

'In this weather? It's lost in mist and very cold. What gave her the idea that ...'

There was no time to waste on words or theories. 'I'm on my way!' Richard said.

Luke ran back to the beach and in the gathering gloom could just make out a figure approaching the beach of the island. The figure wore trousers but he knew it was Rosita. What on earth was she thinking of? Before he began to follow, or even call out, another figure emerged from the shadows and began to move after her. It could hardly be Richard. So who was it?

Rosita stopped and looked towards the island. There seemed to be a pile of wood on the beach. She bent over to continue the half walk, half crawling movement towards it. The stones were covered in green slimy weed and the shallowest pools were already rimmed with frost. She was beginning to feel very cold. She stood and looked towards the pile of wood. So that was it. Luke was building a shelter. Was there going to be a party on the island for their engagement? What fun, so long as he waited until the weather was kinder. But where was he? Why didn't he and Martine show themselves? This was getting silly!

It wasn't like Luke to let her come out here on her own. If he were there, why didn't he come and help her? Perhaps there were others too. Perhaps Richard was in on the surprise and they were about to jump out and cheer as she reached the grassy level. Imaginings urged her on. And her implicit trust in Luke.

She stopped more frequently, trying to warm her hands under her arms as they stiffened with the cold. As she drew nearer she saw that the wood was nothing more than debris brought in by tide and wind. For the first time she began to feel anxious. Had she misread the letter? She did things in such a rush these days. Could she have mistaken the date? She turned and looked back. A figure dropped low and lay still. From where she stood, the shape appeared as inanimate as the rocks around it.

Luke watched from the beach. He knew that, used to the rocks as he was, he could make the journey to the island in half the time taken by Rosita and the person following her. He waited until both shapes had reached the beach and climbed up onto the grassy plateau then he hurried in their wake. Running, leaping with the confidence of familiarity, he set off across the causeway, cautiously watching, ready to drop out of sight the moment one of them looked his way. For the moment he didn't want to be seen by either. Without risking Rosita's safety, he wanted to find out exactly what the other person was planning.

Rosita heard footsteps and turned with a smile of relief. 'Luke! I was wondering where you – Idris? What on earth are you doing here?'

'I want to talk to you.' He took her arm and led her forcibly up towards the cliff edge on the other side of the island.

She began to struggle and he slapped her, the shock confusing her and allowing her to be dragged faster.

'Richard refuses to re-employ me. I think you should persuade him to take me back.'

'Why should I do that?' Confidence was growing, but then she saw how close they were to the edge, the sea below moving against the cliff edge, innocent and quiet.

'Be careful, Idris! Don't push me too close to the edge!'

He pretended to slip and pushed her to the edge of the dangerous drop. They were out of sight from the land and alarm bells were ringing in her head. Alone here with Idris, and her feet slipping on the surface, the sea waiting greedily below. He eased his grip and she moved away, down towards the beach. Idris ran to her, dragged her back and pushed her again, and this time there was no mistaking his intention. His jaw was thrust forward, his eyes cold, his practised charm no longer evident.

He was forcing her towards the sea far below them. She screamed, although it was a reflex action; there was no one to hear her and come to her aid. But miraculously, someone did. Luke appeared and with a growl of rage, he pushed Idris out of the way and grabbed Rosita as she began to stumble.

'Thank goodness you came at last,' she sobbed as, ignoring Idris's frantic denials, she clung to him in relief.

Recriminations and denials, accusations and bluff filled the air as the three people hurried across the rocks to the safety of the land. Idris walked away from them, determined to get to his car, but Richard had raced down the lane and slewed his car across in front of his. Richard stood facing him as he tried to manoeuvre it past.

'I think you'd better explain what you were doing following Rosita and trying to push her over the cliffs,' Luke shouted, so Richard had an idea of what had happened.

'I wanted to talk her into pleading with you to give me a job, that's all,' Idris said. 'Honest, that's all.' Richard was ominously quiet. 'For Kate and the girls,' Idris added. 'I did it for Kate and the girls.'

'He was going to kill me,' Rosita said, in a voice that trembled. 'He was forcing me over the edge.'

Richard took a step towards Idris, who ran past, pushing Rosita and Luke aside. He waded, then swam in the icy water out to where Luke's rowing boat was bobbing gently in shallow water and before any of them reached him, he was pulling on the oars, heading for the dangerous water swirling around the island. The boat caught in a sudden movement of wave crashing against wave and they lost sight of the man inside.

In the alarm of the new disaster, questions and answers were spasmodic and brief. It was clear to both men that Idris was involved and, with Rosita safe, that was enough for the moment.

Rosita borrowed a couple of Luke's pullovers and lit the fire while Luke and Richard searched the dark sea for Idris. At six o'clock, when it had been dark for more than two hours, there was still no sign of him.

Rosita went to tell Mrs Carey what had happened. Luke telephoned the police and the coastguard and reported him missing, presumed drowned. They all knew that in these temperatures he wouldn't survive very long without help.

Chapter Eighteen

'BUT WHERE CAN he be?' Mrs Carey walked up and down in the small living room, her eyes hollow, the creases on her face deepening into a mask of despair. It was after 2 a.m. and since Rosita and Luke had seen him rowing the boat towards Gull Island in the fading light the afternoon before, they had heard nothing of Idris. With Rosita and Richard, she was listening for the arrival of a police car with dread in her heart. Her lovely golden boy was dead, she just knew it.

'He'll be safe, Mam,' Richard said automatically.

'No thanks to you if he is!' She glared at her son. 'Fancy accusing him of trying to kill someone! First you say he stole your money and now this. What's got into you? That's what I want to know.'

'Auntie Molly Carey, we didn't say he was trying to kill me,' Rosita protested. 'But he was making me walk close to the edge and I was feared for my life.'

'Teasing, that's all that was, for sure.'

'If I'd slipped I'd have been in the sea,' Rosita murmured, but she didn't have the heart to argue strongly, to tell Idris's mother the truth. Idris was probably dead and that was enough for the old lady to cope with.

The waiting continued and at five in the morning, Mrs Carey looked at the chiming clock that had followed her from home to home all her married life. 'Where is he?' she wailed. 'If he's safe then why doesn't he come home?'

As she was being comforted, no one heard footsteps approaching, or the door being opened. 'Idris *is* home and has been all night,' Kate said, coming into the room. 'I've just had the police around to see if I – as his estranged wife – could help in the search for him and he's fast asleep in bed after arriving frozen and soaked through. What's been happening, Mam?'

'Wouldn't I like to know!' Mrs Carey glared at Richard and Rosita.

'Idris said he saw Rosita crawling across the rocks to the island and was worried about her.'

'What was he doing there?' Richard demanded.

'I don't know. Does it matter?' Kate asked in her quiet way. When she was told that Idris was accused of trying to push Rosita over the cliff she said very little, but showed a marked coolness towards her half-sister.

'Whatever he does, Idris will always be the innocent with Kate and your mother, won't he?' Rosita whispered to Richard when Kate left to open the Station Row shop.

For the next week Idris enjoyed the tender loving care of his wife, who found it impossible not to forgive him for past deeds when he'd arrived after his untimely swim. Kate was angry with Rosita and disbelieved her accusation, but she continued to work at the Station Row shop, for which Rosita was grateful. She hurried home at lunchtimes to feed Idris and bank up the fire, and to make sure he had all he needed. At the end of the week, she went home one lunchtime to find him gone.

There was no note, the bedclothes were thrown back as though he had just risen and left. His shoes were by the bed. Wherever he had gone, he'd worn slippers. The phone was off the hook, lying on the hall table. He had obviously left in a hurry. She rang Mrs Carey and tried a few friends but no one knew where he was.

She thought of the island. The place seemed like a part of their lives, drawing them to it like a magnet. She remembered that for the Careys it had been home for many years; perhaps that was the reason for its importance. Could Idris have gone back there? Wearing slippers? He might be delirious – but she didn't dare speak to the police again, they'd think the family were all crazy. She wondered if Idris *was* a bit mad. Losing his job might have unhinged him a little. There was a bit of a *tawch* about his explanation of why he was at the island, but that was probably a woman again. She sighed and wondered whether to look for him or wait for him to come home, or change the locks on the doors once again.

It had been a phone call that had made Idris leave so hurriedly. Hattie was in labour and Barbara was unable to drive. The farmer she worked for was away at some market and Barbara insisted the responsibility was his – he had to get her to hospital. Idris had plenty of nerve, but he didn't think it wise to put that in a note for his wife!

The drive to the hospital was terrifying. Hattie was making such a noise; crying, complaining, accusing him of everything and screaming with the pain. Her full, rounded face, so like Graham's, was bright red with the exertion of dealing with pain and perspiration streamed down her cheeks.

Idris was frantic to be rid of it all. He drove recklessly until Barbara told him to slow down or he'd crash and they'd be delivering the baby in a field. That thought added to his fear. Where babies and pain and blood were concerned, he wanted nothing to do with it. His blue eyes were wide open like a victim of shock, which was what he was. He had imagined a gentle ride to the hospital, everyone smiling, Barbara and Hattie calmly thanking him for his trouble and then returning home in time for Kate to get him some lunch. He wasn't expecting anything like this!

The pregnancy had made Hattie very unhappy and she had put on a lot of extra weight. Eating was solace for her. For most of the months of waiting, she had felt frightened and full of regrets, blaming Rosita for her misfortunes on the grounds that Rosita had boasted about seeing what she wanted from life and going all out to get it. Well, she had wanted Idris and see where that had got her! Racketing along country lanes with Idris finding every pothole, and with pain burning her up like a boil about to burst.

When they reached the hospital in a quiet backstreet not far from the centre of the town, Barbara eased her daughter from the car and helped her towards the doors.

'Go on ahead, Idris, and tell them we're coming, will you?' she asked. There was no reply and she turned to see that Idris had reversed the car and was speeding back down the road.

The staff smiled encouragingly, muttering soothing reassurances, and led Hattie away. Barbara sat on a seat in the corridor to allow her heart to stop racing. She was trembling now the need for calmness was no longer important. As she sat there, people came and went, giving her nods and smiles but no information. From the way Hattie had been behaving, she had expected the baby to have arrived within minutes of their reaching the hospital, but three hours later, she was still waiting.

Idris drove to the Pleasure Beach and sat in the car, trembling with shock. The very thought of Hattie going through a birth horrified him. He had kept well away when Lynne and Helen had been born, happily letting Kate and the medical staff deal with it all. He had gone back to live with his mam for a couple of weeks until Kate returned from hospital. Best thing too. And Kate hadn't made all that noise. He puffed nervously at a cigarette as he began to think of the pain. He was a shaken man. He hadn't realized it could be like that.

Barbara sat outside the ward and waited patiently all afternoon and all evening for news of her grandchild. When nothing had happened by midnight, she found a hotel that would take her and slept until 7 a.m. Then she went back to the hospital and sat through a second day, occasionally going in to see her distressed daughter. At four the following morning she saw her grandson, who Hattie had said would be called David, for the first time.

After looking at the tiny, scrunched-up little face for a long time, she went to the Careys' but she didn't go in. It was still very early and no one would be awake. Besides, she didn't want to talk to anyone, not yet.

She walked through the streets oblivious to everything and everyone, and stopped again outside Rosita's Newsagents, Tobacconists and Confectioners, in Station Row. She didn't go in there either. She walked on, uncaring about direction, and found herself on the way to the beach near Gull Island. She sat on the cold rocks for a while, unaware of hunger or even thirst, then walked back to town.

At 5.30 that evening, when the roads were busy with cars taking workers home from their businesses and shops were preparing to close, she went to the building site where Richard's firm was preparing the ground for a small estate of ten houses. Ignoring the mud that rose about her ankles and threatened to suck the shoes from her feet, she made her way to the site office, a wooden shed from which telephone lines and electric cables sprouted.

There was no one there and she hesitated, wondering what to do next. She looked around in that gentle way she had, moving her eyes slowly. She cast her gaze over the untidy mess within the building and felt an urge to tidy it up. Coffee cups, including a battered enamel mug that was fit for the ash bin, were spread over every surface, holding down assorted papers, some of which were plans, some of which were the day's copy of the popular newspapers on which horse races had been marked in pencil. How could something so orderly as rows of perfectly built houses be born out of such a mess?

She heard footsteps squelching through the mud but didn't turn around. She seemed as if she were in a daydream, until Richard said, 'What are you doing here? Don't you know you aren't allowed on site? It's dangerous, there are – Barbara? What on earth are you doing here? Looking for me, were you?'

'I don't know who I want really,' she said in a whisper.

Richard saw that she was upset. 'What's happened?' His guess was that she had been to see Rosita and had been rebuffed. 'Come on, sit down and I'll make us some coffee.' He looked around the office in the hope of finding a clean cup.

'I don't want anything, I just want to sit for a while.'

More for something to do than actual need, Richard picked up the battered mug he'd used since starting to build his first house. He poured hot water onto the powder, added milk from a bottle, sipped and pulled a face. 'Best you don't have coffee after all.' He smiled. 'It's awful. Now, tell me what's upset you.'

'I've just seen the baby. Hattie's baby. It's a boy and she wants him called David.' She spoke in a monotone and he had difficulty hearing her.

'That's good news, isn't it? David ...' He savoured the name. 'I like that. Is he all right? The baby? There's nothing wrong?'

'David is strong and they're satisfied with him, but Hattie—' She broke down then and cried as she said, 'My poor Hattie is dead.'

Richard's first thought was to get Barbara to his mother. She needed a sympathetic soul like Mrs Carey to help her now. His second thought was that Rosita and Kate had to be told immediately. He offered his arm and walked the sobbing Barbara to where his new Vauxhall stood, helped her in and drove to his mother's house.

'Molly, it's my Hattie. She died after bringing her baby into the world,' Barbara sobbed as her friend came to greet her. 'Couldn't stop the bleeding, they said.'

'Oh, my dear girl!' Mrs Carey's arms enfolded her friend.

'What will I do?' Barbara repeated again and again.

'Do? You'll stay here with me until things are sorted. And they will be, believe me they will be. Now, just sit and warm yourself while I find you something to eat. I bet you haven't eaten for hours.' Chattering away, soothing and comforting, Mrs Carey eased Barbara into a chair near the fire and wrapped a blanket around her. 'And get them shoes and stockings off, you're frozen stiff,' she scolded.

She hugged Barbara, then busied herself getting more warm blankets and slippers and soon had Barbara comfortable, with a steaming bowl of soup placed in front of her.

Richard left them and went to find Rosita. She was just putting the finishing touches to her evening meal of a beef casserole that had been gently simmering since midday.

'Richard! There's a lovely surprise! Will you join me? I seem to have made enough for an army.'

'Rosita, I have some very bad news. Hattie's baby was born today and—'

'Oh, that's good news, isn't it? As long as he's all right?' She looked at him and at once saw that all was far from right. 'What is it? The baby? Is he—?'

'The baby is fine, but it's Hattie. She died soon after giving birth.'

'What? But how? Why?'

'I don't know the details. Post-partum haemorrhage I think they said when I rang the hospital. Apparently it happened suddenly, without warning, and although she was attended to at once, there was no way they could save her. Your mother came to the site and told me. By the state she was in and the fact that the baby was born at four this morning, I think she'd been walking for hours. It was almost six this evening when I found her.'

'Where is she?'

'With Mam. I didn't know what else to do. She needed someone to comfort her.'

Rosita threw the plate of food aside and reached for her coat. 'I have to see her,' she said.

The need to comfort her mother over the death of her half-sister was instantaneous yet, as Richard stopped the car outside his mother's house, Rosita was trembling. She hadn't spoken or had any contact with her mother for years. How could she expect to give comfort now? How could her mother greet her with anything but scorn for arriving at such a time? Mam would think her hypocritical, coming to mourn a half-sister she hardly knew and certainly hadn't liked.

She needn't have worried. As she stepped into the room, which had already taken on the atmosphere of grief, Barbara stood up and opened her arms. It was as if the years between hadn't happened, as mother and daughter embraced and cried on each other's shoulder. With a nod to his mother, Richard took her arm and went to find Kate.

Finding themselves alone, for a long time neither spoke, then, as Rosita began to say she was sorry, Barbara touched her lips gently with her fingers and shook her head.

'Let's not try and explain away all that's happened, let's just start again, from now. But first we must grieve for Hattie and that little boy who was orphaned when he was only minutes old.'

They held each other and Rosita's mind took her back in a cavalcade of scenes, half-remembered but returning with new vividness. How she had loved to cuddle into her mother's neck like this. Barbara had always smelled deliciously of wood smoke and freshly baked bread. The remembered scents were always a part of her childhood memories of a mother she had lost when she was five.

When she returned to the school shop later that evening, Rosita rang Luke to tell him what had happened. He listened to the news of Hattie's death with dismay but sighed with relief on hearing that because of it, Rosita and Barbara had met and talked at long last. He asked repeatedly what he could do to help and if Barbara needed anything.

As they were about to ring off, Luke said, 'It's strange, but I was about to phone you. It's about next Sunday. The visit to the cottage for you and Richard to meet Martine is off, of course. I was going to suggest you come anyway, but now, with this tragedy ...'

'Oh, I'm sorry about Martine, Luke,' she said, then added, 'but I don't understand. Last week was when I was invited to meet you, and just me, not Richard. That's why I was on the island, remember?' She laughed. 'Getting very forgetful, aren't you?'

'But I definitely invited both of you, and to the cottage, not to the island. In this weather? And it was the seventeenth I said, not the tenth.'

'Luke, I don't understand. Your letter had been opened by mistake, by Idris, but there was none of it missing. It was just the single page. How could I have made a mistake?'

'Then the letter you received wasn't the one I wrote. It was almost three pages for a start. You know how I chatter on. And my writing is such a scrawl.'

'What does it mean?'

'I don't know, but I think Idris might be able to enlighten us, don't you?'

Luke replaced the phone and immediately rang Richard. They met half an hour later although it was late. When Luke had explained the differences in the two letters, they went back to the house in Walpole Street and without waking Kate, they managed to rouse Idris. He was asleep on the couch, still not allowed back in Kate's bed, although she looked after him in every other way. He grinned ruefully, gesturing to the couch as he found himself a chair.

Without preamble, Richard demanded an explanation.

'If you want the truth then you can have it, but you won't like it, mind,' he said truculently. 'You won't like it at all, brother dear.'

'Did you rewrite my letter and change the date?' Luke asked. 'If so, it puts a different light on Rosita's story that you were trying to push her over the edge.'

'Rubbish, man! She made it all up. It was she who persuaded me to meet *her*. Daft about me she is and even my being married to her half-sister didn't worry her.'

Richard rose threateningly. 'Now you're talking rubbish.'

'She's always felt attracted to me,' Idris continued with a confident smile. 'You don't think all those visits to Station Row to fix a bit of cracking plaster were genuine, do you? Be fair. When I fixed a piece of plaster it stays fixed. Calling me back time after time and always at lunchtime, mind, when the shop was closed. Well, you know what some women are for a bit of illicit sex.'

Richard stood up and this time he hit Idris so he fell backwards, sliding on the upturned chair until it stopped against the far wall. Silently, Luke handed Idris a handkerchief to hold against his nose.

'Told you you wouldn't like it, didn't I?' Idris said thickly. 'You've never been exciting enough for a woman, Richard. I had the charm ration for both of us, haven't you noticed?' He went to the bathroom to wash his face and stem the blood seeping into the handkerchief.

Silently, Richard and Luke left.

Idris looked into the bathroom mirror and smiled. His foolish fantasy of murdering Rosita was just that, a foolish fantasy – he'd never have the nerve to harm anyone. But it had been fun. He could never have pushed Rosita to that terrible death. It was just his imagination giving him ideas he could never fulfil. He had enjoyed the teasing, though, it had made him feel strong and powerful, watching her frightened face. Besides, by stirring things a bit he might still prevent or at least delay the marriage that would deprive him of Richard's wealth.

If Richard didn't marry, he'd have to leave his money to someone. With the rest of their brothers spread far and wide with little contact with the family, his girls would benefit one day, even if he didn't. All he had to do was prevent Richard from marrying Rosita. He smiled again at his reflection. That mightn't be too difficult.

It made him feel quite a lad, arranging for a fortune to come to his girls. What a great father he was.

Rosita was surprised at how well she and her mother got on. Instead of the ogre she had invented to ease her misery, she found Barbara to be as gentle and kindly as Kate and a very long way from the sister who had so tragically died. The new baby helped, it was something to share; the visits to the hospital to see him, admire him and consider him more beautiful than the others in the row of identical bundles in the identical cots.

Kate grieved with them yet held back from tears, remembering how her sister had ruined her marriage. The day before the funeral, she met her husband at his mother's and tried to persuade him to admit the truth about Richard.

He laughed and said, 'What's so wonderful about the truth? There's plenty who'd be happier without it. I know Rosita wanted me and I told Richard. That's the truth and he definitely didn't want to hear it. Best I keep silent on the rest.'

'Truth? That isn't the truth!' Kate scolded. 'Rosita has always loved Richard.'

'You have to admit it's taken him a hell of a long time to do anything about it. No wonder she was tired of waiting. Thirty-odd years, for heaven's sake. Hardly an irresistible passion, is it?'

*

Barbara and her two daughters went together to arrange the funeral and, each day, they went to see the baby, who had remained in hospital being cared for by the nurses.

Unknown to Rosita, Richard also found time in his day to call and see baby David. He would stand for a long time and stare, marvelling at the perfection of the tiny child.

On the day of the funeral, the Careys' door was propped open to allow anyone who wished to call in. The first visitor was Luke. He and Barbara hugged each other and shed a few tears like the friends they were.

'Are you and Rosita friends again?' he whispered. Barbara nodded. 'At least something good has come out of this excruciating pain. A child is irreplaceable and it's ironic that it took the loss of one to regain another.'

She looked at him with her dreamy and beautiful eyes and said softly, 'Oh, Luke. Stay with me and help me through this.'

'I will, my dear. I promise.'

Rosita found she was unable to miss a day without going to see the tiny person that was called David Prothero. After a few days she was allowed to hold him. He seemed to fit into her arms as if made for that special place. She began to think very seriously about his future.

Hattie's funeral was a small one, with only the family and a few neighbours returning to the house, where Mrs Carey had prepared food. Afterwards, Rosita and Kate sat close to their mother, together in their grief, comforting her, making her feel less alone. Then Rosita and Richard went out to walk along the sands of the deserted Pleasure Beach, leaving Barbara in the capable hands of Molly Carey.

It was raining and the shelters, usually filled with the colourful extravagances of summer, looked drab and fitting for the sadness of the day.

'What are we going to do about Idris?' Richard asked. 'I don't trust him. What if he tries something else to harm us?'

'He's all talk, too much of a coward to take chances. Don't worry. Whatever he says, we'l41 know better than to believe him. He lives in a dream world of high adventure but makes sure he holds on to the reality of Kate.'

'Did your mother tell you there was £300 found among Hattie's possessions?' Richard asked quietly.

'Three hundred? Where would she have got such a sum?'

'Well, I could never prove it, but it was three hundred I suspected Idris of stealing. It doesn't need much imagination to put the two together, does it? She was carrying his child and he didn't want to admit it. The easiest way out was to pay her for her silence – with my money.'

They were both silent for the rest of their walk, Richard seething with anger against his brother and Rosita holding on to the thought that if Idris had paid Hattie all that money, then the child must have been his and not Richard's.

Idris was fed up. Firstly there was the discomfort of sleeping night after night on the narrow couch in his own kitchen, where he and Hattie had spent so many illicit and happy hours. And besides that inconvenience, since Barbara had been staying with her, his mother had very little time for him.

When Kate had thrown him out and he had gone back to his mother, it had been like reverting to the later years of childhood, with plates of food being put before him at regular intervals and with his every wish not only granted but improved upon. Now, worse than the rest, he was frequently ignored.

Just like Dad treated me when I was a boy, he thought irritably. For Dad it was Richard and no one else. I was invisible to him. But Mam treated me like a young god and would now, if it weren't for that Barbara Prothero butting in!

On Sunday afternoon, a week after Hattie's funeral, Rosita was relaxing, reading the newest edition of the *Bookseller's Review*, the magazine which kept her up to date with what was happening in the trade, when Richard called. She could see from his face that he had something important to discuss.

'Come for a drive? I thought we'd go and see Luke,' he said. 'He's sure to be at the cottage.'

When they reached there, Luke was wandering across the beach gathering firewood and for a while they helped him. Then, when they were sitting in his comfortable room, Richard brought up the subject he wanted to discuss.

'I'm considering setting Idris up in a business of his own,' he told them. 'What d'you think? A sort of handyman. He'll never make a fortune but he's quite good at small building jobs and – let's be honest – he does attract the ladies and it's those who need the occasional plumber or carpenter. He could do quite well.'

'He'd have to do a better job than he did on the plastering he did for me,' Rosita said. Richard glanced at Luke and tightened his lips but said nothing.

'It would be expensive,' Luke warned. 'He'll need tools and a vehicle.'

'I can afford it.'

It would keep him busy,' Rosita mused, 'and he'd like being his own boss. There's a certain prestige in working for yourself, as I well know.'

'There'll be problems too. For a start, he wouldn't get paid unless he worked.'

Richard thought about the plan for a while then he decided to make the announcement. He found Idris, Kate and Helen and Lynne in his mother's house. Rosita was there too, sitting on the couch beside Barbara.

'I've decided to do what we discussed,' he said to Rosita and turning to his brother he went on, 'I'm offering you a lump sum to buy tools and a van to start you in a business of your own. I can find you a few jobs at first, small things that need doing but which I don't have the time or manpower to deal with. After that you're on your own.'

Mrs Carey was delighted and went out into the kitchen at once to find the port left from Christmas. But Idris's reaction was odd. He seemed surprised at Richard's generosity after the disagreements and suspicions of the past months.

'What's in it for you?' he asked ungraciously.

'Peace of mind knowing you aren't scrounging off Mam if you must know!' Richard snapped. 'I know she's been giving you handouts these past weeks. Perhaps you should have kept that £300 instead of giving it to Hattie.' He handed his brother a sheaf of papers. 'The van is waiting for you with your name on the side. If you aren't happy about it just let me know and I'll have it painted out.' He gestured for Rosita to follow him and they walked out, leaving Mrs Carey staring in pride and pleasure at Idris.

'There's lovely,' they heard her say as they left. 'You'll be a proper businessman, working for yourself. Come on, then, let's go and see your ol' van with your name an' all!'

'I'll be getting back home,' Kate said. She and the girls left, while Idris fussed about, getting his mother to put on a coat before walking out to the kerb where Richard had parked the newly painted van. He offered his arm; Molly Carey was getting very frail.

'All right,' she said, 'don't rush me. Just like a child with a new toy you are.'

Idris was pleased when he saw the van. Although old, it had been smartly painted in cream with his name, Idris Carey, and below it the legend, 'Handyman', in brown.

He tossed the keys and grinned at his mother. 'Go on, get your handbag or whatever else you can't travel without, and we'll go for a spin.'

'Lovely. Can we go over to the beach house, where we lived when you were small?' she pleaded, and, after getting her a scarf and some warm boots, they set off.

'Fancy the old green van being given a new lease of life,' he said with a grin. 'It won't last long, mind, but it'll do for a while, until I make my fortune and buy a brand new one twice the size of this old wreck.'

'Now you be patient, Idris. Best to walk before you run, mind.'

From the town, he didn't drive straight to their destination but first took his mother on a sightseeing trip. He knew she loved to see places where she and his father had spent their hard but happy youth. Out through country lanes, to the lonely but beautiful stone-built Merthyr Dyfan church where she and Henry had married, where she stopped to look and revive memories he didn't share.

He drove on, between slowly greening hedges, where a large flock of goldfinches flew across their path.

'A charm of goldfinches,' she said. 'They'll soon be pairing up for the spring.'

'Lucky sods,' Idris muttered.

Leaving the narrow lanes, they headed towards the busy main road into Cardiff. He stopped once or twice for her to look at places she remembered, then suggested they went back towards the Pleasure Beach before going on to Gull Island. He enjoyed giving her this treat, reminding her he was her favourite, her golden boy.

The day was surprisingly warm for early spring, with skies clear and blue. People on the pavements had lost the urgent, bent-forward, hasty walk of winter and were strolling, enjoying the sweet fresh air. The road back to town was very steep and a lorry was slowly chugging its way up towards them in a low gear. Idris slowed near the top for her to look across the docks and the sea beyond, then eased his foot off the brake and swooped down.

'Don't!' Mrs Carey laughed excitedly. 'You'll frighten me to death!'

He laughed too, pleased that she was enjoying her unexpected outing. Then, after slowing again, he touched the accelerator to frighten her and add to the fun and somehow the wheel slipped in his hand and the van shot across the road, touched the wing of an approaching lorry, bounced off and careered over, to stop against the wall of the school.

The contact was severe and his mother catapulted forward and hit her head on the facia. Another few miles per hour and she would have gone straight through the windscreen. Idris hit the screen but miraculously it didn't break. The rear-view mirror caught the side of his face and blood ran in a fast stream down his face.

Stemming the flow with a handkerchief, he helped his mother out and ran to phone Richard. He wanted to call an ambulance but she insisted that he phoned Richard.

'I'm only a bit shaken,' she said. 'Richard will know what to do.'

A householder invited them inside but Idris stood by the gate and waited for his brother, preparing his story. Mrs Carey sat inside, sipping tea in trembling hands, her arms shaking like a drummer on a final roll. Richard arrived in less than fifteen minutes and he carried his mother to his car and took her to the hospital. He said nothing to Idris, saving his fury until he knew his mother was safe.

Unbelievably, Mrs Carey wasn't seriously hurt, but the doctor advised her to stay overnight, in case of delayed shock or other damage revealing itself. Idris was bandaged and then insisted he was well enough to go home.

He walked into the house with an unnecessary limp, and saw with relief the look of alarm and horror that crossed Kate's face. Exaggerating his discomfort just a little, he allowed himself to be put to bed and fussed over.

Kate couldn't turn him from her bed any longer. He was difficult, completely unreliable and untrustworthy, but the naughty-boy charm always got to her. Something within her still felt the strong emotional ties of marriage and, she had to admit it, love. She didn't have much difficulty persuading him to stay.

Mrs Carey stayed in hospital for three days and in that time had more visitors than the rest of the ward together; including Rosita, Kate and Richard, and a contrite Idris who brought flowers and fruit and a huge box of chocolates far beyond a sweets ration – refusing to explain how they were acquired!

Rosita and Richard still went daily to see baby David and having met twice at the hospital, no longer without telling each other. Although they talked about him a lot, they didn't discuss his future, but knew the time was coming when a decision would have to be made. In a wheelchair Mrs Carey also visited the nursery and admired the child. One day she was there when Richard arrived.

He approached the cot and smiled at his mother. 'He's a funny little chap, isn't he?' he said after kissing his mother. 'I feel drawn to him somehow. He looks so helpless and alone in there.'

'He's a Carey, in spite of not carrying the name, and should be our responsibility.' Mrs Carey sighed. 'And there's Kate not willing, and me too old to do anything about it.'

Luke drove from Cardiff and after parking his car beside the cottage, looked along the beach and saw someone sitting on the steps of the Careys' old house. He knew at once that it was Barbara. He went into the cottage and prepared a tray of tea and, balancing it carefully, he made his way across the uneven rocks, to sit beside her.

'I have so many memories of this place, Luke,' she said as she took a cup of tea. 'Remember how we used to walk out here? The youngest Carey sitting on the bogie cart? Often barefoot, dressed in clothing that was rarely a proper fit. We used to drag firewood back the two miles home. Me surrounded by the Carey clan. And the picnics we enjoyed! Very different from the picnics people would have today. A loaf and a scraping of margarine and a jar of jam, Marmite or bloater paste. Remember?'

'I remember,' Luke said softly. 'I once came here looking for you to ask you to marry me.'

She turned her face to him in surprise, her beautiful eyes widening. Her face showed the signs of too much wind and sun, the still-thick hair more grey than brown. To Luke she had never looked more beautiful.

'I'd decided that the best for you and Rosita was for you to marry me. I came here, couldn't find you and was eventually told by Mrs Carey that you'd become Mrs Graham Prothero. I went that same day and lied my way into the army and was sent to France.'

'What a different life we'd have had if I'd delayed my decision for a week or two. Poor Rosita. I let her down badly.' She leaned towards him and his arms held her close.

The evening drew in and an offshore wind moved the warmed air from the land out onto the colder sea and covered the scene in a chilling mist. The island disappeared as though a curtain had been drawn over it. There was no one else around, just the two figures locked together on the steps of the ruined house. It was a long time before they moved.

Mrs Carey knew there was something wrong between Rosita and Richard. Nothing had been said, but looking at them now, each pretending to look at a newspaper, tense and unhappy, she thought there must have been a quarrel. When would they ever learn to accept their differences?

Barbara had telephoned; said she had met Luke and would like to bring him back for supper. They were sitting waiting for them to arrive.

'What is it with you two?' she demanded when she could stand the silence no longer. 'Ever since I asked you to stay and eat with us, the atmosphere has been as thick as a boiled sock!'

Rosita smiled and assured her that everything was 'just fine'. Mrs Carey glared at Richard's miserable face and 'humphed' to show she wasn't convinced.

Barbara and Luke arrived and were soon followed by Kate, Idris and the girls and there was a mood of celebration. Mrs Carey was home from hospital, Idris was wallowing in Kate's loving attention. It was only from Rosita and Richard there was a lack of joy.

Unaware of the tension, Barbara said, 'Well, you two, have you a date for the wedding yet?'

'Richard and I won't be marrying after all. Too many complications. We want different things.'

'You've had another quarrel!' Mrs Carey said in exasperation.

'Not a quarrel, Auntie Molly Carey. I have other plans.' She smiled at her mother and said, 'I've been in touch with the authorities and applied to adopt baby David.'

White-faced, Richard stood up and stared at her. 'They won't let you,' he gasped. 'A single woman? No, they'll never agree!'

'He's my sister's child, and because there's a family connection they are considering it.'

Richard glared at her and stormed from the room. Rosita stared after him, ashamed at the way she had broken the news in front of everyone. Last evening she had told him she couldn't marry him but hadn't explained her reasons. Hearing of her intention to adopt or at least foster Hattie's orphan son had been more of a shock for him than she had imagined.

She reached for her coat and went after him. As she reached the door she saw his car leaving the kerb opposite. Running to her Anglia she drove after him. His car was more powerful and if he wanted to he could easily leave her behind.

He drove out of town and, hardly registering any surprise, Rosita realized he was heading for the beach at Gull Island. It was dark and frosty and the swath of her headlights made the hedges unreal, like scenery in a play. He parked near the beach and pushed open the car door. She parked near and ran towards him. His passenger door was unlocked and she sat beside him, panting as though she had run all the way.

A moon lit the scene, casting its eerie glow over the rocks and trees around them. To their left, Luke's cottage showed a yellow light. The island looked larger in the moonlight, rising out of a calm sea, its colours muted and dull.

'Why, Rosita?'

'I have to,' she said simply. 'The baby needs me. I can't allow him to grow up among strangers. Kate refuses to take him. Even with her compassionate nature, she's unable to accept her husband's child into her home.'

He didn't reply, but just sat, looking out across the water.

'Richard, I'm sorry. But my own childhood, with all its trauma, makes it impossible for me to leave him. I just can't allow David to be brought up with no one of his own. He's my nephew.'

'And mine,' he said.

'I didn't want arguments. I just know I can do the best for him. You see that, don't you, Richard?'

'Why do you never trust me? Or is it that you don't need me any more? Have Barbara and baby David taken all the love you can spare and there's none left for me?'

'You know I love you. All my life I've held on to the hope that one day, you and I – But this changes everything. I can't ignore the helpless, adorable little scrap. I can't allow him to go to strangers and, well, I can't expect you to feel the same.'

'But I do. I want him too!' Richard turned to look at her, hardly visible in the strange light. 'What makes you think you're the only one to feel compassion and love for a helpless child? I want to look after him, keep him safe and surround him with love. Can't we combine the love we have for him. Care for him together?'

'You mean it?'

'Of course I mean it, woman! I've seen him every day since he was born. I can't explain it, but I want him.'

'You wouldn't resent him, being Idris's child?'

'Would you?'

'Never!'

'Rosita, I believe David's best chance of a happy childhood is with us, you and me, plus a child of our own. D'you think you could manage two very young children?'

He opened his arms and with a sigh of relief, Rosita slid into them. 'With you beside me, I can manage anything.'